Naked Justice

By William Bernhardt

William Bernhardt

◆ ◆ ◆

NAKED
JUSTICE

BALLANTINE BOOKS ◆ NEW YORK

http://www.randomhouse.com

Library of Congress Cataloging in Publication Data
Bernhardt, William, 1960–
Naked justice / William Bernhardt.
p.   cm.
ISBN 0-345-38685-X
I. Title.
PS3552.E73147N35   1997   96–38209
813'.54—dc20

Manufactured in the United States of America

First Edition: February 1997

10   9   8   7   6   5   4   3   2   1

Once again, for Kirsten,
because she deserves it

When I was a child, I spake as a child, I understood as a child, I thought as a child, but when I became a man, I put away childish things.

—Saint Paul, 1 Corinthians 13:11

PROLOGUE

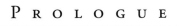

◆ ◆ ◆

As the Barrett family drove from City Hall to the ice-cream parlor, they could scarcely have imagined that soon thousands, if not millions, of people would be scrutinizing, criticizing, and debating what really happened during those final hours.

"I want chocolate chip!" Alysha shrieked, with the breathless anticipation only an eight-year-old confronted with the prospect of ice cream can muster.

"Now, honey," said Caroline Barrett, Alysha's mother, "you know chocolate stains your clothes. Why don't you get vanilla?"

"Want chocolate. Chocolate! Chocolate, chocolate, chocolate!"

"Me too," chirped Annabelle, Alysha's baby sister.

They both looped their arms over the front seat of the car. "Daddy, we want chocolate! Can we have chocolate?"

Daddy was a large, broad-shouldered black man who still had essentially the same physique he'd had fifteen years ago when he played college football. "Sure, sweethearts. Whatever you want."

Caroline glared at him. "What do you think you're doing?"

"Honey, it's just ice cream."

"It is *not* just ice cream. You're undermining my authority."

"Oh, honey . . ."

"This is what you always do. You make me play the heavy so you can be the fairy godfather!"

He glanced at the children in the backseat. "Let's not do this here."

"Don't tell me when I may or may not talk. This is an important issue. You're sending all the wrong messages."

Daddy's jaw stiffened. "The only message I'm sending is that they can have whatever kind of ice cream they want." He pulled into the parking lot across from the Baskin-Robbins.

"You're teaching our children that they don't have to obey me. That they can get whatever they want by running to Daddy."

"This is ridiculous." He popped open the car door and slid out of the driver's seat. Alysha jumped toward him as he reached across the backseat and released four-year-old Annabelle from her car seat.

Carrying both girls in his strong arms, he strode across the parking lot to the Baskin-Robbins. Caroline remained several steps behind.

"Honey," he said, "why don't you pop into Novel Idea and check out the new books? I can handle this."

She gave him a stony look. "You'd like that, wouldn't you?"

He sighed, then carried the girls into the ice-cream parlor.

The man behind the counter, who was wearing a white apron and a white paper cap, rose to attention and saluted. "Afternoon, Mr. Mayor."

"Afternoon, Art. How're you doing?"

"Can't complain."

"How's Jenny? And that smart little boy of yours?"

"Oh, they're fine, sir. Just fine."

Alysha and Annabelle approached the front counter, pressed their noses against the glass, and surveyed the rich variety of flavors.

"All right, little ladies," the man behind the counter said, "what can I get you?"

The two girls looked at each other, then turned their eyes slowly back toward their parents. There was a pronounced silence. Art, the scoop man, would later testify that he had never felt such tension in the air, particularly when the only question pending was what flavor ice cream to order.

"Get whatever you want, girls," Daddy said finally.

"Except," Caroline added, laying emphasis on each word, "chocolate."

"Ho*ney* —"

"Don't start with me, Wallace. Don't start."

Wallace Barrett threw up his hands. "Well, I don't see the point of telling them they can have a special treat and then not letting them get what they want."

"I told them they couldn't have chocolate. We have to be consistent."

"This isn't consistent. This is just mean."

"Oh, right. And you, their great hero, are going to ride in and save them from their heartless mother. Is that it?"

"No, but—"

"I'm tired of being treated like what I say doesn't matter!" Her voice was rising; her eyes were red and watery. "You can't just trample over me like a tight end on the opposing team. I deserve some respect!"

Wallace Barrett's eyes moved from the ice-cream man to the four customers standing nearby. "Caroline," he whispered, "you're creating a scene."

"Do you think I care?" Her voice became thin and shrill. "Do you think I care what people think? This is important to me."

"I thought we were talking about the children."

"You were wrong. This is about *me*. But the only way I can get to you is through them! You don't give a damn about me!"

His face seemed to solidify. His eyes narrowed to near invisibility and his cheekbones twitched. "Shut up."

"Don't tell me what to do, you selfish pig! You're not mayor over me."

"I'm warning you—"

"Go to hell."

"Shut up!"

His voice boomed through the small store like a thunderbolt from Olympus. The other customers jumped away, startled. Witnesses would later say that time seemed suspended for the next several seconds, as if everything was happening in a horrifying slow motion. His voice reverberated along the walls and the ceiling, and as it did, Wallace Barrett reared his thick, muscled arm back, then jerked it forward with a practiced quarterback snap. His fist hurtled around, splitting the air like a knife, moving with impossible speed toward his wife's beautiful ebony face. Her eyes widened in sudden, paralyzing fear, a fear so vivid and immediate that everyone agreed she must have experienced it many times before. She was terrified, but there was no time to move, no time even to scream, before . . .

His fist stopped barely an inch from her face.

They stared at one another, their eyes locked together. The large woman eating the brownie sundae would later describe the sentiment conveyed as pure, undisguised hatred.

"You'll regret this," Wallace Barrett said in the barest of whispers. His arm was still suspended in the air. It began to tremble, and the trembling spread up his neck to his face, then throughout the rest of his body.

At last his arm dropped to his side. "C'mon, girls," he said. "Let's go home."

They scampered toward him. "But, Daddy—"

"No whining. Let's go."

"But, Daddy—" Annabelle insisted.

Barrett's hand swept around in a wide arc and popped her once on the backside. She quieted immediately.

"We'll come back later, Art," Wallace Barrett said. "I'm sorry."

He carried his girls out of the ice-cream parlor. A few awkward moments later, Caroline Barrett followed.

As soon as she was gone, everyone in the store released a communal sigh of relief. Art went on about his business and tried to forget the incident—until later, when the hordes descended on his little store, prying and probing and offering him large sums of money to remember.

The girls did not return later. Not Alysha or Annabelle, or for that matter, Caroline. Because only a few hours later, they were all dead.

I'll Be Judge, I'll Be Jury

◆ ◆ ◆

CHAPTER

1

BEN KINCAID STARED blankly at the woman in the black robe, not quite certain he had heard her correctly.

Judge Sarah L. Hart cleared her throat. "I repeat: What else would she be doing with a frozen fish?"

"Oh," Ben murmured. "That's what I thought you said."

The judge smiled. "Can't you help me out here?"

Of course, Ben mused silently, if he could have, he would have. Some time ago. Judge Hart had an unerring knack for cutting to the heart of the matter. That, he knew, was why she was one of the best judges in Tulsa County. Of course there were times when you didn't necessarily want the best judge in Tulsa County . . .

"Your honor," Ben said, coughing into his hand, "the fish was not actually frozen. It was . . . preserved."

"I'm not sure I understand the difference."

"These are freshwater fish. Bass. Trout. They're kept in a freshwater tank."

"Ah. How ignorant of me. Why didn't they cover this in judge school?" She removed her eyeglasses and massaged the brim of her nose.

"Ben?" He felt a tugging at his jacket. It was his client, Fannie Fenneman, the fisherwoman under discussion. Ben tried to ignore her.

She tugged harder. "Ben. Psst, Ben!"

"Still here, Fannie." Realizing it was futile, he asked the judge for a moment to confer with his client. "What's the problem?"

She leaned close to his ear. "I don't think this is going so well."

"Really. What was your first clue?"

Fannie tugged uncomfortably at the dress Ben had made her wear rather than her customary overalls and waders. "The judge seems very confused."

"Wouldn't you be?"

"Mr. Kincaid," Judge Hart said, "if I might have your attention again . . ."

"Yes, your honor. Of course, your honor."

"I thought perhaps you could help me sort this all out."

"I'd be delighted to try."

"Good. Let me pose a few questions."

Ben was mentally posing a few questions of his own. Such as: Why am I here? Why do I always get these cases? Why did I go to law school?

"Your client has obtained some renown as a . . . er . . . fisherperson. Is that correct?"

"World-famous," Fannie said emphatically.

"World-famous," the judge echoed. "In fishing circles, presumably. Your client has won numerous tournaments during the past several years, right?"

"All of them," Fannie answered.

"Ms. Fenneman," Judge Hart said, "are you sure you need counsel? You seem so able to defend yourself, your counsel can barely get a word in edgewise."

Fannie lowered her eyes and buttoned her lip.

"Now," the judge continued, "the tournament officials say Ms. Fenneman cheated, and they've brought criminal charges. Am I still on track?"

The assistant district attorney, Martin Edwards, rose to his feet. "That's right, your honor. She's wrongfully taken over six thousand dollars in tournament prize money. It's fraud. Deceit."

"I see. And so you decided to crack down on this dangerous . . . fish faker. Stop her before she fishes again. Is that it?"

Edwards adjusted his tie. "I . . . probably wouldn't have used exactly those words."

"I suppose all the triple homicides and depraved sex crimes on your docket pale in comparison with this fish fraud?"

"Your honor, a crime is a crime."

"Of course, of course," Judge Hart said, holding up her hands. "We can't be making exceptions." She shuffled a few papers. "Next thing you know, we'll have people telling fish stories all over the place. Why, the very phrase *fish story* could come to mean a tale that is exaggerated and not to be believed."

"Your honor, we have this woman dead to rights. We found a freshwater tank in the back of her truck. The scheme was, she would wait until after the tournament began and the other anglers had shipped out, then sneak back to her car, pull a fish she bought beforehand out of the tank, and claim she caught it."

Fannie leaped to her feet. "That's a filthy rotten lie! I never saw that tank before in my life!"

Ben pushed her back into her chair. "It's not our turn."

"But he said—"

"Sit *down*."

Fannie grudgingly obeyed.

Edwards continued. "Realistically, your honor, how could the same woman win all these tournaments year after year? I mean, it's not as if there's a lot of strategy involved. You sit in a boat and wait for a fish."

"Says you," Fannie muttered.

"Perhaps," Judge Hart speculated, "the secret lies in her wrist action as she casts the line."

"Right," Edwards replied. "Or maybe she charms them with her good looks."

Fannie could contain herself no longer. "It's the bait."

All heads in the courtroom turned to Fannie.

"I beg your pardon?" Judge Hart said, peering down through her glasses.

"Bait," Fannie repeated. "I make my own. The fish can't resist it."

"Well, there you have it," Judge Hart said, falling back into her chair. "I'm convinced."

Fannie folded her arms angrily across her chest. "I don't like this judge," she whispered to Ben. "I think she's trying to be sarcastic."

Trying? Ben thought.

BEN LISTENED CAREFULLY as the prosecution brought forth a series of experts from the glamorous world of professional fishing. The court learned about sonar fish detection, fiberglass rods, and chemically enhanced aphrodisiacal bait. All the experts agreed, however, that an unbroken string of tournament successes such as Fannie's was unprecedented and rather unlikely. On cross, Ben dutifully required each witness to admit that winning forty-seven consecutive tournaments was not, strictly speaking, totally and utterly impossible. Somehow, though, he doubted this "admission" was helping her case much.

For their final witness, the prosecution called a man named Ernest Samson Hemingway. ("No relation," he said as he was sworn in.) Mr. Hemingway was a frequent tournament participant and the organizer of the last competition in which Fannie participated. He was also the man who disqualified her and restricted her from further league competitions. He had instigated the investigation against her and ultimately found the chief piece of evidence being used to establish Fannie's guilt.

Edwards conducted the direct examination, delivering every question in somber tones suggesting the matter at hand was as momentous as the quest for world peace. "Mr. Hemingway, what did you do after the tournament began?"

"I followed the defendant. Miss Fenneman."

"Ms. Fenneman," Fannie muttered.

"And why would you do that?"

"Well, me and the boys've been suspicious of her for some time."

"Why?"

"Well, you know, her winning all those tournaments, one right after another. T'ain't natural. Hell, I've been fishin' all my life, and I ain't never come up with a fish like the ones she showed up with every dadburned time."

"You couldn't catch a fish in an aquarium," Fannie whispered. Ben jabbed her in the side.

"So," Edwards asked, "you suspected skulduggery?"

Hemingway straightened his shoulders. "I suspected she was cheatin', if that's what you mean."

"Indeed it is." Edwards turned a page in his outline. "So what did you see when you followed her?"

"Well, you hafta understand, we was in the water, each in our own boat, and I hadta keep a distance so's she wouldn't know she was bein' watched. Still, I managed to keep an eye on her. Got me a souped-up pair of binoculars. Canon 540s."

"And what did you see?"

"At first she sailed out with everyone else. She found her spot, tossed in her line—all natural-like."

"And then what happened?"

"Well, I hadta wait about thirty, forty minutes, while she did nothin' in particular but sit there and fish."

"Yes. And then?"

"Well, I saw her pull in her reel and look all around to make sure no one was watchin', real suspicious-like. Then she revs up the boat and heads for shore. But not fast, you see. She goes real slow and quiet, so's not to make any noise. Then she gets out of her boat and disappears."

"Disappears?"

"Well, she went onshore."

"Did you see where she went?"

"Naw. I couldn't get close enough."

Edwards began to look a bit worried. "So . . . you don't know what she did next?"

"I know this. Ten minutes later she was back in her boat. And thirty minutes after that she sailed back to port with the biggest blamed rainbow trout I've seen in my life."

"So what do you think she did onshore?"

"Objection," Ben said, rising to his feet. "Calls for speculation."

Judge Hart nodded. "Let's limit the testimony to what he saw and heard, Mr. Edwards. Trust me, the story is riveting enough without supplementing it with conjecture."

Edwards smiled thinly. "Mr. Hemingway, what did you do after the defendant returned to port with this large fish?"

"Well, I hopped into my truck and drove out to the spot where I saw her get out of the car. And what do you suppose I found?"

"Uh ... traditionally, I ask the questions and the witness gives the answers."

"Oh. Right."

"So what did you find, sir?"

Hemingway leaned forward. "Not a hundred feet from where she got out of the boat, parked behind a tree, I found Fannie's flame-red Ford pickup truck. Mag wheels and nylon gate."

"Did you search the truck?"

"I most certainly did."

"What did you find?"

"Objection," Ben said. "No probable cause to search."

"Nice try," Judge Hart said. "But Mr. Hemingway isn't a member of the law enforcement community, is he? His activities do not constitute state action."

"But his testimony is being used by the government."

"Yes, so it is. Tough how these things work out sometimes, isn't it? Overruled." She nodded toward Edwards. "Please proceed."

"Mr. Hemingway, what did you find inside the truck?"

He leaned back, obviously pleased with himself. "That's when I found the freshwater tank."

Edwards introduced the State's Exhibit A, an oversized portable freshwater tank. Just right for a jumbo trout.

"What did you do after you found the tank?" Edwards asked.

"Well, at that point, it was obvious she'd been cheatin'. What else could I do? I disqualified her and told her to return all the prize money. When she refused, I went and had me a little talk with the assistant DA."

His brother-in-law, Ben recalled.

"Thank you," Edwards said. "No more questions."

Judge Hart swiveled to face the defendant's table. "Any cross-examination, Mr. Kincaid?"

"Uh, yes." Ben scrambled to his feet.

Fannie gave him a little shove. "Go get 'em, tiger."

Ben tried to restrain his enthusiasm. "Mr. Hemingway, my name is Ben Kincaid, and I represent Ms. Fenneman. I'd like to ask you a few questions."

Hemingway dipped his chin. "Shoot."

"Mr. Hemingway, the fact is you didn't actually see Ms. Fenneman take anything out of that tank, did you?"

"Well, no."

"You didn't see what she did after she got out of the boat?"

"That's true."

"Would you be surprised to learn that she went onshore just to . . . well . . ." Ben's face flushed. ". . . to relieve herself?"

A slow grin crept across Hemingway's face. "Well, I wouldn't be surprised to hear that she *said* that."

"Just answer the questions, sir." Ben's eyes darted around the courtroom. He knew he was just covering the obvious material; nobody appeared particularly impressed, and rightly so.

"Pssst."

Ben heard the hissing behind him, but resisted getting dragged into another expression of Fannie's outrage. "Mr. Hemingway, isn't it true—"

"*Pssst!*"

Ben plowed dutifully ahead. "Isn't it true that you never—"

"Excuse me." This time the voice came from the foreground. It was Judge Hart. "Counsel, I believe your legal assistant is attempting to get your attention."

Ben turned to face Christina McCall, who was leaning across the railing that separated the gallery from the court. Her hand was outstretched and she was clutching a scrap of paper. Ben snatched the paper and opened it.

Judge Hart peered down curiously from the bench. "Fan mail from some flounder?"

"Uh . . . not exactly." Ben stared at the note, which contained two words: HE'S LYING.

"Your honor, might I confer for a moment—?"

"Will it speed the trial along?"

"I'm sure it will."

"Then by all means."

Ben walked to the back of the courtroom. Christina was in her pan-European phase; she was wearing a red-and-blue-checked French-schoolgirl dress tucked into black leggings, which Ben supposed was intended to make her look as leggy as a woman barely five-feet-one was ever likely to look. "Christina, I think you're becoming more eccentric and mysterious every day."

She smiled. "Did you read my note?"

"Yes. What does it mean?"

"Just what it says." She tossed her head back, making her vivid red hair, which was tied in a ponytail, swish between her shoulder blades. "He's lying. Vis-à-vis the tank. It's a frame."

"A fish frame. How?"

"I don't know how."

"Then how do you know he's lying?"

"Because I am a *femme du monde*—or a *femme*, at any rate."

"Stifle the French and tell me your theory. I find this very hard to believe."

"That's because you've been assuming your client is guilty."

Ben avoided her eyes. "Well, her success record is pretty amazing."

"Right. No woman could ever be that good."

"I didn't mean that."

"You didn't. But look at the guy in the stand." Ben glanced back toward the front at Hemingway, in his flannel shirt, his jeans, his palm-sized belt buckle, and his baseball cap advertising Shakespeare fishing gear. Hmmm.

"So you think he didn't like losing forty-seven times in a row?"

"I think he didn't like losing to a competitor with no chest hair."

Ben continued staring at the man in the witness stand. If he had learned nothing else in the years since he'd been out of law school, he'd learned to trust Christina's instincts. She was a far better judge of people than he would ever be.

"Ready to proceed?" Judge Hart asked.

"Yes. Thank you, your honor." Ben folded up his prepared outline. He was going to have to wing this one. "Mr. Hemingway. You've been a participant in some of these tournaments yourself, haven't you?"

"I like to cast a line every now and again."

"You probably didn't much care for losing all those tournaments to my client, did you?"

"Objection." Edwards was on his feet. "This is not relevant."

"Your honor," Ben interjected. "I'm trying to establish—"

Judge Hart cut him off. "No windy speeches, counsel. I know where you're going. Overruled."

Ben turned back to the witness. "Answer the question."

"Well, I'd prob'ly rather win than lose, if that's what you mean. I don't much cotton to losin'."

"Especially to a woman, right?"

Hemingway's eyes darted away. "I don't know what in the Sam Hill that's got to do with anything."

Ben took a few steps toward the witness. "Mr. Hemingway, you put that freshwater tank in Fannie's truck, didn't you?"

His voice swelled. "I sure as—" He glanced at the judge, then checked himself. "I mean, I certainly did not."

"You're under oath."

"I'm aware of that."

"And you're stating under oath that you did not put that tank in Fannie's truck?"

"You got it, shyster. Hell, I've never had one of those tanks in my life. Never even seen one till I found Exhibit A in her truck."

"And you wouldn't want to damage Fannie's reputation as a fisherwoman?"

"Couldn't care less about that."

"Hmm." Ben took a step back. "Mr. Hemingway, when was the last time you actually won a fishing tournament?"

"It's been . . ." His eyes floated to the tops of their sockets. "Well, it's been a while."

"A while . . . meaning years?"

"Yes."

"How many years?"

"I don't rightly recall."

"You must have some idea."

"Five years, eight months, and thirteen days, okay?" He was leaning slightly forward now, balancing on his fingertips.

"What tournament was that? That you won, I mean. Five years ago."

"That was the Beaver Invitational, for your information. Damn tough tournament, too."

"I see." The neurons were firing in Ben's brain, but he hadn't yet pieced everything together. Beaver. Beaver. That place rang a bell, and not just because it was the cow-chip-throwing capital of the world. There was something he had read in the witness files . . .

He glanced to the back of the courtroom and saw a red ponytail bouncing above the pews. Christina was already digging in the files, way ahead of him.

A few moments later, she returned with a newspaper article they had obtained during discovery from the prosecution. The accompanying photo showed Hemingway holding an impressive bass. The sun was setting in the background, casting a rosy hue over the lake.

Ben handed the article to Hemingway. "Is this the tournament?"

Hemingway glanced at the picture. A smile of recollected pride crossed his lips. "Yes. I won that tournament. That was before *she* hit the circuit."

"Nice-looking fish you caught there."

"Aw, she was a beauty."

"Nice gloss. Good color."

"Yeah."

"Thing is . . . don't fish start to get kind of . . . well, groady, after they've been out in the sun for a while?" Ben was hardly an expert, but once Christina had dragged him out on a fishing expedition in Arkansas.

"Well," Hemingway answered, "the coat tends to dry up. Scales flake off. They rot, like anything else."

"But, Mr. Hemingway, that fish looks beautiful. You said so yourself."

"The picture was prob'ly taken just after I caught him."

"I don't think so."

"Musta been."

"No." Ben pointed to a line in the article. "Paper says you caught him at twelve-forty P.M."

"Well then, this was prob'ly right after that."

Ben pointed to the photograph. "Look in the background. The sun is setting."

"Well . . . yesss."

"This was during the summertime in Oklahoma. Sun sets, what? About eight-thirty? Nine?"

"Yesss . . ."

"So this photo was taken seven or eight hours after you caught the fish. But he looks like you just dragged him out of the water."

Hemingway shifted his weight. "Well, you know, them photographers are real talented."

"You're suggesting trick photography? Maybe some airbrush work? I don't think so, Mr. Hemingway. I think you bought him."

"I did not buy him!"

"You must've."

"I didn't!"

"You must've caught some other fish and then substituted the fish you bought just before this picture was taken."

"I did no such thing!"

"Your denials are futile, Mr. Hemingway. The photo speaks for itself."

His fists were balling up. "It's a lie."

"Face it, sir. You cheated."

His voice rose. "I did not!"

"The evidence is right in front of you. Stop denying it."

"I did *not* cheat!"

"Then how did the fish stay fresh all afternoon?"

He sprang to his feet. "Because I kept it in my—"

Hemingway stopped suddenly and froze. He looked both ways at once, mouth gaping, then slowly dropped to his chair.

Ben eased away from the witness stand, his eyes dancing. "Is the word you're searching for by any chance . . . *tank?*"

CHAPTER

2

BEN DIDN'T MAKE it back to his office until later that afternoon. It was a downtown cubbyhole on a street full of pawnshops and loan offices (GET THE CASH YOU NEED QUICK—NO QUESTIONS ASKED). The yellow brick of most of the buildings harkened back to an era when these offices formed Tulsa's line of demarcation between the prosperous white oil barons to the south and the equally prosperous Black Wall Street to the north.

Ben pushed open the door and stepped inside. For once the office seemed relatively peaceful. No bill collectors blocking the entrance, no strapped clients explaining why they couldn't pay, no disgruntled opponents seeking revenge.

Jones, Ben's office assistant, sat at a desk in the center of the lobby area, one hand clutching a phone receiver and the other tickling the keyboard of his computer.

Jones covered the mouthpiece when he saw Ben enter. "Congratulations, Boss."

"You heard?"

Jones nodded. "Fannie told all. She's in your office waiting for you." He smiled. "Said you carved up the prosecution's main witness on cross."

"She's exaggerating."

"No doubt."

"Who's on the line?"

Jones pointed at the computer screen. "I found another small New England college on the Net this morning. They have several graduate programs in nursing."

Ben's interest was immediate. "Really?"

"Relax, Boss. Just because they have a program doesn't mean your sister is in it. I'm trying to bully my way into the admissions records."

Ben crossed his fingers. After a few moments he heard a voice buzzing on the other end of the line. Jones replied, not in Oklahoman, but in a clipped British accent. "Jolly good, old chap. Are you certain about that?" After a few more such exchanges, Jones hung up the phone.

"Ronald Colman?" Ben asked.

Jones grinned. "A tony British accent can occasionally charm some answers out of these New England universities."

"And?"

Jones shook his head. "Sorry, Boss. She isn't there."

Ben tried not to let his disappointment show. "Well, keep trying." He started toward his office.

"Boss—"

He stopped. "Yeah?"

"Not that it's any of my business, but—"

"But you're going to butt in anyway."

"Don't you think it's time you gave up this search? Your sister obviously doesn't want to be found."

"We don't know that for certain."

"She told you she was enrolling in a graduate-level nursing program in Connecticut. But we've searched every Connecticut college on the map and she isn't there."

"She might've gotten her states confused."

"Get a reality check, Boss. She fled. Vanished. After dumping her baby on you." Jones clicked the mouse on the computer. "How old is Joey now?"

"Thirteen months."

"So she's been gone for almost six months. And she's never called once to check on her kid. Face it; she's history."

Ben knew any refutation would sound desperate and lame. "Still . . . it doesn't hurt to keep looking. When you have the time."

Jones frowned. "You're the boss, Boss." He handed Ben some papers. "Here's your latest draft of the summary judgment brief in the Skaggs case. It's due today."

Ben checked his watch. "Today? The courthouse closes in less than an hour!"

Jones turned back to his computer. "Have a nice day."

"Swell." Ben shoved the brief under his arm. "By the way . . ." He made an awkward coughing noise. ". . . did the payroll . . . ?"

Jones shook his head.

"Oh. Well." He shuffled toward his interior office.

Just as Ben tried to step in, another, much larger figure stepped out.

"Whoa!" the man said as he quickly ducked out of the way. "Sorry, Skipper. We nearly had a head-on collision. We coulda flattened each other."

Except, Ben thought, since Loving outweighed him by about a hundred and twenty pounds, mostly muscle, Loving would've done most of the flattening. "Working on some big case?"

"Not at the moment. Things are kinda slow." Loving was Ben's private investigator, although he often worked independently when clients had need of his services. "I was chatting with your client. Nice gal."

Ben suppressed a smile. "I thought you might like her."

"By the way . . ." The hesitance in his voice told Ben exactly what was coming. "I know you've been busy and all, but can you tell if the payroll . . .?"

Ben shook his head. "No."

"Oh. Well, I understand."

"I'm sorry, Loving. Work really seems to have dried up, and my clients aren't paying—"

"Don't worry about it, Skipper. It ain't your fault."

"It ain't?"

"Nah, it's the whole international banking conspiracy thing."

"The—what?"

"The banking conspiracy."

Ben frowned. "Perhaps I should start reading the papers."

"All the bigwigs in all the major industrial countries, the Trilateral Commission, the Illuminati, the power elite—they're all sucking up the world's cash. Trying to make paper currency worthless."

"And why would they want to do that?"

" 'Cause they own all the gold, of course. Cash goes down, gold goes up."

"That's incredibly paranoid."

Loving chuckled. "Yeah, that's what JFK said, too. And look what they did to him."

"I beg your pardon. I thought the CIA, the FBI, the Mafia, the Cubans, and the military-industrial complex were behind that one."

Loving smiled knowingly as Ben entered his office and closed the door. "That's what they want you to think."

Ben made his way to the tiny desk in the corner and tossed the Skaggs brief on top.

"Ben Kincaid, my hero."

Ben glanced up. Fannie was standing awkwardly in the center of the room. She was back in her trademark overalls and was fidgeting nervously with her hands.

"Oh. Hello, Fannie."

"Ben, you were wonderful in the courtroom today."

Ben slid into his desk chair. "I really didn't do anything."

"I think you did. You salvaged my professional standing. My reputation."

Ben undid the top button of his shirt and loosened his tie. "Fannie, I don't want to seem rude, but I need to review this brief pronto."

"Oh." She knotted her fingers together. "I was hoping we could . . . talk."

"Well . . ."

"It's real important."

"I'm sorry, but—"

"It's about your . . . payment."

Ben suddenly had a sinking feeling. "Well, I can do more than one thing at a time. You talk, I'll read."

"Oh. Sure." There was a long pause. "Ben, I'm so grateful for all you've done for me. I mean it. You've saved my good name. You've redeemed me."

Actually, Ben thought, the fact that Hemingway planted the tank in her truck didn't necessarily mean she hadn't been cheating, but he decided to keep that thought to himself.

"I owe you everything. Problem is . . . I don't have anything."

Ben's eyes squeezed closed. *I knew it.* "What happened to all that prize money?"

"Well, to tell you the truth, I'm a bit too fond of that Creek Nation Bingo Parlor."

I can't stand it, Ben thought. I just can't stand it.

"I know I owe you, Ben. I owe you a lot."

"It was nothing," Ben mumbled, "nothing at all."

There was a sharp intake of breath. "Well, never let it be said that Fannie Fenneman doesn't honor her debts." There was a pause, followed by a metallic clinking noise. "So I've decided to pay my bill in trade."

Ben's eyes stopped moving across the brief. Slowly his head raised.

Fannie was standing in the center of the office, stark naked, her overalls in a pile around her feet.

"Uh, Fannie . . ."

"Now, don't you worry, Ben. You'll get your money's worth."

"I'm sure . . . I mean, I never doubted . . ."

"Well, come on, Ben." She wrapped her arms around herself. Ben thought perhaps she was embarrassed, but the external evidence indicated she was cold. "I'm ready and waiting."

Ben eased out of his chair. "Fannie, I don't think this is a good idea."

"It is, Ben. I promise." Her body vibrated in a singularly impressive manner. "You won't be sorry."

"I already am." He took his suit coat off the hook on the door and held it out to her. "Here, put something on before—"

"Ben, no." She brushed the coat away and grabbed his arm, pulling him to her. Before he could stop himself, Ben collided into her. She wrapped her arms around him. "Don't fight it, Ben. It's the only way."

"Fannie, please!"

Just then, the office door swung open. Christina poked her head inside. "Ben, can I—" She stopped short, her eyes widening like balloons. "Oh, my—I had no idea. I'm so sorry." She vanished.

"Christina! Wait! It isn't—" Ben pushed himself out of Fannie's arms. "Excuse me." He ran toward the door.

"But, Ben!" Fannie cried.

He whirled around. "And put your clothes back on!" He stepped through the door and found Jones and Loving staring at him. "What are you two looking at?"

Both pairs of eyes immediately darted down to their desks.

Ben stomped across the lobby. "Have you seen Christina?"

"She blew out of here like a rocket. Can you blame her?"

"Jones, it isn't what you think—"

"Jeez, Boss"—his look was one of pure amazement—"you don't even have carpet in there."

"Jones—"

"There is that one chair, I suppose. Or the desk. Man, you must really like it rough."

"*Jones!*" He ran to the front window and looked both ways down the street. Christina was nowhere in sight. "Look, Jones, if you see Christina, tell her . . ." He searched his mind for the right words. "Never mind, I'll tell her myself. The Skaggs brief looks fine, by the way. Can you file it?"

"I could," Jones said, "but don't you have to be going that way, anyway?"

"Me? Why?"

"To get to Forestview. Joey, remember? I mean"—he glanced back at the office door—"if you're up to it."

Ben glanced at his watch. "It's not five yet. I still have—"

Jones interrupted him. "Parent-teacher conference. Four-thirty sharp."

Ben slammed his fists together. "Blast! I totally forgot."

"Well, you've had a lot on your mind."

"Would you stop that!" Ben grabbed his briefcase.

"Look, Boss, I've got a ratty old sofa at home. It isn't much, but if you like, I could put it in your office."

Ben raised a finger. "I don't have time for this. I'll talk to you later."

"I can't wait. Stay out of trouble, Casanova."

3

BEN SAT IN a molded plastic chair in the small conference room at Forest-view Country Day School. He was trying his best to remain calm.

"I'm afraid I just don't see the problem."

Ms. Hammerstein, the head teacher in the infant care room, sported an unchanging placid smile. "Well, first of all, Mr. Kincaid, let me tell you what a wonderful child Joey is. So smart. Such a delight. We all love him very much."

"Ye-es . . ."

"He's a truly special individual."

Ben refrained from drumming his fingers on the table. "Why do I feel like I'm waiting for the other shoe to drop?"

Ms. Hammerstein's visage barely fluttered. "I'm sure I don't know what you mean."

"The woman on the phone said there was a problem. That's why we're having this meeting, according to her. Because there's a problem."

"Well . . . yes." Ms. Hammerstein opened the blue notebook on the table before her. "There have been a few . . . issues that have arisen. I wouldn't have used the word *problem*—"

"The woman on the phone did."

She scanned the page in her notebook with Joey's name at the top. "Most of these—let's call them observations—are what I would group under the general heading of compliance issues."

"Compliance?"

"Yes."

"Meaning he doesn't do exactly what you want exactly when you want it."

"Now, Mr. Kincaid. We try to be very flexible."

"Doesn't sound that way."

"Mr. Kincaid . . . I assure you . . ."

"I'm sorry." Ben realized he was acting like a typical father. How dare you suggest that my child has a flaw? "Let's cut to the chase. What are these issues?"

"Well . . ." Ms. Hammerstein turned another page in her notebook. "Joey just . . . isn't like the other children."

"Why should he be?"

"He doesn't play with the other children."

"So he prefers his own company. Is that a crime? He's shy."

"He wanders off by himself."

"God forbid. Let's sic the robot dogs on him."

She took a deep breath. "He doesn't talk. Doesn't even babble. Doesn't engage in imaginative play like the other children."

"Has it occurred to you that Joey has perhaps had a slightly more traumatic infancy than the other children?" Like being born to a mother already divorced for the second time. Like being abandoned when he was barely seven months old. Like being dumped on Uncle Ben, who didn't know squat about how to take care of a baby. Like being placed in this concentration camp cum country day school so Uncle Ben could eke out what he laughingly called a living. "I think we should cut Joey a little slack."

"I'm perfectly willing to cut him as much slack as he needs, Mr. Kincaid. But I am not willing to jeopardize his personal safety."

"What are you talking about?"

"I've already told you. Joey wanders off. He doesn't listen. He doesn't do as he's told. It's dangerous. Whenever we go outside, we have to watch him every second. If we blink, Joey wanders off by himself. He could get lost or hurt. There are only two teachers in each classroom, and twelve children. We can't afford to have one person permanently assigned to preventing Joey from hurting himself."

"Why not? God knows your tuition is high enough."

"Mr. Kincaid, this isn't about money. It's about the fact that . . . that Joey isn't like the other children."

"So this isn't about compliance at all. It's about conformity."

Ms. Hammerstein's head tilted to one side. "Joey . . . does march to the beat of a different drummer."

"But you'll soon have him goosestepping with the other soldiers. Is that it?"

"Mr. Kincaid!"

Ben tried to get a grip on himself. He wasn't being rational and he knew it. He took a deep breath and swallowed. "So what do you recommend?"

"I would like Joey to be examined by a professional."

"*What?*" His shout practically lifted the ceiling.

"Nonintrusive, of course. The doctor would just come to the school and observe Joey."

"The *doctor*? What kind of doctor?"

"Well . . ."

Ben's jaw clenched together. "A shrink, right? You want to send him to a shrink."

"I would like him to be observed by a specialist in pre-adolescent personality disorders—"

"He's only thirteen months old, for God's sake!" Ben leaped out of his chair. "What kind of people are you?"

"Mr. Kincaid, please stay calm. I assure you this is as hard for me as it is for you."

"I doubt it!" Ben bounced back into his seat, hands folded across his chest. "I refuse to believe a thirteen-month-old kid can have some deep psychiatric problem."

"I hope you're right. If you are, then we can eliminate that possibility and explore some other possible cause. But we can't reach any diagnosis without help."

"I can't believe you want to foist some headshrinker on my boy."

"But he isn't your boy, is he, Mr. Kincaid?"

That slowed him down a beat. "What do you mean?"

"Mr. Kincaid, I'm familiar with your situation. And believe me, I admire what you have done under such difficult circumstances. But at the same time, I can't help wondering whether Joey might not be better off in . . . well, a more stable home environment."

Ben felt his eyes narrowing. "What do you mean?"

"Please don't think I'm being critical, Mr. Kincaid. I don't mean it that way. But you are single, right?"

"Yes."

"You live in a small apartment in a boardinghouse?"

"Yes."

"You work full-time."

"Right."

"Your practice is . . . what's the word?"

"Struggling?"

"Good. Struggling. And your work often requires you to be away from home at night."

"Well, when I have a case in court."

"And that happens . . ."

"Not as often as I'd like."

The placid smile returned to Ms. Hammerstein's face. "Don't you see, Mr. Kincaid? Joey has had such a traumatic first year. He needs constancy. He needs to know there are people he can count on day in, day out."

"He has a nanny—"

"He needs a parent." She closed her blue notebook. "Maybe even two."

Ben didn't respond for several seconds. Dark thoughts raced through his head. "I don't know what you want me to do."

"Well, before we do anything drastic, let's get a doctor to see Joey. See what he says. Then we'll go from there."

"Fine, but I don't want Joey to know he's being tested."

"He won't, I assure you." She reached across the table and placed her hand on Ben's shoulder. "You're doing the right thing, Mr. Kincaid."

Ben wished he could bring himself to return the peacemaking gesture, but he couldn't. "I hope you're right."

BEN PICKED UP Joey in the Rocket Room. He swept the boy into his arms and they hugged. Or to be more accurate, Ben hugged Joey. Joey never hugged. He didn't resist, but he didn't hug. He was just there.

Ben held Joey up to his face and smiled. "Hey, pardner! Can you say hi to your uncle Ben?"

Joey didn't answer. He was gazing off into space, at nothing in particular.

"Joey, say hi. Can you say hi?"

If he could, he didn't. His head tilted, as if he were contemplating the great mysteries of the universe.

"Joey, can you answer me?"

Joey's eyes glazed.

"Joey. Please say hi!"

Still no answer.

"Joey!" Ben took Joey by the chin and forced him to look his way. Joey quickly averted his gaze. He never made eye contact. "Will you please say hi to your uncle Ben?"

He continued staring off somewhere over Ben's shoulder.

Ben sighed, then set Joey down on the ground and took his hand. "Let's go to the car."

Ben led him down the corridor. He scanned the hall for the mayor, Wallace Barrett, who usually picked up his kids about the same time. Barrett had been mayor for the last three and a half years. The city's first black mayor. Some pundits had speculated that the color barrier would never be broken in Tulsa, but Wallace "The Wall" Barrett had done it by being smart, articulate, and hard-working. Of course, being a former University of Oklahoma football star, in a state where more people went to football games than voted, didn't hurt any.

Barrett didn't seem to be around today. Come to think of it, Ben had heard something on the car radio about Barrett holding a press conference, announcing his intent to run for reelection. That probably explained his absence.

Barrett had two daughters, both beauties. Ben recalled seeing them the previous Friday, when one of them had been so anxious to get to her father that she crashed into Ben's leg.

"Hey, slow down," Ben had said.

The girl ignored him, rushing on down the corridor. "Daddy!" she screamed. When she reached the end of the hallway, she leaped into her father's arms. Her father scooped her up, hugged her tight, then swung her around in a circle.

"Hey, Kincaid! Sorry about my little crash pilot." A second girl clutched Barrett's leg.

Ben and Barrett had met at school functions and had become nodding acquaintances. Barrett was the kind of person who never forgot your name, your wife's name, your kids' names, or anything else.

"I'm fine, Mr. Mayor. Don't worry about it. You've got a great pair of daughters."

"Don't I know it." He scooped his other girl into his arms and beamed at the both of them. They were practically identical, but for the difference in their ages. Slim and pretty, with curly black hair.

Barrett squeezed his daughters till they burst out laughing. They threw their arms around his neck and hugged him. He kissed them both on the cheek. Ben had seen the love in his eyes, the love so freely and enthusiastically returned by his daughters.

Barrett grinned from ear to ear. "I must be the luckiest man on earth."

Ben nodded. "I think you're probably right."

A tug on his arm snapped Ben back to the present. He looked down at Joey, who was still holding his hand and gazing off into space. Ben crouched down eye to eye with him. "Joey," he said hesitantly, "you're not . . . I mean, you don't—Joey?"

Joey seemed to have taken an intense interest in the aquarium.

Ben took Joey's chin and gently guided it around to face him. "Joey, I know you didn't have any choice about staying with me, but you're not . . ."

He swallowed, then tried again. "I know you don't show it much, but deep down you really do . . . don't you?"

Joey stuck his finger between his lips and explored the roof of his mouth.

"Right. Well. Anyway." He stood up again and took Joey's hand. "Let's go, pardner." They pushed through the front doors. "What sounds good for dinner tonight? I was thinking we might make spaghetti."

CHAPTER

4

LATER THAT EVENING, Harvey Sanders peered through the curtains of his upstairs window at the house next door and shook his head sadly. They were at it again.

Seemed like it was almost every day now. Rain or shine, come what may, he could count on his famous neighbors having some terrific row before the day was over. Harvey hated to think of those lovely little girls being subjected to this barrage of hatred. Must be hard trying to tell yourself that Mommy and Daddy love each other after you've witnessed something like this day after day. Those poor kids.

Harvey closed the curtains, turned off *Little House on the Prairie*, and walked downstairs to the kitchen. He took a beer out of the fridge and popped the lid into the sink. As he did, he passed an open window that overlooked an equally open window in the Barretts' house. Man alive, they were really going at it now.

"Shut up, you stupid cow!"

Harvey couldn't hear them any better if they were in the next room. Wally had one of those deep booming voices; it carried. There was some more shouting, some general clamor. Then he heard some crying. Damn. One of the girls. "Daddy! Daddy!"

The crying swelled till it was almost piercing, then it seemed to fade. The girl was moving away from the window.

The fight continued. "I know you care about them, or pretend to. What about me?"

There was some reply Harvey didn't catch.

"You're damn right! *Me!*"

The next sound startled Harvey so that he dropped his beer bottle on the linoleum. It was a sharp, quick sound, like the popping of a paper bag.

Or a slap across the face. Flesh against flesh.

There were several more exchanges he couldn't understand. Then: "Don't drag the children into this!"

"I don't have any choice!"

There was another noise, loud enough to make Harvey flinch. A great, crashing noise—Harvey couldn't even think of anything that would make a noise like that. Dishes? Furniture? Or worse?

Harvey strolled into his living room. Well, what would his excuse be this time? Perhaps a shard of Anasazi pottery? Or perhaps a toilet that needed attention? Either would do.

He'd give them a little cool-down time before he went over and interjected himself into the situation. He really wasn't the nosy neighbor type, not some sitcom cliché, sneaking up to windows and holding a glass against the wall. He didn't like to butt into other people's business. But back where he came from (Dill City, Oklahoma, to be exact—population 632), people cared about each other, and tried to be there for each other, and didn't get nervous about walking in and offering help when folks were needing it.

Here in the big city (Tulsa, Oklahoma, to be exact—population 503,000) he had learned to be more circumspect. He'd moved out here twelve years before, after his grandmother passed on and left him this great house in a ritzy neighborhood. In that time, he'd found that folks got a little nervous when you started asking personal questions. Back in Dill City, doors were never locked and people expected to be visited. No one thought twice about dropping in unannounced on a neighbor. Here, seemed like neighbors never called on each other unless they had made an appointment days in advance and had some super-special reason. So he had learned to have reasons.

Harvey had moved to Tulsa after he got out of college (University of Oklahoma, to be exact—Class of '85). Harvey wanted to be an actor, but to tide himself over until fame and fortune called, he took a job at the world-famous Gilcrease Museum of Western Art. Twelve years later, he was an assistant curator, which was as high as he cared to rise on the totem pole. Why would he want to be curator? That was just a fund-raising position. Harvey didn't want to have lunch at Southern Hills. He wanted to play with the toys.

And Gilcrease had the best toys. Western art, yes—Remingtons and Carys and Morans, sculptures and paintings. But what Harvey really loved were the artifacts. Artifacts of the Old West, artifacts of Native American cultures. Great stuff. The museum's holdings were so vast they couldn't all be displayed at once. The artifacts in deep storage had to be maintained. Harvey took care of that. He loved working with the goods, and it gave him a legitimate excuse to take some of them home occasionally, just for a day or two. Which in turn gave him a great excuse to take them over to the Barretts. Show-and-tell for grown-ups.

"Hey, Wally, look at this great kachina doll!" he'd say as he strolled in through the kitchen door. Actually, he wasn't sure the mayor cared a bit about kachina dolls. He wasn't sure he much cared for being called Wally, either. Didn't matter. It got Harvey through the door, where he could keep an eye on things. That mattered.

And if museum curios couldn't do the trick, there was always home repair. One ruse he could count on—there was always something in the Barrett home that needed to be fixed. Back in Dill City, he had learned how to take care of most home emergencies himself, including the plumbing, because there was usually no one else to do it. These were useful skills, and skills that Wally had never managed to acquire, thus leading to another easy entrance into the Barrett home.

"Harvey!" he remembered Caroline saying not too long ago, when he delivered himself to their kitchen, "what brings you over here?"

"Well, the kids were tellin' me there was a leak in the . . ." He snapped his fingers. "Oh, the . . ."

"The shower?"

"That's right. The shower."

"You mean the shower drain."

"Right, that's what I meant. Well, I brought my tools."

"So I see."

"I'll just get to work. So how's everything going?"

Worked like a charm. Let him stay vigilant, maybe prevent a few knock-down-drag-outs, and maybe make Caroline's life a little easier. Which was important.

The truth was, Harvey harbored a secret, one he admitted only to himself. Sure, he cared about the kids, and he worried when their parents fought like cocks in the henhouse. But that was only half the story.

Truth was, Harvey was in love with Caroline Barrett.

It was nothing tawdry or unseemly or disgusting. He didn't lust after her from afar or take pictures of her to bed or anything. He just loved her, that was all.

Who wouldn't? Caroline was a gorgeous woman, one of the most natural beauties God ever saw fit to put on the face of this earth. Tall, thin, well-dressed, with high cheekbones and long legs that went from here to forever. She was a knockout's knockout. Why she'd want to get hitched up to some old jock-turned-politico he couldn't imagine. Couldn't resist the limelight, he supposed, such as it was. What could you say about a culture that made millionaires out of football players and paid museum curators twenty-two thousand a year?

It wasn't so much the fighting that worried him. All couples quarrel, though most didn't do it as often, or as mean, as those two. But he had noticed that in the last six months or so, Caroline had occasionally taken to wearing sunglasses when she went outside, and the sun just wasn't that bright. One afternoon when he caught her out in the garden, she had a bruise on her cheek so discolored no amount of makeup could hide it. She told him some lame story about bumping into the shelves in the attic.

That worried him.

One afternoon not too long ago, he'd been at the neighborhood block party and the Barretts were there too, and there was some jerk who had just moved into the area and had drunk too much for his own good who was hanging around Caroline, smirking and winking and drooling and touching her arm and generally trying to cozy up in a none-too-subtle way. Wally saw what was going on, marched over, stepped between them (cutting the jerk off), and just stared at her. He didn't say a word; he just stared. But man, his was a stare that could chill Death himself. It had given Harvey shivers all up and down his spine.

That worried him.

Harvey watched television for a while, but found he couldn't concentrate on it. There was something odd about this business today, though Harvey couldn't quite put his finger on what. He pushed off the sofa and returned to the kitchen. He stood by the window for a while, but didn't hear a peep. That was it—that was what was odd. Earlier he'd heard such a terrific hullabaloo, and now he heard nothing. How long ago was it he heard the big noise? An hour? But now he heard nothing. Less than nothing, actually. It was absolutely silent over there. Deathly silent.

That should be good, shouldn't it? That should mean the fight was over. So why was his skin crawling?

Harvey put the empty beer bottle in the trash and strolled out onto his front lawn. It was no different. No sign of activity at the house next door, or anywhere else, for that matter. He should've been relieved by that. This was supposed to be a nice, upper-class neighborhood, but lately, he'd noticed people he didn't much like the looks of. Not that he sat around all night peering out the windows or anything, but still. Occasionally there were vagrants. The last several nights he'd seen what he called the Odd Couple: some grungy-looking man wearing fatigues and a young girl—mid to late teens, he'd guess—wearing a tank top and big hoop earrings and a blue headband. They walked up and down the street, real casually, looking the neighborhood over. Or casing it, he suspected. Let those druggies in and you might as well move out.

The eerie silence was shattered by a piercing, howling noise. What the hell? He eased across the lawn toward the Barretts' house. Suddenly, as if in answer to his question, Harvey saw Wallace Barrett race out the front door.

"Wally!" Harvey shouted.

Barrett didn't answer, didn't even seem to hear, as far as Harvey could tell, even though they were less than twenty-five feet apart. Barrett was running at top speed, flexing those leg muscles that made him the best rushing quarterback OU had ever seen. His shirt seemed to be torn, and there was something bright smeared across one side of his face.

"Wally!"

No use. Barrett leaped into his Porsche parked on the curb—had that been there before?—and slid into the driver's seat. In a few seconds the car was powered up and Barrett was halfway down the street.

Now that was very odd, Harvey thought. Odd, and worrisome.

I need to get in that house, he told himself. I need to know . . . what? He wasn't sure. But the short hairs on the back of his neck told him something unusual was happening. Or had happened.

It was so quiet over there.

The window on the side of the Barrett home was still open. Maybe if he just sidled up to it casually . . .

No. What would he say, after all, if they saw him? He didn't have his tools and he didn't have a kachina doll. The place was probably a mess. The kids were probably upset. It would just be an embarrassment to everyone.

Well, he told himself, the police were supposed to handle this sort of thing, weren't they? So let them. He could call in a domestic disturbance anonymously. The cops had to answer, even if they didn't think there was anything to it; he'd read about that in the paper. They could check on Caroline and the kids, and no one need know he had called them in.

It was tempting just to go in now, to march in there and make sure everything was fine. That's what he would've done back in Dill City.

Hmph. And these big-city types thought they were so much more sophisticated. Sometimes he thought they didn't know anything at all, not about the things that were really important.

The doorknob was so close. He could just reach out . . . step inside . . .

But he didn't. He turned around and walked back to his house.

If he had gone in, he would surely have been overcome by the sickly sweet smell of blood, so thick that it permeated the air in every room of the house. He would have noticed the swarming flies, drawn by the smell through the open window, circling the grisly remains. He might've called the police a lot sooner than he did, had he remained conscious afterward, which is doubtful.

Things like this never happened back in Dill City.

5

BEN PULLED HIS aging '82 Honda Accord onto the side of the street. The brakes squeaked and squealed, but they did manage to stop the car. This time, anyway. He patted the dash affectionately. Two hundred thousand miles and still ticking. What more could you ask for?

He scooped Joey out of his car seat and carried him across the street to the boardinghouse where Ben had one of the second-story apartments. As he approached, he saw Mrs. Marmelstein out front. She was on her knees, facing away from them, puttering in her garden.

"How are the tulips doing?" Ben asked.

Mrs. Marmelstein brushed a straggling strand of steel-gray hair out of her face. "Well, they're doing their best, but that late frost didn't do them any favors. How's my favorite boy?"

Ben held no illusions that she might be talking about him. She pushed herself creakily to her feet, drawing herself up to her full five-feet-four height, and tweaked Joey on the nose. He batted her hand away.

Mrs. Marmelstein leaned into his tiny face. "Are you my little pumpkey-wumpkey?"

Joey looked off into the distance.

Ben gave Joey a gentle shake. "Joey, say hello to Mrs. Marmelstein."

Joey didn't.

"C'mon, Joey. If you're rude to the landlady, we could end up sleeping under the Eighth Street bridge."

"That's all right." Mrs. Marmelstein pinched Joey on the cheek. "We're just not very sociable today, are we?"

Or any other day, Ben thought. "Well, we'd best go on in. I expect Joni is waiting—"

"That reminds me. There's something I'd like to discuss with you, Benjamin."

"Really?" he said, fearing the worst. A few months before, he had taken her to a doctor's appointment, and the man had pronounced the word they had been dreading—Alzheimer's. Mrs. Marmelstein had always been a bit dotty, but that diagnosis had put her occasional eccentricities in an entirely new light. Sometimes, she was totally lucid. But at others . . . "What is it?"

"Well . . ." She glanced at Joey, then back at Ben. "It's an adult matter."

That piqued his curiosity. He spotted Joni, the teenager who watched Joey when he wasn't at school and Ben couldn't be at home. She was standing in the front vestibule of the house. He dropped Joey to the ground. "Okay, pardner. Joni will take you upstairs. I'll be in to start dinner in just a few minutes. Okay?"

Joey waddled up the front porch where Joni was waiting for him.

"Okay," Ben said after Joey was inside. "What's this adult matter?"

"Well . . ." Her voice dropped to hushed tones. ". . . it's about Joni."

"I thought you liked Joni."

"I adore Joni. You know that. And goodness how she has matured since you asked her to be Joey's nanny. But I do believe she's been having"—Mrs. Marmelstein rocked forward on her toes and whispered—"gentleman callers."

Ben suppressed his grin. "You mean Booker?"

She fidgeted with her trowel. "I mean the black gentleman, yes."

Ben placed his hand on her shoulder. "Booker's okay, Mrs. Marmelstein. I have the utmost confidence in him."

"You don't think he . . . consorts with the wrong element?"

Well, there was that minor business of being a member of a North Side gang, but he seemed to have extricated himself from that mistake. "I think he's fine. And he's a great playmate for Joey. Very energetic."

"But that's just it. Having him around so much . . ." She turned to one side and stared down at the grass. "Mind you, I don't want to be the kind of landlady who's always interfering in her tenants' business."

"Oh, heaven forbid," Ben said with a straight face.

"At the same time, I can't help but worry that, with the two of them together in your apartment so much"—her voice dropped to the point of near inaudibility—"people will think there's something romantic going on."

In fact, there had been something romantic going on for the past six months, but Ben suspected that this was not the time to bring Mrs. Marmelstein up-to-date. "You know, Joni's parents have the apartment just next door to mine. And she and Booker are both eighteen now."

"I don't care if they're eighteen or eighty. I don't allow any hanky-panky in my house. You know that, Benjamin!"

"Yes, yes, I know. But I think it will be okay. And you know how I depend on Joni. I would never have been able to keep Joey without her."

"Well, yes . . ."

"And you like having Joey around, don't you?"

"You know I do. He's such a sweet little thing. Such a mind of his own."

"And you wouldn't want me to lose him, would you?" Being just a tad manipulative, Ben told himself, but any port in a storm.

"Of course I wouldn't."

"Good. So let's not bother Joni and Booker. I promise I'll personally police the situation and ensure that nothing untoward occurs."

She hesitated a moment. "I suppose it might be all right then."

"Good. I'd better get dinner going." He started toward the porch.

"Oh, Benjamin, today was my baking day. I put a nice fresh fruitcake on your kitchen counter."

"Thanks . . ."

"Don't eat it all yourself. Give some to Joey, too. Little boys love cake."

"Actually, I think it's a choking hazard." Ben wondered if he could use the same excuse for himself.

CHAPTER

6

APPRENTICE POLICE OFFICER Kevin Calley still held illusions that he might get home early when the squawk of the police radio shattered his dream.

He snapped up the handset. "Yes?"

"Ten-four, Kevin. This is the Box." The Box was the name given to the daytime switchboard officer for reasons long lost to antiquity. "Gotta 986 at 1260 South Terwilliger, which I believe is on your way home. And since you are technically still on duty . . ."

Calley silently swore. There went the early Friday night on the town he and Marie had planned. Boy, would she be pissed.

He took down all the details and made a minor course correction toward Terwilliger. Not that he minded working; it was, after all, why he had become a policeman. It was just that this was the end of his first week on the job—first week out of the academy, first week driving his own patrol car. Mostly traffic work, but that was all right for now. You couldn't expect to catch the Kindergarten Killer the first week. But he and Marie had planned a little party to celebrate the successful conclusion of his first seven days as a peace officer. They and a few friends were going out to In Cahoots, out at Seventy-first and Memorial, to down a few tall cool ones, cut a two-step, get a little rowdy, and generally have a good time. He'd signed out early—after arranging for someone else to cover for him—just so they could get a start on the evening, get there before all the good booths by the dance floor were taken.

It was great going home to Marie these days. There was a real gleam in her eyes when he came home in the evening wearing his shiny new uniform . . . and she had other memorable ways of showing her pleasure as well. She was proud of her little boy in blue. It had made a great difference in their marriage. No question they'd gone through some rough patches, especially in the early days. Things were looking up, though. He used to sneer when his father told him money made the world go round, but the fact was, a steady paycheck could eliminate a hell of a lot of marital stress. After a year or so, he'd have Marie out of the trailer park and into a real honest-to-God house like she deserved.

Why did it have to be a domestic disturbance, though? He could live with issuing a traffic ticket on his way home. A warning, if he was pressed for time. But like all cops, he hated domestic calls. They were never easy, never satisfying. If you caught a bank robber, well, great, job well done. But you got no applause from a domestic call. Sometimes it wasn't serious, just some spouse trying to up the stakes in an ongoing fight by calling in the police. When it was serious, though, the issues were even more complicated. If you arrest a wife beater, at best you've spared some people some violence at the cost of breaking up the family. More often, though, the police were put in the position of trying to convince a battered woman to prosecute, which they usually wouldn't do. Even if the police had been out several times before. It was amazing how many women would allow themselves to become punching bags—covering up, telling lies, denying reality, even when it smacked their face like a bare fist.

Well, best to get it over with. He pulled his black-and-white up into the driveway of 1260 South Terwilliger. Nice house. Nice neighborhood, in fact.

Barrett, the name on the mailbox read. Barrett. Good God, this wasn't the mayor's place, was it? He'd heard rumors about him down at the police station. Some of the boys had been called out to his house before, but so far, it had all been hushed up.

He radioed his arrival to the Box and climbed out of his car. He noticed a man in the upstairs window next door watching him. Dollars to doughnuts he was the one who made the anonymous call.

Calley rang the bell and waited. He rang it again.

No answer.

Now that was odd. According to the Box, the altercation in progress had been so loud it could be heard outside the house. But Calley didn't hear a thing.

Calley tried to remember what he had learned at the academy. Did he have probable cause to enter without a warrant? It was a tough call. He could easily see some lawyer arguing that he didn't. He didn't need a black mark on his record the first week.

He rang the bell again. Still no answer. Damn.

It was probably just a mistake or a prank or a false alarm. He should just get back in his car, make his report, and drive on home.

But what if something was going on in there? The Box had told him there were supposedly a woman and two kids involved.

Damn! Marie would be so angry if he got suspended. He wouldn't get laid for a month.

He rang the bell again. "Police," he barked.

No answer.

He pressed his ear against the door. He didn't hear anything, but the pressure of his head nudged the door open. It hadn't been shut, at least not all the way. Like someone had thrown it closed in a hurry.

The door creaked open about a foot wide. Well, hell, Calley thought. You can't have any reasonable expectation of privacy when your front door is gaping open, can you?

He pushed the door the rest of the way open and stepped inside. "Police," he repeated, but there was still no answer. There was a smell, though, a pungent, putrid smell. Well, he thought, I'll just make a quick tour of the house and make sure there hasn't been any—

He turned a corner and drew in his breath.

There she was. The lady of the house. The first lady of the city.

Formerly, anyway.

She was sprawled backwards over a dining room chair, her feet on the floor, her hands above her head. Her face was bruised in several places; her lips were cracked and caked with dried blood. Her blouse was torn, exposing her left shoulder and brassiere. Blood was smeared all over her body and formed dried puddles on the floor. Her lips were parted and her eyes were wide open, staring at him.

Calley pressed his hand against his mouth, suppressing his gag reflex. What the hell had he stumbled into?

His brain raced. His respiration quickened; panic began to overwhelm him. What should I do? He tried to think; he knew he should do something. He should get to a phone and call headquarters. No, that would leave prints. He'd use his car radio. No, he couldn't leave the house. What about the kids? What if the killer was still here?

Calley fell to his knees and started retching huge dry heaves. It was more than a minute before he could stop himself. What was he doing here? He didn't know anything about homicides. He'd never even seen one before, except in pictures. Why did it have to be him? On his first goddamn week on the job!

Calley took deep, cleansing breaths and tried to steady himself. Pull yourself together, Calley, he told himself. Think of it as a test. A test to see how good a cop you're going to be. When the going gets tough, the tough get going.

He would like to get going, he thought, way far away from this place. But he knew he couldn't. He had to check the rest of the house. He had to make sure . . . *God!* He couldn't even think about it.

Slowly he covered the rest of the downstairs, making a wide berth around the dining room. Nothing else seemed unusual. With his heart pounding in his chest, he started upstairs.

The first room on the left clearly belonged to a little girl. It was covered with stuffed animals and pink chiffon and Barbie doll accessories. But where was the girl?

There she was. She was lying on top of her bed in the middle of a sea of teddy bears and lions and giraffes. She was barely bigger than they were.

Calley knew even before he touched her that she was gone. Unlike the woman downstairs, there was no sign of blood, no obvious indication of violence. But she was motionless and still—much too still for a little girl. Her skin was pale, as if she'd been drained of blood. Her eyes were closed.

Her wrist was ice cold. Calley searched for a pulse, but there was nothing. He held his hand over her mouth and nose. Nothing.

She was dead. Just like Mom.

Calley pushed himself out of the room. His gorge was rising and he honestly, sincerely didn't know if he was going to make it. His eyes were clouding and the walls were beginning to spin. He was losing what little equilibrium he still had. But he had to press on. A test, he told himself. And you don't want to fail.

He continued taking deep, steady breaths, but he still knew he was going to be sick. He pushed his way toward the bathroom he had passed in the hall. His foot made a crackling noise when he lifted it. There was something sticky on the floor. Dark and red and sticky. He followed the sticky trail into the bathroom.

And found the other one. Sprawled inside the tub, her blood splattered across the porcelain. Everywhere.

Calley turned and ran. All notions of logic and duty and honor had been erased by the hideous sight in the bathtub. All he knew now was that he had to get out of there. He had to run and run and run until he couldn't run anymore, until he couldn't remember, until he had purged this grotesque madness from his brain.

He jumped over the banister at the halfway point and crashed down into the living room. Scrambling to his feet, ignoring the ankle he twisted upon landing, he bolted across the room. He careened into a small end table and knocked it over, sending a small framed photo flying across the room until it smashed into the opposite wall, the glass shattering into pieces.

Calley never noticed. He was already outside. He knew he needed to get to his car and call this in. But he couldn't. Not yet, anyway. For now, he just had to escape. To get away. To keep putting distance between this house of horrors and himself until there was nothing left to see, nothing left to know, and most of all, nothing left to remember.

CHAPTER

7

BEN ENTERED HIS apartment and carefully threaded his way through a minefield of toys, trains, tracks, blocks, action figures, board books, stuffed animals, and security blankets. Joey was sitting on the floor in a corner, arranging his small plastic animals in a straight line. When he finished, he would take them one by one to another corner and line them up there. Sometimes he did this for hours.

"Where's Joni?" Ben asked. Joey, of course, didn't answer, but Ben's nose inspired him to investigate the kitchen.

In the kitchen, Ben found Joni stirring a copper pot on the stove. Her boyfriend, Booker, was sitting at the table.

"How's it going, Booker?"

"All right, my man." They slapped hands.

"How's the shoulder?" Booker's shoulder was slowly mending from an injury he'd received in Ben's living room several months ago. He'd managed to save Christina and Joey's lives, but he'd gotten a nasty knife wound in the process.

"Only hurts when I laugh." Booker was a big, muscular man; he worked out regularly at a gym downtown. "And I only laugh when Joni does her striptease routine."

"Booker!" Joni whirled around, aiming a wooden spoon at his head.

"Just a joke, Joni. Just a joke." He turned his head and gave Ben a pronounced wink.

Joni was wearing jeans and a T-shirt (R.E.M. RULES!) that covered her tall, lean figure like a drape. The ensemble was completed by ten-hole utility boots and the usual baseball cap turned backward. Her short black hair was tucked behind her ears. Joni had a twin sister, Jami, but since Joni had cut her hair, they had gone from being seemingly identical to being barely discernible as members of the same family.

Ben leaned over the stove and inhaled. "Boy, that smells good. But you're not supposed to do the cooking. That's my job."

"Well, you had that conference today, so I knew you'd probably be late. So I started dinner."

"That was very considerate of you. I didn't know you could cook."

"Actually, Booker did all the cooking. All I've done is stir."

"Booker! You?"

Booker shrugged. "What can I say? I'm a Renaissance man."

"Evidently." Ben took another deep whiff. "What is it, anyway?"

Joni peered intently into the pot. "Uh . . . soup."

"Soup. Good. What kind?"

"Uhhh . . . you know . . . just soup."

"Just soup? C'mon, what is it?"

"I'm not clear on all the details."

Booker interrupted. "Beer cheese soup. The best."

"Beer cheese? As in beer?" Ben frowned. "We don't have any alcoholic beverages in this house."

Booker smiled. "Brought my own."

"But we can't give Joey something that has beer in it!"

Booker smiled. "I prepared young Master Joseph the usual assorted vegetable platter."

Along with his other eccentricities, Joey had an astounding (for his age) preference for food that was actually healthy. "Well, still. You know I don't approve of having alcohol in the house."

"Relax, Ben. We just put in a smidgen. And we poured the rest down the drain. And sterilized the drain with Lysol." She poked him in the stomach. "What an old woman you've become. You're worse than Mrs. Marmelstein."

"I don't mean to be a pain. But it's a big responsibility, looking after a little kid."

"You don't have to tell me," she said. "After all, I'm his nanny."

And a darn good nanny she had been, too. Ben had had doubts when, out of desperation, he had promoted her from occasional babysitter to full-fledged nanny status, but she had proven herself time and time again. Almost overnight she had gone from goofy, irresponsible teenager to dedicated, mature caregiver. She fed Joey, bathed Joey, changed Joey, and put up with his odd behavior whenever he wasn't at school and Ben couldn't be at home.

Ben felt a furry nuzzling at his feet. "Hi there, Giselle." Giselle was his cat, a black Burmese who was a past birthday present from Christina. "Are you telling me that you love me, or that you're hungry?"

Foolish question. Ben took a can of Feline's Fancy out of the cupboard and scraped it into her bowl. She gobbled it down in well under a minute, then plodded out of the room.

"Not very friendly today," Ben commented.

"Giselle is undergoing a lot of stress," Joni explained. "She's never had a rival for your affection before."

"A rival?"

"Joey."

"Oh. Has she been . . . misbehaving?"

Joni laid down her spoon and turned off the heat. "Let's just say it's best to keep them in separate rooms."

"I had no idea. Thanks for the tip." He glanced into the soup pot. "Is dinner about ready?"

"Ten more minutes," Joni replied. "Why don't you get out of the monkey suit?"

"Deal." Ben left the kitchen and walked toward his bedroom. On his way, he noticed Joey in the living room. He was still playing with his animals, obsessively lining them up. The expression on his face suggested that he was deep in thought, contemplating some weighty matter. But what?

Ms. Hammerstein's words came back to him unbidden. *He isn't like the other children.*

Ben could fuss and fume all he wanted in public, but privately he knew she was right.

I can't help wondering whether Joey might not be better off in a more stable environment.

Well, who wouldn't be? Ben threw his coat onto his bed. Where was his box, anyway?

He lay down on the hardwood floor and reached under the bed. A moment later, he withdrew a shoebox-size wooden box.

Ben lifted the metal clasp and peered inside. This was his childhood treasure chest, the place where he kept his most cherished belongings. There was a Captain Action action figure, a Frisbee, and a Magic 8-Ball. An almost complete deck of Mars Attacks trading cards. A toy phaser. A genuine Superman Krypto-Ray gun. There was a picture of Ben in the third grade, gap-toothed and towheaded.

All the treasures of his childhood. All the things he loved best. Sorted and counted and organized a thousand times over.

Memories were so unreliable. Sometimes he felt like this was all he had left of his childhood, all that remained. He had been a very shy kid, very quiet. Didn't socialize, didn't play well with other children. Seemed to be in a world of his own.

Hmmm.

Ben closed the box. He didn't have time for this indulgence. He should be out there playing with his nephew, trying to engage him, to draw him out of his shell. Being the best substitute daddy he could be, and ignoring . . .

I can't help wondering whether Joey might not be better off in a more stable environment. You want what's best for Joey, don't you?

He did, of course.

Ben wanted to do the right thing.

But sometimes it was hard as hell to know what that was.

CHAPTER

8

HE GRIPPED THE steering wheel with such intensity that the cold white knuckles of his hands shone in the moonlight. His face was flushed and sweaty; his head was pressed forward so far his nose nearly touched the wheel. He drove in a blind panic, with no conscious thought in his brain except the one central overwhelming one that was more instinct than thought.

. . . gotta go . . . gotta get out . . . gotta go . . . gotta get out . . . gotta get away . . .

He still couldn't sort it out in his head. It had all been so violent, so fast and final. He tried to retrace the events of the day, the afternoon, the evening, but it was all a blur, a confused random assortment of images he didn't understand, like a computer that had short-circuited and spewed out all its data in one instantaneous jumbled mess. The only thing he remembered clearly was the one sight burned in his brain—Caroline draped over the chair, blood dripping from her mouth.

Oh my God. Oh my God.

. . . gotta go . . . gotta get out . . . gotta go . . . gotta get out . . . gotta get away from here . . .

Where was he going? He didn't know. Where could he go? Where could he go that he wouldn't be recognized, wouldn't be identified, wouldn't be reported? They had to be looking for him by now. What with all the noise and the screaming and goddamn Harvey next door, they must know by now. Can't keep secrets in this town, no sirree. He'd learned that a long time ago.

He clenched the steering wheel all the tighter. They'd be looking for him.

. . . gotta go . . . gotta get out . . . gotta go . . . gotta get away from here . . . gotta get away from here before it's too late . . .

In the dead center of the turnpike, he saw a red pickup aimed straight for him, headlights blinding. He clenched his eyes shut and swerved to the right. The pickup whooshed past, missing him by inches. He suddenly realized he'd been driving down the center of the highway. Driving down the center, going about ninety, not knowing the difference.

He was going to die tonight, wasn't he? Jesus God, that was what this was all about. Meeting his Maker. Paying for his sins. It wasn't fair that they should die and he should live. He had to die, too. That's what he was doing out here in the dark on the turnpike. He was going to kill himself.

He realized he was breathing in gasps, practically hyperventilating. Go ahead, he told himself. Do it. That would be a nice touch. And you'll die all the quicker.

His hands were so wet they kept slipping off the wheel, sending him careening in one direction or the other. I wonder if it's made the news yet? he thought. Wonder if I'm getting a good spin?

One way to find out. He snapped on the radio. He didn't have to wait long.

" . . . police are chasing Mayor Wallace Barrett down the Indian Nation Turnpike eighty miles south of Tulsa. Reports indicate that he is driving at an excessive speed in an extremely erratic manner, and that he does not respond to overtures from the police caravan. Conflicting reports continue to come in from the scene of the crime. Once again: Mayor Barrett's wife, Caroline Barrett, and their two young children, Alysha, age eight, and Annabelle, age four, have been murdered. We will continue to update this story as new information emerges."

He shut it off. Police caravan? What the hell were they talking about? He checked the rearview mirror.

The bright, almost blinding glare of headlights shone back at him.

As he rose up the next hill, he spotted at least four separate sets of headlights.

They'd found him. In almost no time at all.

He rolled down his window, sending the car swerving back and forth across the center line. The wind rushed past his head, making a thundering noise, blotting out almost everything else.

"Pull your vehicle to the side of the road!"

The command came from the cop car just behind him, practically tailgating, as close behind as they could risk getting to a car going ninety, anyway. Someone barked another command, but he couldn't make it out. Didn't matter. He couldn't stop now. Couldn't.

. . . gotta go . . . gotta keep going . . .

He heard something else, something that had been there all along but was so drowned out by the wind he hadn't distinguished it. A chopping noise. From overhead.

He stared up into space. It was a helicopter! But not a police copter. The huge channel number painted on the side glistened in the darkness. Someone was speaking to him through an electronic megaphone. He could barely make out the words.

"Mister Mayor!"

Yeah, that's me. Mister Mayor—that was what the reporters in town always called him. So they not only knew where he was, but who he was.

"Mister Mayor!" The wind swept the words away, making them almost unintelligible. "Did you do it?"

Jesus God. They knew everything. And they had minicams. He knew the new infrared models didn't need much light. He was on television! The whole goddamn stupid chase was on television. He saw the cameras, saw the blinking red lights. Two of them, at least. Hell, it was a better turnout than he had for his last press conference.

He heard some static from behind, barked commands from the cop cars. The police were trying to get the press to stay back. It wasn't working.

"Pull your vehicle to the side of the road!"

He rolled up his window. What was the point? He had to figure out what he was going to do. What the hell was he going to do?

He'd never be able to lose them. And he was coming up to the tollgate. He couldn't stop. What was he doing to do?

All these unresolved dilemmas were suddenly blotted out by the appearance of a semitrailer truck dead on the horizon. It was barreling toward him, seconds from impact. Small wonder; he was more in the semi's lane than in his own.

The semi driver laid on his horn. He couldn't possibly move that huge heavy truck in time. Barrett knew it was up to him. He twisted the wheel around, jerking his Porsche to the right. He lurched out of the path of the semi at so sharp an angle he was practically perpendicular to the road. He careened off the shoulder and onto a nearby embankment.

He saw the brick tollbooth just ahead, illuminated in his headlights. He smashed his foot down on the brakes, but it was too late, much much too late.

"I'm coming home, Jesus!" His hands rose off the wheel and covered his face. The white brick wall filled his field of vision and he screamed for just an instant before the thunderous impact silenced him and everything around him faded to black.

9

HOMICIDE DETECTIVE MIKE Morelli pulled his Trans Am onto Terwilliger and searched for the house. The hardest part was not reading the numbers on the curbs; it was keeping his sagging eyelids pried open.

"Jeez, Tomlinson," he groaned at the man in the passenger seat, "how long have we been awake?"

"Twenty-five hours and counting," Tomlinson replied. Tomlinson was Mike's protégé, a detective in training.

"Christ. How many murders can one little town in the heartland have? First that poor schmuck in the bathroom at the River Parks. Then a homeless man living in a cardboard box under the West End Bridge. And now the mayor's entire family. Who's next."

"It's been a tough night."

"That's for damn sure." Mike massaged his face. "I don't understand it."

"Oh, I do," Tomlinson said matter-of-factly. "Sunspots."

"I beg your pardon?"

"Sunspots. Lots of sunspot activity today. I heard it on the radio. Crime always soars during high sunspot activity periods. It's like the full moon."

"Do tell."

"Has something to do with shortcircuiting the synapses in our neural networks. All those little ganglia go *snap*! Tempers flare, and suddenly you've got a crime wave on your hands."

"This is a fascinating theory, Tomlinson. Perhaps you should write this up for one of the police journals."

"It's been done. Well, not in the police journals, but in other influential publications."

"Like the ones they sell at supermarket checkout stands?" Mike cruised to the end of the street. "Ah. This must be it."

Cars were parked all around an impressive two-story brick house on the north side of the street. Swarms of people were streaming in and out of the house. A crowd was huddled on the front lawn; some people were even taking snapshots.

"What the hell is going on?" Mike put the car in neutral and jumped out, leaving Tomlinson to park.

Mike grabbed the first available cop he saw. "Who's in charge?"

A young fresh-faced cop, who obviously knew who Mike was and knew better than to mess around with him, snapped to attention. "Lieutenant Prescott, sir."

Mike's teeth ground together. "Jesus God. Why did it have to be Prescott?"

"I don't know, sir, I just arrived a few—"

Mike cut him off. "Why hasn't this crime scene been cordoned off?"

"I—I don't know, sir. I guess Lieutenant Prescott—"

"Is what? Incompetent?" Mike stomped up to the front porch. "Where the hell is he?"

The young cop lifted a shaking hand. "Inside," he whispered.

Mike pushed his way through the door, bumping into a large man wearing shorts and a T-shirt. "What the hell are you doing in here?"

The man seemed startled. "I just wanted to have a look-see. I live two streets down. Always wanted to see the inside of this place."

Mike grabbed the man by the shoulders and shoved him forcibly toward the door. "Get the hell—"

He stopped when he noticed the man was hiding something cupped in his hands. "What is that?"

The man reluctantly opened his hands. "Just a little souvenir." It was a pair of cuff links bearing the insignia of the mayor's office.

Mike snatched the cuff links. "You're taking evidence from a crime scene?"

"No, no, I found this in the mayor's bedroom."

"Get out of here!" Mike shoved him right through the door and down the front steps, then whirled around and stomped into the living room. He found another police officer talking on the phone.

"Sure, honey, I should be home by eight—"

Mike pushed down the interrupt button and canceled the call.

"Hey, I was talking—" A flash of recognition lit in the man's eyes. "Lieutenant Morelli!"

"I assume you dusted that phone for prints before you rubbed your sweaty little paws all over it?"

"Well—"

"Goddamn it, why didn't you use your car radio?"

"Well, I—I mean, Lieutenant Prescott—"

"Of course. Lieutenant Prescott. Do you think Lieutenant Prescott is going to be able to save your ass once I put you up for suspension?"

"Well, sir—"

"Goddamn it!" He grabbed the man by the lapels. "Why isn't there any paper on the floor?"

"I guess we didn't see the point."

"The point?" He grabbed the officer's head and pushed it down. "Look at that floor! There's probably been about a thousand or so people stomping through here. Any blood or footprints or other trace evidence has been destroyed. This crime scene is contaminated."

A voice sounded behind him. "Look, Morelli, if you have to play the tough guy, why don't you pick on someone your own rank?"

Mike whirled around. "Prescott!"

Prescott was a fair-haired, somewhat stocky man, almost a head shorter than Mike. What he had lost in height, Mike thought, he made up in swagger.

"What the hell is going on here, Prescott? Why hasn't this crime scene been secured?"

Prescott smirked. "Relax, Supercop. This one's in the bag."

"What are you talking about?"

"We know who did it. And we've got him in custody. Our esteemed mayor was seen fleeing the scene of the crime, blood all over him. And everybody saw him trying to escape last night. We've got him cold."

"You stupid little prick. That doesn't matter." He stepped forward till he was practically hovering over Prescott. "If you screw up the crime scene, we could lose everything. This whole case could be thrown out of court."

"That isn't going to happen," Prescott said calmly.

"Says you." Mike glared at him. "What the hell are you doing here, anyway? Last I heard, I was the head man in Homicide."

"As I understand it, you were busy interviewing vagrants under the West End Bridge. Obviously, someone needed to take charge of this case immediately."

"So Chief Blackwell sent you?"

"Think higher."

Mike swore silently. "The council."

Prescott touched his nose. "Bingo."

Mike's jaws clenched together so tightly he was afraid he might pop a filling. This went to the very heart of why he hated Prescott—besides his obvious incompetence. Prescott had never risen through the ranks like the other men in his department. He had been brought in from another county, not by anyone in the police department, but by special appointment of the city council. He was their man. Whenever they wanted something done, whenever they needed some information, they called Prescott.

"And why is the council involved in this?"

"That shouldn't be too hard to figure out, even for you. And soon as word

came down that the mayor's family had been murdered, and the mayor himself was being hunted by the police, the city council called an emergency
meeting and took charge of the situation. They contacted me directly and
asked me to handle the initial investigation."

"To preserve the evidence? Or destroy it?"

"I resent your uninformed implication—"

"All I know is what I see, Prescott. I'm standing in the middle of a
totally botched crime scene. Any evidence that may have once been here is
worthless."

"I told you already, we have the killer in custody. We don't need your
Sherlock Holmes routine this time, Morelli. We've already got our man."

"Yeah, well, I just hope you don't lose him"—he leaned right into
Prescott's face—"by being such a goddamn incompetent fuck-up!"

The police officers on duty froze. Everyone knew about Lieutenant
Morelli's temper, but this was extraordinary even for him. The entire room
fell silent. Except for a soft whirring noise.

Prescott grinned back at Mike. "Smile. You're on *Candid Camera*."

Mike turned slowly and saw the truth. The cameraman from Channel
Eight had caught the whole exchange.

"This is a crime scene!" Mike barked. "Get out of here!"

The camera continued to whir.

"I'm going to take that goddamn camera and smash it—"

The cameraman ducked and scurried out the door.

"Good. And as for you, Prescott, you're off this case."

Prescott's face contorted. "You can't do this."

"Just watch me."

"You don't have the authority."

Mike's face flushed an angry red. "I'm still the head of Homicide. You are
my subordinate and you are *off this case*!"

"I'm going straight to Blackwell with this. And beyond."

"You do that."

Prescott glared at Mike for a few more moments, then stomped out of the
house.

"All right," Mike said, addressing all the uniforms in the area, "we're
turning this into a real crime scene starting right now. I want paper on the
floor immediately. Covering all walkways." He pointed to the officer closest to
him. "That means you. And I want you all to keep your grubby hands off
everything till the print team has a chance to dust. Then we'll let the trace evidence team see if they can possibly find any remaining traces of hair or fiber or
blood or DNA. I want pictures of the whole house, from every possible angle,
especially where the bodies were found. And I want all unauthorized personnel out of here!"

"Mike."

It was Tomlinson. "What is it?"

He pointed through the front windows. "I think there's something going on outside you should know about."

Mike peered through the front windows. Prescott was still on the scene, standing on the front lawn, talking to several reporters and minicams.

"I don't believe it," Mike murmured. "He's giving a goddamn press conference!"

Mike rushed out the front door just in time to hear the tail end of Prescott's remarks.

". . . because Lieutenant Morelli's conduct has been questionable for some time, and this latest incident will only intensify the ongoing investigation. Rest assured, however, that the guilty man is in custody—"

Mike plunged between Prescott and the cameras. "What do you think you're doing?"

"Just answering a few questions for the folks at home," Prescott said wanly.

Mike faced the reporters. "Turn those cameras off. I said *off*!"

The cameramen wordlessly obeyed.

Mike whirled on Prescott. "I told you you were off the case!"

"So I'm off. Doesn't mean I can't answer a few questions."

"You idiot. You can't tell people who's guilty before there's been a trial. You'll get the department sued, not to mention prejudicing the whole investigation."

"I keep telling you, there's no investigation. We have the killer in custody."

"You stupid—Prescott, you're on probation."

"What!"

"You heard me. You're suspended until further notice. Don't come to the office. And don't talk to the press!"

Prescott's eyes narrowed. "I have a lot of friends, Morelli."

"Well, you'd better, 'cause if you're still in my face five seconds from now, you're not going to have a job."

"We'll see." He whipped around and stomped down the driveway.

"Sorry about that disturbance," Mike told the reporters. "We'll give an official press conference this afternoon in time for you to make the five o'clock news. Thank you."

Mike hustled back to his car to call in the forensic teams. Jeez, what a day. At this rate, he'd have his first heart attack before he made captain.

Maybe it was sunspots, after all.

10

HARD AS SHE tried, Deanna Meanders found she could carry only three of the four bags of groceries at once. She could go inside and ask Martha to help, she supposed. Argue and cajole and finally order her out. Martha would be put out and argumentative ("I'm not your slave!"); she'd say something that would irritate Deanna, Deanna would say something back, and they'd kill a couple of hours being crappy to one another.

Nah, she'd get it herself.

It was already after seven. Deanna had had a hell of a time getting out of the office. Mr. Coughlin dumped yet another one of his emergencies on her at the last possible moment. "We've got to have this faxed to San Diego before six!" And as well she knew, when he had an emergency, everyone in the office had an emergency. "We all have to pull together." Translation: no one goes home till I do. "Emergencies come with the territory." Translation: I put it off till the last minute.

When she finally escaped, she made an unavoidable run to Bud's for groceries. And now she was late, damn it. It wasn't so much that she worried about Martha; she was sixteen—old enough to look after herself. But the later Deanna got home, the less time she had to spend with her. Martha got older and older and busier and busier, and as the time passed they grew more and more distant.

Being a single mother was hell. Sometimes it seemed like all she ever did was work and worry, and neither did her much good. Certainly Martha didn't appreciate either. "How come you can't come to school today for the play like the other mothers?" Or, alternately: "Mother, get a life of your own, okay?" Sure, she was just a typical teenager. But it still hurt. Martha thought her mother had all these choices, that she could decide for herself what to do. The truth was, she had no choices. She had to work to keep this family unit afloat. Martha depended on her, whether she knew it or not. Not to mention the fact that, the second Deanna screwed up, that son of a bitch she divorced would be right back in her face trying to get custody again. And she couldn't let that happen. No matter what.

Deanna walked toward the front door. The windows were open, and she could hear voices inside. Including one that wasn't supposed to be there. Quietly she crept up to the window.

There he was. Buck, the banished boyfriend. Well, if not exactly banished, certainly keenly disapproved of. He hadn't shaved, like always, and he was wearing those loose green fatigues, like always. He looked like someone you'd expect to hit you up for a quarter downtown. And this was Martha's one true love. God, life was cruel sometimes.

Deanna hadn't known what to do the first day she came home and found Buck in her living room, feet on the sofa, snuggling up to Martha and drinking a beer. A *beer*, for God's sake! Did they meet at school? No, turns out Buck isn't in school. He got expelled a long time ago and he never went back. Not to worry. He had plenty of money. Except that worried Deanna even more—how did a high school dropout with a crummy no-talent job manage to have so much cash all the time?

Deanna had never uncovered Buck's true age. He claimed to be twenty, but she suspected he was older. What did it matter? Twenty was too old to be seeing a sixteen-year-old. Martha hadn't really dated before, and now she was going with some guy old enough to . . . well, to drink beer, among other things.

Deanna considered this pairing totally unacceptable, but at the same time, she knew what would happen if she made a big thing out of it and forbade Buck to come around any more. Tempers would escalate, lines would be drawn, and this budding romance would turn into some Romeo-and-Julietesque grand passion. Deanna knew quite well how headstrong Martha could be. She'd rebel, and soon she'd run off with him, maybe even get married. Or worse, get pregnant. And Martha's whole future would be ruined.

She couldn't risk it. So after much deliberation, she had said that Martha could continue to see Buck, but only during certain hours, and only when they were chaperoned. That way, she hoped, the romance would run its natural course. Eventually Martha would become disenchanted with his ignorant insolence; she would realize that his half-grown goatee was really pretty ugly; and she wouldn't think it was funny anymore when he belched in her face.

So Deanna had hoped, anyway. But the relationship had been raging on for three months now, with no sign of abating. And now he was in their house when he wasn't supposed to be, when Deanna wasn't home.

Buck. Jesus Christ, what kind of a name was that for a human being, anyway?

Martha and Buck were sitting at the kitchen table playing a card game, that strange one with the special illustrated cards. Magic: The Gathering, they called it. All Deanna knew was that the game was ungodly complicated and it cost a fortune to collect enough cards to have a good deck.

Martha laid a red card in the center of the table. "I'm going to use my red mana to summon a Fireball and do nine damage to you."

Buck's eyebrows knitted together. "Against me? Why me, woman?"

Deanna winced.

"Don't attack me," he said. "Go after my Juggernaut."

"I don't want your Juggernaut. I want you, handsome."

"But I've only got ten life points left."

"And now you've got one. I've already done it."

His voice acquired an edge. "And I'm telling you not to, woman."

"C'mon, Buck. Play the game. You have one life point."

"But I told you—"

"Buck, take your turn!"

"You stupid *bitch*!"

Deanna felt the air rush out of her lungs.

"Calm down," Martha said.

"Don't you tell me what to do, woman. You stupid, stupid bitch!" He threw all the cards in his hand at her. "You screwed up my whole game."

"I tried to win, if that's what you mean. Aren't you supposed to try to win? Isn't that the point?"

"Yeah, well, fuck you. Bitch," he added again, as an afterthought.

Deanna clutched at her chest. Omigod, omigod, omigod. How did I let this happen?

"Same to you," Martha snarled back at him, and for added emphasis, she shot him the finger.

Buck's lips pressed together. "Don't you point that finger at me, woman."

"Don't tell me what to do." The finger remained.

"I told you not to do that!" He jumped out of his seat, reached across the table, and swung at her. He might have been aiming at her hand, but the blow passed barely an inch from her face.

Deanna had seen enough. Too much, actually. She bolted into the house and ran into the kitchen. "What the hell is going on in here?"

Both Martha and Buck jumped out of their seats. "Mom! How long have you been here?"

"Long enough. Buck, I want you out of my house."

"Mo-*om*!"

"Now!" She pointed toward the door. "Out!"

Buck settled into the kitchen chair. "Like, isn't it Martha's house, too? Doesn't she have any say in this?"

"No." Deanna marched forward till she was standing right over him. "Get out! Or I'll throw you out!"

A small smile crossed Buck's lips. He looked Deanna up and down, as if conducting a smug appraisal. "You're going to throw me out?"

"Damn straight." She picked up the kitchen phone and punched 911.

"Mo-om! Stop this! Buck is my guest."

"You're not allowed to have guests anymore." Deanna spoke into the phone receiver. "Yes, I'm calling about a trespasser. Housebreaker. Whatever. An unwanted person who won't leave. Can you send out a patrol car? We may be in danger."

"Christ, all right already." Buck stood up and pressed the interrupt button. "I'm going, I'm going."

"Good." She pushed him toward the door. "And don't come back!"

"Look, woman, Martha and I are going steady."

"Not anymore. Your relationship is over." She pressed a finger against his chest. "And don't you ever—*ever*—call me *woman*!"

He ambled toward the door, smirking. "Martha, your old lady is crackers." He winked. "I'll call you."

"Don't even think about it!" Deanna shouted.

Buck sauntered out the door. A few moments later, she heard his motorcycle rev up and saw him zoom down the street.

Martha ran into the living room and flung herself onto the sofa. "I am never speaking to you ever again. Never! *Never!*"

"Honey, it was for your own—"

"I have never been so humiliated in my whole life! My life is ruined!" Deanna saw tears trickling in the corners of Martha's eyes. "I can't believe you made him leave."

Deanna flopped down at the foot of the sofa. "Honey . . . he's a jerk."

"I happen to love him, Mother, for your information."

"Oh, you do not. You just think you do."

"Who are you to tell me whether I love someone?" She pounded her fist into a sofa pillow. "What's so bad about Buck, anyway?"

Deanna stared at her, flabbergasted. "Are you kidding? I saw the way he talked to you, the way he treated you."

"He didn't mean it."

"He called you—the b-word. I won't stand for that."

"He can't help it. He grew up around his dad, a dumb metalworker who can barely read. It's what he learned. You always said we shouldn't treat underprivileged people like they were worse than us. Right?"

"Honey . . . he tried to hit you."

"He did not."

"I saw it."

"Well, I shouldn't have given him the finger."

"True, but that's no excuse for him trying to hit you."

"Where do you get off telling me what I can and can't do, anyway?" Martha leaped to her feet. "It's not like you've made your life such a giant success."

Deanna mentally counted to ten. "Martha, I'm only doing this because I love you."

"Bull. I think you do it because you're jealous. Jealous!"

"Sweetheart, please calm down."

"That's why you were spying on us through that window. Is that how you get your cheap thrills? Are you that hard up?"

"Honey, I looked through the window because I heard Buck, who as you know perfectly well is not supposed to be over here when I'm not around."

"You said he could come over after dinner."

"Right. And we haven't had dinner."

"Wrong. I have. You haven't, because you're late."

"I had to work late."

"You always have to work late. You care about your job more than you care about me. You don't even like me. You only got custody to spite Daddy."

"Martha!"

"I hate you!" she shrieked. "I *hate* you!" Martha ran across the living room toward her bedroom. "And I'm never speaking to you *again*!" She disappeared inside the interior hallway.

Well, Deanna told herself, you certainly handled that well. God, why didn't anyone ever tell me parenting would be so hard? And thankless. And why can't I ever, just for once, handle something right?

Best to let Martha cool off, she decided, before she tried to talk to her again. She'd listen to reason later. Perhaps Deanna was overreacting, but she didn't think so. That kid was a potential abuser. Potential—hell, he was there already. She'd seen the look in his eye when he talked to her. Contemptuous, superior. Violent. It was a look Deanna had seen before.

She would not let Martha have her life ruined by some abusive son of a bitch.

One time in this family was enough. Two was too damn many. This was a vicious cycle she was not going to allow to repeat.

She walked outside to recover the groceries. She thought she was handling this right, she really did. She had to be tough. Still, something about Martha, something about the look in her eye when she ran out of the room, chilled her to the bone. What if she did something stupid?

She closed her eyes and said a silent prayer. Please, God. Please, no. Take care of my little girl. Because I'm not sure I can do it alone.

And if she spends any more time with that bastard Buck—anything could happen.

11

BEN WAS LATE getting to his office the next morning, not that that was unusual. What was unusual was that his entire office staff—Christina, Jones, and Loving—were standing shoulder to shoulder just inside the front door waiting for him.

"Let me guess," Ben said. "You're on strike. Look, I don't blame you, but until some of our clients pay their bills—"

He stopped. The huge ear-to-ear grins on their faces told him that wasn't it. "Okay, what, then? Is today my birthday or something?"

"Where have you been?" Christina said, wrapping her arm around his shoulder and pulling him into the office.

"At Forestview. I had to take Joey to school, and then there was this big sign-up for the spring bake sale—"

"Never mind that." Christina pushed him into a chair while the other two huddled around. "We've been trying to get hold of you all morning."

"Why?"

Jones leaned forward. "I got a call the minute I came into the office, Boss."

"And?"

"The mayor wants you!"

Ben fell deep into thought. Was this about that incident with his daughter at Forestview last Friday? It was just a little bump. And she ran into him . . .

"Can you believe it, Skipper?" Loving grabbed him by the shoulders and shook him. "The mayor wants you!"

"That's nice . . . I guess."

Christina cut in. "Ben, do you even know what we're talking about?"

"Well, actually . . . no."

"The biggest cause célèbre to hit Tulsa in years, and you're totally clueless. What were you doing last night?"

"Well, let me see. I had soup for dinner, then I read *Goodnight Moon* to

Joey about eight thousand times. After he went to sleep, I finished my Trollope novel . . ."

She slapped her forehead. "I can't believe it. Everyone in the state watched the chase last night. Except, of course, you."

"Chase? What are you talking about?"

"Ben, the mayor has been charged with murder."

"Murder!" The light slowly dawned. "And he wants me to get him off?"

Christina and Jones and Loving all exchanged a glance. "Well," Christina said, "he wants you to represent him, anyway. *Entre nous*, I wouldn't get your hopes up too high on the outcome."

"What do you mean?"

Christina grabbed his arm. "I'll brief you while we drive to the jailhouse."

BECAUSE MAYOR BARRETT had specified that he wanted to see Ben alone, Christina (after considerable protest) agreed to cool her heels outside while Ben went into his cell to talk to him.

"Don't worry about me, Christina," he told her. "I'll be fine."

"I'm not worried about you. I'm worried about us."

"Come again?"

"I'm afraid you'll do something idiotic like not agree to represent him."

"In fact, I do have some reservations . . ."

"See! It's starting already. You're going to veer off on some wacky ethical tangent, and we're going to go hungry."

"Just let me talk to him. Then we'll see."

She grabbed him by the lapels. "Ben, promise me you'll take this case."

"We'll see."

"Ben!"

"We'll see."

Ben allowed the guard to lead him down the long metallic corridor. Mayor Barrett had the cell at the far end, a private suite, such as it was. A five-by-seven cell, with a bunk bed, a sink, and an open-faced toilet. Not exactly the mayor's mansion.

He was lying on the bottom bunk, his hands covering his face. When he moved them, Ben saw black and red lacerations on his face, and a bandage wrapped around his jaw and the back of his head.

The guard let Ben into the cell, locked the door behind him, then disappeared.

"How do you feel?" Ben asked.

"Better than I have a right to feel."

"My legal assistant told me you were in a traffic accident."

Barrett tried to smile, although between the bruises and the bandages, his face didn't have much give in it. "I crashed into a brick building with four cop cars, two television helicopters, and about half the world watching. Like I said, I'm better off than I have a right to be."

"Jeez. What were you doing?"

"Trying to kill myself," he said, with a matter-of-fact air that caught Ben by surprise. "As it was, I didn't even break a bone. Goddamn air bags."

Ben paced nervously around the tiny cell. There was nowhere to sit, so he stood awkwardly by the cell door and contemplated the dominant question.

This was a part of criminal defense work that Ben particularly hated. Most criminal defense lawyers never asked the question. Since defending a client you knew was guilty raised a million ethical difficulties, most lawyers preferred not to inquire.

Ben, however, wanted to know the truth. He wanted to know where he stood. If he was going to put his name and reputation on the line, particularly in what was certain to be a high-profile case, he wanted to know he was doing the right thing. As his old mentor Jack Bullock used to say, he wanted to be on the side of the angels. But with such a horrible, heinous crime, how could he possibly ask?

Barrett sat up suddenly, hands on his knees. "Ben, I want you to know something up front. I didn't do it."

Ben gazed at him, his face, his eyes.

"I did not kill my wife. I did not kill my two precious daughters. How could I?" His eyes began to water, but he fought it back. "I couldn't do anything like that." He stared down at his hands. "I couldn't."

"I've read the preliminary police report. Neighbors say you and your wife had a disagreement yesterday afternoon."

Barrett nodded. "That's right. We did. I'm not going to pretend we didn't." He spread his arms wide. "It was that kind of marriage. We fought sometimes, like cats and dogs. But we still loved each other."

"What was the fight about?"

Barrett shrugged. "I hardly remember."

"The prosecutor will want to know."

"It was something about the kids. She thought I was spoiling them, giving them everything they wanted. Undermining her authority. And not paying enough attention to her. We'd had this argument before."

"How many times?"

He shrugged again. "I don't know. Many."

"Were these fights . . . violent?"

He twisted his head around. "Violent? You mean, did I hit her? Absolutely not."

"Well, I had to ask."

"Look, I don't know what people are saying about me now, but I would never hurt my wife. Or my girls. They're the most precious things in the world to me." His voice choked. "Were. I couldn't hurt them. Don't you think that if the mayor of the city was a wife beater, it would've come out before now?"

"I suppose." Ben pulled a small notebook out of his jacket pocket and began taking notes. "So you had an argument. Then what?"

"I can barely remember. It's all such a blur. And smashing into a brick wall didn't help."

"Just tell me what you recall. We don't have to get everything today."

"Well, I got mad. That doesn't happen often; most times I can just laugh it off. But this time she really got my goat, suggesting that I was hurting the girls and all. So I stomped out of the house."

"You left?"

"Right. Got in my car and drove away."

"How long were you gone?"

"I don't know exactly. Not long. Maybe an hour. I got a Coke at a Sonic—you can check that if you want—and I started to feel bad. So what if we disagreed on a few minor points. I loved my wife, and I loved my family. I didn't have any business running out like that. A strong man stands up straight and faces the music. So I headed back home."

"What happened when you got there?"

"I was in such a hurry, I left my car on the street and ran into the house. And—"

"Yes?"

He hesitated. "And then . . . I found . . . them. What was left of them."

"They were already dead?"

"Oh, yeah." His eyes became wide and fixed. "My wife was spread out like . . . like some sick human sacrifice. And my little girls . . ." Tears rushed to his eyes. His hands covered his face.

"I'm sorry," Ben said quietly. "I know this is hard for you."

Barrett continued to cry. His whole upper body trembled.

Ben took a deep breath. He hated this. He felt like a vulture of the worst order, intruding on this man's grief with these incessant questions. Guilty or not, he was clearly grief-stricken. "Can you tell me what you did after you found the bodies?"

"I freaked." He wiped his nose and eyes. "I don't know what I was thinking. I just freaked. Ran out to my car and tore off. Without a word to anyone. Stupid, I know. But I wasn't thinking clearly. I wasn't thinking at all. I just knew I had to get away from all that awful, hideous—death. And that blood. I kept thinking, I gotta go, I gotta get away from all this. It was like a chant, an order, running through my brain. Like maybe, if they weren't right there in front of me, it didn't really happen."

"I can understand wanting to leave. But I can't understand what you were doing on the Indian Nation Turnpike."

"I don't know, man. I was just running scared. Trying to escape reality."

"Some people have suggested that you were running to Mexico to hide out from the police."

"Well, they're wrong. I just had to get my head clear. Had to admit to myself that they were really"—he stopped short of the word, then spoke its euphemism—"gone."

Ben cleared his throat. "My office assistant told me you were seeking representation."

"Let's put our cards on the table, okay, Ben? I don't want representation. I want you."

"So my secretary said. I have to tell you—I'm a little surprised."

"Why?"

"We don't know each other that well."

"I know your reputation. That comes with being mayor."

"There are dozens of good attorneys in town. With more experience than I have. You could hire anyone you want. Forgive me, but . . . this just doesn't make sense."

There was a small change in Barrett's expression, not a smile, but a tiny tugging at the corner of his lips. "Can I be blunt?"

"Of course."

"My case is going to be assigned to Judge Hart."

"How can you know that? The assignment won't be made until after the preliminary hearing."

"Ben, I'm the mayor, okay? I know." He stretched out his arms. "Now my sources at the courthouse tell me there are a lot of good attorneys, and a lot of attorneys that Judge Hart likes. But, they say, you're a particular favorite."

"I don't know about that."

"I do. It's a fact."

"Even if that were true, it wouldn't matter. Judge Hart is a smart, professional judge. She's not going to give you any breaks just because she likes me."

"I'm sure she would never intentionally show any favoritism. But when all is said and done, all other things being equal, wouldn't you rather be represented by the guy the judge likes than the guy she doesn't?"

Ben couldn't argue with that logic.

"Look, I'll give you whatever you want. How about a ten-thousand-buck retainer up front? You can charge me a hundred and fifty an hour, even though I know you normally don't get half that much, when your clients pay at all, which from what I hear isn't that often. So when can you start?"

Ben fidgeted with his briefcase. "I haven't decided—"

"What's to decide?"

"Well . . . it's very complicated . . ."

Barrett's eyes slowly narrowed. "You think I did it, don't you?"

Ben averted his eyes.

"You think I killed my wife. You think I killed my two little girls."

"It doesn't matter what I think. It's what the jury thinks—"

"Yeah, but that's why you won't take the case. Right?"

Ben met him eye to eye. "If I don't believe your story myself, how can I make a jury believe it?"

"What is it you don't believe?"

"Everything. Leaving at just the wrong moment and coming back to find them all dead."

"That's how it happened!"

"Well, whether it did or didn't, a jury will certainly have difficulty believing it."

Barrett folded his arms. "All right. So that's one problem. What else?"

"The crime itself is a problem. Forgive me. I know you must be upset about all this, but I have to speak honestly. Everyone in your family was killed except you. The public hates survivors; they always assume there must be a reason why one survives when others don't. And who can blame them? They can believe a father—an athlete—in the heat of passion loses his head and kills his family. But if you didn't kill them, who did? Who else could possibly have a motive to eliminate your entire family?"

"Ben," Barrett said, after a long pause, "how much do you know about politics?"

"Very little."

"Well, it's a dirty game."

"What are you saying—that your political enemies did this?"

"I just announced I was running for reelection."

"I can't believe anyone would commit such a horrible crime for political reasons."

"That's only because, as you just admitted, you know very little about politics."

"Why would anyone kill your family?"

"To put me right where I am now." He spread his arms wide. "Look at me. I'm in jail, not likely to get out any time soon. My reputation is shot. Even if I'm acquitted, most people will assume I was probably guilty. My political career is ended. Over. Hell, if they'd killed me, they'd just get my chosen successor. This way, they've rubbed the Barrett administration right off the map."

"I can't believe anyone would do that."

"You can't believe someone would commit murder to make millions of dollars?"

"Millions? But you said—"

"I'm talking about kickbacks, Ben. Municipal construction contracts that always seemed to end up in the same hands. Until I came on board and cleaned things up. Believe me, there are some heavy hitters in this town who want me gone, erased, and the sooner and more thoroughly the better. They don't like having their hand taken out of the cookie jar. Especially," he added, "not by a black man."

"But a crime like this." Ben shook his head. "Three murders . . ."

"Oh, hell, the creeps I'm talking about wouldn't do the murders themselves."

"Then—"

"Ben, you're not really this naive, are you? These days you can hire a hit man for a thousand bucks. Hell, you can find their advertisements in the backs of magazines."

"You're saying a professional hit man did this?"

"Is that so incredible?"

"Frankly, yes."

Barrett was quiet for a moment. "Ben," he said finally, "did you read the description of the murders in the police report?"

"I did."

"So did I. You remember what it said about my little"—his voice trembled, then cracked—"my little Annie?" He clenched his jaw and steadied himself, fighting back the tears. "She was killed by a single incision. A thin blade inserted at exactly the right point through her ribs and at the base of the heart. Caused immediate death. Now I ask you, could I do that? In the heat of passion, no less?" He paused. "Or did that require . . . a professional touch?"

"But that was just one of the murders. The other two—"

"I know. Something must've gone wrong after the killer got Annie. But the point remains—I could not have committed that murder."

"The jury will assume that you could. Or that you just got lucky."

"Lucky? That I got *lucky?*"

Ben wished he could will those stupid words back into his mouth, but it was too late.

Barrett's whole body shook with anger. "I . . . did . . . not . . . get . . . lucky. I lost my *family.* I'm a *victim!*" He took several deep breaths till he had steadied himself. "I could not have committed these crimes. They were done by a professional."

"Well—"

"Let me tell you something else. I think I've seen him. I've seen someone prowling around our neighborhood. An oily-looking creep in green fatigues. Nasty. Usually hanging around with a younger woman. A girl, really. Wears a headband. I saw this guy wandering around several times, but I didn't know what to make of it. Now I do. Now I realize he was casing the neighborhood, waiting for just the right moment. As soon as he saw me run out of the house yesterday, he made his move."

"How many times have you seen this man?"

"I'm not certain. At least four or five times. Other people in the neighborhood must have seen him, too. Ask around."

Ben batted his pencil against his lips. "I suppose I could do that."

"Don't make up your mind whether to accept the case now. Take some time. Ask some questions. Go to a city council meeting."

"City council?"

"Oh, hell, yes. They're the ones behind this. They've been out to get me since day one."

"I suppose it wouldn't hurt to ask a few questions." He turned toward the cell door.

"But, Ben"—Barrett grabbed his arm—"get back to me as soon as possible, okay?" He peered deeply into Ben's eyes. "I need you, Ben."

Ben tugged at his tie, not answering.

"I know what you're thinking. You don't want to represent me because you think I'm some rich, fat-cat, ex-jock politician. You like the ones you consider tough cases. A man with no money. A retarded boy. A woman getting railroaded by the FBI. I'll tell you something, Ben, and I hope you'll hear what I'm saying. Those are the *easy* cases. You take those cases, you come out looking like a hero, win or lose. But, Ben, even if I'm not particularly underprivileged, I *am* a victim in this case. I'm the one who's had his family taken from him, his career, his liberty. And now the police and the press are going to try to convince everyone that I'm a hideous baby-killing maniac. Well, I'm not! *I'm not!*" He placed his hands down on the thin mattress. "And I want you to prove it."

Ben broke away and moved awkwardly to the cell door. "I'll get back to you." He motioned for the guard and left, leaving the mayor of the city and a million unanswered questions in his wake.

12

WHEN BEN ARRIVED at the mayor's mansion, it bore all the unmistakable traces of a crime scene: yellow tape cordoning off the area, uniformed patrolmen posted at all entrances, professionals shuffling through their appointed duties with a somber deliberativeness. Perhaps the most distinctive characteristic, however, was a marked stillness, a stillness in the midst of the hustle-bustle, a stillness that seemed to distinguish the house from all the other houses where life continued without interruption.

Ben nodded at Detective Tomlinson, who was just inside the front door. They knew each other well now, well enough that Tomlinson didn't question whether his boss would allow Ben onto the crime scene. As he knew, Ben Kincaid and Mike Morelli had been college roommates and had played as a musical combo in college-town niteries—Ben on piano, Mike on guitar. He also knew that Mike had married Ben's sister, then been divorced by her, a series of events that had put a distinct strain on his and Ben's friendship.

"Where—?" Ben didn't have to finish the question. Tomlinson pointed to a hunched figure crawling around on the hardwood floor in the living room.

Ben crossed the room, careful to remain on the protective sheets of butcher paper. Mike was crouched down on all fours, his nose to the floor, his rear end to the ceiling.

"Lose a contact?" Ben asked.

Mike cocked one eye to see who was there. "No."

"Trick back gave out again?"

"If you must know, I'm applying luminol to a smear of dirt to see if I can raise a footprint."

"I see. I don't suppose you've found anything?"

Mike rested his weight on one elbow. "For your information, I've found dozens of footprints. Unfortunately, they all came from police officers' boots."

"Didn't you put down paper after you cordoned off the scene?"

"Yes, of course, *I* did, but—" He stopped, then pushed up onto his knees and brushed off his hands. "What are you doing here, anyway, Ben? I chased off all the other thrill-seekers." His eyes narrowed. "You're not mixed up in this case, are you?"

"No. Not yet, anyway."

"What on earth does that mean?"

"Mayor Barrett has asked me to represent him."

Mike's eyes widened. "He asked *you*?"

"Is that so incredible?"

"I just thought he would want someone . . ."

Ben drummed his fingers. "Yes?"

"I mean, I thought he would want someone . . . someone . . ."

"I'm waiting."

"I thought he would want someone . . . taller. Yeah, that's it. Taller."

"Uh-huh, right. Let me clear up your obvious mystification. Someone seems to have given Mayor Barrett the misguided notion that I might have some influence with the judge he anticipates will be assigned to the case."

"Ah. Now that I can believe."

"That I have a lot of sway with the judge?"

"No. That Barrett would hire someone he *thought* did."

"I don't follow."

Mike stood up and shrugged. "Barrett is a politician. You know how they are. Their entire world revolves around politics. For them, it's more important to know the right people than to do the right thing. They'll choose influence over talent every time."

Ben lowered his chin. "Gee, thanks."

Mike smiled. "My point is that politicians want someone they think has the inside track. And apparently, this time that means you. So, have you accepted the case?"

"Not yet."

"What are you waiting for?"

"Well, I was hoping you could give me some insight. The . . . inside track, so to speak. I have to admit I have a few concerns."

"Like the fact that Barrett is obviously guilty?"

Ben looked away. "Of course, it would be inappropriate to discuss a potential client's innocence or guilt . . ."

"Yeah, that's you, Ben. Always playing by the book." He smirked. "I gather Barrett isn't confessing?"

"Far from it."

"What's his explanation? Unless that's privileged."

Ben shrugged. "I can't go into the details. But he contends he may have been framed by enemies on the city council."

Mike brushed the dirt off his unseasonably heavy trenchcoat. "And his much-publicized joyride down the Indian Nation Turnpike?"

"Panicked. Didn't know what he was doing."

"Ri-ight." He laid a hand on Ben's shoulder. "Have fun in court."

"I gather you think he's guilty."

"I pride myself on not jumping to conclusions about someone's guilt, even when the evidence against him is overwhelming. Which it is."

Ben nodded. This was not exactly what he wanted to hear.

"Win or lose, this is going to be a high-profile case. Local reporters have already started swarming, and it's just a matter of time till the nationals hit the scene. This case has star quality, plus all the lurid details the press loves. City's first black mayor, inner-city kid who made good, college athlete, accused of murdering his entire family in a gruesome manner." He whistled. "This is going to be one major media circus."

"And this business about the city council?"

"Well, Barrett does have enemies on the council. You know, even after the city government was restructured a few years ago, the council is still dominated by well-to-do whites. Some weren't too keen on taking their lead from a poor kid from the North Side."

Ben nodded. "Anyway, appreciate your help. If I do take the case, I'll cut you some slack on cross."

"Oh, it won't be me up there."

"Aren't you in charge of the crime scene?"

"Now, yes. But the first detective on the scene was Lieutenant Prescott."

"Prescott!" Ben had heard all about Prescott over beer and pizza. He knew Prescott's reputation well enough to avoid him. "Why on earth would you assign Prescott to such a big case?"

"I didn't. I was out of the office on another case."

"Chief Blackwell? I thought he didn't like the man any better than you did."

"Actually, according to Prescott, he was sent to the crime scene by"— Mike stopped short—"by friends on the city council."

Ben raised an eyebrow. "No kidding."

"Mmmm."

"How did Prescott do?"

"Oh, he—" Once again Mike stopped himself. "Well, I needn't go into the details."

"Uh-huh. He botched it, didn't he? That's why the footprints are screwed up."

"Ben." Mike looked supremely uncomfortable. "I am a member of the police department, you know. I report to the DA."

"This is more important than what team we're on, Mike. A man has been charged with murder."

"I know. But I can't endanger a pending case by criticizing a fellow member of my department. Not even . . ." His lips curled as if he had an unpleasant taste in his mouth.

"Mike, if it becomes important to the case—"

"I'm not saying I won't answer your questions. Just don't ask me to criticize a fellow officer, okay?"

"All right." Ben sensed he had already pushed his friend far enough. Better to wait for another time, another place. "If I take the case, I'll send word."

"Ben." Mike stepped closer to him and lowered his voice. "This is off the record, just buddy to buddy. I know it's tempting to take a high-profile case. But honestly, this one's a loser. The press is already acting as if Barrett's guilt is a foregone conclusion, and people believe what they hear on television. You remember the line from Lewis Carroll?"

"Which?"

" 'I'll be judge, I'll be jury,' said cunning old Fury / 'I'll try the whole cause and condemn you to death.' "

"Well . . ."

"That's what's going on now, Ben, with the police, with the press, and with however many millions of spectators out there who have already made up their minds. You're going to be taking heat from all sides—the media, the black community, the white community—and the end result will be the same. You could come out of it looking ridiculous."

He shoved his hands into the pockets of his coat. "I know better than to try to tell you what to do, Ben . . . but I can tell you what you should do. It's not as if Barrett couldn't get another lawyer. He can buy anyone he wants."

"Thanks for the advice." Ben started for the door.

"Hey," Mike called after him, "have you located your wayward sister?"

" 'Fraid not."

Mike nodded. "She's pretty good at staying out of sight when she doesn't want to be found. When she dumped me and took off for Montana with that schmuck professor, it took me months to track her down. And I'm a detective."

"I'm sure she'll turn up in time."

"Yeah. How's Joey?"

"Oh, he's . . . fine."

"He's a cute kid. As kids go. I like that little squirt."

You should, Ben thought. Blood will tell. Despite the story Julia had told when she first appeared with the baby, Ben was almost certain Mike was Joey's father. He had considered telling Mike a million times, but before he took that major step he wanted to be certain, and he couldn't be certain until he had tracked Julia down and gotten her to confirm his suspicions.

"Give him a hug for me, okay?" Mike said.

"I will," Ben answered as he walked outside. The sudden glare of sunlight made him squint.

I'll give him a hug, he thought. But when will Joey hug back?

13

THE INSTANT BEN opened his apartment door, he was assaulted by the distinctive and unusual smell of seafood. Ben hated seafood. It made him break out in hives.

"Hi, Joni," Ben said as he laid his briefcase on the kitchen table. Joey was in his playpen fiddling with a busy box. "Thanks for picking Joey up at school."

"No problemo."

"I had to run down some information on a possible new case—"

"I know. The mayor. *Wowzah!*"

"It's not that big a deal."

"Oh, right. Mayor Barrett assembles his own dream team, and you're it. No biggie."

"It's really not—"

"I always tell my sister, Jami—I say, you underestimate our Benjamin. He might make something of himself one day."

"Well, how nice."

"Granted, he is a lawyer, and he does spend a lot of time hanging out with cops, but still, give him a chance—"

"I get the drift. By the way, I haven't seen Jami lately. How is she?"

"Oh, very slack."

Ben blinked. "I beg your pardon?"

"Well, maybe I never noticed so much before I became a responsible caregiver, but she's not exactly making a difference in our society. She's been very gloom-ridden since she lost her job at The Body Shop. Can't get those discounts on exotic herb shampoo anymore. She mostly sits around on the sofa in the same skanky clothes and channel-surfs. She's become a mistress of time suckage."

"I'm sorry to hear that. Thanks again for picking up the kid."

"I was glad to do it. Gave me a great excuse to borrow the family wheels. I had a few errands to run."

Ben's head tilted a tiny degree. "Errands?"

"Right."

"And you took Joey along?"

"Right."

"Uh . . . Joni . . ." He loosened his tie. "You wouldn't take Joey any-where . . . inappropriate, would you?"

"Inappropriate? What did you have in mind? An adult book store? An opium den? A biker bar?"

"Joni, be serious. You know I'm responsible for him."

"Boy, you can say that again." She dropped her spoon and turned the heat up. "Exhale, Ben. What do you think I am, some tweaked-out bimbo? We went to Bud's for groceries."

Relief washed across his face. "What'd you get?"

"Paprika. For the shrimp tarragon."

Ben leaned over her shoulder and stared into the pot. "I suppose that has . . . shrimp in it?"

She smiled. "There's that keen analytical mind of yours again, Ben. Some-times it's scary."

"Ha-ha." He inhaled the aroma emanating from the stove. Yup, definitely seafood.

"Dinner will be on in five minutes. I can't wait to see what you think. I've never tried anything like this before."

"Really."

"I hope it's good. I mean, I'll be so disappointed . . . But I don't want to apply any pressure. I want an honest appraisal."

"You know, Booker might be a better judge . . ."

"He's working all night. And Mrs. Marmelstein has a cold. Nope, you're my man, Ben."

"Oh, gee." He decided to change the subject. "How's Joey?"

"His usual quiet self. I do have some concerns about him, though."

Ben felt a tiny clutching at his heart. "What, has he been unhappy?"

"Not that I've noticed."

"Doesn't seem to fit in? Doesn't follow instructions?"

Joni turned away from the stove. "Ben, what's wrong with you?"

"Then it isn't—"

"The only concern I have is about Joey's clothes."

"Oh." Ben plopped down in a chair. "What about them? We just bought him several outfits."

"That was five months ago, Ben. He's a kid. He grows. And he wears them out. Look at the knees on those overalls he's wearing."

"All right," Ben said, "what are my choices?"

"There are no choices. Only a single imperative. Baby Gap."

Ben appeared perplexed. "Is that a store?"

Joni's eyes rolled. "Jeez, Ben, you are totally clueless."

"I've just never cared for clothes shopping. My mother used to take me on these endless expeditions to—"

"Please! Don't burden me with the nightmarish tale of a rich kid forced to buy beautiful clothes against his will. My heart doesn't bleed for you."

"You never had to go to a birthday party wearing a cravat."

Joni returned to her cooking. "Just leave me some money, Ben. I'll take the little darling out to Woodland Hills tomorrow and fix him up."

"If you say so."

"I do. Remember, Ben, we're not just caretakers. We're responsible for his inner being. We have to make sure he can evolve."

"Right." Ben lifted Joey out of his playpen. "How's my little man evolving today?"

Joey didn't appear displeased to escape the playpen, but he didn't show any great happiness in it, either.

"C'mon, Joey. How 'bout a little smile for Uncle Ben?"

No smile was forthcoming.

"Okay, how 'bout a tiny titter of merriment?"

No change.

"A modest display of enthusiasm?"

Nope.

"Could you wink your right eye for me?"

Joey began picking his nose.

Ben swung the boy through the air and deposited him in his high chair. "There you go. Almost time for din-din."

Ben leaned close to Joey's ear and whispered. "You are glad to see me, though, aren't you, pal?" Ben peered deeply into the child's bright blue eyes. What he wouldn't give to see a flicker of recognition in there, a glimmer of appreciation, a tiny reflection of his own love. But he couldn't kid himself. He didn't see it. He didn't see anything at all except his own desperate face reflected in the iris.

"Here it is," Joni announced. She placed the main course in the center of the table, laid plates, and gave Joey his vegetable platter. "Eat up. Oooh! This is so exciting!"

Ben calmly scraped a reasonable portion of shrimp tarragon onto his plate. Well, what were a few hives among friends?

AFTER DINNER, BEN made a few unsuccessful attempts to play with Joey, then settled for playing the piano for him, which Joey seemed to like, or not dislike, anyway. Ben played some Mozart (because he had read that children's IQs could be raised by listening to Mozart). Then he played a Christine Lavin tune, "Old-Fashioned Romance," and a James Taylor favorite he and Mike had performed back in their college days, "If I Keep My Heart Out of Sight." By the end of the last, he noticed Joey's eyelids beginning to droop. He gave his nephew a quick bath, tucked him into bed, and read several storybooks to him. When Joey was asleep, Ben turned on the Natural Sounds comforter (HEAR HIGH TIDE IN YOUR OWN BEDROOM!) and left the room.

Ben was tired, but he knew he couldn't sleep yet. He had a decision to make first. He would've liked to have had more time, but it wasn't fair to keep Mayor Barrett in the lurch. He had to decide immediately if he was taking the case.

Not that it was necessarily so hideous to represent someone who was guilty. He'd taken cases before for people he—well, if he didn't know they were guilty, he certainly had strong suspicions. But this was different. The charge was murder. Murder of the defendant's own family. A heinous, absolutely unforgivable crime. The thought of being in the same room with someone who could do such a thing made Ben's blood run cold.

The media exposure was another factor. Mike was right; it was going to be a circus. He'd dealt with the press before, usually ineptly, but never on this level. Of course, publicity might be advantageous for a struggling attorney. On the other hand, he couldn't stand the thought of being labeled by millions as the guy who represented the Family Killer. The Baby Murderer. He'd rather go broke.

And why not admit it? He'd thought about it often enough during the day. What would his mother say?

He knew there were ethical reasons why he should take the case, but he still didn't want to do it. He wanted to be on the side of the angels.

So why hesitate? Just say no and be done with it. But there was something nagging at him, something he hadn't quite put his finger on yet.

Sighing, he pulled his box out from under his bed and sorted through his childhood treasures till he saw what he needed. He lifted the black orb with both hands and flipped it upside down.

"Oh, Oracle of the Magic 8-Ball, guide me in this moment of crisis. Should I take this case?"

He peered down at the white letters shimmering through the inky blue fluid: NO ANSWER AT THIS TIME.

That wasn't much help. He asked the question again and flipped the 8-ball.

TRY AGAIN LATER.

Well, thanks a hell of a lot, Oracle of the Magic 8-Ball.

Maybe while he was at it, he should ask for advice on what to do about Joey. He still couldn't believe that Joey was unhappy, that there was something wrong. Perhaps something serious. But the evidence was becoming harder to ignore. Tonight, when he had gazed into that little boy's eyes . . .

Wait a minute. Something glimmered in the far reaches of Ben's memory. Gazing into his eyes . . .

His memory hopscotched back past Joey, beyond the evening, to the Friday before. Back at Forestview, before Barrett was arrested, before the tragedy.

Of course. He could see it clearly now, almost as if it was happening all over again. He saw Barrett picking up his two little girls. He remembered it so well because he had been so jealous. Jealous of the adoring way those two girls beamed at their daddy.

And the way he beamed back at them.

Barrett loved those little girls. Loved them with all his heart, all his soul, all his mind. Loved them with every ounce of his being. It was as if all the love he had to muster crystallized and glistened in his eyes.

And the eyes don't lie.

The man Ben had seen would never hurt his little girls. Absolutely never.

Ben put the 8-Ball back in the box. Wallace Barrett did not kill his daughters. He was certain of it.

And if Barrett didn't, that meant someone else did. Someone who was still on the loose. Someone the police weren't even looking for.

Well, someone should be.

Ben slid the box back under his bed, picked up the bedroom phone and dialed. "Christina? . . . Yeah. Yeah, we are. Look, here's what we're going to do."

Two

The Eyes of the World

◆ ◆ ◆

14

NOTHING COULD HAVE prepared Ben for the reception that awaited him the instant he stepped out of his car in the courthouse parking lot. Reporters descended upon him from nowhere and circled tightly around, blocking his access to the courthouse door. His vision was obscured by microphones bearing the insignia of all five local television stations, one from Oklahoma City, one from New York, and one from CNN. The same journalists who had been bombarding his office with phone calls and interview requests since his decision to represent Barrett had been made public.

"Mr. Kincaid!"

"Can you give us a statement?"

"How are you going to plead?"

Ben tried to push his way through the mob, keeping his lips zipped. He was aware that any muttered comment or offhand remark would be picked up by one of the microphones currently thrust in his face and replayed continuously throughout the day.

"Can you give us a clue about what's going to happen inside?"

Ben pushed through the electronic thicket and headed resolutely toward the front door of the courthouse.

"How do you feel about representing a guilty man?"

Ben stopped. "Who said that?"

The reporters quieted. They looked from one to another.

"Come on, this isn't a playground. Who said it?"

One of the local reporters, a young man with blond permaplaqued hair, took a step forward. "That was me."

Ben covered the microphone with his hand and blocked his camera with his briefcase. "Let me give you a little remedial Civics 101, pal. Here in America, everyone is presumed innocent until proven otherwise. No one is guilty until a jury says so."

"But—"

"No one. No exceptions. And suggesting otherwise could have some serious legal ramifications. Got it?"

The reporter nodded. Ben turned and walked into the courthouse, this time unimpeded.

Shouldn't have done that, Ben told himself. You'll regret it. The first time that blow-dried blowhard gets a chance to shaft you on the air, he will. But the guy could do a lot more damage if he went on the air blatantly assuming Barrett was guilty. Oh sure, he would never say it in so many words, but his coverage would be slanted and the feature would be structured and timed and edited in such a fashion as to make everyone watching suppose Barrett must be guilty. And some of those couch potatoes, the ones who still think the way to find out what's going on in the world is to watch the local news, would end up sitting on the jury. He had to do everything possible to preclude that kind of reporting before the jury pool was irremediably tainted.

Four men from the sheriff's office were waiting outside a courtroom on the seventh floor with the mayor, now defendant, Wallace Barrett. Today the mayor had eschewed his usual Armani pin-striped three-piece suit in favor of standard-issue loose-fitting bright orange coveralls, designed to attract attention in the event of an escape because they were so garish and ugly. Quite a comedown.

The instant Ben stepped into the frame beside Barrett, a flurry of flash-bulbs illuminated the hallway. The page one money shot.

"How're the boys treating you?" Ben asked.

Barrett smiled, revealing a tiny glimmer of the charisma that put him in office. "Not bad for city employees."

"Well, they're overworked and underpaid."

"I know. I've been trying to get the council to approve a twenty percent wage increase for them for three years."

The officers on either side of him studiously scrutinized their shoes. It was true; they all knew it.

Ben took Barrett by the arm and led him into the courtroom, sheriff's men close at his heels. The instant they entered the courtroom, they were met by a loud, enthusiastic response—all of it negative. The courtroom was packed, no surprise, and with the exception of the press, everyone in the room appeared to be hissing and booing and snarling at their mayor, now the disreputable-looking defendant in the ugly orange garb. There were a few shouts from the far corner, a few loud calls for impeachment, a few racist slurs.

"Ignore it," Ben commanded sotto voce. "Face forward. Don't give them the satisfaction of responding."

Barrett nodded his understanding.

Unfortunately, the judge was not yet in the courtroom, so there was no immediate demand for order in the court. They would just have to ride it out.

Jack Bullock was at the prosecution table, emptying his briefcase studiously. Ben wasn't surprised; he had anticipated that Bullock would want to handle this one. Ben caught Bullock's eye for a glimmer of a second; Bullock looked quickly away.

Too bad. Ben had known Bullock since he was in law school, back when he had interned at the DA's office in Oklahoma City. They had worked together back then, two minds with a single idealistic goal: making the world a better place. But since they had both moved to Tulsa, and Ben had become known (to the extent he was known at all) principally as a defense lawyer, Bullock had refused to have anything to do with him. He had made it abundantly clear that he considered Ben a "disappointment," a defector from the cause of the good and the righteous.

Ben considered forcing himself on the man, but decided against it. He needed to focus on his client, and how he could best use this arraignment to his client's advantage. He couldn't get all caught up in his emotions about his former mentor.

A few moments later, the court bailiff instructed everyone to rise and the door opened on the Honorable Edwin H. Hawkins, affectionately known as Hang 'em High Hawkins. Hawkins, as Ben knew all too well, envisioned himself as a modern-day Judge Roy Bean, a hanging judge for the Nineties. The only good thing Ben could say about Hawkins handling the arraignment was that it guaranteed he wouldn't be handling the inevitable trial.

Judge Hawkins ran briskly through his preliminaries, doing his best to cut the fine figure of a judge. Unlike his usual slouched, rather cynical demeanor, today he was sitting up straight, enunciating clearly, projecting his voice, and basically conducting himself in a dignified manner. Ben realized Hawkins had been tipped off to the fact that several rows of the gallery were filled with reporters, probably more press than he had seen in his courtroom for all his previous cases combined.

The bailiff called the case, and Hawkins asked Ben if his client would waive the formal reading of the charge. He did. This was all procedural rigmarole. Although required by the state constitution, the reading of the arraignment, usually long and cluttered with difficult to comprehend legalese, only slowed things down.

Judge Hawkins now peered down at the defendant. "Mr. Barrett, you have been charged with three separate counts of first-degree murder. Do you understand the charges that have been made against you?"

"I do," Barrett answered in his usual deep baritone, like James Earl Jones with a head cold. Ben could answer for his client and usually did, but Barrett had told him beforehand that he could and would answer for himself. He was also apparently not unaware that there were reporters in the gallery.

"And have you been advised of your rights as the accused?"

"I have."

"And have you had an opportunity to consult with counsel with regard to the charges that have been made against you?"

"I have."

Hawkins lifted the papers on his desk and bounced them into a neat stack. "Very well, sir. How do you plead against these charges?"

"I plead not guilty," Barrett said emphatically. And then after a moment he added, "I didn't do it."

There was an audible sound from the gallery, not a buzz, but certainly a distinctive murmur. The sound of many pencils in motion.

Hawkins stared down at the defendant, his lips slightly parted. "You plead not guilty?"

"I do, sir."

The model of professionalism, Hawkins lowered his head and scribbled on his legal pad. He obviously wanted to say something, but was too smart to say it here and now.

"Got anything more to say?" the judge asked.

"I'm sick at heart about this, judge." Barrett's face was firm but earnest. "We must catch whoever committed this horrible crime. It wasn't me, but the police aren't looking for anyone else. I'm specifically asking this court to use its influence to order the police department to continue its investigation."

"I'm afraid that's outside my jurisdiction." The judge shuffled a few more papers, then turned to Bullock, standing just to the side of the defendant. "Mr. Prosecutor, when can you be ready for trial?"

"As soon as your honor wishes," he replied crisply.

"The prosecution is ready?"

"Completely."

"You've got all the evidence you need?"

A faint smile played on Bullock's lips. "Hasn't everyone?"

Hawkins quickly lowered his head, to conceal, Ben suspected, the faint smile now playing on his own lips. When his head rose again, he had re-applied his poker face. "Very well. The court will set the preliminary hearing for Thursday at nine o'clock. The defendant is committed to the care of the county sheriff's—"

"About that, your honor," Ben said. He hated to interrupt, but he also knew that after a judge had made a ruling, it was almost impossible to get him to reverse it. "We move that the defendant be released on bail pending the hearing or trial. We're willing to post any reasonable amount."

"The state objects in the strongest possible way," Bullock said. "The defendant has been charged with three counts of capital murder."

"Nonetheless," Ben said, "Mr. Barrett is one of the leading citizens in our community—"

"Was," Bullock interjected.

"Mr. Barrett is one of the best-known individuals in this city. In this state, for that matter. He could hardly just disappear."

"Your honor," Bullock said, in his usual calm but insistent voice, "the defendant has already tried to flee once. Surely we are not going to give him another opportunity."

"That's not fair or accurate—"

Hawkins waved Ben quiet. "The court agrees with the prosecutor, counsel. These charges are so serious, so"—he paused, apparently searching for a word that would convey his meaning without suggesting that he had lost his neutrality—"so profoundly disturbing that bail could be denied on those grounds alone. Moreover, the defendant has demonstrated a clear disposition for flight. I believe I have no choice but to deny bail. The defendant is remanded to the custody of the county sheriff until further notice."

He pounded his gavel for emphasis. "If there is nothing more, I'll see you gentlemen on Thursday. By the way, I've granted approval to Court TV to televise the hearing and, pending approval of the judge assigned to the case, the trial. Other networks will have equal access to the footage, as will you."

"Your honor," Ben said, "I object—"

Barrett tugged on Ben's arm. "No, it's all right."

Ben lowered his voice. "Wallace, I don't think this is a good idea."

"It's okay." He nodded, evidently trying to avoid any embarrassment to Ben, but still determined to have his way.

Ben turned back to the court, frowning. "I withdraw my objection."

"That's what I like to hear. We're dismissed." Hawkins pounded his gavel and left the courtroom.

Ben took his client to a private corner for an impromptu discussion of trial strategy. "What were you doing back there? I was making an important objection."

Barrett shrugged. "I don't mind the cameras."

"You should. Televising trials is a bad idea. The media presence will distort the process."

"I can handle it. The cameras like me. Besides, I might want to have a career again after this mess is over."

Ben leaned into his client's face. "Stop worrying about your approval rating and start worrying about this trial. Don't you know what we're up against? Didn't you hear the reaction when you came into the courtroom? Can't you read the expression on everyone's face? The whole world thinks you're guilty!"

"That's just it," Barrett said quietly.

That caught Ben off guard. "I don't follow you."

"You said it. Everyone thinks I'm guilty. Basically, they believe what the media tell them, and the media are telling them I'm guilty. They want a good story, the more dramatic, the better. Right now, the best story in town is the one about the ex-jock mayor who goes nuts and kills his wife and kids. That's a ratings winner. 'Family slaughtered by unknown assailant who will probably never be caught' isn't half as compelling. That's why they're focusing on me. Ten years from now, when I'm doing time for a crime I didn't commit, the press might get interested in a 'has-justice-been-denied?' story. But for now, making me look guilty is the juiciest game in town."

"So what's your point?"

"Just this: everyone in town is going to be bombarded with media coverage suggesting that I'm guilty. I want them to hear someone arguing that I'm innocent. And the only place they're going to hear that argument is inside this courtroom—from you. So I want it televised."

Ben pressed his lips together. He still thought it was unwise, but he could see the man's point. "I hope you're not making a big mistake here."

Barrett chuckled. "Well, if I am, you'll fix it, right? That's what lawyers are for."

THE SHERIFF'S MEN escorted Barrett back to his cell. Ben stayed behind to pack his briefcase. He noticed Bullock was still at his table, lingering for no apparent reason.

"Well, Ben, you must be very proud of yourself." His tone suggested more than a little irony.

"For what?"

"For getting this case!" Bullock spread his arms wide. "What a plum! So much publicity. It's a defense lawyer's dream. Soon you'll have every baby murderer in town coming to you."

Ben slung his papers into his briefcase. "Jack, I'm not in the mood."

"What, are we sensitive today? I thought you gloried in representing maimers and slaughterers."

"That remark doesn't even deserve an answer."

Bullock grew quiet. He stood, then walked beside Ben. He lifted his hand briefly, then lowered it, as if he had fleetingly considered placing his hand on Ben's shoulder.

"I can't believe that the same smart, fresh-faced kid I used to work shoulder to shoulder with, putting away the bad guys and throwing away the keys, is going to defend the man who has committed what is quite possibly the most hideous, most horrifying crime I have ever encountered."

"Jack, he hasn't been found guilty yet."

"Don't give me that kindergarten crap. I don't care what bullshit story you're cooking up for the jurors. It's perfectly obvious what happened."

"If I've learned anything in the time I've been practicing law," Ben said, "it's that things are not always what they appear."

"You're deluding yourself." Bullock shook his head sadly. "You know, Ben, I don't mean to hassle you every time I see you. Afterward, I go home and kick myself. I just can't help it. I'm so . . . *sad* about this. I feel a loss, deep in my gut."

Ben felt a distinct itching at his eyes.

"You used to know the difference between right and wrong."

They stared into each other's eyes, sinking deeply into pools of recollection. They both knew what he was referring to now.

"You were willing to make personal sacrifices for your beliefs. You knew what was important."

"Did I?"

"Oh, yeah." Bullock's half-smile returned. "I still remember the day you came into my office for the first time."

So did Ben.

BEN HAD BEEN more than a little nervous when Marge Cunningham, the secretary for all the law students clerking at the Oklahoma City DA's office that year, had informed him that Jack Bullock wished to see him. Most days Ben stayed in the library and did his work with as little social contact as possible. He tried to stay out of trouble, stuck to his research assignments, and scrupulously avoided anything that might land him in a courtroom.

So he was startled, first, that Marge would even speak to him, and second, that he had been summoned by Jack Bullock himself. Bullock had quite the reputation in the DA's office; he'd been there longer than the DA. District attorneys, after all, were elected; they came and went depending upon which way the political wind blew. Bullock had outlasted them all because he was smart and because even the district attorneys who didn't like him didn't want to find him sitting at the table on the other side of the courtroom. He was good.

It was late in the evening. Only a few staff members were still there; all the other interns had long since left. Ben tended to work late, in part because he revised his written work endlessly and in part because he didn't particularly want to go home.

Ben lifted his hand to knock on the closed door to Bullock's office. He was embarrassed to see that his hand was trembling. Good grief, he told himself, you're about to be a lawyer. Get a grip on yourself.

"Come in," a voice from inside the office bellowed.

The office was mostly dark; a single banker's lamp on the desk illuminated the room. Jack Bullock sat in the chair, pushed all the way back, feet propped up on the desk, legal pad on his lap.

Ben stood in the doorway. "Um . . . Marge said . . . I mean, Marge, she's the secretary—"

"I know who Marge is." His voice was firm and precise; every word seemed to have an edge.

"Oh, well, yes, of course you do." Ben took a deep breath. "Marge thought you wanted to see me, although I'm sure it was just some crazy mistake. I'll close the door on my way out."

"Stop."

Ben froze, pinioned in the doorway.

"It was no mistake. Have a seat." He gestured toward a chair on the other side of the desk.

Breathing rapidly, Ben stepped into the office and slid into the chair. He wished to God he could stop his legs from shaking, but it didn't seem to be within his power.

Bullock's face was half in the light, half out, silhouetted by the lamp. "You're the one who got caught between the doors, aren't you?"

Ben felt his heart sink into the pit of his stomach. He should have known. He would never be allowed to live that one down.

It had happened the first day of work. He'd stayed late, hoping to make a good impression by getting all his work done right off the bat. About nine, he stepped beyond the outer office door, looking for the men's room. All he found was the outer office door, which was locked. He turned to go back, but the inner office door had closed behind him and locked. There was a keypad by both doors, but Ben had no idea what the code was. He was trapped. He banged the doors and shouted for help, but no help came. He ended up being stuck between the doors for over four hours, till the cleaning staff showed up and set him free. Of course word got back to the other interns, who proceeded to rag him mercilessly every day thereafter, in part because it was so ridiculous and in part because they knew that anyone who was already staying late on the first day could be a serious pain in the butt.

"It was just a stupid mistake," Ben blurted out. It just wasn't fair. He liked working here; he didn't want to lose the job over this. "I didn't know about the security system. Nobody told me. It won't happen again. It was no big deal."

"I think it was."

"I don't know what you heard, but I don't do stupid things all the time. Certainly not all the time—"

"What I conclude from this incident," Bullock said, interrupting effortlessly, "is that you were willing to put in long hours. Even on your first day."

"Well . . . yeah . . ." Ben's hands were making ridiculous flopping gestures. He sat on them.

"Is that still true?"

Ben looked up. "Well, yes."

"Haven't I seen you in the corner carrel in the library during the lunch hour?"

"Uh, yeah . . ."

"Drinking mineral water out of a bottle?"

"Right." Ben wasn't sure which part was the offense—being in the library during lunch or drinking mineral water. "Well, it's not like I *have* to drink mineral water. It's just that the tap water here is so bad."

"You grew up in Nichols Hills, didn't you?"

Ben frowned. "How did you know?"

"Not hard. It's written all over you. Plus, everyone knows Nichols Hills has the worst water supply. The best houses and the worst water. I'd drink mineral water, too, if I lived in Nichols Hills. Which I never will." His eyes lowered. "Will you?"

Ben stuttered. "Th-that's not my principal goal in life, no."

Bullock's head tilted to one side. "You're not related to that Nichols Hills cardiologist, are you? Edward Kincaid. The Baptist Hospital hotshot. The one I always see in the society pages at some fund-raiser or the other."

Ben was tempted to lie, but he knew it would be simple for Bullock to learn the truth. "That's my father."

"You get along well with dear old dad?"

Ben could feel himself blotching up, as he always did when an uncomfortable subject was broached. "We've had our differences."

"Like?"

Ben shrugged. "He wasn't too keen on my becoming a lawyer."

Bullock made a small snorting noise. "Doctors never are. Lawyers frighten them. They consider them a threat to their God-given right to make tubs of money. And they like to tell themselves that all those lawsuits against them are brought by lawyers. It's easier than acknowledging the reality that those lawsuits are brought by their patients. Maybe if they spent less time hating lawyers and more time caring about their patients, they wouldn't have that problem."

Ben didn't say anything. He really wished Bullock would change the subject.

"I'm looking for an intern," Bullock said suddenly.

"Oh, well." Ben's voice cracked. "That's no problem. We have ten interns in the office this summer."

"I need only one." Bullock pushed himself to his feet. He was taller than

Ben would have guessed—lankier, but still imposing. "I need a personal assistant. Someone to work exclusively with me, to help me cope with this mindnumbing caseload the DA has dropped in my lap."

"That shouldn't be a problem," Ben said. "I think any of the interns would be honored to work with you."

Bullock leaned across his desk. "I was rather thinking you might like the job."

Ben was flabbergasted, and it showed. "Me?" His hands escaped from under his legs and pressed themselves against his chest. "Why me?"

"Because of this." Bullock picked up a thick document and tossed it across his desk. It was the trial brief Ben had written for a case styled *State of Oklahoma v. Raymond Rogers Browning*. Browning was a low-level drug dealer who'd been caught with a stash of junk in his parents' basement. Ben had written the brief, and it had been filed virtually unchanged. "How long did you spend on that brief, Kincaid?"

Ben wondered whether he should be honest, but he knew he was a pathetic liar. "Two weeks. A little more." Probably three times as long as most of his fellow interns spent on a single brief. "Mostly nights."

"So you could keep up with your other work during the day."

Ben nodded.

"I suspected as much."

Ben leaned forward. "I'm sorry about this, Mr. Bullock. I'll be more efficient in the future. I promise. It's just that, this was a very special case."

"I quite agree," Bullock said quietly.

"You . . ." Ben stopped, surprised. "You do?"

"Oh, yes. I've been trying to convince everyone in this office of the importance of this case. But no one else can see it. They say, it's a first offense. Blow it off. Plead it down. Assign the brief to an intern. That's what they say."

"I know it's Browning's first offense," Ben said. "At least, the first time he's been caught. But the man was peddling drugs to schoolchildren. *Grade* school children. And he stashed the stuff in his parents' house, obviously implicating them. And he lied to his parents about it." Ben's face lowered. "That's just unforgivable."

"I couldn't agree more."

"You do?"

"I do. A person who would do what this man has done could do anything. The man is a sociopath. He doesn't care about anyone other than himself; he thinks he is the measure of the whole world. If we had pleaded him down, or let him off with time served, he'd be back in custody within months. The only difference would be that he'd have more time to ruin more children's lives. I wasn't willing to let that happen." He stepped around his desk, closer to Ben. "And judging from this brief, you weren't either."

Ben didn't say anything. He didn't know what to say.

"Mr. Kincaid, let me lay it on the line for you. I still believe in good and bad, in black and white, in right and wrong. I believe the guilty should be punished. I believe the law enforcement community has an obligation to make the world a better place, a safer place. And I believe that with dedication and hard work, everyone can make a difference. Even lawyers."

"So do I," Ben said, so quietly it was barely audible.

"So what do you say, Kincaid?" He held out his hand. "Wanna work with me?"

"Yes," Ben answered, clasping his hand. "Very much."

Bullock shook vigorously and smiled. "Mr. Kincaid, I think this is the beginning of a beautiful friendship."

And it was. For a while.

CHAPTER

15

ON HIS WAY to the office the next morning, Ben checked the newspapers in the stand at the corner. The Wallace Barrett case took the headline and filled the top half of the page in the Tulsa and Oklahoma City papers. It was respectably featured on page one in *The New York Times* and *The Wall Street Journal* and got a nice blue-lined box in *USA Today*. No doubt about it—the eyes of the world were upon them.

Ben bought one of the local papers and carried it back to his office. The banner headline read: MAYOR SICK AT HEART ABOUT MURDERS. Beneath that, a smaller headline read: DA REP SAYS AIRTIGHT CASE READY FOR TRIAL. In the center of the page, a photo showed Barrett in his baggy orange coveralls, hands cuffed behind his back, looking away from the camera, out the corner of narrowed eyes. No doubt about it; he looked like a criminal. Correction: they made him look like a criminal. It was clear to Ben that, despite the fact that there must've been hundreds of photos of Barrett in their morgue, the paper intentionally chose the one that made him look the most unsavory. The most guilty.

At the office, Jones was dealing with the news reporters that had been calling the office night and day. He was juggling two different phones, one in each ear. He was talking into one with another of his seemingly endless array of accents.

"Kincaid? No one by that name here, mate. No, we're wallaby breeders. Cute furry things. Can I sign you up? You're sure? Well, put another shrimp on the barbie for me."

Ben rolled his eyes. At least as authentic as your average *Crocodile Dundee* movie. Before he could interrupt, Jones had started in on the other phone.

"Ahh, no, no, sahib. No Kincaid here. Pakistani Embassy. Yes, quite, quite certain. Can we perhaps be issuing a visa for your humble self?"

Ben sighed. When did dramatic arts become a secretarial skill?

After Jones hung up the phone, Ben collected Christina and Loving and started his pretrial strategy session and pep talk.

"I think Christina has already told you that I've decided to take the Wallace Barrett case. Now I know you might have misgivings about this, but it's important that we work together as a team—everyone pulling in the same direction. Still, I'm not going to force you to do anything that twists your conscience. So if you want out, I understand, but you need to tell me now."

Christina, Jones, and Loving remained stone-faced. No one spoke.

"I don't hear anything," Ben said. "Jones, what about you?"

Jones tapped the side of his head thoughtfully. "I don't know, Boss. This dilemma raises serious moral and ethical issues. Can I ask you a question?"

"Of course."

"Is he paying us up front?"

"He's giving us a sizable retainer, yes."

Jones nodded. "I'm in."

"Well, that was easy. Loving, what about you? I know you may not believe Barrett is innocent—"

"I do."

"You do?"

"Oh, yeah. This whole thing stinks. It's got government cover-up written all over it."

"Well . . ."

"Are you sure Barrett is safe?"

"Safe? He's in the county jail."

"That may not be good enough."

Ben folded his arms across his chest. "I'm . . . not quite sure I follow you."

"This is just like what they did to Marilyn."

"Uh, Marilyn?"

"Sure. First they discredited her, then they bumped her off."

"I thought Marilyn died of a drug overdose."

Loving guffawed. "Oh, right. You probably think Jim Morrison died of a heart attack."

Ben decided not to respond. "Christina?"

"Oui," she chirped.

Ben smiled, pleased and relieved. "All right, then, here's what I want everyone to do. Jones, get on the Net and start digging up everything you can find on this case. I'd like complete backgrounds on our client, his wife, his kids, his immediate family. See if you can get me a breakdown on the most important political issues he's supported, proposals, legislation, whatever. And especially anything that relates to his relationship with the city council or any other political enemies. I want to know anyone who might've had a motive for killing Barrett's family, including the possibility that it was done to discredit Barrett himself. Remember, for once we have an actual honest-to-God paying client, so be thorough. Don't leave any stone unturned."

"Got it, Boss. Does Barrett have an e-mail address?"

"I don't know. Why?"

"I know the Tulsa city offices have computers and are wired for e-mail. If I could read all the messages Barrett has received over the last few months, I might find some clues."

Christina frowned. "But wouldn't they be deleted by now?"

Jones raised a finger. "Actually, no. See, this is the mistake everyone makes. They think that once they've deleted an e-mail message from their computer, it's gone. But it isn't. The central computer system makes backup copies of all messages, and the copies remain in the system until they are physically erased and written over."

"But could we use that?"

"Federal law allows employers to monitor employees' e-mail, and e-mail can be used as evidence in civil lawsuits. I don't see why this should be any different."

"All right, see what you can do." Ben turned toward his investigator. "Loving, I'd like you to focus on the city council angle. Get members' names and run them by all your friends with connections to, um, not necessarily legal activities. If you get my drift."

"Loud and clear."

"And see if anybody knows anything about the possibility of a hit man coming to town. Someone who might've been hired to kill Barrett or his family or both, or who might've been lurking around Barrett's neighborhood."

"If it was a hit man, someone in town would know. The trick is findin' the one who knows."

"I have faith in you, Loving. If he's out there, you'll find him. And while you're at it, check on Barrett's wife. I understand she was originally from Crescent, Oklahoma. Do you know where that is?"

Loving smirked. "Of course I do, Skipper. What do you think, I live in a cave? Crescent is where Karen Silkwood lived. Before the Feds ran her off the road."

"Ri-ight."

"And what about me?" Christina asked. "I assume you have an assignment that will make full use of my numerous and varied talents."

"Christina, I need you to help me get ready for trial. The preliminary hearing is a foregone conclusion; we know perfectly well Barrett will be bound over for trial. There's more than sufficient evidence, and even if there wasn't, given the current atmosphere in this town, a judge would have to be crazy to set him free. So we gear ourselves toward the trial."

Ben stepped back and addressed all three of them. "We have to be ready for anything and everything. We're going to be scrutinized like never before. We're going to be under a gigantic media magnifying glass, with millions of people watching every move we make. I want you to hassle the prosecution mercilessly till they turn over all their files, all their evidence, all the potentially exculpatory evidence. Don't let them get away with anything. I know this is going to be hard. We're going to be under constant pressure. We've got to ignore all that and pull together and win this case. All right?"

Loving thrust his fist in the air. "All right! Let's go, team!"

Christina and Jones followed his lead. "Go, team, go! Win, team, win!"

"Wait a minute," Ben said. "This is serious."

They didn't stop. "Go, go, go! Win, win, win!"

"Hey!"

Christina laid a hand on Ben's shoulder. "It's no use. You know how stirred up Loving gets when you do these Knute Rocknesque pep talks." Jones and Loving continued chanting in the background.

Ben grabbed his briefcase. "While you clowns finish your pep rally, I'm going to visit Mike."

They continued unabated. "Two, four, six, eight, who do we appreciate? Be-e-e-e-n!"

By the time they got to "Rah-rah, sish-boom-bah," Ben was halfway to police headquarters.

16

BEN PUSHED OPEN the door bearing the M. MORELLI nameplate and found his friend barking commands into the phone. "And I want it now, which means you're already late!"

Ben took a seat and waited for Mike to complete his latest effort to increase efficiency through intimidation. At last Mike threw the receiver into the cradle with disgust. "Incompetents!" Mike bellowed. "Be glad you got out of government work, Ben. It doesn't matter what department you're in. It's all just one big miasma of bureaucrats and bullshit. You know what Balzac said."

"I do?"

"Bureaucracy is a giant mechanism operated by pygmies."

"Right. I knew that." Ben took the nearest seat. "You don't seem very jolly this morning. Barrett case giving you headaches?"

"Like you wouldn't—" Mike paused. "You're taking his case, aren't you?"

"Yup. Filed my entry of appearance and everything. How did you guess?"

"Oh, hell, I knew you would the minute you mentioned it."

"I didn't."

"I did. After all, it's stupid, irrational, fruitless, and almost certain to do you more harm than good. In other words, a case you couldn't resist."

Ben smiled wryly. "How's the investigation going?"

Mike opened his desk drawer and jammed a toothpick in his mouth. He'd been off tobacco for six months, but he still needed the oral security of a wood sliver in his mouth from time to time. "There's no investigation. We have our man. The evidence says he's guilty. We're taking him to trial."

"And no one is considering any other angles?"

"What other angles?" Mike spread his arms across the desk. "Ben, you know me. I don't jump to conclusions or try to take the easy way out. There is simply no evidence indicating anything other than the obvious: Wallace Barrett killed his wife and kids."

"Okay. Tell me about this evidence."

Mike shook his head. "You're in the wrong office. Bullock is upstairs."

"C'mon, Mike, you know how Bullock is. He's not going to give me anything without making me refight World War Two. We'll have motions and hearings and it will take days."

Mike rolled the toothpick to the other side of his face. "Maybe you should sweet-talk him."

"It wouldn't help. He seems to be a bit angry with me."

"He's angry at *you*?" Mike's eyes widened. "I'm surprised you'll even speak to him, after what he did to you."

Ben shrugged. "We need to put the past behind us." Ben scooted his chair closer to Mike's desk. "So anyway, old buddy old pal, what can you tell me about this case?"

Mike glanced at the open door. "What do you want to know?"

"What about the victims? How were they killed?"

"Dr. Koregai can give you more details, but basically, they all suffered fatal knife wounds."

Ben nodded grimly. Knives would not be the typical weapon of choice for a professional hit man. Of course, that might well be why it was chosen. "Were the bodies moved?"

"Nope. D.R.T." As Ben knew, that meant they were Dead Right There.

"Have you found the knife? Or knives?"

Mike shook his head no. "And frankly, we don't expect to."

"Why not?"

"Well, Ben, there's a lot of ground between here and that tollbooth he smashed into on the Indian Nation Turnpike."

"When I was in the Barrett house, I didn't notice all that many signs of struggle."

Mike shifted his weight uncomfortably. "By the time you arrived, much of the evidence had been photographed and removed. But you're right. There were a few overturned chairs, vases, a coffee table. But not much."

"Any prints?"

"Yeah, lots. All family members. Barrett's prints were all over the place, but I suppose we can't hold that against him, since he lived there." Mike paused. "Have you seen the video?"

"Excuse me?"

"The video. It's easy to get. There are three different versions on the market now. *Wallace Barrett's Flight from Justice. Horror in the Heartland.* I forget the other one."

"No, I haven't seen it."

"You'll want to. It's very exciting."

"Do you think the prosecution will use it?"

"Would you?"

Ben nodded. Stupid question. "Anything that suggests a possible motive?"

"Motive might be too strong a word. Theory, I'd say."

"Okay, what's your theory, Sherlock?"

Mike paused. "Have you had any discussions with your client? Like about his relationship with his wife?"

"A little. Not much. Why?"

"You . . . might want to do that."

Ben leaned forward anxiously. "What are you getting at, Mike?"

Mike hedged. "Again, the coroner can tell you more than I can. But some of the bruises we found on the wife's face . . . don't correlate to the knife wounds."

Ben felt a fluttering sensation in his gut.

"We've had some reports from people who observed Barrett with his wife in public. Parties and such. And a rather detailed report from their neighbor."

"Mike, you know that any time someone famous is arrested, a thousand would-be talk-show guests crawl out of the woodwork claiming to know something about them."

"That's true."

"Be realistic. Wallace Barrett was a celebrity. If he was a wife beater, word would've gotten out."

"I don't know, Ben. Sometimes the darkest secrets stay hidden the longest. You know what Charles Churchill said."

"Intimately."

"Keep up appearances, there lies the test / The world will give thee credit for the rest. / Outward be fair, however foul within / Sin if thou wilt, but then in secret sin."

Ben frowned. "Do you stay up late memorizing these things just so you can make me feel inferior?"

"Actually, yes." Mike flashed a brilliant smile. "It's my revenge for all those times you blew the intro to my big make-the-girls James Taylor number."

"Mike, I don't believe the mayor of the city could keep a history of domestic abuse secret. And I don't think a jury will, either."

"I don't know, Ben. We've had 911 calls about alleged domestic disturbances sending us to Barrett's place twice in the last three years. And then there's the business about the picture."

"The picture? What picture?"

"Didn't you notice? The framed photo smashed against the wall in the living room."

"What?"

"A picture of Caroline Barrett. And someone smashed it into a million pieces."

Ben tried not to react. "Anyone could've smashed a photo."

"Yes, anyone could, but why would they? Smashing a photo—that goes beyond rational motivation or murder for hire. That's just mean. Hateful. It doesn't make any sense. Unless you believe that Barrett lost control—"

"Well, I don't."

"We've had a lot of reports. Apparently he was notorious for his temper."

"Everyone has a temper. But no one kills their daughters. That's just—unthinkable."

"Wrong. Everyone's thinking it. And every member of your jury will be thinking it. And you're not going to sway them unless you have some damn convincing evidence."

Ben scooted forward. "Mike, I don't want to tread on your toes, but apparently the crime scene investigation was pretty seriously botched. If that's true, and the evidence is tainted, I need to know."

"That's why God invented cross-examination."

"Mike, you know Bullock believes it's his civic duty to get a conviction, no matter what. I can't stand by and let him railroad an innocent man." Ben leaned across the desk. "Will you help me?"

Mike's toothpick rolled to the other side of his mouth. "I'm sorry, Ben. I can't."

"But—"

"Ben, I'm a cop. I work with the DA."

"But—"

"*No.*" He pressed his hands against the desk. "I'm sorry."

"I'm sorry, too," Ben said quietly. He grabbed his briefcase and headed toward the door.

"Of course, every competent defense attorney knows to scrutinize the blood evidence very carefully."

Ben stopped.

"Particularly with all this new DNA stuff that no one understands. You can't be too careful."

Mike was staring out the window, not talking to anyone in particular.

"And only a fool would pass up a chance to talk to Caroline Barrett's sister. Man, what a looker. Almost as pretty as her sister. The DA loves her."

A smile crept across Ben's face. "Thanks, Mike. You're a good friend."

Mike turned suddenly. "Are you still here? I thought you left hours ago."

Ben nodded. "I did."

CHAPTER

17

DEANNA WOULD HAVE been lying to herself had she pretended she was anxious to get home that day. Not that work was any great delight, but home was bound to be worse.

Last night had been sheer hell. Martha had locked herself up in her room and didn't emerge until morning. Even then, she made a great point of ignoring Deanna, walking in wide circles around her, saying nothing, keeping a lofty and sullen expression plastered on her face. Social boycott, from your sixteen-year-old daughter. Ain't life grand?

Tonight would undoubtedly be worse. Mom and Martha alone together, all night long. What fun!

She dropped her briefcase in the front hallway. "Martha. I'm home."

There was no response. Well, that wasn't a tremendous surprise.

Martha wasn't in the living room. Normally, absent Buck, she would be watching one of those tabloid TV shows this time of the evening. But the living room was silent.

I suppose she's holed up in her room, Deanna thought, protecting herself from undesirable contact with me. Well, enough's enough. I didn't change her diapers for three years so she could treat me like an untouchable.

She banged on Martha's bedroom door. There was no answer. No noise, no stereo, no radio.

The short hairs on the back of Deanna's neck stood on end. That was very odd. She tried the door.

It wasn't locked. And Martha wasn't inside. *Damn!*

She ran back to the kitchen to check the refrigerator for messages.

Nothing there. Not a word.

Maybe the note fell off, she told herself, trying to stave off the incipient panic. Maybe Martha didn't fasten it securely . . .

She bent down on her hands and knees and examined the floor. There was no note. But on the other side of the kitchen, under the table, she did notice something. A small flat colorful something.

She crawled under the table. There were two playing cards that evidently had fallen off the table and gotten lost. One was Sewers of Estaark. The other was the Vesuvian Doppelganger. Magic cards.

He'd been here.

And now Martha was gone.

Omigod, omigod, omigod. She pressed her hands against her chest, trying to calm herself. Don't make too much of this, she thought. Don't jump to any stupid conclusions. Wait for the facts.

What facts, you fool? Martha's *gone.*

She threatened to run away, and she did.

What a stupid ignorant sorry excuse for a mother she was. How could she be so blind? She had practically pushed her daughter into that arrogant, abusive creep's arms. She had been too protective, too smothering. And what did she have now? Nothing.

She laid her head down on the table. What a loser I am. My life is over. Just let me die now, before I do any more harm.

It was just about then that she heard the back screen door open.

Her head snapped up. She blew out of her chair, stumbling on a table leg, limping into the living room. "Martha!"

Martha was coming in from the backyard. Her face was flushed and glowing. She lifted her chin and made a wide arc around her mother.

"Oh no." Deanna grabbed her arm. "What have you been doing?"

Martha slowly lowered her eyes and focused daggerlike on a point in the middle of Deanna's face. "I was trying to get a tan. Is that all right with you? Or did I need your permission first?"

Deanna held out the two Magic cards. "I found these on the kitchen floor."

Martha snatched them away. "Thanks."

"Where did they come from?"

Martha looked at her as if she had lost her mind. "For your information, I was playing a solitaire game before I went outside."

"Solitaire?"

"Right. As in, by myself. That should make you happy." Martha jerked her arm free, then sulked away to her bedroom.

Deanna didn't know whether to laugh or cry. A good argument could be made for either. She returned to the kitchen table, laid her head down again, and let the tears flow. God, she had been so scared. So afraid. Why didn't anyone ever tell you how hard it was to raise children?

Because it would be the end of the human race, she realized.

A laugh broke out, involuntarily. She began to regain her composure. She had been so scared.

She laughed again, not really knowing why, and unfolded the evening paper. Perhaps the agonies of the world would take her mind off the agonies of the home.

She scanned the front page. The whole office had been abuzz about the mayor's being arrested. She couldn't get through the first paragraph without wincing. Those poor little girls. They would have been utterly lost, confused, and terrified. What they must have thought. Especially if their killer really was their own father.

She scanned the article to see if the police were pursuing any other suspects. There were some quotes from a press conference given by a Lieutenant Morelli in which he made it rather clear the police thought the mayor did it. A reporter had spoken to a neighbor who had seen the mayor dash out of his house around the time of the murder.

But the neighbor had more than that to say to the reporter. Deanna read the passage twice, just to make sure she got it right. The neighbor complained that he had seen suspicious persons in the neighborhood for several days—one male, one female. She read the descriptions.

Tall, lanky. Goatee. Fatigues. High-top sneakers.

She couldn't have described Buck better herself.

And the girl?

Short, dark. Tank top. Blue headband.

She folded up the paper and slid it into her briefcase, as if hoping to hide the evidence. Could it be a coincidence? The descriptions were very general.

But both of them? Together?

She knew Martha and Buck had gone out together sometimes in the afternoons, even though they weren't supposed to. But what on earth would they be doing in the mayor's neighborhood?

A shiver trickled down her spine. Where the hell did Buck get all that money, anyway? He didn't exactly look as if he were descended from royalty.

Deanna felt a cold, icy sensation oozing through the marrow of her bones and chilling the blood in her veins. What was happening here? What was happening to their lives?

She couldn't sort this out. She couldn't think clearly. All she could think about was the one central question that kept racing through her mind.

Her eyes darted involuntarily toward her daughter's bedroom door. *Martha—!*

Was it really you?

18

CHRISTINA MET BEN at the door. "I found the sister," she announced, beaming.

"That was quick."

She fluttered her eyelashes. "Am I not your faithful aide-de-camp? Am I not resourceful beyond measure?"

"Uh-huh," Ben answered. "But seriously, how did you find her?"

"You know what they say. *Cherchez la femme.*"

"Christina!"

"She was listed in the phone book."

Ben smiled. "Amazing."

"Now this is odd," Jones muttered from behind his computer.

Ben and Christina crossed the office to his desk. A steady ping, every second or so, was coming from the computer. "What's up?"

"I've been doing some research online," Jones explained. "Follow-ups on the city council, like you wanted. I sent out a lot of feelers on the Web and to some of the big databases and search engines on the Net."

Ben leaned toward the computer screen. "Did you get a response?"

"Oh, yeah. According to my e-mail folder"—he clicked his mouse twice—"I received exactly four thousand eight hundred sixty-six responses."

"You're joking."

"And they're still coming in."

Christina crowded between them. "I can't believe there are that many computer hackers with titillating stories about city councilmen."

"I don't know what these messages are about. Look for yourself. They're not addressed to me. They're addressed to the Boss."

Ben saw his name headlining a tall, staggered stack of cyber-envelopes: BENJAMIN KINCAID, ESQ.

"To me? That doesn't make any sense," Ben whispered. "I don't know any of these computer hackers."

"You may not know them," Jones replied. "But they sure know you."

"Four thousand of them?"

"And counting. They're still coming in."

The computer suddenly erupted with a series of beeps and bells. Screens flashed. The stack of cyber-envelopes expanded to infinity. "What's going on?"

Jones was frantically pushing keyboard buttons and clicking the mouse. "I don't know. The computer seems to have lost its mind. It's showing hundreds of messages coming in at once. No, make that thousands. The computer's jamming up."

"Get rid of them," Ben said.

Jones continued banging the keyboard. "I can't. That's just it. Whoever is sending these messages is tying up the modem connection. I can't get rid of them and I can't get past them to do anything else. I can't even exit." He turned suddenly. "Boss, this is computer warfare."

"Huh?"

"Sabotage. Someone doesn't want me to be able to do my work. Correction: doesn't want *you* to be able to do *your* work."

"How could anyone send so many messages all at once?"

"Our friend must have a program or subroutine that generates them spontaneously. Spamming, we call it. This is pretty sophisticated stuff. Someone is trying to screw you up but good."

Ben got an uncomfortable feeling in the pit of his stomach. "Let's look at one of them," he suggested. "Can we do that?"

"I think so." Jones clicked on the top envelope in the computer window. A short message was revealed: SICK HEART.

"That's it?"

" 'Fraid so."

"Let's look at the next one."

They looked at the next message, and the next and the next, but they were all the same: SICK HEART.

"This is really weird," Jones said.

"Second the motion," Ben murmured.

"Look," Christina said, "we need to know where these messages are coming from. Can you trace them?"

"That's way beyond my capabilities," Jones answered. "There aren't many skid marks on the superhighway."

"Well, can you tell who's sending it?"

"I can get his online name and e-mail address, but almost no one uses their real name." He punched a few buttons on the keyboard. "The sender has direct access to the Net. He's not using CompuServe or Delphi or any third-party carrier."

"Sick Heart?" Christina said aloud. "What does that mean?"

"It's what Wallace Barrett said the other day in court," Ben replied. "He said he was sick at heart about the killings."

"Apparently someone else is, too," Jones said. "Someone who isn't too happy that you took Barrett's case."

"Let's not jump to any conclusions," Christina said. "It's not like this is the first time Ben ever represented an unpopular defendant. Ben's made a lot of enemies these past few years."

"Oh, thank you very much," Ben said. "Now I feel much better."

"Look, it's probably just a prank. I mean, it's not as if it threatened you."

"No. Not yet."

"I think the best thing is to just ignore it."

"I can't ignore it," Jones said, throwing his hands into the air. "My keyboard is totally locked up."

"Can't you block messages from this source?"

"Not without access to the keyboard. I can't do anything right now."

"Then pull the plug."

Jones looked horrified. "Boss! Do you know what you're saying?"

"It's not a living being, Jones. It's a machine."

"Says you."

"I don't think you have any choice. It's no good to you like this."

Jones sighed. "True. But unplugging it won't make the interference go away. The messages will just stack up in my mailbox until they can be delivered."

"We'll get a new phone line put in and get a new e-mail address. Will that take care of the problem?"

Jones shrugged. "I guess. Till Sick Heart gets the new number, anyway."

"Let's hope he doesn't."

"In the meantime, how will I get my work done?"

"I've still got my old college typewriter in my office."

Jones looked aghast. "Are you joking? Me? A typewriter? As in typing paper? Return bars? Liquid Paper?"

"I don't see that we have any alternative."

"Well, this is just beyond the pale."

Ben didn't hear Jones's dismayed protestations. He was still staring at the flickering computer screen.

Sick Heart. Sick Heart. Sick Heart.

CHAPTER

19

MIKE MORELLI RACED to finish his paperwork. He had reports to complete pertaining to the still-unsolved murder of the homeless man, plus he needed to get the Barrett murder report finished while it was still reasonably fresh on his mind. He knew that his report would be closely scrutinized by judges and reporters, and worst of all, by lawyers, and it would probably end up as Prosecution Exhibit One, so it had better be done right.

The city council had finally allocated funds for the purchase of computers for the Tulsa police department, and Mike now had one on his desk. He had never used one before and probably wouldn't have started if Chief Blackwell hadn't complained about the time Mike wasted battering out reports on typewriters. So Mike had agreed to give the computer a try. So far, his work was taking about four times as long to complete. Last night, he had inadvertently deleted an entire day's work. Why didn't they tell you up front that you had to save before you could turn off the computer? With a typewriter, when you were done, you were done.

Mike had resorted to reading the manual, the last refuge of the desperate. He found it far from illuminating; indeed, he began to wonder if it was perhaps written in some foreign language, Urdu maybe, and was not intended to be understood by outsiders.

Finally he slammed the manual shut. This was simply not going to work. He'd finish the reports in crayon if he had to.

A flutter of activity in the doorway caught his eye. "What the hell are you doing in here?"

Detective Prescott smiled a smarmy smile. "Just wanted to see how your report is coming along."

"Get out of my face before—"

Jack Bullock strolled into the office a step behind Prescott. "Good afternoon, Lieutenant Morelli."

"Are you two traveling together now?"

"Does that bother you?"

"I would've thought you had better things to do at the moment."

Not waiting for an invitation that would not have been forthcoming, Bullock flopped down into one of Mike's chairs. "Doing what?"

"Well, for starters, taking care of the Barrett prosecution."

"Ah, but that's exactly why I'm here." He steepled his fingers in front of his face and peered through them. "To make sure you don't screw it up."

"If you have a complaint about my work, take it to Chief Blackwell."

"Oh, believe me, I already have. But even he can't influence what you write in your report."

An unhappy smile thinned Mike's lips. "Is that why you're here?"

"In part."

"You'll get a copy of my report at the same time as everyone else."

"That's not good enough."

Mike felt the steam inside rising. He gritted his teeth. "In case you've forgotten, Mr. Prosecutor, I don't work for you."

"Cut the macho cop crap," Prescott said, intervening between the two of them. "Bullock's trying to help you."

Mike fixed Prescott with his glare. "You put him up to this, didn't you, Prescott? You're trying to cover your ass."

"We're trying to cover everyone's ass," Bullock said, "because everyone's ass is going to be on the line if this Barrett prosecution goes sour. Including yours."

"Being a bit melodramatic, aren't you?"

"Not at all. The eyes of the world are on us, Morelli. Did you realize this story is being tracked on CNN? Fact. Did you know Court TV has been granted gavel-to-gavel coverage rights? Fact. If we live to be a hundred, we'll never see another case with this high a profile. So naturally, the city council is very concerned that everything goes right."

"Meaning?"

"Meaning that the great city of Tulsa, and its government employees, not come off looking bad."

"Meaning?"

"Meaning we've got to get a conviction, you stupid son of a bitch," Prescott interrupted. "Meaning we've got to lock this sorry bastard up and throw away the fucking key."

Mike calmly placed a toothpick in his mouth. "That's what I thought it meant."

"So you can see where we might be concerned about your report," Bullock continued. "We don't want anything in it to impede the prosecution."

"I am not going to lie in my report," Mike said firmly.

"I'm not asking you to lie," Bullock replied. "I am an officer of the court, after all. At the same time, there's no reason to include unnecessary details that might impair our case."

"Like the fact that Prescott totally screwed up the crime scene?"

Prescott's fists clenched. "That's not true, you—"

"It is true!" Mike snapped back. "You did the most half-assed job of controlling a crime scene I've seen in my entire career. You went in assuming you already had the culprit, so it didn't matter whether you preserved the evidence. That was a stupid, stupid mistake."

"Gentlemen, please." Bullock raised his hands. "Everyone in this room knows that mistakes were made. Why on earth do we need to parade that fact before the media and the defense?"

"I am a member of this police force, Bullock. My job is putting bad guys behind bars. It's what I do. What makes you think I would do anything that would hurt the prosecution?"

Bullock paused. "Detective Prescott saw Ben Kincaid coming out of your office earlier today."

Mike glared at Prescott. "Are you spying on me now, you sorry excuse for a—"

"It was purely a coincidence, I'm sure," Bullock cut in. "Just in the right place at the right time. But it does raise some disturbing questions. Why on earth would our investigating homicide detective be chatting with the lawyer for the defense?"

So that was it, Mike thought. Now this whole charade was starting to make sense to him. "He came to me because you've been so damn uncooperative."

"I consider that part of my job."

"Well, it isn't. You're legally obligated to provide all potentially exculpatory evidence to the defense. You're required to identify your witnesses and exhibits in advance of trial. When you screw around and lie and hide the ball, you cheapen all of us."

"Very stirring speech," Bullock replied curtly. "But unfortunately, it only reinforces my suspicion that, for whatever perverse reason, you may be sympathizing with the defense."

"Well, you're wrong," Mike said defiantly. "I know the law and I follow it. That's all there is to it."

"I disagree. This raises some serious ethical issues. After all, he's the lawyer for the defense, and you're a lead witness for the prosecution."

"Witness? When did I become a witness?"

"You're the investigating officer at the scene, Lieutenant. I need you to explain to the jury"—he gave emphasis to each word—"that everything at the crime scene was done exactly as it should have been done."

"Like hell!"

"Look, I'm aware that you and Kincaid have some history."

"I believe you and he have a little history, too," Mike snapped back.

"That has nothing to do with this."

"Doesn't it? Isn't that part of the reason you're so determined to win this case?"

"You're barking up the wrong tree, Lieutenant. I'm trying to preserve the reputation of this city. I'm trying to make it a safe place to live, to raise children. These petty motivations you suggest have nothing to do with it."

"I'll just bet."

Bullock rose slowly out of his chair. "Lieutenant Morelli, you may not work for me directly, but the police department is answerable to the district attorney's office. I expect your full cooperation on this matter."

"You'll have it," Mike answered. "To the full letter of the law."

"I'll have it, period." Bullock replied. "Do you understand me?"

"I understand what you're saying, yes."

"If I come to believe for one moment that you are not giving me your complete cooperation, I will see that your employment with this city is terminated immediately."

"You don't have the power."

"How much power do you think I need?" He leaned across the desk till he was practically nose to nose with Mike. "Chief Blackwell is already considering sacking you."

"That's not true."

"The city council is considering the wisdom of your continued employment, too," Prescott added. "They have some grave concerns about your conduct."

"Thanks to you, no doubt, you weasel. I haven't done anything improper—"

"Chief Blackwell disagrees," Bullock said.

"What?"

"Chief Blackwell was not at all amused by your little on-camera diatribe at the crime scene," Bullock said. "Cursing and screaming at a fellow officer. While the cameras were rolling, no less."

Mike felt his lips run dry. "They ran that? But—"

"They did not run it, thank God. But a copy was supplied to Chief Blackwell. He was very unhappy about it."

A light slowly dawned in Mike's brain. "You're trying to blackmail me into being your toady on this case. To cover up the truth."

"You can call it whatever you like, Lieutenant. Either you play ball with me or you'll be playing ball in the streets." He turned and headed for the door. "And if I see you anywhere near Kincaid before this case is over, you'll be fired on the spot. Come on, Prescott."

Prescott headed out the door, but not without first giving Mike his best *so there* look.

"Get out of my office," Mike growled.

"So long, Morelli," Prescott said, smiling. "I'll be watching you."

20

BEN PEERED THROUGH the windshield of his beat-up Honda Accord. "Where is this place, anyway? I don't usually get this far south. And you still haven't told me where it is exactly that we're going."

"We're almost there," Christina said enigmatically. "Turn onto Yale and head south."

The light at the intersection was green, so Ben swooped through and hit a hard right.

"And you might want to slow down."

"Nothing personal, Christina, but I hate passengers who try to tell me how to—"

Suddenly the road before him made a sharp ninety-degree swerve to the left. Ben twisted his steering wheel around, barely making the curve. As soon as he successfully completed the maneuver, he saw another equally sharp hairpin curve, this one twisting to the right.

Ben pulled the wheel hard the other way and hit his brakes, barely making the second turn. "Jiminy Christmas," he muttered. He slowed down to about twenty and cautiously threaded his way through the equally sharp remaining curves. "What is this place?"

"Dead-Man's Curve, Tulsa style," Christina explained.

"Man, if I'd been going any faster, I would've gone right off the road."

"A sad fact that has been discovered by many before you. How do you think the place got its name? This stretch between Eighty-first and Ninety-first is one of the worst in the city, especially at night. People who weren't even aware they were speeding have totaled their cars here."

"Well, next time you steer me toward Dead-Man's Curve or anything else with a grim nickname, give me some warning, all right?"

"I don't want to affront your manhood."

"Christina—"

"After all, I know how you hate passengers who try to tell you—"

"Christina!"

She smiled, and didn't say a word for the rest of the drive.

Ben peered through the glass window in the door. "You've got to be kidding."

Christina frowned. "You said you wanted to talk to her."

"Couldn't you arrange a nice normal interview? Like in an office, maybe?"

"She refused."

"So you came up with this!"

"*Pardonnez moi.* It was the best I could do."

"Christina—"

"It was this or nothing, Ben. Take it or leave it."

Ben sighed. He peered through the window to the main studio in the Midtown All-American Aerobic Salon. Ten women were scattered through the studio in rough formation facing a full-wall mirror. They were all stretching, warming up. They were dressed in leotards, mostly pink and purple, and body suits that wrapped around their torsos and thonged over their backsides. Headbands were de rigueur.

"This is not going to work," Ben murmured.

"C'mon, Ben, give it the old college try. These women do this three times a week. Surely you can survive it once."

"I'm not complaining because it's too hard. I'm complaining because it's stupid!"

"Right."

"Look, you want me to do push-ups, I can do push-ups. You want sit-ups, I'll do sit-ups. I can do jumping jacks all night long. But I'm not going to do all this swishy-wooshy, dancy-wancy, pseudo-sweaty stuff."

Christina laid a hand on his shoulder. "Ben, you may not be the most coordinated guy in the world . . ."

"That is not what I'm complaining about!"

"Uh-huh. Look, when I contacted Cynthia Taylor, Caroline Barrett's sister, she absolutely refused to talk to the lawyer representing Wallace Barrett, whom she despises. I tried every trick, every fib, every canard I know, but she wouldn't change her mind. Short of sending Loving over to threaten her with bodily harm, I saw no way to change her mind. But after a little investigation, I discovered that she's the instructor in this aerobics class."

"And your brilliant plan is that if I sweat with her for half an hour, she'll agree to talk to me?"

"No. But after each session, she makes herself available for private counseling with members of her class . . ."

Ben shook his head. "I'm not going to forget this, Christina."

"You don't have to thank me."

"That isn't what I meant."

BEN ENTERED THE aerobics studio dressed, thanks to Christina's prior instructions, in his green gym shorts and Beethoven T-shirt. He noticed everyone else was wearing snazzy name-brand exer-outfits with sparkling white high-top tennies. His sneakers, which were at least ten years old, were scuffed and brown and had holes over both big toes.

He did not blend in.

Ben took an unobtrusive position in the far corner.

"Psst."

Christina again. She was standing in the next row over, holding a large rectangular block. "Don't forget your bench."

"My what?"

"Your bench. This is a steps class."

Ben walked to the far wall where the rectangular blocks were stacked. "What does that mean?"

"You'll see. Don't forget to get a set of weights, too."

Ben obliged.

A few moments later, Cynthia Taylor bounced into the room. As might be suspected, she was tall and thin and perfectly shaped. Her headband was a pastel tie-dye.

"All right, class!" she said, clapping her hands. "Let's *gooooo!*"

She punched a button on a tape deck resting in a folding chair, and a dance tune with lots of synthesizers and a prominent beat burst out.

"What is that?" Ben asked, wincing.

"That's music, silly," Christina shouted back. "To help you keep the rhythm."

"I don't know what it is," Ben replied, "but it is definitely not music."

Ben diverted his attention from the painfully loud and bizarre lyrics ("Se's a maniac, maaaan-i-ac I know . . . ") and tried to follow Cynthia Taylor's fancy footwork. She was doing a sort of reverse box step, with the bench in the middle. Left foot floor, right foot up. Switch around, left foot up, right foot down.

Ben tried to copy her movements, but he was about three steps behind and soon was totally confused. He looked in the mirror and suddenly realized that the entire class was facing the other direction. He was facing the mirror; they were facing him.

"Don't forget the switchback on the horseshoe," Cynthia Taylor shouted.

"The what?" Ben said, but his words were lost in the general clamor. The music switched from one raucous rhythmic number to another that, as far as Ben could tell, was musically indistinguishable from the first.

"Keep in step for the pirouette," Cynthia said. "Here we *goooo!*"

Ben watched as the rest of the class leaped on top of their benches with one foot down and the other outstretched behind them, arms reaching forward. They looked like the figure of Mercury in the FTD logo. That was followed by another involved box step on the ground. Then they switched legs, kicked forward, drew their knee up to their chin, and started over again.

"Okay," Cynthia shouted. "Everyone got it? Let's *goooo!*"

Ben's protestations to the contrary, the class kicked into high gear. The music's tempo accelerated, as if someone had switched a record player to the 78 speed. The class whirled through the complex motions faster than Ben could follow. Tasmanian devils in stretch pants.

He jumped up on the bench left foot first, but with a bit too much force, and flew off to the other side, bumping into a petite brunette.

"Oops. Sorry," he said, turning a bright crimson. The woman laughed, along with about half the rest of the class.

Ben checked Christina to see how she was handling this complicated barrage of movements. Unfortunately, she seemed to be doing great. She was following the steps in perfect rhythm, making it appear effortless.

"Well, if she can get it," Ben thought sullenly, "so can I. Not very coordinated indeed."

He launched back into the routine. He held out his right foot and leaped toward the block, careful this time not to overdo it. Unfortunately, he undershot the mark. His toe hit the block but the rest of his foot did not. He slid backward, tumbling onto his backside and rolling into a gray-haired woman in the row behind him.

"Omigosh," Cynthia said, running over to check on him. "Are you all right?"

Ben was still in a heap on the floor. "I'm just fine," he said icily. "Don't stop for me."

"Well . . . all right." She returned to her bench.

The woman he had practically tackled bent down and outstretched her hand. "Looks like you're having a spell of trouble, sonny. Can I help?"

"No, thank you."

"It's important to stay in shape, you know," she said. "You don't want to be trampled by us grandmas."

AFTER THE SESSION was over, Ben huffed and puffed out of the studio, leaning against the wall for support.

"Let's get out of here," he gasped.

"Get out? Have you forgotten why we came?"

"No." He tried to slow his breathing and swallow more air. "I'm just not capable of doing it."

"Give yourself a minute. You'll come around."

A thought occurred. "You seem to be doing all right. In fact, you're barely sweating."

Christina smiled, bouncing her full red hair around her shoulders. "Well, I work out regularly, you know."

"No, I didn't."

"Not at a fancy place like this. At the Y downtown. This was a breeze compared to"—she stopped suddenly—"Oh, I mean, not that this was easy or anything."

"Thanks." He grimaced. "Shouldn't we shower before we see her?"

"No. She'll only be in her office for ten minutes. Then she has another class."

"She's going to do this again? What is she, a masochist?"

Christina led Ben to Cynthia Taylor's small glass-enclosed office. They knocked, then stepped inside, Ben in the lead.

"Oh, my goodness," Cynthia said, rushing forward. "How are you? Does your foot hurt? Have you taken your pulse recently?"

"I'm fine," Ben insisted, with not a little irritation. "I'd like to talk to you, if you don't mind."

"Of course not." She positioned herself behind her small desk. "You know, there's a beginner's class that meets on Tuesdays and Thursdays you might be interested in. Of course, most of the other participants are children, but still—"

"I didn't actually come for exercise counseling," Ben said. Christina jabbed him in the side. Apparently she had hoped for a more subtle approach.

"Oh?" Cynthia said. "Then why?"

"To tell you the truth, I wanted to ask about your late sister. And your brother-in-law."

Cynthia's face became stony and cold. "I'm sorry. I'm not here to satisfy the perverse curiosity of thrill-seekers."

"I'm not a thrill-seeker," Ben said. "I'm a lawyer."

Her eyes narrowed. "You're not the one who's had people pestering me all week, are you? The clown representing Wallace?"

Ben tilted his head to one side.

"You sorry son of a bitch. You think I'd help the man who killed my sister? I want you out of here now."

"Ms. Taylor," Ben said calmly, "I just want to talk."

"I'm serious. If you're not out of here in five seconds, I'm calling Security."

"Ms. Taylor, because you are a witness for the prosecution, I could subpoena you. But I'd rather not do that."

"What makes you think I'm going to testify?"

"Let's call it a strong hunch. Are you?"

She folded her arms across her chest, covering the sweat-drenched triangle on the front of her leotard. "Damn straight."

"May I ask why?"

"Why? Because I want that sick bastard put behind bars. I want him executed. He thinks that because he's such a goddamn big shot he can get away with murder. I'm going to prove he's wrong."

"But what are you going to say? You weren't there at the time of the murder, were you?"

"No, of course not."

"Did you ever hear Wallace say he was going to kill your sister?"

"Not in so many words."

"Then what are you going to testify about?"

There was a protracted silence before she spoke again. "I'm going to tell the jury the truth. I'm going to tell them that Wallace Barrett was a wife beater."

Damn. He'd been afraid of this. "When?"

"Repeatedly. All the time. He got off on it."

"I can't believe a man as prominent as Wallace Barrett could be beating his wife without people knowing about it."

"Some people knew." Her voice was quieter now. "I knew. And the police knew."

"The police?" Mike's warning returned to Ben's mind. "Had she called them?"

"Yes, twice. He was such a bastard."

Ben glanced at Christina. He could see the tension in her face. She could live with representing a murderer, but a wife beater was an entirely different kettle of fish. "Can you tell me about it?"

"One night about eight months ago, he flew into a rage because—get this—he couldn't find the tie he wanted to wear to some party. He ripped her dress off, beat her up. She had bruises all along her arms, legs. Even her face. Then he pushed her outside and locked the door. She was trapped out on the front lawn, wearing nothing but her bra and panties, in front of everyone. All the neighbors must have seen. Finally, she went to the man next door's place—Harvey, I think his name is—and called the police."

"Did you see the bruises?"

"No. I was living in Chicago at the time. But she told me about it the next day on the phone."

"So why didn't the police lock Wallace up?"

Cynthia's eyes went down toward the desk. "She wouldn't press charges. There was nothing they could do."

"What about the neighbors?"

"None of them would talk. Said they hadn't seen anything."

"Ms. Taylor, did it occur to you that that might be because they really *didn't* see anything? Because your sister made the story up?"

Her eyes lit like fire. "I've known Wallace Barrett since the week Caroline met him. He's always been an abuser. He's never cared about anyone other than himself."

"And none of this has ever come out? Even when he ran for mayor?"

"Don't underestimate Wallace. He's a very smart man. He knows how to . . . stifle dissent."

"Come on, this is almost as paranoid as—" Ben stopped himself. Almost as paranoid as Wallace Barrett talking about how the city council was out to get him. What was wrong with these people? "What was the second incident?"

"Barely a month ago," Cynthia replied. "This time he was in a jealous rage because she'd had the audacity to talk to some man she met at a party he dragged her to. He went out of control, screamed about how she was having an affair, sleeping around. Called her a whore, a bitch. Then he socked her right in the eye. She had to wear sunglasses for weeks."

"Were you present during this incident?"

"No. But I saw the black eye."

"She could've gotten that any number of ways."

"Bullshit. In case you haven't noticed, there's no jury in the room, so spare me this crap."

"You understand, I have to consider all possible explanations."

"I know exactly what you're trying to do." She drew in her breath. "I don't know how you can live with yourself."

"If Caroline Barrett was being battered, as you claim, it's difficult for me to believe she wouldn't tell anyone."

"She did tell someone. She told me."

"You know what I mean. The district attorney. The media."

Cynthia fell back in her chair. "How much do you know about battered women, Mr. Kincaid?"

"Not that much," he admitted.

"It's a recognized syndrome. A disease, really. It stems from our inherent genetic fight-or-flight response. When a woman is frightened or in danger, she goes through a series of emotional reactions. Avoidance mechanisms. Unconsciously she finds ways of dealing with the threat, like denial, repression, minimization. It's all been documented."

"Excuse me," Ben said. "Are you a psychologist?"

"I'm working on my degree at TU," she answered.

Ben made a note.

"Some women go through a sort of seesaw effect—anxiety rises until avoidance and numbing set in. Other women experience both symptoms simultaneously, creating conflicting emotions that make it almost impossible to act."

"Still, Caroline Barrett was rich, pretty, smart. She doesn't fit the image of a battered woman."

"That's not an image you're talking about. It's a stereotype. And it's wrong. Many battered women have successful careers and are perfectly capable of expressing anger when they don't believe they're in danger. Some are even aggressive, or are perceived by friends as domineering. Abuse occurs in every race, ethnic background, educational level, and socioeconomic group. And don't believe that right-wing hogwash that domestic violence is exaggerated. If anything, it's underexaggerated, because it's underreported. And when it finally comes to the surface, the response is almost always the same. They avoid, they deny, they pretend it didn't happen. And they don't report the son of a bitch who beat them."

"Yes, but getting back to this case—why didn't Caroline just leave?"

"They don't leave because leaving doesn't stop the violence. Often it intensifies it. These creeps are terrified of separation; the woman walks out and they become stalkers, harassing her at every opportunity. Studies have shown that a woman's life may actually be in more danger after she leaves. And if you have two small children in your care, that may be a risk you simply cannot take."

"I gather this will be the gist of your testimony?"

"That's up to the district attorney. I'll answer whatever he asks."

"Are you a member of any organizations, Ms. Taylor? Any women's groups, perhaps?"

"I'm the president of the local chapter of DVIS—the Domestic Violence Intervention Services."

Ben nodded. "DVIS would probably love to have a high-profile case that would dramatize its cause, wouldn't it?"

Cynthia glared at him. "So that'll be your pitch. You're a great human being, Mr. Kincaid."

"I was just asking a question. Look, my client tells me he didn't beat his wife. He says the city council is out to get him. I have to believe him until the evidence proves otherwise."

"The evidence is all around you. You're just not seeing it."

"That's what everyone says. You're all so anxious to convict you don't consider the alternatives. I'm not going to fall into that trap."

"My sister was the one in the trap!" There was a stuttering noise, a catch in her throat. "I—tried to talk to her. I tried to get her out of there, to get her somewhere safe. But she wouldn't listen." Her voice flattened, as if all the air went out of her. "And I didn't insist. I thought there was still time. If only I had known . . ." Her steely eyes became soft and watery.

"I'm sorry, Ms. Taylor," Ben said quietly.

Her chin rose. "Don't be sorry. Give up the legal shenanigans and let them give Wallace Barrett the lethal injection he deserves."

Ben folded his notepad. "You really want to see him convicted, don't you?"

"Do I want the man who beat and killed my sister to pay for his crimes? You're damn right I do."

"You'd be willing to do almost anything to see him punished, wouldn't you? Or say anything?"

Cynthia's eyes burned across the desk to Ben's. "Was there anything else, Mr. Kincaid? I have a class to teach."

"No. Thank you for your time." Ben led Christina outside to the weight-lifting area.

"Ben," Christina whispered once they were outside, "I have some real problems—"

"We'll work it out later."

"But—"

"We'll work it out, Christina. I promise. But later."

I'll work it out for you later, he thought to himself, because first I have to work it out for myself.

AS SOON AS Ben and Christina left the office, Cynthia Taylor picked up the receiver to her, a large office desktop phone with a million buttons and an LED readout. After the line connected, she gave the receptionist an extension number. A few minutes later, she reached the party on the other end of the line.

"Yeah, it's me. Cynthia." Slight pause. "I don't care what you told me, I need to talk to you now, and this is where you are."

A loud and angry voice grated on the other end. "Yeah?" she answered. "Well, it is an emergency. Guess who was in my office? . . . Wrong. The creep who's representing Wallace . . . Right. In my office."

There was a burst of static. "Of course I didn't invite him here. I didn't even know who he was. He huffed and puffed his way through one of my classes, then came to my office during the counseling period and started asking questions." Pause. "Yeah, well, I thought you'd want to know."

She listened patiently while the voice on the other end of the line spewed forth for more than a minute.

"Well, whatever you're planning to do, you'd better do it fast and do it well. I think he knows a lot more than you think he does." She slammed the receiver down, grabbed her towel, and headed back to her class.

As soon as Cynthia Taylor was out of sight, Ben and Christina stepped out from behind a tall stack of plastic mats.

"And you accuse me of having wacky ideas," Christina groused. "Why are we still here?"

"There's something she wasn't telling me," Ben said. He led her toward the now-empty office.

"I thought the same thing," Christina replied. "But it doesn't explain why we were crouched behind the gym equipment."

"It's hard for me to believe she could be part of this purported conspiracy," Ben explained, "especially if it culminated in the death of her sister. Still, there was something odd about the way she acted. If she is involved or feels guilty for any other reason, then our visit might've shaken her up. If we shook her up, she might report in to whoever she's working with. And did you notice what she did the second she thought we were gone?"

Christina nodded. "She made a phone call."

"Right." He checked both ways down the corridors. They were empty. He grabbed the doorknob to Cynthia's office and ducked inside. "Come on."

Christina followed, closing the door behind him. "Do you know what will happen if we get caught?"

"So don't get caught." Ben scanned the desktop. "We'll only be in here for a minute. I just wanted to see if we could figure out who she called."

"Well, Sherlock, if I were you—"

"Don't try to talk me out of it. We won't be in here long."

"Fine, but—"

"Shh. I'm thinking."

Christina folded her arms and arched an eyebrow.

"I know." Ben picked up a pad of paper on the desktop. "Maybe she scribbled down the number."

"But why would she—"

"Shh." Ben picked up a pencil and lightly drew across the sheet. "Maybe we can pick up an imprint."

"Ben, this is pathetic."

"Don't be so negative." He continued scribbling. Nothing appeared. "Rats. Didn't work."

"Ben, if you want to know—"

"Would you stop already? I'm detecting."

Christina tapped her foot.

"I've got it." Ben grabbed an open phone book on the corner of the desk. "Maybe she looked the number up. Maybe she left an imprint or smudge next to the number."

"Ben, you've been watching too many late movies."

"Always the skeptic." He held the book up to his nose and scanned the pages. "Blast. I don't see anything."

"Ben, if you want to know—"

"Shh. I'm working."

She threw up her hands in disgust. "I can't stand this any longer." She walked up to the phone console and pressed the Redial button. Half a second later, a seven-digit number appeared on the LED readout. The phone began dialing. "There's your number, Sherlock. Hope I didn't waste too much of your valuable detecting time."

Ben stared at the readout. "I was going to try that next."

"No doubt. Shall we see who it is?" She pushed the Hands-free button for the speakerphone. A few seconds later they both heard the line answered.

"Good afternoon. You've reached City Hall. The city council is now in session. How may I direct your call?"

CHAPTER

21

THE PRELIMINARY HEARING took less than a day, and probably wouldn't have lasted that long if the press hadn't been there in force. Ben had known all along there was no question about whether Barrett would be bound over for trial; there was more than enough evidence to take him to trial, and even if there hadn't been, a judge would have had to be suicidal to set him free in the midst of the constant barrage of media attention and scrutiny, almost all of which had at least implicitly assumed Barrett was guilty. Judge Hawkins bound Barrett over for trial and set a court date barely three weeks away.

"So this is it," Barrett murmured to Ben under his breath. "Now it really begins."

Ben nodded somberly. Barrett had not seemed his usual self today. Even when the TV cameras began rolling, he remained reserved, even cool.

Ben wondered what had happened. Was the inherent stress of being charged with murder getting to him? Had he moved beyond the denial stage and realized that his life was actually in danger? Or was there something more?

"What now?" Barrett asked.

"Now we get ready for trial. No holds barred."

"The judge thinks I did it."

"No, the judge simply ruled that there was sufficient evidence to make you stand trial. And frankly, there is. Don't let that worry you. The standard for conviction is much higher. You can't be convicted unless the jury finds you guilty beyond a reasonable doubt."

"I can't believe all these people think I could do such a horrible thing." His eyes seemed tired, almost beaten. "That I could hold my own precious little girls' lives in my hands and take them away. It's just . . . inconceivable."

Ben wished there was some way he could alleviate Barrett's distress, but he knew there was none. He'd seen this before. Being a criminal defendant was like going through the stages of grieving. First there was denial, which Ben had seen plainly enough when he'd visited Barrett in his cell. But he was past that now; Barrett was beginning to realize that he was actually going to be on trial—for his life. He was coming to grips with the fact that his entire family was gone, and that most people thought he was to blame. If they didn't correct that misapprehension, Barrett would end up sentenced to death.

"Is there anything else the court should take up before we adjourn?" Judge Hawkins asked.

"Your honor." Bullock rose to his feet. "The state would move that the parties be permitted to submit juror questionnaires prior to voir dire to obtain more detailed information about the prospective veniremen."

"I oppose that motion," Ben said.

Hawkins turned his way. "Why?"

"That's my question," Ben answered. "Why? What does a questionnaire get us that voir dire can't? I don't think we have to blindly adopt every new judicial flavor of the month. Just because questionnaires are all the rage in California is no reason for us to follow suit."

"I think there is a reason," Bullock interjected. "Time. I don't want to waste it. Time-wasting may be part of the defense strategy, but it's not mine."

"This won't save time," Ben argued. "It just adds one more very long step to the selection process."

"It *will* save time," Bullock insisted. "If we cover a lot of questions in advance on paper, we won't have to waste time on voir dire covering the same territory."

"It hasn't saved time in California," Ben said. "To the contrary, trials in California run twelve times as long as they do in Oklahoma."

"Your honor." Bullock stepped closer to the bench and used his quieter, lower "sincere" voice. "We all know perfectly well how hotly contested jury selection will be in this case. We know that neither party will leave any stone unturned"—he glanced over at Ben—"especially the defense. Given that we're going to cover a huge amount of material, why not get through some of it in advance on paper?"

"I'm inclined to agree," Judge Hawkins said. "I think it will save time and eliminate repetition, especially in a case of this nature. Of course, the final decision will be up to the trial judge, but I see no reason why you can't begin drafting your questionnaires." He peered down through his glasses. "I might also remind all the attorneys in the room that this is not California, and it would be best not to forget it. None of the judges in this district have forgotten why trials have judges. We will take control of the courtroom. If you think we're going to protract this trial with an endless parade of witnesses or interminable examinations, guess again. It won't be permitted." He pushed back his glasses and looked toward Bullock. "That being said, your motion is granted."

"Thank you, your honor," Bullock said, bowing his head slightly. He turned to the cameras in the gallery and smiled, doing his best to provide a lovely Kodak moment.

"All right, then," Hawkins said, rapping his papers on the bench. "Anything else?"

"Yes, your honor." Ben stepped forward. "The defense has two motions in limine pending."

"Those are motions to suppress," Bullock said, making sure the press understood what Ben was doing without having to translate the Latin. "More evidence that proves Mr. Kincaid's client is guilty. So of course he doesn't want the jury to see it."

"Objection," Ben said.

The judge nodded. "Sustained. Mr. Kincaid, why don't you take your motion up with the trial court judge?"

"A provisional ruling would be very helpful, your honor. We only have three weeks. I'd like to know what we're going to be up against."

Hawkins sighed. Ben knew he hated to make any ruling that was remotely difficult or controversial, but it seemed there was no escaping it. "Very well, counsel. Proceed."

"Thank you, your honor. My first motion concerns some blood traces taken at the scene of the crime that I would like kept out of the trial."

"Wouldn't he, though?" Bullock said softly, but not so softly that everyone in the courtroom couldn't hear it.

"The blood traces in question were found inside Mr. Barrett's home, near the front door. According to the prosecution's exhibit list—and I phrase it this way because I still have not been permitted to examine the evidence myself—the blood traces outlined a footprint—shoe print, actually—pointing toward the door. The print corresponds roughly to the size of Mr. Barrett's foot."

"Meaning?" Judge Barrett asked.

"Meaning the man killed his family, tracked the blood on the floor, and fled," Bullock said.

"Let me thank the prosecutor for demonstrating the great prejudice which this misleading bit of evidence could create if it were admitted into evidence," Ben said, not missing a beat. "In fact, the print proves nothing of the sort, but if the court allows it into evidence, Mr. Bullock will undoubtedly twist and contort reality to reach some such unwarranted conclusion."

Judge Hawkins frowned. "And can you please explain to me why this print doesn't tell us exactly what it appears to tell us?"

"Certainly, your honor." Ben opened the folder that contained the product of several days of Loving's hard work, tracking people down and getting their words on paper. "I've filed a number of motions pertaining to the manner in which the crime scene was preserved, or rather, wasn't preserved. I've submitted nine different affadavits"—he pulled them out and passed them to the bailiff—"which are certified and on file. These are from neighbors, journalists, and even members of the police force. What becomes immediately apparent is that the crime scene was contaminated and not preserved because the police believed—wrongfully—that they had already apprehended the culprit."

Hawkins began drumming his fingers. "Get to the point, counsel."

"Your honor, I have identified over twenty-five people who were permitted entry to the crime scene before it was sealed."

Hawkins snatched the list from the bailiff. "Twenty-five?"

"That's right, twenty-five. They are identified by name. Your honor, the crime scene was irremediably tainted. This fact demands the expulsion of all blood samples found on the premises, if not *all* evidence from the crime scene."

Judge Hawkins said nothing, but his conservative brow was decidedly furrowed.

"With so many people tromping through the house," Ben continued, "we have no way of knowing who left that bloody footprint behind."

"Well . . ."

"No one could have gained entrance to the home without walking through that entryway. It could have been anyone. Since the evidence is not probative, and since the flaws in its reliability were created by the state's own incompetence, I move that the evidence be excluded."

"Your honor, may I be heard?" Bullock scurried toward the bench. "If the evidence is subject to multiple interpretations, counsel may explore that on cross-examination."

"If the evidence is more prejudicial than probative, it should be excluded," Ben rejoined. "That's what the evidence code says. I'm only asking that the court apply the law of the state."

Bullock ignored him and spoke directly to the judge. "There may have been people in the home that morning. Frankly, your honor, I don't know. That is startling new information—which, I might add, Mr. Kincaid did not bother to share with me in advance. I can assure you I will fully investigate these charges before trial. But the blood must have come from Barrett."

"He's assuming Barrett was guilty," Ben said. "That's a false assumption."

"Wrong," Bullock said. "Blood remains viscous enough to be smeared or tracked or dripped for only an hour, maybe two. After that, it coagulates and dries. It had to be Barrett."

"You're still assuming his guilt."

"I'm pointing out that the blood traces were left before your purported swarm of people descended. Given that we know Barrett was at the crime scene at the time of the murders, I think it's a probative indicator of guilt."

The judge nodded. "I tend to agree, Mr. Prosecutor. The motion will be overruled. Counsel is of course free to use cross-examination to try to impeach the evidence as best he can." He turned to Ben. "Was there something else?"

"Yes." Ben returned to the podium for his other folder. "I also have objections to the use of purported DNA evidence by the prosecution."

Hawkins rubbed his hands against his face. "Great. Here we go."

"Your honor, as you know, there is still some question whether the Supreme Court of this state has found that DNA fingerprinting meets the Frey standard of reliability sufficient to allow it to be used in our courts."

"This is a nonexistent issue," Bullock insisted. "Everyone uses DNA nowadays. The only reason we haven't used it here more often is that we didn't have the proper laboratory facilities."

"They still don't," Ben said. "They've hired it out to a third party."

Bullock shifted uncomfortably. "It's a reliable firm, your honor. Cellmark Laboratories. They're experts in the field. They're preparing our exhibits."

"For a fee," Ben interjected.

"The use of paid experts is hardly a novel development," Bullock said. "Defense lawyers do it all the time."

"Paid experts, yes," Ben said. "Paid evidence, no. This is entirely different. This is a firm that basically goes around to prosecutors saying, 'Pay us money and we'll create some pseudoscientific evidence no one else understands and get you a conviction.' "

"Balderdash," Bullock grunted. "Much ado about nothing. So long as the evidence is probative, who cares where it comes from?"

"I do." Ben leaned closer to the bench. "Your honor, the U.S. Court of Appeals was disturbed when the Von Bulow family in effect hired a private homicide investigator. It suggests that someone is being prosecuted only because his enemies are wealthy."

"So?" Bullock said. "We're not asking anyone to foot the DNA bill. This is entirely different."

"This is exactly the same. Only the motivation is different. Here, extra money is being spent and extraordinary efforts are being made because the eyes of the world are upon us. The law should be the same for everyone. It shouldn't get worse because you're rich and famous and the prosecutor is afraid of screwing up on national television."

"Your honor, this is offensive in the extreme." Bullock was wearing what Ben recognized as his disgusted-with-opposing-counsel expression. "Mr. Kincaid is clearly desperate to find some footing in a case where the evidence is overwhelmingly against him. But to resort to this slanderous hyperbole is truly outrageous. I will not hear anyone casting aspersions on my department. We work solely in the interests of the community."

"I know," Ben said. "You just work a lot harder when the minicams are running."

Hawkins sat up straight. "I find this philosophical debate very stimulating, but we're getting rather far afield from Mr. Kincaid's motion. Grounds for keeping the DNA evidence out of the trial would only arise if the evidence was unreliable or did not conform to current scientific standards of trustworthiness. Neither can be proven until the evidence has actually been produced."

He pointed his gavel at Bullock. "You will make the evidence available to opposing counsel as soon as possible, understand? No foot-dragging, no messing around."

"Yes, sir."

The gavel shifted to Ben. "After you've reviewed the evidence, we'll hear your motion. I'll set a hearing the day before trial, to be heard by the trial judge."

Ben tried to protest. "But that won't leave me any time—"

With a firm look, Hawkins dared Ben to say another word. "I've ruled." He banged his gavel and rose to his feet. "Court is in recess."

The reporters filed out of the courtroom and made their way to the outer hallway where they would receive Bullock's usual press conference and Ben's usual "no comment." Before he left the room, however, Bullock stopped by Ben's table.

"I'd like copies of those purported affadavits you were waving around."

"I put your copies in the mail," Ben said.

"I'd like them now."

"Fine. I'll trade you copies of the affadavits for all the evidence on your list that you haven't shown me yet."

"Well . . . I'm not prepared to hold an evidentiary summit."

Ben slapped his briefcase closed. "And I forgot to make extra copies of the affadavits. Darn." He tried to make his way past to his client, but Bullock blocked his way.

"Thought you were going to pull a fast one, didn't you, Kincaid? Thought you were going to pull the rabbit out of your hat again. Well, the judge didn't buy it."

"Not yet, anyway," Ben said. "The trial judge may feel differently."

"Don't count on it. She may find you cute when you're defending teen prostitutes and petty thieves, but she'll feel differently when it's murder and the whole wide world is watching."

So Bullock thought Judge Hart was going to get the case also. Guess that made it official.

"I can't believe you would try to sweep away the evidence by pretrial ruling," Bullock added. "Even as far as you've fallen, you've never tried anything that low before."

Ben pushed away. "Jack, this is different."

"Yes, you always wanted to make exceptions. Put a bleeding heart before a sick society. Won't you ever learn?"

Ben would have liked to imagine he didn't know what Bullock was talking about, but of course he did. It was always the same with Bullock; like some twisted rogue elephant, he never forgot.

DURING THE TIME Ben worked with Bullock at the DA's office, their work habits had almost instantly become routine, like two old bachelors who had lived together for years. When Ben didn't have classes, which was most of the time, they both arrived at the office before seven. Ben made the coffee; Bullock opened the mail. They reviewed the cases in progress, pending court dates, imminent deadlines. They strategized and calculated how to bring their charges and make them stick. Ben was principally responsible for any briefing or paperwork that needed to be done, while Bullock handled the courtroom end. At the end of the day, they retired to Bullock's office, Bullock with his beer, Ben with his chocolate milk, to review the day's work and plan for tomorrow. Neither of them was ever home before nine.

Until March. After the first of the month, Bullock informed Ben that he had a new case breaking, a major prosecution with multi-state ramifications. The DA had asked him to handle it personally, but had insisted that Bullock tell no one, not even his intern. So Ben was shut out.

Ben still had plenty to do, but he couldn't help but wonder what Bullock was working on. He was holed up in his office almost all day with the DA and police officers and OSBI agents. They even called a grand jury. None of the interns knew why, although the word in the hallway was that something big was in the offing.

Curiosity was killing Ben. But even when he managed to get Bullock's ear for a moment or two, he couldn't persuade Bullock to give him the inside scoop.

It was his friend Mike Morelli who finally told him. By that time, Mike's marriage with Ben's sister, Julia, had already broken up. Ben rarely saw either of them; Julia had run off to Montana with an English professor and Mike was playing cops and robbers in Tulsa. Ben was quite surprised, therefore, when Mike showed up one night at his apartment.

Mike got straight to the point. "It's your dad."

"I don't believe it. You must be mistaken."

"No mistake. Some of the boys at the station have been working directly with the DA. I know these guys, and they know what they're talking about. Your dad is the target."

"But why?"

"I don't know. But, Ben, how is he going to take it?"

Ben knew exactly what was troubling Mike. Throughout his life, Ben's father had been plagued by a violent temper. It was more than personality—it was pathological, or to be more specific, neurological. Sometimes a sudden rage would overcome him to such a degree that he simply could not control himself. His whole body would tremble and shake, sometimes he would even pass out.

The deleterious effects of this rage on his health were profound. According to the specialists, these enormous bouts of anger triggered internal chain reactions releasing adrenaline and other stress-related compounds, as well as decreasing the number of immune cells and inducing abnormal electrical activity and aberrant heartbeats. Blood saturated with these damaging hormones destroyed his arterial walls, interfering with the flow of blood to his heart. He had already suffered three minor heart attacks, and was at considerable risk for a fourth.

"And you're sure it was the DA's office? *Here?*"

Mike nodded grimly. "Absolutely positive."

Ben jumped into his Honda and drove downtown. Night had already fallen, but he knew that Bullock would still be at the office. He had to get some answers.

Ben stomped into Bullock's office at full tilt. There were two OSBI agents there, but he didn't let that stop him from asking what he wanted to know.

To his credit, Bullock didn't even attempt to deny it.

"I'm sorry we had to keep you out of the loop on this one, Ben, but I'm sure you understand—"

"I do not understand!" Ben surprised himself with his anger, and his ability to express it. A month, even a week earlier, he could never have imagined himself talking to his boss—hell, his hero—in this manner. "We're talking about my father!"

"Ben, I'm afraid we're going to be asking the grand jury to consider some very serious charges against your father and some of his business associates. The evidence against him is overwhelming."

"How long has this investigation been going on?"

Bullock glanced at his two companions. "Months. The OSBI contacted me in December—"

Ben found himself so enraged he could barely talk. "I can't believe you would investigate my own father behind my back."

"Ben, be realistic. We couldn't tell you. The potential conflict of interest is obvious. Still, now that you know, there's no reason why you can't help."

"Help? Help you prosecute my own father?"

"Well, you are a member of my staff."

"You must be joking."

"Ben, I don't think you understand the gravity of the charges."

That quieted Ben, however briefly. "What charges do you expect the grand jury to return?"

"At the very least, criminal fraud. Maybe murder."

"Murder! There's no way—"

"Yes, Ben, there is. Let me tell you about the case."

"You're going to have the grand jury indict my father for murder?"

"Well," Bullock hedged, "we don't know that we'll get it."

Ben knew better than to believe that line. He'd been around long enough to know that the grand jury room was the prosecutor's playground. The defendant wasn't even entitled to have a lawyer present.

And Bullock was very skillful.

"I can't believe this," Ben said, pressing the side of his head. "I can't believe it."

"Really, Ben, I didn't expect you to react in this emotional manner. Frankly, I didn't think you even liked him."

"Like him or not, he's still my father." Something about the way Bullock had said it, though, triggered a memory in Ben's brain. "You felt me out about my father the very first night we met." A growing realization dawned with disturbing clarity. "You knew even then. You knew you were going after him even then!"

"Now, Ben—"

"Admit it! You've known all along!"

Bullock stared back at Ben, then sighed. "All right. I knew he was under investigation. Even then. Of course, I didn't know whether charges would be brought."

"And you never once mentioned it to me?"

"I couldn't. It might have imperiled the investigation."

"But I know my father. He couldn't possibly—"

Bullock looked away. "If that's true, then he won't be indicted. But I can't stop the investigation."

"But he's my father!" Ben turned away. He was getting too emotional; any minute now he would be crying, and that was the last thing he wanted Bullock to see. "I thought I could trust you."

"Ben, the public trust is what matters. We have an obligation to the people we serve."

"That doesn't justify—"

"That justifies everything. What we're doing is for the common good. People have been hurt. People have died."

His words hung heavily in the air between them.

"I'm out of here," Ben murmured. He headed for the door.

"Wait." As always Bullock expected his one-word imperatives to be instantly obeyed. "I need a commitment from you."

"A commitment?"

"You're a member of my staff. I need to know where you stand. Are you with us or against us?"

"If you're asking if I'm going to help you lock up my father, no."

Bullock was silent for a moment. "I'm disappointed to hear that, Ben. I thought we understood each other. I thought we believed in the same things."

"We're talking about my *father*!"

"We can't make exceptions. Once you start that, you tumble down a slippery slope that doesn't end until the foundations of our society have been totally eroded. Either you're the defender of the law or you're not." He lifted his head slightly. "I guess you're not."

Ben stared back at his mentor, his lips slightly parted, frozen.

Bullock turned away. "As of this moment, Kincaid, consider yourself on the other side of a Chinese wall. You are to have no contact with this case or with anyone who is working on this case."

"But—"

"That's all there is to say. Now if you don't mind, we have a lot of work to do before the grand jury hearing tomorrow."

And that was how it ended. Like a translucent soap bubble, beautiful but fragile, the Bullock-Kincaid crusade for justice disappeared. That was the last time Bullock had ever spoken a civil word to Ben. Their friendship, their partnership, was over.

But, as Ben learned the very next day, the nightmare was just beginning.

22

WHEN BEN RETURNED to his office after the Barrett preliminary hearing, Loving was waiting for him, his eyes eager with anticipation. "How'd it go, Skipper?"

It occurred to Ben that if he could win murder trials, play all twenty-five Chopin preludes by heart, and recite "Annabel Lee" without error, he ought to be able to persuade Loving to stop calling him Skipper. But so far, not.

"Well, as I anticipated, Barrett was bound over for trial. We got a start date in about three weeks. And the judge denied my motion to suppress."

"Damn!" Loving slammed one huge fist into the palm of his hand. "Did you show him the affidavits? You didn't forget to show him the affidavits, did you?"

"I assure you, I remembered."

"Jeez, I worked my butt off gettin' those guys to sign up."

"I know, Loving, and I appreciate it."

"They didn't wanna do it, you know. 'Specially the cops."

"Really. How did you persuade them?"

Loving shrugged. "I gotta lot of friends with the boys in blue. So do you, believe it or not. Even if you are a lawyer. They ain't forgotten how you put yourself on the line to help catch the Kindergarten Killer. And none of them are too crazy 'bout Prescott. I can't believe the judge turned down your motion." He snapped his fingers. "It must be 'cause of all them reporters. You know how the media distort everything. They're the ones who really pull the strings in this country."

"Are they? I thought it was the military-industrial complex."

"Jeez, you're behind the times. The media bosses control everything now. They can make people believe anything they want. Look how they framed Tonya Harding."

"What?"

Christina whirled around in her chair and pushed away from her desk. "I've gone through the prosecution exhibit list with a fine-tooth comb, Ben."

"Good," he said, happy to change the subject.

"I've identified all the evidence that hasn't been produced. There's definitely a pattern. Almost all of it came from the crime scene. They must be hiding something, but I don't know what it is."

"I do." Ben threw his briefcase on top of her desk. "I knew as soon as I announced in court that the crime scene hadn't been properly preserved. I knew from Bullock's reaction."

"He was surprised?"

"No. I've seen Bullock surprised before, and that wasn't it. Oh, it was a good fake, but it didn't fool me. He might've been surprised that I already found out, but he wasn't surprised to hear that the crime scene was corrupted."

"So why the big stall?"

"The less time we have to examine the evidence, the less time we'll have to determine the extent of the corruption. He doesn't want to fight any more evidentiary motions than necessary." He turned back toward Loving. "How's your snooping on the city council going?"

Loving frowned. "Slow. I made a list, talked to some of them. These are high-profile respectable citizen types, natch. No one volunteered that they'd hired a hit man."

"Well, that's no surprise."

"I made some notes. Jones said he'd type them up."

"Where is Jones, anyway?" Ben turned around. Jones was standing over his desk beside the phone. He seemed stricken. The blood had drained out of his face.

"Jones?" Ben walked beside him and laid a hand on his shoulder. "What's wrong?"

It took Jones more than a moment before he could respond. "I . . . just . . ." He shook his head, licked his lips. "I just got back from lunch." His eyes drifted down toward the answering machine. "Thought I'd listen to the phone messages."

Ben's brow creased with concern. "And?"

His voice trembled a bit as he spoke. He was obviously shaken. "Listen."

Jones turned the volume up to the highest setting. He pushed the Messages button. After a loud beep, they all heard the same two words repeated in a hushed, guttural monotone.

"Sick heart. Sick heart. Sick heart. Sick heart. Sick heart."

The message was repeated again and again until the caller finally hung up. A harsh beep signaled the end.

"That's . . . odd." Ben said quietly.

"That would be one word for it," Jones murmured.

"It must be the same creep," Ben said. "The same nut who shut down your computer. But why? What's the point? At least the computer trick interfered with our investigation. One message is hardly going to tie up the phone line."

Loving shook his head. "He didn't do this to tie up the phone, Skipper. He did this to scare the hell out of you. This is a threat."

"Against Barrett?"

"No way. It ain't that hard to get messages into the jailhouse. If he'd wanted it to go to Barrett, he would've sent it to Barrett." He turned and faced Ben. "This was for you."

CHAPTER

23

DEANNA RUMMAGED THROUGH the cluttered collection of teenage effluvia on the floor of Martha's closet. She'd already searched her dresser, her desk, and the pockets of her dirty clothes. She found Martha's diary, too, but so far she'd managed to resist that temptation. She had a hunch that resolution would not last long, however. Especially if she didn't find what she was looking for.

Martha had been given permission to go to the movies—her first time out of the house, other than for school, since their big blowout over Buck. Martha had actually seemed slightly grateful, nice even, although perhaps she was just so relieved to be released from incarceration that she was willing to be kind even to the woman who had "destroyed the only love she ever knew." Deanna had dropped her at the Eton Square Cineplex, then returned home to begin the search.

The pile on the closet floor was a mishmash of dirty and clean clothes, old book reports, posters, makeup, shoes, top-secret notes, all piled together like autumn leaves on the carpet. Deanna sifted through it quickly; indeed, it was not long at all before she had found what she wanted.

A red tank top.

Deanna had been almost certain Martha had one, but she wanted to be sure. This was important, after all.

She had thought she might find the blue headband as well, but realistically, that was probably impossible, because it was probably on Martha's head. It always was. She wore it everywhere.

Deanna removed the newspaper article from her back pocket and carefully unfolded it. She reread the description given by one of Barrett's neighbors of the strangers he had seen lurking in the neighborhood prior to the murder. Dark hair, skinny, shaggy, with a goatee and green fatigues. That fit Buck to a tee. And the girl with him? Short hair, five foot two or three, red tank to´ blue headband.

Martha.

The only part of the description she had been remotely unsure about was the tank top, and now she had confirmed it.

Could it really have been Martha? Deanna knew the poor girl thought she was in love, and would probably have been easily influenced by Buck, thug that he was. But to do something like this? To have stalked the mayor and his family? What if the police were wrong? What if Mayor Barrett didn't kill his family? What if—

She pressed her fingers against her mouth. She just couldn't think about it. Couldn't even imagine it. Not her Martha. Not her!

Her eyes returned unbidden to the newspaper article. Something about it clicked in her memory. Her eyes scanned the neighbor's description. He also recalled that on at least one occasion the man had been carrying a black bag. Bigger than a handbag, smaller than a suitcase. Maybe a gym bag.

The suggestion, of course, was that the bag might have contained some kind of weapon.

And the reason it had clicked in Deanna's memory was that she had seen that bag somewhere in this room.

Deanna brushed the dirty clothes off her lap and stood up. It wasn't in the closet. The desk didn't check out, so she tried the dresser. My God, my God, my God. She could feel the panic rising, her blood rushing to her head. What if Martha was involved with some gangster? What if he carried a gun?

What if the gun was hidden in Martha's room?

She was fumbling now, rushing so fast and with such urgency that she was spilling things, knocking them over. She would never be able to put this back together again. Martha would know she had been searched, that her privacy had been invaded.

Didn't matter. This was more important.

She found the bag under Martha's bed, tucked away in the far corner. Its presence alone was an infraction of the house rules; Deanna had ordered the return or disposal of all Buck-related items. This meant she was keeping something of his that she planned to return or he planned to return for later.

Over my dead body. Deanna pulled the bag out from under the bed, unzipped the top flap, and looked inside.

It was not a gun or any other kind of weapon, at least not in the conventional sense. It was a camera.

Deanna reached for it, then stopped herself. God, maybe I shouldn't put my fingerprints on this. She was embarrassed. Starting to think like a character in a dimestore detective novel. Still . . .

She grabbed a Kleenex from the bathroom, then picked up the camera, careful not to actually touch it. It was a .35-millimeter camera—high quality, from the looks of it. Not a snapshot camera. Too complicated, too many dials. This was for someone who was serious about it.

What was Buck doing with the camera? Did it involve Wallace Barrett? Did it involve Martha? Was he part of some conspiracy? Martha had never mentioned that Buck was a photographer, much less that he'd let her borrow his camera. Was he taking . . . pictures of Martha? Pictures they wouldn't want her mother to see?

Enough. Her head was spinning with fear of possibilities. She was sick of speculation. It was time to know.

She advanced the film in the camera. Easy—there were only a few more shots left. She rewound it, then removed the film cartridge. She'd just get this developed. And then she'd see . . .

She clenched her fist around the film. Whatever there was to see.

24

BEN ASKED CHRISTINA to come to his apartment that night so they could coordinate their efforts and make the most of the rapidly diminishing days before trial. Christina stopped at Ri Le's for takeout. Cashew Chicken Delight was a favorite indulgence, but one reserved for times of special need.

After dinner, Joni returned to her apartment. Ben played with Joey for a while, tried unsuccessfully to get a reaction out of him, then gave him his bath and got him ready for bed. He turned out the overhead light, turned on the Goodnight Moon night-light, flipped on the baby monitor, and nestled down in the rocking chair with pajamaed Joey in his arms.

He gave Joey a bottle of apple juice and began to rock. Technically Joey was probably too old to still be drinking from a bottle, but it seemed to comfort him. He drank from a cup during the day, but any variation in the bedroom routine only made the process more difficult than it already was.

"I know you, I waltzed with you once upon a dream . . ." Ben began his usual bedtime routine. Joey had tired of nursery rhymes early, but fortunately, Ben's musical repertoire was vast. They had spent the first three months together singing nothing but the theme song from the Flintstones. Now they had graduated to a series of Disney favorites. Ben liked to start with "Once Upon a Dream," from *Sleeping Beauty*, since the music was Tchaikovsky's and Ben could play it on the piano. Then they moved to *Cinderella*—"A Dream Is a Wish Your Heart Makes" and "So This Is Love."

Joey was restless tonight. He squirmed in Ben's arms, as if trying to get away. He twisted and shoved and tried to sit up.

"Joey, please go to sleep."

Ben gently pushed him back into his arms. Joey immediately pushed himself back up.

"C'mon, Joey. It's bedtime. Sleep."

Joey did not care to sleep. He twisted around, pulling one arm out of his pajamas.

"Joey, stop that. It's bedtime."

Joey began chattering. *Ga-ga-ga-ga* and *ka-ka-ka-ka.* Gurgling and drooling and humming.

"Joey, Uncle Ben has work to do tonight."

Joey was on the floor now, crawling toward his toys.

"Joey! Tonight I don't have time to play Pooh Bear."

Joey stopped momentarily on hearing the familiar words. Then he continued crawling.

"I'm serious, Joey. I don't have time." He tried to scoop Joey up; instantly Joey began to wail at the top of his lungs.

"All right! All right, already! We'll play Pooh Bear."

Joey turned his head slightly. One could almost imagine that he was considering the proposition.

Ben scooped him back into his lap, sat in the chair, and began singing. "Winnie the Pooh—*Pooh!*" On the second *Pooh*, he poked Joey in the tummy. Joey stopped crying. "Winnie the Pooh—*Pooh!*" Ben poked him again. "Chubby little cubby . . ." Ben continued singing the song, stopping for a poke and a tickle on every *"Pooh!"* By the end, Joey's displeasure had disappeared. Even if he didn't make direct eye contact with Ben, he seemed much happier.

"All right, Joey, this time you poke me." Ben pulled up his shirt, exposing his belly button. He sang the song again, pausing after the first *Pooh.*

Joey hesitated, still not looking directly at Ben. Then his eyes turned and he reached out and jabbed Ben in the stomach. Hard.

"Oof!" Ben laughed. He had to. He tried a few more verses, and with each *Pooh,* Joey supplied a strong and hardy poke, each time a little quicker. They had played out this routine several nights in a row now, and it seemed to get better each time. Although Joey never spoke and was still pretty much in his own world, this was as engaged as he had ever become with Ben.

After several more pokes, the routine ended. "All right now, let's calm down. It's bedtime, you know."

This time Joey seemed willing to accept the proposition that the day was at an end. He nestled into Ben's arms and closed his eyes.

"Do you know you're the sweetest widdle boy in the whole wide world? Yes, you are!" Ben rubbed his nose against Joey's. "You are the sweetest, smartest boy in the world, Joey. I love you so much!"

Joey smiled, turned onto his side. In a few minutes, Ben heard the soft rhythmic breathing that told him the child was finally asleep. He tiptoed over to the crib and gently laid him down.

Ben pulled the bedroom door to and joined Christina in the living room. "What are you up to?" he asked.

"Not much. Reading about our esteemed city council. Come here a sec."

Ben's eyebrows knitted. "Why?"

"Don't ask questions. Just come."

Ben walked over to the sofa. As soon as he reached Christina, she yanked up his shirt, poked him in the stomach, and chirped, "Pooh!"

Ben's face flushed a bright crimson. "Ha-ha."

Christina rolled over on her side laughing. Ben looked annoyed and started to walk away.

"Wait!" she said. "I want to do the whole song!"

"Fat chance."

"Aw, Ben, don't be a spoilsport." She segued into baby talk. "You know I think you're the sweetest widdle boy in the whole wide world."

"You're a laugh riot, Christina." Ben opened his briefcase and removed his files. "I can't believe you were spying on us. At bedtime, no less."

"I was not spying. I sat here the whole time."

"Then how—"

Christina pointed to the white plastic receiver on the coffee table. "You turned on the baby monitor, remember?"

Ben whipped open his files. "I hate that thing."

Christina pressed her hands against her chest in mock offendedness. "How could you? I gave it to you."

"Yes, and if I'd known you were going to use it for covert surveillance, I would've given it back. In fact, I think I will." He grabbed the baby monitor and tossed it to her. "Here. Take it with you when you leave. The transmitter, too."

"Ben, it's a safety device. So you can hear Joey crying in the night."

"Are you kidding? He sleeps ten feet from where I do and he has lungs like a whale. I've never had the slightest trouble hearing him cry."

Christina was still laughing. "Whatever you say. After all, you're my pwecious, pwecious widdle baby boy!"

Ben threw his files down on the floor. "Why do I get the distinct impression we are not going to get any work done tonight?"

Christina gasped for breath. "Because you're the sweetest, smartest boy—"

"Stop already!"

She smiled. "Next to Joey, of course."

25

THE NEXT MORNING, Christina led Ben and Loving through the confusing city hall building to the large room in which the city council held its meetings. At the front of the room, the members of the city council were seated behind a table and arranged in a semicircle, with the current chairperson in the center. Microphones amplified their comments and conveyed them throughout the room, as well as over the airwaves of the local cable channel that broadcast the meetings.

They took seats near the back of the gallery. Christina had brought the file she and Jones had assembled with background information on the current city council members.

Christina passed the briefs to Ben. "Since 1989, each member of the council has been elected by a separate Tulsa district. The city government was restructured that year. You may have heard something about it, even though I know you only take the paper so you can tell when movies start."

"I recall overhearing some discussion at the time," Ben said dryly.

"The restructuring came as the result of a thirty-five-year battle, not to mention an NAACP lawsuit. Voters finally approved a change most comparably sized cities had made years before. It was a major brouhaha. Under the old city commission system, the majority of the councilpersons came from affluent white south Tulsa. Now, under the mayor-council system, each equally apportioned city district elects its own representative to the council. This was supposed to make city government more representative and efficient and responsive, although as a practical matter, it hasn't made a heck of a lot of difference."

"Who are these people?" Ben asked, scanning the semicircle before him. "I expected the most prominent citizens in the city. The movers and the shakers."

"The movers and shakers are out moving and shaking. City council is for politicians."

"I don't see any faces I recognize."

"Yeah. Of course you probably wouldn't recognize Hillary Clinton if she was up there. But you're right; these are not, with a few exceptions, the rich and famous. Most were single-issue candidates with a particular political axe to grind. Something that got them elected, or something that made them want to run in the first place. After all, would you want to be on the city council?"

"Well . . . no."

"Of course not. Who would? It's a lot of work for little gratitude or satisfaction. You've got the press watching you all the time, only reporting when you do something wrong or they uncover some bête noire or lurid secret from your past. And the city council level is too small potato to attract any of the— what's the right word?—*benefits* that accrue to politicians at a higher level."

"Someone must be running. I see bodies up there."

"Right. The zealots, the extremists, one-issue wonders. Socially accepted monomaniacs." Christina pointed toward the stage. "See the guy on the extreme left?"

Ben noted the tall man with the shaggy hair and full beard. He wore a T-shirt and jeans with a hole over one knee. "The one who looks sort of like Grizzly Adams?"

"*Oui.*"

"What's his issue? Bad hygiene?"

"No. The environment, natch. Brian Erickson. Deep south district. The wetlands that are being paved over for the turnpike extension."

"Let me guess. He's against it."

"Very insightful."

Ben's eyes shifted over a seat to a medium-size, middle-aged black woman. She was dressed in professional garb and carried herself with a serious, distinguished air. "Who's she?"

"Loretta Walker," Christina explained. "Activist lawyer. North Side district. Grew up in a poor family of eleven. First member of her family to go to college. Graduated Order of the Coif from OU law school."

"And her cause?"

"What do you expect? She wants the North Side to look more like the South Side."

Ben nodded. The chairman rapped his gavel on a podium and called the meeting to order. He was a short, thick man, mostly bald. He wore bifocals at the tip of his nose and spoke in a pronounced monotone. "Could we have a reading of the minutes?"

Loretta Walker, who apparently served as secretary, read the minutes, which were approved with marked disinterest. "Very good," the chairman said. "Let's move ahead to item number one. That's why we're all here today."

The first item on the agenda was what to do about the fact that the city's mayor was currently operating out of a cell in the county jail. "The floor is now open for discussion."

Brian Erickson led the debate. "I think this is a major embarrassment. How can we hope to accomplish anything of importance when our mayor is behind bars? He's supposed to be the city's moral leader, and here he is murdering his own family! No wonder the wetlands are going to hell."

"I will remind everyone," the chairman said lifelessly, "especially since the television cameras are upon us, that the defendant is accused but not yet convicted. Therefore it would behoove us to speak of him as the accused or the suspect rather than the murderer, regardless of how obvious the truth of the matter may seem to be."

"We can't jump to any conclusions," Loretta Walker insisted. "Every time any black person comes to any prominence in this country, the powers that be try to knock him down. Clarence Thomas, Michael Jackson, O. J. Simpson, Wallace Barrett—whoever. It's racism, pure and simple."

"Wait a minute. We're not here to decide whether he's guilty." This came from a man sitting on the right side of the podium. Medium size, dark blue suit, red tie. "We're here to determine how best to lead this city. We're here to do the people's will, and God's will. We're here to lead the way, to be a shining star in the darkness."

"What's he?" Ben whispered. "Some sort of preacher?"

"No," Christina replied, "but he might as well be. Carl Canton. Heads the local chapter of the Christian Coalition. A political action committee. Lots of ORU grads and Pat Buchanan Republicans."

"What's his agenda?"

"God."

"Yeah, but in terms of policy."

"Less welfare, less government, lower taxes. All that religious stuff."

"When I think of all the little schoolchildren out there," Carl Canton continued, "who may have worshiped their mayor, only to see him exposed for the man he truly is, I despair. I truly despair!" His face became flushed; his eyes wide and watery. Ben could see the camera moving in for a close-up. "Our children deserve a leader they can respect. Someone they can trust. To think of what this may do to them"—his voice broke—"it breaks my heart. Just breaks my heart!"

"Good grief," Ben said, "he's not going to cry, is he?"

"No telling, *mon capitaine*," Christina answered. "A few tears would probably get him on the evening news. And sensitive men are in with voters right now."

"We have no *choice*!" Canton bellowed. "We must impeach this man. Immediately and without hesitation."

The councilpersons continued to debate. Another woman, Andrea Potter ("I'm a housewife and proud of it!"), sided with Canton. Christina explained that they were the family issues coalition. Walker, Erickson, and most of the others expressed their disgust over the mayor's situation, but feared that impeachment proceedings would only bring the city more bad publicity than it already had. The chairman managed to shuffle the debate along without committing to any particular viewpoint.

"Who is this chairman, anyway?" Ben asked.

"Bailey Whitman. He's generally considered the most powerful member of the council. He was a college football player at OU."

"I never heard of him."

"That's because he played at the same time as Wallace Barrett."

"That's interesting." Ben cocked his head to one side. "They went to school together?"

"You got it. They're both the same age—thirty-eight."

"Are you sure? Whitman looks much older."

"Yeah. But he isn't."

"Hmmm."

"Yes. Rumor mill says he was planning to run for mayor against Barrett this fall. Two old football teammates going head to head. Pretty dramatic, huh?"

"Yeah. Except that Barrett's going to have a hard time running a campaign from behind bars."

"Which is a nice break for Whitman, because no one thought he had the slightest chance of winning."

"It seems the council is divided," Chairman Whitman said, breaking his silence. "Many of you cannot bear to do nothing, but the rest of you do not want to put the city through the embarrassment of impeachment proceedings. May I suggest a third alternative? The council does have the power to declare the mayor to be incapacitated, and if it does so, it may appoint an interim mayor to serve until such time as the incapacitation is no longer present."

Loretta Walker leaned forward. "Doesn't incapacitation mean being sick? Physically or mentally ailing?"

"I believe," Whitman said, pushing his bifocals up his nose, "that it means whatever a majority of us says it means."

"But I don't think it was intended to apply to a mayor in jail," Walker insisted.

"That's because no one could have possibly anticipated this humiliating turn of events. Still, it has happened, and we have to deal with it."

"If we go your way," Erickson inquired, "who will the interim mayor be?"

"Whomever we appoint," Whitman replied.

"Meaning you?"

Whitman pursed his lips and knitted his brows slightly. "I'm not the only option, although, as chairman of the council, I believe I am the logical choice."

Andrea Perkins spoke. "If we appoint you, would you serve?"

Whitman hesitated. "Although this will of course entail some personal difficulties—yes, I would serve. As many of you know, I was contemplating a run for the mayor's office. I believe there is a strong need for change, for new blood, to sweep out the old guard and the corrupt politics of influence and to set to work making this city a better place. This is perhaps more important now than ever. So I will accept the position. And if I am successful in the coming election, then there will be no need to put the city through another wrenching change of leadership."

After that speech, the meeting moved quickly to its conclusion. By consensus, the council declared Mayor Barrett to be incapacitated, then appointed Whitman to act as interim mayor until such time as Barrett was cleared of the charges against him, if indeed he ever was. Whitman swore to do his best to see that the transition of power was smooth and said a few words about how this was the beginning of a new "time of healing" for the city. The remaining items on the agenda were relatively trivial and the meeting was adjourned.

After the councilpersons and cameras had departed, Christina asked Ben, "So what do you think? Conspiracy to get the mayor?"

"There's not much love lost between them, that's for sure. Almost every one of them managed to malign him. And they didn't hesitate to use this prosecution as an excuse to effectively put him out of office."

"Yeah, but killing his family as part of a conspiracy to get him out of the way?"

"I know. It's hard to imagine. Especially with this bunch. They're so disparate. Different backgrounds, differing interests. It's hard to imagine they could get together to plot anything so involved. Not to mention evil."

"Why d'ya think it had to be all of them?" Loving asked.

"Well, that was Barrett's theory—"

"I don't think so, Skipper. I read your notes on your meetin'. He thought the council was behind it, but that didn't necessarily mean all of them was in on it. Mighta just been a few of 'em. Or even just one."

Ben batted the side of his face with the finger. "Christina, what did you think about Bailey Whitman?"

She shrugged. "You mean regarding Barrett? It's funny." She thought for a moment. "Of all the councilpersons, he probably said the least nasty stuff about Barrett. But I had the impression he probably hates him the worst."

"I had the same impression."

"Ditto," Loving echoed.

"He could actually have the strongest motive. Living under Barrett's shadow at college, and now again in city government. Facing a mayoralty race he couldn't win. Until this happened. It almost makes a certain twisted sense." Ben pondered. "But murder?"

"Hey," Loving said, "you know what my mama always said."

"Actually, I don't."

"She said, 'Son, politics is a dirty game.'"

"Your mother was quite the philosopher."

Loving chuckled. "Well, she may not have gone to college or nothin', Skipper, but she was one smart lady just the same. She knew what she was talkin' about."

Ben rose to his feet, slapped Loving on the shoulder. "Loving, I think you may just be right. Thanks."

"Hey," he said, arms spread wide, "don't thank me. Thank my mother."

26

WHITMAN KEPT THEM waiting for more than an hour. Loving couldn't stand the inactivity and stomped out, promising to meet Ben and Christina back at the office before the end of the day. Another half hour passed before the secretary escorted the two of them in to see Chairman, now Interim Mayor, Whitman.

The moment they stepped into his office, Ben felt as if he should shield his eyes. The office was decorated in a single color—red. A yellowish red, and it was everywhere. Red carpet, red curtains, red pictures on the wall. Even a red blotter on his desk.

Whitman flashed an instant smile, something he apparently could generate at the drop of the hat, or perhaps more accurately, at the flicker of a minicam. Ben introduced himself and Christina. "I gather you're fond of red?"

Whitman nodded. "You could say that. It's the only color I can see."

"Really?"

" 'Fraid so. I was born color-blind, an extreme case. Alizarin crimson is the only color my eyes perceive. Everything else is just gray. So you can see why I would try to surround myself with it. It's the only color, the only visual variation in my life." He leaned sideways against his desk. "I saw you in the gallery during the city council meeting today. What can I do for you?"

"I'm representing Wallace Barrett," Ben explained.

The smile drained away just as instantly as it had appeared. "I don't know what you want with me."

"Just a chance to talk."

"About what? Look, the vote has already been taken. He's out of power. I'm the acting mayor now. He's not my boss."

"I don't care about that," Ben said. "I'm not interested in your political differences. I'm here about the murder."

Whitman gave Ben a long, strained look. He slid behind his desk and dropped to the relative security of his chair. "What can I tell you about that?"

"I don't know. What do you know about it?"

Whitman shrugged. "Just what I see on television."

Ben took one of the chairs on the opposite side of the desk and motioned Christina into the other one. "During the council meeting this afternoon, you seemed pretty positive about Barrett's guilt."

Whitman's face remained bland. "Isn't everyone?"

"But you know him personally."

"If you'll recall, I was the one who cautioned the council not to make any unfounded assumptions of guilt in advance of trial."

"Yes," Ben said. "That was very cautious of you." There was a brief silence as Ben and Whitman scrutinized each other.

Christina took advantage of the silence to jump in with her two bits. "I gather you're not too upset about Mayor Barrett—"

"Former Mayor Barrett," Whitman corrected.

Christina smiled. "More like the deposed Mayor Barrett, from what I saw. Anyway, you didn't seem too upset about his being replaced. By you."

Whitman shrugged. "What do you want, false modesty? Pious regret? Crocodile tears? You won't get them. I won't pretend to feel something I don't. I've made my position on Mayor Barrett public on many occasions. I think the man is a moral quagmire. Always has been. No sense of ethics or propriety. No sense of right and wrong, only win-win-win and how much can I get? An opportunist, willing to do anything to gain immediate advantage. And from what I hear, a wife beater as well."

Ben grimaced. So the rumor mill was starting up already. He supposed it was inevitable.

"I think the absence of moral leadership is responsible for much of the spiritual emptiness that has pervaded this once great city in recent years."

"I gather you intend to make some changes," Ben said.

"Damn straight," Whitman replied. "And you can quote me on that. See, I don't believe in coincidence. I believe everything happens for a reason, even hideous tragedies like the murder of that innocent woman and her children. I believe, to the very bottom of my heart, that God wanted that man out of the mayor's office. And me in it."

Christina pushed forward. "So you're saying God killed those two little girls so you could be mayor?"

"I said nothing of the kind," Whitman replied. "What I said was more in the nature of, well, every cloud has a silver lining."

"That's the most pompous—"

Ben shoved her back into her chair. "So now that you're the acting mayor, what are your plans?"

"I've already developed a detailed ten-point plan to restore Tulsa to the true path, to spiritual and fiscal health. The details will soon be made public. I'll be holding a press conference in about an hour."

"You've known Wallace for quite a long time, haven't you?"

Whitman nodded. "Unhappily, that's true. Since our college days. We played football together."

"And I gather you didn't like him back then any better than you do now."

"What's to like?"

"He was a star, wasn't he? An ace quarterback?"

"He was," Whitman said evenly. "Because that was what they made him."

"They?"

Whitman shrugged. "The university. The coaches. The alumni association."

"It was a conspiracy?"

"Don't be stupid. It was business as usual. Why do you think Barrett came to OU in the first place?"

"I'm afraid I don't know."

"Because they bought him, that's why. He put himself up for auction, and OU was the highest bidder. After all, those were the Switzer years. Anything goes, that was the motto. Even when they got caught on recruiting violations, all they ever got was a slap on the wrists. Even after Switzer lost his job, he was reemployed. No one cares about right and wrong. Not in the world of football."

"When you say they bought him—"

"A new car. A nice apartment off campus. Clothes. Tuition. Grades."

"Grades?"

Whitman snorted. "Of course. Don't you know? Barrett graduated with close to a three-point average, even though the man's as dumb as a post and half illiterate. Now how do you suppose that happened?"

Ben shrugged. "The same way football players always get through college. They take easy courses. They major in phys ed."

"And they cheat." Whitman folded his hands across his chest. "Take my word for it. Barrett couldn't have gotten a degree in basketweaving without help."

"I find that very hard to believe—"

"Why?" Whitman looked at Ben with incredulity. "You believe they'll pay him gobs of money to come, but won't make sure he stays in school. C'mon! They had to protect their investment. Failing students can't play ball, much less win two national championships. So he cheated."

"And never got caught?"

"Who wanted to catch him? The ones who should have been doing the catching were the ones who were helping him cheat!" Whitman swore bitterly. "They gave him everything."

"And," Christina said softly, "they didn't give you anything, right?"

"I thought you wanted to talk about Barrett."

"We do," Ben said. He pulled his chair closer to the desk. "You must've been surprised when Barrett graduated, moved back to Tulsa, became a business success, then the mayor."

Whitman's smile thinned and narrowed. "Disgusted, yes. Surprised, no."

"Being a bit cynical, aren't you?"

"No, I'm simply being realistic. I'm a pragmatist. If a man rises to fame by cheating, he's likely to go on cheating till he gets caught. Or, in this case, arrested for murder."

"Are you suggesting—"

"It's well known that Barrett bought his way into that corporation by agreeing to be their high-profile spokesman. They told him what to believe, and he believed it, at Rotary Clubs and after-dinner gigs and anyplace else that would have him. He made a lot of friends. And you don't want to hear the list of charges brought against him when he ran for mayor. He violated every campaign spending regulation in the book."

"As I recall," Christina said, "all the charges against Mayor Barrett were dropped."

Whitman spread his arms open wide. "Like I said, Barrett's got a lot of friends."

"Mr. Whitman," Ben said, "I have some information suggesting that someone may have hired an enforcer—that is, a hit man—to kill Wallace Barrett's family."

"What!"

"Neighbors have reported seeing unsavory characters casing the neighborhood—stalking the Barretts, perhaps. People who had no business being there. One of them was carrying a bag that could easily have contained a weapon."

"That's absurd!" Whitman pushed away from his desk. "I think this interview has come to an end."

"Look!" Christina pointed toward the window. "Is that a scissor-tailed flycatcher?"

Whitman turned and looked. "What? Where?"

"Out there," she said, pointing.

Whitman turned back. "Do we care?"

Christina sat back in her seat, looking somewhat miffed. "Well, it is the state bird, after all."

Whitman stared at her a moment, then turned to face Ben. "Look, I don't believe a word of this cockamamie fantasy about a hit man. This is some absurd defense you and Barrett have cooked up to cheat his way out of being convicted. Next we'll be hearing that he couldn't help himself because his daddy beat him when he was growing up."

"Mr. Whitman, I'm taking these allegations very seriously. Are you sure you don't know anything about this?"

Whitman slowly rose out of his chair. "What are you suggesting?"

"I've been following a number of leads, and one of them led me to your office. Your phone number, actually." Not precisely true, but close enough for present purposes.

"This is an outrage!"

"I'm Barrett's attorney, sir. I have to follow up all possible leads."

Whitman's eyes burned. He stepped out from behind his desk, arm extended. "I want both of you out of my office. This instant!"

"So you're saying you don't know this hit man?"

"I'm saying I want you out!"

"He's been described as tall, thin, goateed, with long brown hair. Wears fatigues. Know anyone like that?"

"Of course not!"

Ben stood firm. "May I take that as a denial?"

Whitman grabbed Ben by the shoulders and shoved him toward the door. "You may take that as an eviction. Get out!"

"But I still—"

"On the count of three, I'm calling Security! One . . ."

"But—"

"Two . . ."

Christina tugged at Ben's arm. "Ben, I've spent the night in jail before, and it wasn't fun. Let's vamoose."

They closed the door behind them a split second before they heard Whitman's resounding "Three!"

"YOU WERE IN an awful big hurry to get out," Ben said after they returned to the main corridor. "Aren't you supposed to be the fearless one?"

"He wasn't going to reveal anything else. You told him what you know. If he is connected to this alleged hit man, he's sure to contact him."

"Yeah, except there's one minor problem. When he does, we won't be there."

"Yes, but being your faithful aide-de-camp, I have prepared for this contingency."

They continued walking down the corridor. "If you're thinking you're going to try that redial trick again, forget it. We'll never be allowed anywhere near that office. At least not until he's gone."

"True." She grabbed his arm again, and ducked into the ladies' room.

"Wait a minute!" Ben said. "I can't go in there!"

"Sure you can. *Tout de suite.*"

"No!"

"Oh, don't be so prissy." She leaned through the door. "Anybody in here?" There was no response. "See? Coast is clear." She pulled him through the door.

"Christina! Have you lost your mind? This is the *ladies'* room!"

"And here I thought it was some wacky kind of elevator. Thanks for the clarification."

She opened a stall and tried to drag him inside. "Look at you! You're turning beet red. You get so embarrassed about these guy/girl things."

"I do not." He stood firm outside the stall. "I'm not going in there!"

"Well, if someone comes in, do you want to be seen?"

"Good point." He stepped inside and locked the stall behind them. "So what's the deal?"

"The deal is, I want to find out what's going on in Wallace Barrett's office."

"From here?"

"Yes." She set down her huge purse and began rummaging. "With the help of this." With a flourish, she removed the blue-and-white plastic receiver from her purse and set it on the tank above the toilet.

"Have you taken leave of your senses?"

"Nope." She turned the dial, switching the receiver on. A red light shone on the front; low level static emerged.

"Why are you carrying that thing in your purse?"

"Because you threw it at me last night, remember? You told me to take it and I still had it in my purse when we were in Whitman's office."

Ben's eyes lowered. "Christina, I'm getting a sinking feeling I'm not going to like what you say next."

"Remember when I directed his attention to the bird out his window? Except there was no bird?"

"Ye-es."

"That's when I slipped the transmitter under his desk."

"No!"

She beamed. "Wouldn't you say resourcefulness is my dominant characteristic?"

"I'd say insanity is your dominant characteristic. What if he finds it?"

"Shush." She turned up the volume and adjusted the antenna till she got the best reception. There was a pronounced knocking noise, then a softer shuffling sound. "He's pacing," she interpreted. "Thinking. Pounding on his desk. Trying to decide what to do next."

Ben took her by the shoulders. "Christina, this is eavesdropping."

"I suppose that would technically be correct."

"It's like wiretapping. It's an invasion of privacy."

"I don't see anything wrong with listening in here and there to gather useful information."

"You and Richard Nixon. Look, this is probably illegal. Almost certainly immoral."

"And necessary."

"Christina—"

"Ben, listen to me. Did you think Whitman was telling us the truth?"

"Well—"

"No. Of course not. He knows much more about this than he's willing to say."

"But—"

"Ben, zip it up and listen. If he is involved in this, the fact that we came to his office and spilled what we know is bound to make him worry. Maybe enough to do something stupid."

"I still don't think—"

"Shhh." The shuffling noise coming over the monitor had ended. For a few moments, they heard nothing but the hissing of the air-conditioning. Then they heard several rapid-fire clicking noises. About a minute later, the phone rang.

"Whitman." Given the circumstances, the reception was excellent. They could hear every word he spoke into the phone. "Where are you?" A short pause. "Good. Stay that way. No, I don't want you anywhere you can be seen. Especially not here. That's right, that's what I said, so you do it, you sorry son of a bitch. Don't give me any crap. I pay you the money, you do what I say."

Ben and Christina exchanged a meaningful look. Christina nudged up the volume on the receiver.

"Good. That's better. Now listen to me. The first thing I want you to do is get your goddamn hair cut. Better yet, dyed. Shave the crappy beard. And get rid of those idiotic fatigues, for God's sake. Burn 'em."

More static. More air-conditioning noise.

"You want to know why? I'll tell you why. Because you were spotted, you stupid pea-brained stooge. Haven't you read the papers?"

Another long silence. They could hear a faint twitter of the voice on the opposite end of the line, not nearly loud enough to distinguish the words.

"Listen to me, jerk-off. You need to get rid of anything that could link us to that neighbor's ID. Yeah, clothes, too. What about the camera, and all those pictures you took? You what? *What?* "

The receiver exploded with noise. A smashing, then a clattering to the floor. "Threw the phone across the room," Christina whispered. Ben nodded.

Several seconds passed before Whitman spoke again. His voice was low, and the thin, even tone did not disguise the threat that lay behind every word. "Listen to me. You get it back." Pause. "Don't make any excuses. Get it back." Whitman cut the voice on the other end off. "You get it back or I'll break your fucking neck! Understand?"

His shout reverberated through the baby monitor receiver. "Good. I'm glad we understand each other. Now I'll tell you something else. I want you to meet me. Tonight. Don't give me any excuses, you just meet me. That's right. Midnight. Yeah, I know where O'Brien Park is. Fine. I'll meet you there. And bring the goddamn camera!"

The phone smashed down into its cradle. Six fast stomps, followed by a slam.

"He's out of there." Christina turned off the monitor. "I hope he stays gone for a while. I need to get that transmitter back."

Ben crooked open the stall door and surveyed the scene. "We need to get out of here and call Mike. He'll want to be at this midnight rendezvous."

"Think, Ben. Mike is a policeman. Policemen work for the prosecution."

"But this is Mike—"

"And Mike is a good cop, but he still works for the prosecution. We need someone who works for us. Someone we can put on the stand."

"Well, I don't think it should be us. Do you know where O'Brien Park is? It's one of the worst thug hangouts on the North Side."

"Sounds like something Loving might enjoy."

"That's a crazy idea." Ben began to smile. "Crazy in a wonderful sort of way."

"Well," Christina replied, "insanity is my dominant characteristic."

Ben's lips turned upward at the edges. "It's one of them."

"One? What's the other?"

Ben stroked her chin. "Guts."

27

DEANNA PARKED HER car in the driveway and walked to the front door. She stopped to get the mail, sliding it into the bag they had given her at the drugstore. She'd read it later. She had more pressing business now.

She ran through all the possible approaches again in her mind. "I'm only doing this because I'm your mother and I love you." Possible—but so trite it turned her stomach. "I'm sorry, Martha, but you're my child and I have to protect you." Nah. No teenager wants to be protected. "Martha, you're an adult now, and being an adult entails not only privileges but responsibilities." Well, it did have a certain flattering appeal, but Deanna suspected that it wouldn't get her far in the long run, and the consequences of declaring that Martha had new privileges could be disastrous.

Damnation. What was the point? Whatever approach she chose, she knew they'd be off the script the first time Martha opened her mouth. Face the facts, she told herself. You're stalling. And who could blame her? She didn't know what would happen, but the one thing she was absolutely sure of was that it would be unpleasant.

She braced herself, took several deep breaths, and stepped inside the house. "Martha! I'm home!"

No response. And after all, what did she expect? "That's lovely, Mom. Good to see you." Not likely.

"Martha, I want to speak to you," she shouted to a closed bedroom door. She'd give the girl a minute to respond peaceably before she commenced hostilities.

The minute passed. Determined not to lose her resolve, Deanna walked down the hallway. As she approached, she heard Martha talking into the Princess phone in her room.

"I can't find it," she was saying. Her words were perfectly understandable through the door. "I did. I looked everywhere. I don't know what happened to it. It isn't here anymore."

It didn't take three guesses to figure out to whom she was talking. Damn. Should've had that thing disconnected a long time ago.

"I will. I promise. What—" There was a pause, then a gasping sound. An instant later, Deanna heard the call hastily being disconnected.

"Martha?" There was a flurry and rustle. Deanna gave her a few moments, then opened Martha's door. "I said I wanted to talk to you."

Martha was sprawled across her bed reading an R. L. Stine book. "I heard."

"It wasn't optional."

"I'm reading."

"Not anymore." Deanna lifted the book out of Martha's hands and closed it. "We have to talk."

Martha folded her arms defiantly across her chest. "We don't have anything to talk about."

"I think we do. I found the camera under your bed."

Martha's lips parted. She appeared astonished. Apparently, the possibility had never occurred to her. "But it was in my room."

"Right. And I found it, and I took the film out, and I had it developed." She withdrew the photo packet from her purse.

"But this is my room!"

"Right. In my house."

Martha's eyes enlarged, wide and angry. "That doesn't give you the right to invade my privacy!"

"I think it does."

"What is this, Nazi Germany? I'm an American. I have rights."

"Not in my house."

"You can't treat me like you own me!" she screamed. "You can't just come in and . . . and take things that aren't yours!"

"When I'm in my house, I can do whatever I want."

"Fine. Then I'll move in with Buck."

That rejoinder gave Deanna pause. Which, of course, was exactly what it was intended to do. "Look, a civil rights discussion isn't what I had in mind."

"You've been spying on me!"

"I haven't been spying on you." Deanna pressed her hand against her brow. How did this always happen? How did Martha always manage to do this to her? She came in with a perfectly reasonable plan to elicit information, and now she was on the receiving end of a teenage firing line. "I had to know if it was you."

"If what was me?"

"The girl. The one in the papers. The one the neighbor saw."

Martha's eyes crinkled. "What are you talking about?"

"Don't you read the papers? No, of course you don't. Well, where can I start? Are you aware that the mayor's family has been murdered?"

Martha snorted. "Yes, Mo-*ther*."

"And are you aware that one of the mayor's neighbors said he spotted some suspicious-looking strangers casing the neighborhood prior to the murder?"

"So?"

"Do you know where the mayor lives?"

"No. Why should I?"

"He lives on Terwilliger. Near Woodward Park. Just down the way from Philbrook."

A tiny flash of light in the corner of Martha's eyes told Deanna she was beginning to make the connection.

"See if this description rings any bells," Deanna continued. "The man was tall, thin, grungy-looking. Scraggly goatee, green fatigues."

Martha blinked, but didn't say anything.

"The girl was described as being shorter with dark hair. On at least one occasion, she wore a red tank top. And she always wore a blue headband."

Instinctively, Martha's hand shot up toward her headband. Her trademark. "That could be anyone."

"I'll admit, it could be someone other than you and Buck, although it would be a hell of a coincidence. That's why I searched your room. I found the red tank top I was almost certain you had. And I found the black gym bag. The neighbor mentioned that, too. Imagine my surprise when I found an expensive camera inside. Far too expensive to be yours."

Martha didn't answer, but Deanna did have the satisfaction of knowing that for once in her life, she had her daughter's full and undivided attention.

"I had the film developed," she continued. She pulled the photos out of the packet and spread them across the bed. "Could you please explain to me why you were taking pictures of Mayor Barrett's home?"

Wordlessly Martha gazed at the color pictures spread across her bedspread.

"You'll notice that the home was photographed from a wide variety of angles. The front, the back. Close-ups of the doors, the windows. Almost as if someone was casing the joint. Planning some kind of . . . criminal activity."

Martha stared dumbfounded at the photos.

"Martha, I want you to answer my questions. No lying to me—this is important. Why was Buck taking pictures of the mayor's home?"

"I don't know," she said softly. "I mean, I don't know who took these pictures. And I don't know why."

Deanna ignored the feeble denial. "Were you with him?"

"No. I mean—" She stopped, concentrating. "I never saw him take any pictures. I didn't know why he had the camera. He likes expensive toys."

"So you were with him. You did walk with him in the mayor's neighborhood. You just never saw him take any pictures."

"Yeah." Her voice was so quiet it was almost not there at all. "Yeah."

Deanna sat next to her daughter on the bed. She laid one hand on her knee. "Martha, I'm sorry, but I have to ask this question. I have to. Did you have anything to do with . . . with . . ."

Martha turned and stared at her mother, her eyes wide with disbelief. "What are you accusing me of?"

"I'm not accusing you of anything. I just have to know."

"You think I did it!" Martha screamed. "You think I killed that lady and her two girls!"

"No, Martha, I don't. I mean, I hope not. I mean—" She grabbed her daughter by the shoulders. "Martha, I don't know what to think anymore. I want you to tell me. Did you have anything to do with this?"

Tears crept out the corners of Martha's eyes. She turned her head away. "No, I didn't."

"Then Buck did it alone."

"Buck!" Martha leapt off the bed. "So that's what this is about. Accusing Buck. I knew you hated him, Mother, but I didn't know you were desperate enough to accuse him of murder!"

"Honey, I'm just looking at the evidence."

"Buck wouldn't hurt anybody. He's nice, Mother. He's nice to me." Her voice was breaking down. "Buck loves me."

"Martha, please—"

It was too late. Martha bolted out of the room. A few seconds later, Deanna heard the front door slam shut.

Well, Deanna told herself, you certainly handled that well. You practically threw her into that cretin's arms. And if she wasn't totally alienated from you before, she certainly is now.

Deanna collected the photos on the bedspread. Still, if nothing else, she did get something. She got an absolute denial from her daughter that she had anything to do with the murder of the Barrett family. She had stated that unequivocally.

Yeah, Deanna thought. Unequivocally.

Deanna slid the photos back into the bag, then pulled out the day's mail. Maybe there would be some relief from her ongoing misery here. Some sign of happiness in the world. A wedding invitation, perhaps. A graduation announcement.

One envelope caught her attention almost immediately. It was a thin paper preprinted envelope, the kind where you rip off the perforated strips on the edges to get the slip of paper inside. Deanna ripped off the strip and with some effort managed to work out the contents.

It was a formal document, a summons from the Twenty-fifth Judicial District of the State of Oklahoma. Tulsa County.

Deanna read the message, then gasped.

Jury duty.

CHAPTER

28

LOVING PARKED HIS car on the street opposite the park. The nearest streetlight was half a mile down the dirt road; all the lights in the park had been busted so many times the city finally stopped bothering to replace them. This was probably the least safe place imaginable to leave personal property unattended; Loving was glad once again that he had never bothered to replace his well-worn Ford pickup truck. It still ran, although it was more than a little beat-up. Not as bad as the Skipper's car or anything, but it definitely showed its age. Any potential carjackers would immediately realize that this truck wasn't worth the trouble.

He crept quietly into the park, keeping his eyes open for any signs of trouble. It could be anywhere. O'Brien Park was one of the worst, most notorious sites in North Tulsa. Sort of like a heartland version of Central Park, O'Brien Park was a place no sane or law-abiding citizen went after dark. During the day, it might seem like any other park, except that, given its location, it was patronized almost exclusively by refugees from the poor and mostly black neighborhoods surrounding it. On Sunday nights, however, it was a major youth hangout, sometimes cruised by as many as a thousand people a night, in their freshly waxed cars flowing in off North Lewis or Birmingham Avenue. Some of the kids drove in from as far away as Okmulgee to climb onto the hoods of their cars, drink beer, and chill. Shoot the breeze about women or handguns or gangsta rap. The scent of burning marijuana was so strong it would linger for days. The police considered the whole place a keg of dynamite with a lit fuse; they were just waiting for the explosion.

Even when it wasn't Sunday night, this was not a place for a lone white guy, even one built like a refrigerator. Loving knew that. But the Skipper seemed to think this was important, so here he was. Truth to tell, he'd do just about anything for Ben. Ben was a good guy, especially for someone who'd spent too much time in college and too little time in real life. He'd done

Loving some critical favors on more than one occasion, so Loving was more than happy to return one.

He saw something at the north end of the park, just over the hill between the picnic tables and the baseball diamond. One man—skinny, long haired, standing alone. Waiting, unless Loving missed his guess.

Moving stealthily forward, Loving crawled beneath the stone picnic table nearest the man. He could see through the opening between the table and the bench, but someone would have to be looking hard to spot him. With any luck, if they didn't whisper he'd be able to hear as well.

About five more minutes passed before the other party to the rendezvous arrived. He appeared suddenly out of the blackness; he must've parked his car somewhere else, too.

It was Whitman. Loving was surprised he had come himself. Whatever was bothering him, it had to be serious. So serious Whitman couldn't trust it to a third party.

He approached the skinny kid with the long hair. They didn't shake hands. For that matter, they didn't even seem particularly friendly.

Their first few exchanges were mumbled and Loving couldn't pick them up. In less than a minute, though, the discussion had become sufficiently heated for Loving to overhear.

"I told you to cut your goddamn hair!" Whitman said through clenched teeth. "Good God, what if someone spotted us together? You think it would take them long to put two and two together?"

"I like my hair the way it is, man."

Whitman grabbed the dangling tresses on either side of the younger man's head and jerked it forward. "You'll get your hair cut or you're a dead man, you sorry son of a bitch. Do you understand me?"

"Hey, leggo."

Whitman jerked all the harder. "Do you understand me?"

"Hey, like you ain't my mother, okay?"

Whitman wrapped the hair around his hands and pulled down so hard it drove the kid to his knees. *Do you understand?*

He cried out in pain. "All right, all right. You're hurtin' me."

"I can do a lot worse."

"Like, chill already. I got the message."

Whitman released his hair. Strands came off with his fingers. "You'd better."

The kid brushed the dirt off his knees and stumbled back to his feet.

"I've invested a lot of money in you," Whitman growled. "I'm feeding more of your bad habits than I can count. And in exchange, I expect a little cooperation."

"Fine, fine. Whatever you want." Loving noticed that the kid was a hell of a lot more compliant now. Amazing what a little physical pain can do.

"What the hell did you think you were doing?" Whitman said.

"You mean—"

"I mean dragging some stupid girl into this. Have you lost your mind?"

The kid smirked. "Is that what you're so uptight about, man? Then relax. She's cool."

"She should never have been involved."

"I thought she'd make me less conspicuous, okay? Instead of some hood casin' the neighborhood, we just looked like a couple of sweethearts out for an evening stroll. It was perfect. No one even noticed us."

"Someone did, you asshole. Someone told the police."

"Not her."

"Maybe not, but what if someone recognizes her, huh, punk? What then?"

The kid fell silent.

"Have you got the camera?"

The kid passed the camera to Whitman. Which reminded Loving that he had a tiny camera of his own, with an infra-red filter, and he should be using it to record this little meeting.

As soon as Whitman got the camera, he ripped open the back. "Where's the film?" he barked.

"Ah. Well . . . that's a bit of a problem."

Whitman rose to the tips of his toes. "What do you mean?"

"It seems that Martha's mother developed the film. Found the camera under her bed and took the film and developed it. I mean, can you imagine? What a prying bitch."

In a flash, Whitman brought his fist around and hit the kid so hard it literally knocked him off his feet. He fell to his hands and knees.

Whitman grabbed his neck and shoved his face into the dirt. "I want those pictures and I want them immediately. And the negatives. Do you understand?"

The kid sputtered dirt.

"That film could lead the cops to you, and from you to me. I don't want that to happen. Got it?"

The kid tried to speak. "But how can I—"

Whitman rammed his head against the ground hard. "I don't know how you can do it, and frankly, I don't care. You can threaten her or torture her or kill her. I just want that film. Very soon. Otherwise, I'm going to threaten and torture and kill *you!*"

Whitman shoved the kid's face down again into the dirt. The kid rolled over onto his back, groaning. Loving could see blood and dirt smeared on his face.

Whitman yanked his wallet out of his back pocket, ripped out several bills and let them flutter down onto the kid's prostrate form. "Here's some spending money. Just make sure you do whatever you need to get the job done. Got it?"

The kid nodded his head, trembling.

"Fine, asshole. I don't want to hear from you again until it's done." Whitman turned and disappeared into the darkness.

Great. Loving shoved the camera back under his shirt. He'd gotten more than a sufficient number of photos of this meeting. This would break the case wide open. Whitman was totally hosed.

Loving was so pleased with this development that he didn't hear the footsteps behind him until it was too late. He reacted immediately, but forgetting where he was, he sprang upward, slamming his head into the underside of the concrete picnic table. While he reeled from that blow, he saw something jabbing in at the side. He ducked; it barely missed his head. And he knew now what it was—a baseball bat.

Loving forced himself forward, scrambling to get out from under the table. As long as he was pinned down here, there was no way he could fight back. The bat came at him again, this time catching him square against the back and knocking him over. His spine ached; he just hoped it wasn't severed. He heard the whooshing sound that told him the bat was coming at him again. But there was nothing he could do about it. He closed his eyes and prayed for the best. A few seconds later, the bat swung again. His face was knocked forward into the dirt and he saw nothing but darkness.

29

WHEN BEN ARRIVED at the county jail the next morning to visit his client, he was surprised to find Christina already there.

"Have you heard from Loving?" she asked the instant she saw him.

"No, but I haven't been into the office yet."

"I have," she said, "and he isn't there."

Ben read the concern in her face. "I'm sure he's fine. What could possibly hurt him?"

She frowned. "We always act as if we can ask him to do anything, as if he's indestructible. But he isn't."

Ben laid a hand on her shoulder. "If he doesn't turn up soon, I'll ask Mike to put out an APB. He'll turn up." He turned his attention to Wallace Barrett. He looked well—exceptionally well, given the circumstances. Shaved and groomed, he was wearing a tailored suit rather than the usual prison garb. He even looked as if he'd been working out. "Is there some occasion I don't know about?" Ben asked. "I assume you didn't get all spiffed up for me."

"That's true." Barrett didn't quite make eye contact. He glanced at Christina, then down at the floor.

"What is it?" Ben asked. "What's going on?"

Barrett adjusted his tie, then rose to his full height. "Ben, I'm giving some interviews today."

"What?"

"Look, I know you don't like this, but I don't think I have any choice."

"Choice? Of course you have a choice. You can just say no."

"That's what I've been doing. Taking your advice. And look what's happened!" The sudden boom in the bass register of his voice told Ben this was something Barrett felt strongly about. "Everyone in the goddamn world is convinced I slaughtered my own family!"

"That will change at trial."

"You're delusional! Everyone's mind will be made up before we get to trial, if they aren't already. How long do you think people can resist this constant media bombardment, day after day, always insinuating that I'm guilty? Oh, sure, they never use those words, but that's what they're saying. You can see it in the slant, what they choose to report and what they choose to leave out. They don't want the truth. They want a hero turned murderer. That's where the big ratings are."

"But still—"

"How do you think I feel, sitting in the jailhouse every day, listening to the lies they spew out about me? How would you like it if they said those things about you?"

Ben shook his head. "Cases should be tried in the courtroom, not in the media."

Barrett's large hands balled up. "That's pretty damn easy for you to say, Mr. High-and-Mighty. It ain't your neck on the chopping block. People aren't saying you killed your wife, your precious children."

Ben turned away. He didn't know what more he could say. "Christina, come talk to him."

Christina didn't budge. "Sorry, Ben. I think he's right."

"What?"

"In a perfect world, I'm sure what you say would be true. But we don't live in a perfect world. We live in a world where gossip passes for news, and sensationalism passes for journalism. If we don't play along, we're going to lose out."

Ben turned back to Barrett. "Look, I'm your lawyer, not your mother. I can't tell you what to do. But I think this is a mistake. If you do it anyway, remember—anything you say can and probably will be used against you by the prosecution."

"I understand," Barrett replied. "I know how to handle myself. It's not like I've never given an interview before."

"Fine." Ben popped open his briefcase. "Any other little surprises you'd like to spring on me?"

"Actually, yes." The same nervousness Ben had spotted before seemed to return. "I was talking to your legal assistant here."

"Yes?"

He took a deep breath. "I think we should hire a jury consultant."

"Oh, jeez."

Barrett held up his hands. "I know, Christina told me you thought they were a waste of money."

"Worse than that. They can be a real pain in the butt."

"But I think we're going to need some help on this one."

"You mean you think *I'm* going to need some help with this one."

"We all need help, Ben. Now more than ever."

"Christina is an excellent judge of people," Ben noted. "She's better than any professional know-it-all I've seen in my entire career."

"Probably so, but she's got work of her own right now. I want someone who can go out and take the pulse of the people, maybe run some polls, find out what they think. Then we can tailor our defense accordingly."

"Maybe I'm old-fashioned, but I always try to tailor my defense around the truth."

"C'mon, Ben, get with it. Of course we're going to tell the truth, but the consultant will tell us how to tell it. What notes to play, what buttons to push. How to win the people over."

"Wallace, I think you're confused. This is a trial, not a campaign."

"Is there a difference? We're trying to win the votes of twelve people."

"Christina?"

She shrugged. "Sorry, Ben, I—"

"Right. You agree with him." He turned back to Barrett. "Fine. It's your money. You want to throw it away, that's your business. But I don't want him butting in and trying to tell me what to do at trial. Once voir dire is over, he's gone."

"Understood."

Barrett sat down on the lower bunk in his cell. "One last thing, Ben."

"There's more?"

"Yeah. Something I didn't tell you."

Ben didn't like the sound of that at all. "Tell me now."

"There was a time in my life when . . . well, when I was pretty damn depressed. It was after my football career, before I got my business going. I didn't know what to do with myself. No one seemed interested in me anymore. I'd gone from constantly being in the limelight to being nobody. I couldn't handle it."

Ben nodded sympathetically. "Yes?"

"Not too many people know this, Ben, but I had a nervous breakdown. Had to get some psychiatric counseling. In fact, I spent two weeks in a hospital. In—you know. One of those hospitals."

Ben tried not to evidence his reaction, but the possible impact of this little development on the trial was obvious.

"Yeah, I know," Barrett continued. "If the prosecution finds out, they'll say crazy once, crazy always. They'll use my psychiatric history to try to make me look unbalanced, like some psycho."

Ben nodded grimly. He pulled some papers out of his briefcase. "See this? It's a subpoena. They want your medical records."

"Then they already know."

"I don't think so. The subpoena's too vague. This is just standard procedure. They're on a fishing expedition." Ben put the subpoena back in his briefcase and snapped it shut. "We have to see that they don't catch anything."

"Can you do that?"

"I'll do my best. The hearing's just before the trial."

A new voice interrupted. "Excuse me."

It was one of the sheriffs, standing outside the cell door. "Didn't mean to cut in, but there's a message for you, Mr. Kincaid. Looks urgent."

Ben took the message from the man, scanned it quickly. "Oh my God."

Christina's eyes widened. "What is it?"

Ben grabbed his briefcase. "We'll check back with you later, Wallace. We've got to get back to the office." He nodded toward Christina. "Come on."

LOVING WAS IN the lobby, sprawled out in a desk chair. Jones was pressing a large ice pack against the back of his head. "What happened? Are you all right?" Ben asked as he and Christina huddled round.

"Sorry, Skipper," Loving said. Each word seemed to cause considerable pain. "I screwed up."

"Never mind about that. Are you hurt?"

"Aww . . . nothin' serious. Someone bashed me in the head with a baseball bat."

"Oh, is that all? Loving, have you seen a doctor?"

"I don't need no doctor. I've been hurt a lot worse than this before. I'm just sorry I let the creep get the drop on me." He bit down on his lower lip. "They were there at the park. Just like you said they'd be."

"Did you see anything?"

"I saw it all. Whitman and some longhaired creepazoid punk."

"Did he admit that he killed Barrett's family?"

"Not in so many words. But there's no doubt about it—Whitman sent the kid out to Barrett's neighborhood. And he's got cheap hit man written all over his face."

"But can we prove it?"

Loving lowered his head, obviously ridden with guilt and shame. "Not by me. I lost the camera. And the film. Whoever knocked me over the head ran off with it."

Christina put her arm around him. "You never mind about that. We're just glad you're alive."

Loving shrugged. "I'll take the stand if you want, Skipper, but—"

"But who would believe a guy who's working for the defense attorney."

Ben agreed—it wasn't a very promising prospect. Especially since he knew Bullock would run rings around poor Loving. "You just rest and try to get better. We'll figure out what to do later."

"There's something else, Boss." There was a tremor in Jones's voice that wasn't normally there. A tremor he hadn't heard since . . . "This came in the morning mail."

Ben hesitantly took the overstuffed envelope from Jones and withdrew a black videotape. "I gather this isn't the latest episode of *Melrose Place.*"

Jones shook his head. "I borrowed a VCR from Burris's pawnshop next door. It's on Christina's desk."

Ben walked over to the machine, turned it on, and inserted the tape. After a few moments of snow, the picture came to life. The camera was focused on a barren wall, a corner. Nothing was there. But there was a rhythmic sound in the background.

Ben turned up the volume. It was a ticking sound. A clock? No, each tick was more of a double beat. Th-thump. Th-thump. Th-thump.

It was a heartbeat.

On top of the heartbeat, there was the sound of a bell ringing, followed by some sort of clicking noise, like a lever of some sort being tripped. About a second later, they heard a humming noise, like a small engine being activated.

A shrill cry emerged, electrifying the room. The cry went on and on. It was the sound of something in terrible pain, something in more misery than it could possibly bear. A hideous, chilling shrieking.

"My God," Loving murmured. "What is that?"

Christina was holding her hands against her face. "Is that . . . human?"

Jones shook his head. "Sounds more like an animal to me. An animal being tortured."

The shrill, agonized cry continued to peal out from the television. "But what is it?"

A voice suddenly erupted from the tape. It was a deep, dark voice, speaking unnaturally slowly. "What's . . . wrong . . . with . . . Kitty?" There was a pause, then bone-chilling laughter. "Kitty . . . has . . . a . . . sick . . . heart!" There was more laughter, then a sudden crashing noise.

The picture went to black, but the tape wasn't over. They heard a clock ticking, ticktock, ticktock, and a few seconds after that, the sound of a tremendous explosion.

After the rumble of the explosion had finally faded, the deep voice returned and spoke two more words: *You're next.*

Ben turned off the VCR. This time *his* hand was shaking. "I think it's fair to say that our correspondent has progressed from harassment to intimidation."

Christina looked stricken. "But who could it be?"

"Who couldn't it be?" Jones said. "Everyone on God's green earth has heard about this case."

Christina's face did not relax. "Who is he after? Who is he threatening?"

Ben turned slowly. "Do you know if Barrett has a cat?"

"No," Christina replied. "He doesn't."

Ben slowly turned his head. "I do."

30

BEN SPED BACK to his apartment as fast as his well-worn Honda could get him there. The front left headlight was beginning to dangle out of its socket, and his muffler scraped the pavement every time he hit a bump, but he ignored both. He had called first, but there was no answer, which could mean one of two things—and one of them made his heart stop just to think about it.

He parked his car on the street and bolted at top speed toward Mrs. Marmelstein's boardinghouse. Just as he hit the front lawn, he saw Joni coming from the opposite direction. To his relief, he saw she was cradling Joey in her arms.

"Thank God," Ben gasped as he ran up to them. "Where have you been?"

One glance at his face told Joni that he was not inquiring out of idle curiosity. "We went to the mall. Baby Gap. Clothes shopping, remember?"

Ben tried to calm himself down. "How long have you been gone?"

"Pretty much all morning. Why? Should we have stayed home?"

"No. It's just as well you didn't."

"What? Ben, what's going on?"

"I'm not sure. But I think we may have had company." He glanced over at the front window to his apartment. "Doesn't Giselle normally sleep on the windowsill this time of day?"

Joni glanced at the house. "You know, come to think of it, she does. That's funny, she was there when we—"

There was no point in finishing her sentence, because Ben was already gone. He tore up the front wooden steps, barely missing Mrs. Marmelstein's garden. He ran up the stairs, forced the key in the lock, and ran inside.

"*Giselle!*" he cried out, but who was he kidding? She didn't come when he called even under normal circumstances. More drastic measures were required. He bolted into the kitchen and opened a can of Feline's Fancy, Giselle's favorite food. He held the can up in the air, letting the sweet aroma (well, he assumed cats liked it) waft its way through the apartment. Normally, ten seconds would be sufficient to draw her out of the farthest corner of the apartment.

Nothing happened. No cat.

"Giselle!" He set the can down on the floor and began a search. He felt a profound aching in his chest. He had to search, but he was bitterly afraid of what he might find.

"Giselle!" He pushed open his bedroom door and looked all around. Could she be caught in the closet, in a dresser drawer, under the bed? Each possible place turned up empty.

He tried the bathroom. No luck. Then the front living area—under the sofa, inside the end table. Even inside the piano, for God's sake. But she wasn't there.

The sick feeling expanded and rose up Ben's throat. This just wasn't like Giselle. If she were here, she'd have come to him by now.

If she could.

Joni and Joey came through the front door. "Found her yet?" Joni asked.

"No," Ben said. "Why don't you take a look?" But even as he said it, he knew she was no more likely to find Giselle than he had been.

Think, he told himself. Assume that this person did want to hurt him. The point of the videotape was to prolong the pain, to drag out the twisted suspense. And to tell him . . . what?

Ben tried to recall what he had seen and heard on the tape. That was definitely a cat he had heard shrieking. But what were the other sounds? There was a bell, followed by a clicking, followed by a whirring noise. Some kind of engine running. What was this sicko trying to tell him?

Ben ran it over and over in his mind as his eyes scanned the apartment. Click. Bell. Hum. Click. Bell. Hum.

It hit him the instant his eyes moved to the kitchen.

It was a microwave.

You click the door closed, the bell rings, and the microwave hums into action.

A cat in a microwave? The demented mind behind this was probably just the type who would enjoy seeing a sick urban legend brought to life.

His eyes barely open, barely willing to be open, Ben reentered the kitchen. This time he checked the microwave. It was dark inside, but—something was in there.

Ben closed his eyes and slowly, not wanting to but knowing he had to, opened the microwave door.

There was a large shoebox inside. Closed. Taped shut. Just barely fit.

Not breathing, Ben edged the shoebox out of the tight space. He closed his eyes, said a quick and quiet prayer, and opened the box.

Giselle leaped out of the box, claws extended, and clutched onto Ben's shoulder. Ben cried out in surprise, not to mention pain. A piece of cloth had been jammed in her tiny mouth and held in place by adhesive tape. Ben carefully cleared the cat's mouth and a forlorn howl followed.

"Giselle!" Ben reached for her, but she eluded him and bounced down onto the floor.

"Giselle! Are you all right?" Ben held out his arms, but she had already scampered across the floor to the open can of Feline's Fancy. She lowered her nose and attacked the food as if she hadn't eaten for days.

"Well, you don't seem to be in any immediate pain." What a relief. For a moment there, he had been certain . . .

But he was wrong, thank God. He lowered his head to the table. He could feel his blood circulating again, his heart lurching back into action. Who the hell was behind this, anyway? What sort of game was he playing? As if the Barrett case wasn't complicated enough already, now he had some psychopath tormenting him. Someone who had managed to find his office, his apartment, and his cat, with no problem.

And if he could get to Ben's cat, how hard could it be to get to his friends? Or his nephew? Or Ben himself?

And what did the rest of the tape mean? The explosion. And the final words. *You're next.*

Joni rushed into the kitchen, Joey in tow. "You found her!"

"Yeah."

"Thank goodness." She sat in the chair opposite him. "You really had me worried there for a moment. What's with the new jewelry?"

"Jewelry?"

"Yeah. Around her neck. Did you buy her that?"

"I didn't buy her anything." Ben rose out of his chair and walked to Giselle. He was surprised he hadn't noticed it before—but everything had been happening so fast. Giselle had a bright red ribbon tied around her neck in a bow. And dangling from the ribbon beneath her chin was a coin-size gold heart engraved with two words.

SICK HEART.

IT TOOK BEN twice as long as normal to get Joey to sleep that night. It was as if the boy could sense how worried Ben was, how ill at ease. Ben tried to conceal it, at least until he could do something about it, but he apparently wasn't doing a very good job. His mind was racing. Would this stalker continue with the sick pranks, or would he eventually try something serious? Maybe even deadly. Was it safe for them to stay here, and if not, where would they go?

Joey finally closed his eyelids, but only after Ben had run through "Annabel Lee" twice and sung the "A Dream Is a Wish Your Heart Makes" more times than he cared to count. It was just after ten; he decided to turn on CNN.

"Our top story this evening is our continuing coverage of"—a graphic image formed over the newscaster's left shoulder—"Horror in the Heartland." HEARTLAND appeared in large red letters, with what appeared to be blood dripping from them. The picture cut to video of the Utica neighborhood where Wallace Barrett lived. There was a sudden explosive noise—a gunshot—followed by two more in rapid succession. "Can you trust your neighbors? Are you safe? That's what the citizens of the usually sleepy town of Tulsa, Oklahoma, have been asking themselves in this upper-class neighborhood, since their sense of security was shattered by the hideous murder of a mother and her two tiny, defenseless children. The people of this neighborhood thought they were safe; they thought violence couldn't find them here. Little did they know that this illusion would be shattered by a hideous melodrama featuring their own mayor in the starring role."

Ben shut the television off. This he did not need. Obviously, Barrett's decision to speak to the media had not profoundly influenced the general tenor of the news coverage. He thought about playing the piano, always relaxing, but he was afraid to risk waking the baby. He retrieved his box of childhood treasures from under his bed, but somehow, given his current mood, a Magic 8-Ball and a bag of marbles just wasn't going to help. He considered reading; it seemed as if there was some book he was halfway through, but he hadn't read a page since he became embroiled in this case and now he couldn't remember what it was.

Nights like this, he had to admit, it would be nice to have someone else in your life. Someone to talk to, to relax with, watch a movie or listen to a CD with. Whatever. Truth was, he hadn't had anyone like that since Ellen, and that had been an increasingly long time ago. And that had ended in tragedy.

Ben picked up the phone and was halfway through dialing Christina before he stopped and pushed the interrupt button. It wouldn't be right. He monopolized too much of her time as it was during the day; he didn't have any business invading her nights. She probably had a social life, unlike him. She belonged to clubs and support groups and a church and went to parties and all that stuff.

What do I belong to? Ben asked himself. He didn't have an answer.

Without even thinking about it, he began dialing her number. Long distance to Oklahoma City. He was afraid she might not still be awake, but in fact, she answered in less than three rings.

"Hello?"

"Hi. Mother?"

"Benjamin?" There was a brief pause. "Is today a holiday?"

"No, Mother. I just thought I'd see how you were doing."

Her voice could not disguise a certain incomprehension. "You just called . . . to talk?"

"Is it too late? I hope you weren't already asleep."

"You know, Benjamin, when you get to be my age, you don't sleep as much as you used to. How's my grandson?"

"He's fine, really. All in all."

"You don't sound convinced."

"Well, he doesn't talk much."

"Some children don't. Your sister barely spoke until she was three. But once she started, you couldn't stop her."

"Maybe it's genetic."

"What else would it be?"

Ben stretched out on his sofa. "I don't know, Mother. I'm doing my best, but I don't know very much about raising a kid."

"No one does, Benjamin. It's all trial and error."

"Yeah." He sighed. "I just don't want my errors to destroy someone's life."

There was another long pause. "Benjamin, is something wrong?"

"Oh, no. Nothing. I've just been very busy lately."

"Yes, I know."

"You do?"

"How could I not? I see you on television constantly—scowling at reporters and refusing to comment. I can't go anywhere without running into someone who wants the inside scoop. Majel Howard stopped me at Crescent Market yesterday and I thought I would never get away from her. She wanted to know all about my son, the famous celebrity. Can you imagine? My son, the famous celebrity. Who'd have thought?"

"I'm hardly famous. More like notorious."

"Nonsense. But Majel kept pressing for information, so eventually I had to pretend that you and I talk occasionally and that consequently I might know something."

"Mo-*ther*!"

"Sorry, Benjamin."

"The trial starts soon."

"Yes, so I've heard. Do you have your trial strategy mapped out?"

Ben hesitated. "Not exactly. We have a theory, but no way to prove it."

"It must be very stressful. Handling such a high-profile case. Having reporters swarming around you every second."

"Yeah, it is."

"Well, you'll think of something, Benjamin. I know you will."

"I will?"

"Of course you will. We Kincaids aren't quitters, are we?"

"No. I guess not."

"Was there something else?"

There was, of course. What he wanted to say, what he really wanted deep deep down to say was "Mommy, I'm scared. Mommy, I think some bully wants to hurt me and I don't know how to stop him." But he couldn't say that. That would never do.

"Benjamin?"

"Yes?"

"You know . . . sometimes your father would get so busy with his practice and his surgeries and his research that his head would swim. He wouldn't know what to do next. But he never let it get the best of him. He'd smile, put his arm around me, and say, 'We'll get through this. If the creek don't rise.' "

Ben smiled a little. "That's nice. I wish he had said that to me."

"Didn't he?" There was a rustling on her end of the phone. "You know, when I visited you last, I tried to tell you everything I could remember about your father. But you haven't mentioned him since then."

"I'm sure you already know everything I could say."

"But I don't. I don't know anything about when you visited him in the hospital that last time. Or when you saw him in . . . in . . . well."

After all these years, she still couldn't say it. *In jail.*

"There really isn't much to tell, Mother. I barely remember myself."

BEN COULDN'T HAVE been more surprised when his father showed up at his apartment. He had been opposed to Ben's moving out of the family house. Why would you want to live in some grungy old apartment, he asked, when we have one of the biggest mansions in Nichols Hills not ten miles away? He had refused to visit. But now here he was, on Ben's doorstep, just hours after Ben learned that his mentor, his father in situ, was trying to prosecute his father in fact on charges of criminal fraud and murder.

"Ben, I need your help."

"Um, sure, come on in." He was embarrassed by the condition of his apartment: barely any furniture, clothes and books and records strewn all over the place. He knew his father was a firm believer in the tenet that "you can tell a great deal about a person from the way he lives."

"It's not for me. Personally, I think this is all a load of crap. But your mother is quite upset about it, and I know you don't want that."

"No, of course not." Ben pushed some clothes off a chair and motioned for his father to sit. He didn't. "What's the problem?"

"Well, don't you know? You work there, don't you?" A deep furrow crossed his forehead. "Ben, you haven't screwed up another job, have you?"

Ben felt his jaw clenching. "No, I'm still at the DA's office."

"Then you know they're trying to railroad me."

"I found out about the grand jury investigation today."

"You didn't know till today?"

"No. They intentionally kept me out of it."

"Well, hell's bells. And I thought you were going to be such a big help. I've known about it for weeks. I probably know more about it than you do."

"Probably." Good, Ben thought. Let his father think he's a moron. At least he wouldn't ask him to do anything that . . .

"It's like this," his father explained. "You remember me telling you about the EKCV?"

He did. The Edward Kincaid cardiac valve. A synthetic implant designed to regulate and stimulate the flow of blood through the major arteries. For patients with fallen arterial veins or serious heart problems that couldn't otherwise be repaired, it would be a godsend. What made it truly special—indeed, unique—was that although artificial, it was made from new synthetic materials that were all but indistinguishable from natural organic material. Compatibility was virtually universal.

"Last I heard," Ben said, "you were trying to sell stock in a new corporation to raise funds to market the valve nationwide."

"Right. That was Jim Gregory's idea. You know lawyers—they always know how to come up with some cash. Well, except you, of course."

Ben heard himself chanting a mantra like a yogi. Don't let him get to you. Don't let him get to you.

"So he puts out a prospectus, finds a brokerage firm, prepares an initial offering. All that lawyer stuff. Charges me nearly twenty thousand bucks. But boy, did it work. You wouldn't believe it. We raised almost four million bucks on the first offering. Value of the stock shot up almost overnight."

"You must have been very happy."

"Damn straight. It was like a dream come true. Course, then we had to prove the damn thing worked. Make it viable." He paused for a moment, glanced down at his hands. "I don't know. Maybe we rushed it. Some bad information got out. Suddenly there was this big rumor that the emperor had no clothes, you know? Jim kept saying we needed results. Had to stave off a shareholder derivative action. So I agreed to put the EKCV into action."

"You mean—on people?"

"Well, that's the only way to know whether it really works. If you want to use it on people, eventually you've got to try it out on people. We chose our initial subjects very carefully. All were people with serious cardiac problems, people who otherwise had very little chance of living more than a year. All were willing volunteers."

"What happened?"

"They died. Two of them. Not right away. Hell, no. Then we would have known we had problems. No, everything seemed to be fine and dandy for the first three weeks. But then the synthetic materials began to deteriorate. We still don't know what caused it. Maybe it was stomach acids, maybe respiratory fluids. We just don't know."

"People died?"

"It happens. Experimentation always has risks."

"But . . . they *died*."

"They knew what they were getting into. They volunteered of their own free will. And we had every one of them sign waivers, thank God, or we'd be up to our armpits in civil suits. With the waivers, I thought we were free and clear. Who would've thought the DA would try to press criminal charges? They're making a big deal out of the fact that we didn't get FDA approval. And the hell of it is, they won't even say what it is they're going to charge me with. Don't I have a right to know the charges against me?"

"For the moment, there are no charges against you. That's for the grand jury to decide. What the DA plans to try for is a matter of strategy."

"Strategy. That's what I'd like to know about."

The gnawing in Ben's stomach intensified. "What do you mean?"

"You know what I mean. Hell, they won't tell us anything. I'm supposed to go into that jury room tomorrow all by my lonesome and they won't tell me beans about what they want to know. How am I supposed to prepare?"

Ben tried to choose his words carefully. "If you don't know the answer to a question, or don't recall, just say so."

"Oh, right. That'll look good, won't it? The grand jury will charge me in a heartbeat."

"The truth of the matter is, grand juries usually do whatever the prosecutors want them to do. You should focus on the trial."

"What a defeatist attitude. Typical of you."

"What?"

"Face it, Ben. You've never had much fight in you. You'd rather run from a fight than win it. Do you know this pissant Jack Bullock?"

"Uh . . . yes."

"What's he got up his ass, anyway?"

"I'm not sure what . . ."

"This seems to be a vendetta for him. Has he got some problem with people who are richer than he is?"

"I don't think so. He just can't stand to let . . ." He struggled for a neutral word. ". . . people he believes have committed crimes get away with it."

"A zealot, huh? Great. Just what I need, some goddamn whacked-out civil servant on my case."

"He's not—"

"Ben, I want to know what the DA is planning. I'm particularly interested in whether they've talked to a guy named Perkins. Andrew Perkins. I want you to find out for me."

"Me?"

"Yeah, you. Why not? You work there, for God's sake. Hell, I helped you get the job."

"You— No, I interviewed like everyone else."

His father smirked. "Right. I bet that's what won them over. You have such a dynamic personality." He laughed. "I had Senator Abrams put in a good word for you."

"You didn't have any business—"

"You wanted the job, didn't you?"

"Yes, but—"

"This is beside the point. You're in the DA's office, and I need help. From the inside. So are you going to help? If you hate me so much you can't bring yourself to do it for me, do it for your mom. She's really torn up over this thing."

Ben bit down on his lower lip. "In the first place, they've kept me isolated from this case, so I don't have any idea what they're planning. In the second place, even if I did, I couldn't tell you. I have an ethical obligation of confidentiality to the client I work for. And my client is the State of Oklahoma. Not you."

"Shit." Ben's father threw his hands up in the air. "I should have known."

"What's that supposed to mean?"

"You must be loving this. At long last you have a chance to lord it over your dear old dad. For the first time, you have something I want. Something I need. So you're not going to give it to me."

"That doesn't have anything to do with it!"

"In a pig's eye. You've always been this way, Ben. Since day one. You take and take and take, but you never give."

"That's not—"

"What the hell did I send you to law school for, huh?" His rage was boiling. His face was turning a hot, vivid crimson. "Why did I pay all those bills, so you could throw your life away being a government whore? I tried to get you into a respectable occupation, and you, in your usual obstinate petty way, insisted on becoming a goddamn scum-of-the-earth fucking whore *lawyer!*" He picked up a chair pillow and threw it across the room. "And now that I actually *need* a lawyer, now that you could actually help the family and pay me back for all I've done for you, you refuse!"

The aching in Ben's gut was so intense he could barely stand. "I don't have any choice. I can't help you."

"Can't? Or won't?"

Ben hesitated. "Sometimes there isn't any difference."

Ben's father exploded with white-hot rage. "Do you know what they'll do to me?"

Ben didn't answer, but he had a pretty good idea.

In the space of a heartbeat, his father's fist was in the air. In the same instant, Ben flashed on every time he had seen that fist before, every time he had trembled and fallen into line in its presence. He held up his hands in front of his face.

"You goddamn coward. You disgust me." His father's hand dropped to his side, the threat unfulfilled. He took several deep breaths through great heaving lungs, slowly bringing himself back under control. The trembling throughout his body subsided.

He strode to the door, but stopped just before he passed through. "I don't want anything more to do with you, Ben. Ever. Don't even think about coming crawling back to me. It's done. Over. I won't even speak your name. You're out of my will; you're out of my life."

And just before he passed through that door, he added one final sentence, one that haunted Ben then and still did today, years afterward, as he talked to his mother on the phone, every time he talked to his mother. It was the sentence she had never heard. It was the sentence Ben heard every day of his life.

"I don't want anything to do with you," he had said. "From now on, I don't have a son."

BEN SAT UP and cleared his eyes. "I'm sorry, Mother, I didn't mean to keep you up so long. I'll let you go."

"Benjamin—"

"Yes?"

"I know I've said this before, but—it would make me very happy if you would just let me help you."

"Financially? No."

"Well, you can't fault me for trying." Another long pause. "Benjamin?"

"Yes."

"Feel free to call. Anytime. Then I'd have something to tell Majel Howard next time I see her."

"All right. I'll try."

"And, Benjamin?"

"Yes?"

"Try not to worry so much, all right? You've always taken things so hard, so . . . seriously. Problems have a way of working themselves out. I truly believe that. Things will turn out all right in the end."

"I hope so, Mother. I hope so. And—"

"Yes, dear?"

The tiniest of smiles tugged at the corners of his lips. "Thanks."

CHAPTER

31

BEN HAD HEARD the phrase *media circus* bandied about by lawyers, but it had never had any real meaning for him until now. As he approached the plaza outside the state courthouse at Denver and Fifth, the press descended on him. Flashbulbs burst in his eyes; minicam spotlights blinded him. A multitude of microphones were thrust under his nose, many of them bearing call letters he couldn't even identify. This many reporters hadn't been gathered together in one place in this state since the Oklahoma City bombing. And the trial hadn't even started yet.

"Mr. Kincaid! Would you care to give us a comment?"

"No." Ben tried to push past them, but he was massively outnumbered.

"Mr. Kincaid! Tell us what you expect to happen in there today."

"No."

"Don't you have a responsibility to the American public?"

"No."

"Your client was willing to talk to us. Why won't you?"

"If you'll excuse me." Ben tried to push out of the circle, but no one was budging.

"Look!" A voice emerged from somewhere behind them. "Wallace Barrett's in the courtroom! And he's got a gun!"

As one, the reportorial massé broke and ran toward the courthouse, practically trampling Ben in the process. When they were gone, only Ben and Christina, the one who had sounded the alert, remained.

"Since I know Barrett isn't being brought from the jailhouse for this hearing, I suppose he isn't waving a gun around either, right?"

Christina blushed. "I thought you looked like you needed some help."

"You were right." Ben took her arm and escorted her into the courthouse. They took the stairs, which allowed them to avoid the reporters and were probably quicker than the elevators anyway. At the sixth-floor landing, just outside the stairwell door, they found Jack Bullock propped up against the wall.

"Hiding out?" Ben asked.

Bullock almost smiled. "Just taking a breather."

"I thought you liked the press."

"All things in moderation." He pushed himself away from the wall. "You sure you still want to go through with this, Ben?"

"Well, it seems a bit late in the game to fold."

Bullock shook his head sadly. "I just don't see any upside in this for you. All you're going to accomplish in there is the absolute and final destruction of your reputation. And when it's all over, Barrett's still going to spend the rest of his life in prison. Assuming he avoids the lethal injection."

"Jack, tell me something. Off the record, away from the press. Have you even considered the possibility that you might be wrong? That Barrett might be innocent? After all, your case is entirely based on circumstantial evidence."

"Most murder prosecutions are. So what? I've got DNA and blood evidence linking him to the scene. I've got a neighbor who saw him fleeing from the scene. And I've got about half a billion people who saw him running from the police. If it walks like a duck and talks like a duck . . ."

"Right. Never mind." Ben opened the door and the three of them stepped out into the main hallway. Before he could move, the elevator bell dinged and the doors parted. Cynthia Taylor emerged. Her face was red and blotchy and she was clutching a tissue, trying to blot the steady stream of tears running down her face.

"What's she doing here?" Ben asked.

"Witness for the prosecution," Bullock murmured.

"At a hearing?"

Bullock shrugged. In other words, he wasn't telling.

Almost as soon as Cynthia emerged, the print and television journalists swarmed around her. A barrage of questions came at once.

"Ms. Taylor, who do you think killed your sister?"

"Was your sister a battered woman?"

"Is the report in the *Enquirer* that Wallace Barrett threatened your sister's life true?"

"Please," she whispered. She held up her hands, trying futilely to push them away. "I don't want to answer any questions."

The questions continued to fly, so quickly Ben couldn't even understand what was being asked. Instead of backing off, they were pressing forward, taking advantage of her inability to fend them off. Cynthia was dissolving, overcome by grief and tears.

"Please," Cynthia sobbed. "I just want to be left alone."

One of the telejournalists from Channel Eight jumped forward, tugging her cameraman close behind her. "Ms. Taylor," the reporter said, "according to the coroner's report, your sister was stabbed twenty-seven times. How does that make you feel?"

Ben felt his teeth grinding together so hard he could practically taste his fillings. His whole body began to tremble with anger. Enough.

He marched into the center of the commotion, grabbed the minicam perched on the operator's shoulder, and threw it across the hallway. It slammed against the opposite wall, fell and shattered into pieces.

"What the hell do you think you're doing?" the female reporter shrieked.

"Ending the interview," Ben replied.

"Do you have any idea how much those cameras cost?"

"Bill me." Ben took Cynthia by the arm and escorted her to the court- room. He seated her on the front row behind the prosecution.

"Thank you," Cynthia whispered, dabbing her eyes.

"No problem." Ben headed toward the front of the courtroom.

"Thanks for the assist," Bullock said as Ben passed. "Although, you know, they'll crucify you now on the evening news."

Ben threw his briefcase down on his own table. "Life is full of little trade-offs."

Bullock tilted his head to one side. "Since when did you start doing favors for prosecution witnesses?"

"She isn't just a witness," Ben said. "She's a human being." Ben dropped into his chair and tried to get a grip on himself. His body was still trembling. What had come over him? It was as if he had suddenly been seized by an unstoppable rage; he had totally lost control. What he had done might seem heroic to Cynthia Taylor, but he knew it was just nuts. Utterly uncalled for. What had come over him?

The reporters flowed into the courtroom, setting up at their various sta- tions. Ben scanned the panorama in amazement. It really *was* a three-ring circus. How could anyone imagine that any serious work could be done in the midst of all this showbiz fol-de-rol? How could anyone pretend that their presence wouldn't affect the proceedings, that lawyers and judges and wit- nesses wouldn't want to—wouldn't be forced to play to the cameras? They were taking a system imperfect at best and making it a joke.

He'd never seen anything like it, he thought, but almost immediately he realized that he had. He had been involved in one other case that received inordinate media attention—far more than it deserved, in fact. Or perhaps it just seemed so, because everything about it was so personal.

WHEN BEN ARRIVED at the Oklahoma City courthouse on the first day of his father's trial, he was instantly plunged into a sea of chaos. The hallway was jam-packed with people; there was barely enough space to breathe, much less move. Bailiffs tried to maintain order, but it was mostly futile. Anything could happen in here, and there was nothing anyone could do to stop it.

Ben went to the courthouse with his mother, trying to be the strong shoulder he knew she needed. She was in worse shape than he had ever seen her; she seemed to have aged ten years in two months. That steely facade, that impenetrable fortress had been breached. Social contacts had thinned; invitations had almost dried up altogether. He wondered if she would ever recover herself.

It wasn't that she had been ostracized; she was just in purgatory. They were waiting to see what happened. "After all," she had explained to him earlier, "almost every successful man faces something like this in the course of his career. The small-and-lowly love to bring down the high-and-mighty."

The prosecution had been merciless, and the press had lapped up everything they said. Everything Ben read left little doubt but that his father knew the EKCV was not ready for implementation, but nonetheless proceeded with the sale of stock using falsified data to fill out the prospectuses, and then, in order to appease the shareholders hungry for results, began human experimentation even though it had not been nearly well enough researched, resulting in two deaths. The charge was manslaughter in the second degree.

Ben escorted his mother down the hallway toward the courtroom. "Oh, no," he whispered.

Outside the courtroom, he saw the surviving families of both of the men who had died with the EKCV faltering in their chests. He recognized their pictures from the newspapers; they had been interviewed repeatedly. One man, Herbert Richardson, left behind two grown daughters and a tiny grandchild. The other man, Tony Ackerman, was much younger; he left behind a widow in her early forties and a boy only thirteen years old.

Who the hell had allowed these people to flank the only entrance to the courtroom? Stage-managed by the press, no doubt. Some photojournalist looking for a tense moment to fill out the evening newscast or the front page, never giving a thought to what effect this manipulation might have on the principals. Including Ben's mother.

He continued walking at a steady pace, gripping his mother's arm. They couldn't avoid them; they could only hope to get it over with as soon as possible.

They passed closest to the Ackermans, the woman and the boy. She was holding up well; she did not react overtly, but her face showed the strain and her eyes told Ben she knew who they were. The boy was in much worse shape. Tears streamed down his face; he was choking and gritting his teeth.

"Just keep walking," his mother whispered, but Ben found that he couldn't. He had to reach out; he had to make some attempt to let them know how he felt.

He looked down until he caught the boy's eyes. "I'm so sorry," he said quietly.

The boy's mouth trembled. "I hate you," he said, in a cracked but strong voice.

Ben froze, unable to respond. Hate me? *Me?* But I didn't have anything to do with—But of course, the boy didn't know that. As far as the boy was concerned, this was one gigantic, cynical money-making scheme, and Ben was one of the primary beneficiaries.

Mrs. Ackerman laid her arm across the boy's chest, trying to push him back. He didn't budge. Instead of retreating, he repeated himself. "I hate you."

Ben made one more attempt. "If there's ever anything I can do for you . . ."

Before Ben could complete the offer, the boy's face curled up in an angry, twisted snarl. He pursed his lips and spit.

It caught Ben just below the shoulder. He closed his eyes and brushed it off with his hand. It was a childish gesture, exactly the sort of thing you would expect from a kid.

But it hurt just the same.

There was a commotion at the other end of the hallway. The attention of the spectators turned from the mini-spectacle at the doorway to something altogether more compelling. Ben's father was being escorted to the courtroom by two guards from the sheriff's office. He paused as he approached them.

"Hello, Lillian," he said to Ben's mother cordially, if rather formally. Ben almost expected him to shake her hand.

His eyes turned for the barest of moments to Ben, then moved quickly onward. He didn't say a word to Ben, didn't even acknowledge his presence.

He had meant what he had said.

The first day of trial was a disaster for the defense. Everything went against them. It was obvious that the prosecutors had not simply been boasting in their press conferences. They had a well-researched, well-evidenced, well-organized case. No surprise there—Bullock always did professional work. By all indications, the trial was going to be a slam dunk.

It was just a matter of time.

OF COURSE, IF Ben had bothered to poll the countless representatives of the press in this courtroom gallery, almost all of them would have said they expected the Barrett trial to be a slam dunk as well. Ben was determined to prove them wrong.

He popped open his briefcase. The instant the lid raised, a booming noise exploded from the briefcase. Ben jumped quite literally out of his seat, clutching his chest.

A small puff of smoke arose from the briefcase. Ben waved it away, still trying to catch his breath. When the smoke cleared, he saw the tiny sign dangling from the top of the briefcase:

BOOM!

And in smaller letters beneath that:

YOU'RE NEXT.

Slowly Ben eased back into his chair. Given the general commotion in the courtroom, almost no one had noticed the small but potent explosion, and the few that did quickly turned their attention to more interesting matters.

His heart was racing. *Who was doing this to him?*

Whoever he was, he had made his point. He could get to Ben anytime, anywhere. Any way he wanted to.

The bailiff stepped through the chambers door and brought the court into session. A heartbeat later, Judge Sarah L. Hart entered the room.

Finally seeing her was almost anticlimactic. Ben wondered if she had known she would be assigned to this case as long as everyone else in town seemed to have known. If she had, it didn't seem to have fazed her.

Judge Hart took her seat and scanned the gallery. "Well," she said, stacking her papers, "I'm glad to see so much interest and enthusiasm for the judicial process. We've got more people here for this minor evidentiary hearing than attended my daughter's wedding." She turned her attention to the lawyers. "Are there any matters we can take up now before the trial begins, counsel?"

Bullock rose to his feet first. "Yes, your honor. We issued a subpoena to the defendant seeking the production of certain documents we believe could be critical to the prosecution case. They have not complied."

Judge Hart turned toward Ben. "Is this true?"

"Yes, it is."

"Was the subpoena properly served?"

"Yes, your honor. I have it right here."

"And he hasn't honored it," Bullock added.

"Right, I got that part. What's up, Mr. Kincaid?"

Ben squared his shoulders. "Your honor, this subpoena is nothing but a shameless fishing expedition. They're seeking all medical records, nothing specific. They're just hoping that if they swim around in my client's medical history long enough, they'll find something they can use to embarrass him."

"That's not correct," Bullock said. "We believe there is ample indication that the defendant has possible medical and . . . psychological history that could be of relevance."

"What's your basis for that belief?"

"Well, the crime itself . . . the grisly manner in which it was perpetrated. . . . There may be some prior history."

Ben approached the bench. Bullock followed, and they continued the argument out of the earshot of the reporters. "You see what they're doing, your honor. They're assuming guilt to fabricate probable cause."

"It does seem that way," Judge Hart agreed.

"What they're really hoping for," Ben continued, "is to find some history of psychological treatment, not because it's in any way probative, but because they can use it to smear my client at trial and in the press."

"What the press does is not my concern."

"I think it is," Ben continued. "Regardless of how you rule today, the press will report that the prosecution was seeking records of Barrett's psychological treatment. Most people will assume from that that Barrett has received psychological treatment. Just by making the request, the prosecution has successfully tarnished the defendant in the eyes of the world. And twelve of the people exposed to this intentional smear will be selected for the jury."

"Your honor," Bullock said, "I can only assume that the pressures of handling a major case have caused defense counsel to become paranoid and irrational. He's seeing plots that don't exist."

"Nonetheless," the judge said, "I'm not going to let you prowl around in this man's medical history unless you can give me a good reason."

"Your honor." Bullock stepped away from the bench. The volume level of his voice sharply increased. "Surely you're not going to prevent the prosecution from learning the truth about the man who committed possibly the most heinous crime this city has ever seen!"

Judge Hart pointed her gavel at him. "Talk to me, counsel. I'm the one that matters in this courtroom."

"Of course."

"If I ever think you're talking to anyone other than me in this courtroom, you won't be talking in this courtroom any more."

"Understood, your honor." Bullock bowed his head, seemingly chastised.

"As for your subpoena, it seems to me rather obvious what you're hoping to find, and even if you were lucky enough to find it, I wouldn't let it in, because it doesn't tell us anything about what happened the afternoon of the murder. Call it character evidence or habit or psychological disposition or what have you, it still feels like a smear to me. And I'm not going to have that in my courtroom."

"Very well, your honor."

Ben smiled. Hallelujah, he actually won one. And the one his client was most concerned about, at that. Maybe his luck was turning. Maybe this would be a good time to address the other big issue.

"Your honor, there's also the matter of my motion in limine."

"Right. I've read your briefs, Mr. Kincaid, but I'm afraid I'm not inclined to exclude the DNA evidence."

"Your honor, this evidence was bought and paid for."

The judge nodded. "A fact you can and no doubt will bring out at some length during cross-examination. If the jury feels the payment of money biases the evidence, they will disregard it accordingly."

"But, your honor." Ben knew it was bad form to continue arguing with the judge after she had made a ruling, but this was an issue of such importance he couldn't restrain himself. "The principal problem isn't the payment of money. The principal problem is that DNA evidence doesn't speak for itself. It must be interpreted. That requires experts."

"So hire experts. I don't believe your client is a hardship case."

"No, but there is nothing I can do that matches the impact of prosecution evidence presented by some Ph.D. spouting scientific technobabble and statistics that the jury can't possibly understand, drawing conclusions about the ultimate question of guilt or innocence."

"Again, these are all issues for cross-examination."

"By that time, the damage will be done. This is a new and still uncertain science. It doesn't prove anything; it just suggests circumstantial evidence via statistical probabilities. But juries don't know that. They see some guy in a suit with a closet full of degrees take the stand, babbling a lot of jargon they don't understand, and he tells them the defendant is guilty. Who are they to disagree?"

"The jury is always free to disregard evidence."

Ben decided to try another tack. "But, your honor, don't you see what's happening here? The jury isn't drawing its own conclusions. They're drawing the conclusions they're told to draw by some high-dollar expert. Juries lose more power every day; all the important decisions are made by prosecutors and experts and the press, all telling them what to believe. With all the hubbub, how can we go on pretending that people are being judged by a jury of their peers? We need to draw the line."

"An intriguing argument, Mr. Kincaid, but alas, not a successful one. I'm going to let the evidence in. If there's nothing else"—she slammed her gavel on the bench—"we're in recess. The trial will begin Monday morning at nine o'clock sharp." She glanced up at the cameramen. "That's Central Standard Time."

The bailiff brought everyone to his feet and the judge beat a hasty retreat. Before Ben could make it back to his table, he found Bullock under his nose.

"Must be feeling pretty cocky with your pet judge on the bench, huh?"

"You're fantasizing. Judge Hart is emminently fair—perhaps that's why you're worried."

"Remember, Kincaid, the eyes of the world are on Judge Hart. They're on all of us. This is the big time." Bullock stepped so close Ben could feel his breath on his face. "I'm going to put that filthy baby-murdering client of yours in prison, if not in a graveyard. That's a promise." Bullock whipped around and stomped to the back of the courtroom, where he was greeted by a horde of reporters.

The eyes of the world, Ben thought. Now that was the scariest thought yet.

He packed his briefcase and headed out, hoping he could avoid the press. The stage was fully set now. Judge Hart wouldn't be giving him any breaks. She couldn't, not this time. Neither would the press. And Bullock would be doing everything in his power to get a conviction.

And Ben? All he had was a few hunches, none of which he could prove in a court of law. That would have to change. Ben didn't know how, but somehow, that had to change.

Otherwise, Wallace Barrett didn't have a prayer.

CHAPTER

32

JONES WAS WAITING for Ben and Christina when they returned to the office.

"How did it go?" Jones anxiously inquired.

Ben walked right past him. "Don't ask."

"Does that mean not well?" Jones inquired.

"You can never tell with Ben," Christina replied. "He's so moody. The judge scowls at him and he thinks he's lost the case."

Jones stopped Ben before he could duck into his private office. "Did you quash the subpoena?"

"What?" Ben snapped out of his reverie. "Oh, that. Yeah, I did get that."

"Congratulations!"

"But I lost the DNA motion."

"No kidding. Did you really think the judge was going to exclude the most incriminating evidence in the case?"

"Well, I had hoped . . ."

"Then you were dreaming. You'll still figure out some way to prove Wallace is innocent."

"Is that right? I wish you'd explain how. Did you contact Whitman?"

"Yeah. He denies being anywhere near O'Brien Park last Thursday night. Says he has at least ten witnesses who will testify he spent the night at home. Says if we go public with these accusations, he'll sue."

"A great American. What's Loving doing?"

"Trying to find the man who met Whitman at the park, or someone who can identify him."

"Any luck?"

"Not yet."

"So, basically, the trial starts Monday morning, and we have no defense."

"We have Wallace Barrett."

"No one will believe him."

"You do."

"I don't watch television." Ben opened his office door and tossed in his briefcase. "Once that DNA evidence gets in and the jury starts hearing Ph.D.s babble about probabilities and gene identifiers and whatnot, the jury will be so confused they'll end up believing exactly what the media has been telling them to believe for weeks. That Wallace Barrett killed his family."

Christina laid her hand on his shoulder. "You'll think of something. You just need to reflect a bit. Seek out inspiration. View the world through your third eye."

Ben grimaced.

Jones stepped in. "Here's the morning mail, Boss."

Ben took a stack of letters and a book-sized package. "Thanks. Hold my calls."

"Okay. Why?"

Ben smiled faintly. "I'll be busy reflecting and seeking out inspiration."

Ben closed the office door behind him, threw off his suit coat, and slumped down into the chair behind his desk. Never in his life had he dreaded a trial like the one he was facing now. Never had he felt so powerless. Never had he seen the shortcomings of the judicial system as keenly. He knew Barrett had not killed his family. He knew it! And Loving had gathered strong evidence indicating who did. But he was almost totally unable to prove it in court. The truth would not be heard. And even if it was, it would not be believed.

Ben sorted through the phone messages Jones had stuffed into his hands. Most of them were from reporters requesting interviews. Even some of the network television people were interested. Gee, he thought, Katie Couric is awfully cute. And smart, too . . .

But no. The media were in this case far too deeply already. He was barely able to breathe as it was. How could you conduct a defense, investigate, plan—how could you *think*?—when you knew, to use Bullock's phrase, the eyes of the world were upon you constantly? Can you give a man a fair trial inside a pressure cooker?

Ben rubbed his fingers against his temples. He needed to see Barrett, to give him a report on the hearing, but he just wasn't up to it. He couldn't face a trip to the jailhouse right now. He never liked doing that.

He never liked doing that because he never once did it without remembering his first visit to a jail cell, the one that had ended so horribly, the one that had literally changed his life.

The time he had gone to visit his own father.

IF BEN HADN'T known so many people in the sheriff's office, as a result of working at the DA's office, he never could have gotten in. The fourth day of trial had run late and visiting hours were long since over.

His father greeted Ben as he entered the cell. "What the hell are you doing here? I didn't ask for you."

"I thought we should talk."

"You thought wrong. Guard!"

"Relax. We won't be disturbed for ten minutes, no matter how much fuss you make. They've gone for coffee."

"Oh, you've got it all arranged, haven't you? Bully for you."

Ben stood awkwardly before him. There was no place to sit, no place to put his hands. "So . . . how's it going?"

His father made a snorting sound. "You're the goddamn lawyer. You tell me."

Bad start. Ben tried again. "I see *The Daily Oklahoman* is running front-page editorials on the case."

"Yeah, well, they do that sort of thing."

"The trial isn't going too well, is it?"

"No, it isn't. That should make you very happy." He turned away. "Maybe your client will give you a raise."

Ben cursed silently. He struggled for words, struggled for air. "Look, I don't know how to do this or say this, so I'm just going to spit it out. You wanted to know about Perkins?"

Dr. Kincaid lifted an eyebrow.

"An Andrew Perkins. You wanted to know whether the prosecution knew about some guy named Andrew Perkins? Well, they do. He's going to testify, probably as their last witness, about"—Ben averted his eyes—"that report he wrote on the EKCV before it was implemented. Apparently he feels he made it clear to, um, those concerned, that the device was not safe." Ben cleared his throat awkwardly. "Report shows your name on the distribution list."

Dr. Kincaid's lips thinned. "Are you actually trying to help me?"

"Well, I just heard something in the hallway and I thought—"

"You're trying to help me. You finally decided maybe it would be all right to do something for your dear old dad, right?"

Ben's eyes searched unsuccessfully for his father's. "Yes, I'm trying to help you."

"Well, it's too goddamn late!" His hand came around so fast, Ben barely had a chance to register it, much less prevent it. He slapped him hard with the full power of his considerable weight, with such force that it left an immediately visible mark.

"You stupid lazy little toad. Don't you think I know that already? Do you think I've spent these weeks idly twiddling my thumbs while your prosecutor friends tried to crucify me? Do you think I just sat on my hands while you wrestled with your dainty little conscience? I needed to know about Perkins weeks ago, for the grand jury hearing. That's when you could have helped me.

We could've undercut his credibility early, when it counted for something. Now the secret is out. Hell, Perkins is on their witness list."

"I'm sorry," Ben said. His jaw ached when he moved it. "I didn't know. I just . . . wanted to help."

"Well, you fucked it up, Ben. Like always. You're a stupid, stupid fuck-up. You always have been and you always will be."

"I know you don't mean that. You're just upset, worried—"

"Worried? Damn straight I'm worried. Do you know what they want to do to me? They want to lock me up and throw away the key. They want to tell people that I'm a murderer. Do you understand that? I'm a *doctor*. I save people's lives! Can you imagine how it feels to have people saying that you're a murderer!"

"I'm sure it must be difficult—"

His teeth were clenched so tightly he could barely speak. "No, it isn't just difficult, you stupid pansy prick. It's impossible! It's more than I—than *anyone*—" His whole body began to tremble, energy radiating from every inch of his person. "It isn't fair!"

It was as if the previous Dr. Edward Kincaid had disappeared, had been replaced by some entirely new version, like a snake that had shed his skin. He crossed the tiny cell with such speed, such ferocious anger, that Ben had no chance to respond, much less protect himself. His father struck him again, this time with a clenched fist, dead center on his face. Ben fell forward, losing his balance and his legs all at once.

"My nose," he gasped. He wrapped his arms around his father, trying to prevent his fall.

"Let . . . *go of me!*"

His father tried to push him away, but Ben held tight. "Stop it. You're not in control!"

"You're . . . damn . . . *right!*" Dr. Kincaid raised his knee into Ben's stomach, breaking his armlock. Ben teetered back and forth, trying to stay on his feet.

Ben swung his arm around, trying to protect himself, but his father easily avoided it. Dr. Kincaid raised his fist and delivered another blow to the pulpy part of Ben's face.

This one knocked Ben to his knees. "Stop," he murmured breathlessly. "Don't . . ." The room was swimming around him. "I think my nose is broken."

"Good." The rage boiled up and out of his father's face, his eyes. He was shaking violently and tight as a drum. "Stupid . . . pansy . . . prick." His father reared back his foot and kicked Ben dead in the gut. Ben fell flat on the floor of the cell.

"Wrestle with your conscience. I'll give you something to wrestle!" His foot reared back again. Ben was beyond speaking, beyond any reaction other than feeling the rending deep inside him, the excruciating pain being delivered again and again and again.

"Please . . . stop." Ben barely managed to get the words out. His head lay limply on the cell floor.

And then it passed. Almost as suddenly and violently as the rage had arisen, it passed. Dr. Kincaid collapsed on the cot in the corner of the cell, his head pressed against the pillow, staring at the gray stone wall.

With great effort, feeling the agony caused by each movement of his muscles, Ben pushed himself up on his hands and knees. "Dad?"

To his astonishment, he realized that his father was crying.

"Get . . . out," his father said, not looking at him.

Ben wiped the blood from his face and slowly crawled to the cell door. By the time the guard arrived, he had managed to pull himself to his feet, although it was painfully obvious what had occurred. Ben didn't say a word.

Sometime after Ben's departure and before the next time the guards checked on their prisoner, Dr. Edward Kincaid suffered a massive heart failure. According to the surgeons who treated him, stress-related hormones had saturated his blood, causing enormous damage to the arterial walls. Obstructed arteries hampered the heart's ability to pump, choking off the flow of blood to his heart. They emphasized that this was the fourth heart attack the man had suffered, that uncontrolled anger had plagued his entire life, that Ben shouldn't blame himself.

But of course he did.

The next day Ben resigned from the district attorney's office. Six weeks later, two weeks after his father died and the day after the doctors removed the bandage from Ben's nose, he moved to Tulsa to take a job with a large law firm. He was starting fresh, putting all that unhappiness and failure behind him.

Or so he thought.

BEN PRESSED HIS hands against his forehead. Tears spattered into his hands. My God, Ben, he told himself. You'd think you'd be over it by now. It's been years. *Years.* Your father is dead. There's nothing you can do for him now. It's over.

But it wasn't, of course. It wasn't over, and it seemed it never would be over, no matter how much time passed.

Tick, tick, tick, tick, tick . . .

Time kept marching on. Instead of leaving his baggage behind, Ben kept piling it up, stacking it on top of his head like some demented Sherpa. Years of unhappiness, years of guilt. All the *I wish*'s, all the *if only*'s. If only I had tried to get to know him better. If only I had told him how I felt. I wish . . .

Damn.

Tick, tick, tick, tick, tick . . .

He thought he was leaving it all behind when he ran down the turnpike and set himself up in Tulsa. What a joke. He ran to a big law firm. When that didn't work out, he ran to a big corporation. Took him years before he believed he could make it on his own. If he believed it. Took him years before he realized he couldn't run away far enough or fast enough because the one he was really trying to run away from was himself.

You loser.

Tick, tick, tick, tick, tick . . .

You killed your father.

Tick, tick, tick, tick, tick . . .

It was all your fault. He hated you.

Tick, tick, tick, tick, tick . . .

And another thing, Ben thought to himself. I hate that goddamn clock.

Tick, tick, tick, tick, tick . . .

Except . . . Ben shook his head and tried to clear away the bitter cobwebs. Except, he repeated to himself. Except for one teensy-weensy problem.

He didn't have a clock in his office.

Boom! the voice on the videotape had said. *You're next.*

Ben jumped out of his chair and bolted into the lobby. "Everybody out. *Now!*"

Christina dropped a stack of papers. "What the—"

"No questions. Come on!" Ben turned her around manually and pushed her toward the door. "You, too, Jones. Out!"

Jones was staring at his computer screen. "Just give me five seconds to save."

"No. *Now!*" Ben hauled him up by the lapel and herded both of them through the door. Arm in arm they raced across the street.

And not a second too soon. They were barely halfway across the street when the explosion burst through the office windows and ripped across downtown Tulsa. There was a sudden flash of white-hot light followed by a gust of hurricane-force winds so strong it slammed the three of them into the white brick building on the opposite side of the street. The sound was ear-shattering—painful and intense. The ground shook, knocking them to their knees. Wood and metal splinters flew through the air. Glass shattered, not just in Ben's office but in every storefront up and down the street.

Ben turned his head and peered through the dense black cloud of smoke. An intense fire burned brightly in the hollowed shell of his office. The now-visible foundations began to creak, then crumble. Bent, molten steel dripped to the ground, bringing everything attached with it. A few aftershocks followed, of lesser, but still earsplitting, intensity. Then the walls collapsed; bricks tumbled inward into the inferno.

And then, finally, it was over. The explosive tumult was followed by a silence; an eerie, suspended silence. Only the crackling of the flames remained.

"Are you all right?" Ben whispered.

Christina nodded. Her face was red and bruised from being scraped against the brick building. Her forehead was bleeding in two places. But she was alive.

"Jones?"

He tried to smile. "I'll live. But what the hell happened?"

Ben didn't have an answer for him. All he could do was struggle to his feet and stare at the billowing cloud of smoke and fire that thirty seconds ago had been his office.

Boom! The message had said.

You're next.

THREE

The Family Trademark

◆ ◆ ◆

33

JUDGE HART'S BAILIFF reached into the hopper and withdrew the first name. "Elizabeth MacPherson."

A young woman, probably in her mid-thirties, in the third row of the gallery, put down her paperback novel and walked to the jury box. As directed, she took the first seat on the far end of the back row.

"Harrison James Denton." This one was more attentive, more eager, more wide-eyed. He jumped to his feet and hurried to the jury box, long hair flying behind him, an anxious grin on his face.

"He knows," Harold Sacks whispered into Ben's ear. Ben nodded his agreement.

And so the trial finally began. After all the legal wrangling was over, after all the motions were ruled upon and the countless heated arguments in chambers were done, it finally came down to this: the selection of the twelve persons (fourteen counting alternates) who would decide Wallace Barrett's fate. Whether he lived or died; whether he became a free man or spent the rest of his life in prison.

The weekend had been an unmitigated nightmare for Ben, beginning with the destruction of his office and going downhill from there. Christina had some minor cuts and abrasions, and the docs had removed some glass slivers from Jones, but they were all alive and functioning. The worst part was the psychic aftershock; no one came away from a near-miss violent death like that without feeling some trauma.

The explosion had obliterated his office and done serious damage to the pawnshop and the diner on either side. According to the preliminary reports from the Tulsa Metro Bomb Squad, the explosion was triggered by a device that was probably in that package Ben had received in the mail but had never opened—thank God. The principal ingredients in the bomb were two common chemical liquids that could be found in virtually every kitchen or laundry room in Tulsa. Separate, they were harmless. But the bomb allowed one to trickle into the other, a slow-burn mixture that would eventually and inevitably result in a terrific explosion. Mike had taken a personal interest in the case and had assured Ben the police would investigate to the best of their abilities, but the simple truth was, they had no significant clues. No one had the slightest idea who had planted the bomb. And given the enormity of the pretrial press attention given the Barrett case, the bomber could be almost anyone.

Ben would have liked to have indulged in an extended recuperative period, maybe a few weeks on a Mexican beach, but he didn't have time. He had a case going to trial. He couldn't count on Judge Hart giving him an extension, especially not with the eyes of the world upon her and Bullock breathing down her neck and already accusing her of being biased in Ben's favor. No, he had to be ready.

Fortunately, for once in his life, Ben was representing a client who actually had some money. They had set up shop in a suite in the Adam's Mark Hotel near the courthouse. Of course, this expense would eat away at Ben's fee, but under the circumstances, he had little choice.

There was one lucky break—Christina had taken most of the trial exhibits and notebooks to Kinko's for copying, so they weren't destroyed in the explosion. But all of Ben's notes were. As well as all their office equipment. And all the information Jones had stored on his computer. They didn't even have a working typewriter. Christina, resourceful as ever, had managed to rent the most critical equipment and had it delivered to the hotel suite. But Ben didn't have tenant's insurance and his landlord wasn't sure his policy covered terrorist acts. So all of this simply magnified their ever-increasing expenses.

The worst part of the weekend, though, possibly even worse than the explosion, was dealing with Harold Sacks. Sacks was the jury consultant Barrett had insisted they hire. He was a short man from Boston—overbearing, overconfident, and apparently accustomed to having every word he said treated as if it had been handed down from Mount Sinai.

"The way I see it," Sacks had said just after he'd swiped Ben's last slice of toast from his room service breakfast, "we need black jurors. As many as possible. Make all twelve black if you can."

"That isn't going to happen," Ben informed him. "We're in Tulsa County. You'll be lucky if we get two. Three, tops."

"Well," Sacks said, smiling the odious little smile Ben had come to detest, "that depends on how many white jurors you get dismissed, doesn't it?"

"Judge Hart isn't an idiot. She's not going to dismiss anyone for cause unless there are bona fide reasons. And I'll probably get six preemptories. Like I said, two, maybe three black jurors, tops."

"Hmm." Sacks tapped his forehead and engaged in thought processes Ben suspected were more reminiscent of Machiavelli than Clarence Darrow. "Maybe we can do something about that."

"What's this obsession with black jurors, anyway? Are you saying black jurors will be more sympathetic just because the defendant is black?"

"In a word, yes."

"I don't believe it."

"Look at these polls I've taken." Sacks had spent the previous week polling, at the cost of a mere thirty thousand dollars of Barrett's money. "African Americans who were polled showed significantly higher propensities for believing that Barrett either is or might be innocent. This shouldn't come as any great surprise. Need I remind you of the O. J. Simpson experience?"

"Well, we're still not going to get an all-black jury, no matter what your polls show."

"My second-choice demographic category is young white women."

Ben blinked. "I thought the stereotype was that women tended to be more likely to convict."

"That's true, particularly if the defendant is a woman, and particularly with older women. But in this case, with young white women, we have a special appeal."

"And what's that?"

"Sex."

Ben blinked twice. "Care to explain that?"

Sacks nudged him in the side. "Oh, come on, Ben. You're not as naive as you pretend."

"I'm not?"

"It's obvious. We've got a very handsome man for a defendant. A media star. A husky, strapping athlete. A big black stud, basically. White women crave black lovers. You know what they say. Once you go black, you'll never go back."

"That's the most offensive—"

"Even the ones who have never had a black lover probably fantasize about it. Probably two, three times a day."

"How would you know?"

"I've done my research. Studies have proven this is all true. I've got statistics." He winked. "Why do you think I get the big money?"

"Because rich defendants will try anything to keep themselves out of jail."

Sacks folded his arms. "Well, I wasn't aware that you were handling this case gratis yourself."

Touché.

It only got worse on Sunday afternoon, when the sheriffs delivered the juror questionnaires that had been completed by all the people in the prospective jury pool. Each candidate had been required to complete a detailed forty-five-page list of questions about themselves.

"All right," Sacks said to Ben, gripping several of the completed questionnaires in his hand. "Let's try a mock voir dire."

Ben thought his facial expression surely made any verbal response superfluous.

"Kincaid, let me help you. Please. Tomorrow, when you stand before the jury, you'll be on your own."

"You know, I've got a lot to do . . ."

"I'm not sure what to think about your attitude, Kincaid." Some time during the course of the weekend, Ben had been demoted from *Ben* to *Kincaid.* "Don't you know that voir dire is the most important part of the trial?"

Ben threw down his pencil. "Well, I know it's one important part of the trial. But see, I, unlike you, have to prepare for all the other parts as well."

"Come on, come one. Let's just run a few test cases." He glanced down at the top questionnaire in his hand. "Okay, this guy drives a big black pickup with a bumper sticker that reads: IMPEACH CLINTON AND HER HUSBAND. Do you want him on your jury?"

Ben shrugged. "I'd have to know more about him."

"Wrong. You know you don't want him just from the fact that he has a pickup with an obnoxious bumper sticker."

"Half the people in Tulsa have pickups with obnoxious bumper stickers."

"Then that's the half we don't want." Sacks flipped to the next questionnaire. "What about this guy? He's white and in his mid-fifties, he's a pediatrician, he wears a Mickey Mouse watch with diamond studs, and he has a backyard swimming pool. Do you want him on your jury?"

Ben tried to play along. "Doctor, huh? Well, then he's probably intelligent."

Sacks threw the questionaire at him, laughing. "Give me a break. As if intelligence is a quality you want in a juror. You're on the defense, remember?"

"That doesn't mean—"

"You're going to claim that Barrett was framed, aren't you?"

"Well, sort of . . ."

"That it was all a big conspiracy? That people were out to get him?"

"That's true."

Sacks jabbed Ben again and winked. "Trust me. You don't want intelligent jurors."

"But the truth—"

"And what's more, he's a rich white doctor. You know who they really hate?"

"Lawyers?"

"Yeah. But you know who rich white guys hate even more than lawyers? Rich black guys. Guys who had the audacity to crawl out of the ghetto where they belong."

Ben stared at him in disgust. "This is scientific analysis? It's nothing more than a bunch of stereotypes and bigotries cobbled together and sold as science for sixty thousand dollars!"

"Kincaid, there's a reason why stereotypes become stereotypes. It's because they're true!"

"Sometimes, yes. But sometimes not. That's why we have voir dire. And that's why all this pseudoscientific hugger-mugger is a waste of time. When all is said and done, you don't know who will be chosen tomorrow. You can't read their minds. You can't see inside their hearts. All we can do is ask them the right questions, look them in the eyes, and take our best guess."

"Kincaid, you go in there tomorrow and . . . *guess*"—he spat out the word—"and you might as well buy your client a one-way ticket to death row."

"I'd rather do that than face a panel of prospective jurors and assume that they're all disgusting, close-minded bigots!"

It went downhill from there. Technically, they were still speaking, but relations were strained to say the least. Messages to and fro were couriered by Jones. Separate cars were taken to the courthouse.

The marshals ushered Barrett to the defendant's table before the jury arrived. He seemed impressively calm and collected, given what was about to begin. Ben knew he had to be tearing himself apart inside.

Once the bailiff had called all the names, the prosecution, a team of three headed by Jack Bullock, would have a chance to address the jurors directly. And after him, Ben. And then it would be time to pick.

Thank goodness Christina was here, Ben thought. Her instincts he trusted. He could only hope to keep Sacks at bay, to keep his statistics and studies from tainting her.

The bailiff had called the last name, but no one moved. All eyes scanned the courtroom.

"Are you here?" the bailiff asked.

Ben spotted a woman in the front row of the gallery—slender, mid-forties, with a look of great deliberation on her face. Something was going on in her head. Whatever it was, she couldn't make up her mind.

"Let me try it again," the bailiff said. He glanced down at the slip of paper in his hand. "The last juror is Deanna Meanders."

CHAPTER

34

DEANNA REALIZED SHE needed to do something, and quickly, but for some strange reason she couldn't get her feet to move. What was she doing here? She should never have come; she should've gotten her boss to say she was indispensible or pleaded dependent children or something. Stupid or not, though, she was here now, and the man was calling her name, and she needed to get off her butt and move.

She pushed herself to her feet and took her seat in the jury box. Well, surely she wouldn't actually be selected for the jury. What were the odds? She knew scores of jurors were excused in these big capital murder cases. They would find some reason to boot her. Especially after she told them . . .

Ah, there's the rub. Would she tell them? She knew she should, knew she was morally obligated to tell them.

But would she?

Well, she told herself, she wouldn't volunteer anything, but if they asked the right questions, she would answer honestly.

Right. She almost laughed out loud. What could they possibly ask that would unravel her secret? Excuse me, ma'am, but by any chance is your daughter involved with a man who you think may actually have been responsible for the slaughter of the defendant's family? Somehow she just didn't think that one was going to come up.

Did she think she could consider the evidence presented, forgoing all outside knowledge she might have, and reach a fair verdict? No way in hell.

The question then was, would she keep quiet about it, or would she do the right thing?

And the problem was, if she did the right thing, what would happen to Martha?

She couldn't believe that Martha had knowingly played a part in the murders. Despite all the heartache they'd shared these past few years, she knew Martha was fundamentally a generous, caring person.

But the district attorney, of course, did not know Martha. If Barrett was acquitted and the DA had to find another suspect, he might just stumble onto Buck. And from Buck, it would be a short hop to Martha.

Would he go after Martha as an accessory? Of course he would. He would have no choice. The public would demand it. The media would cry for it. They much preferred conspiracies to lone gunmen, after all. Conspiracies were so much sexier, so much more intriguing.

Martha would go to prison. Maybe not forever, but long enough to irreparably ruin her life. Scars like that you didn't bounce back from.

So would Deanna do the right thing?

How could she? She was a mother, for God's sake. Her whole life was based on the premise that she must take care of her daughter, protect her, shepherd her, help her find a happy and productive life. She couldn't let this tragedy happen. She just couldn't. Even if . . .

She turned her head slightly and gazed at ex-mayor Wallace Barrett sitting next to his attorney at the defense table. He was trying to be strong, she could tell, but he was worried. She could see it in his face. Who wouldn't be? With what he was going through. What, in part, she was putting him through.

She looked away and stared at her hands.

Yeah. Even if.

35

BULLOCK, AS LEAD attorney for the prosecution, got the first shot at the panel of prospective jurors. He approached them with his usual calm demeanor. He was very good in front of juries, as Ben well knew. He was also smart, knowledgeable, and determined, but most of all, he had that special quality that evoked a positive response from the jury. A certain confidence, perhaps, or an air of truthfulness. Whatever it was, it was something that couldn't be learned or taught. You either had it or you didn't.

Bullock did. Ben didn't.

Many times Ben had tried to emulate the man's bearing, his approach, but it never worked. In fact, it was futile to try. All he could do was be himself, and hope for the best.

The usual problem with voir dire was that it was tedious and time-consuming—a too-long prologue before the main event. The jurors were ready to get on with it; but instead, they had to sit through hours of questioning. It was immediately apparent that this would not be a problem today, however. This case was anything but dull, after all, and the jurors were all bright-eyed and bushy-tailed and eager. They wanted to be on this jury. Who wouldn't? It was the trial of the century.

Bullock looked the jurors square in the eye and began. "You know why you're here," he said.

He paused, allowing the words to sink in. "Personally, I wish you didn't. It would make this business of choosing a jury much simpler. But I know you do know. You know what case this jury will hear. And you know . . . the importance of what we are trying to do. The importance of seeing that justice is done."

Ben had to marvel at Bullock's cleverness. He was not making an argument—well, not exactly, your honor—and he was not urging them to convict—well, not exactly, your honor. But close. Close enough that they couldn't possibly miss the point.

"The defendant in this case is a man named Wallace Barrett." He gestured toward the defendant. "Is there anyone here who does not know Mr. Barrett?"

No hands rose.

"Now, that's a problem. We prosecutors always worry about trying celebrities. When people see a man on television or in some sporting event, they start to feel like they know him. They don't, of course. They don't know anything about what he's really like. But they think they do. He's that smiling face on the television screen in their living room. They like him. And that makes it a lot harder to convince them that he may have done something wrong." His voice slowed and dropped an octave. "Even when the crime committed is as hideous as the one in the present case."

Bullock strolled confidently to the opposite end of the jury box. "So I have to ask you this question. Is there anyone who feels that what they already know about Mr. Barrett—or what they think they know—would prevent them from judging the facts and evidence of this case with an open mind? Anyone? Please be honest. I won't put you on the spot. I just want to know."

An older woman in the back row, Marilyn McKensie, hesitantly raised her hand.

"Mrs. McKensie. You think you might have a hard time giving us a fair shake?"

She pursed her lips together, speaking slowly. "No. I'm just afraid . . . Well, I've heard so much about all the awful things he did to his family, I just don't know if I could believe anything he or his lawyer had to say."

A loud buzz rose from the press section. Ben jumped to his feet. "Your honor—"

Judge Hart nodded. She knew very well the prejudicial nature of the remarks the woman had just made in the earshot of every prospective juror. Remarks like that could end the trial before it had begun.

Judge Hart leaned toward the jury box. "Mrs. McKensie, you must realize that no one has proven that the defendant has done anything. He is presumed to be innocent."

"Oh, right. But everyone knows—"

"Mrs. McKensie," the judge continued firmly, "in this state, defendants are innocent until proven guilty. No evidence has yet been adduced against the defendant. That means that at this point in time he is innocent and you must be able to consider him as such. Do you understand?"

"Yes, I know the rules, but—"

"There are no buts. That's the way it is."

Mrs. McKensie licked her lips, fell back into her chair, and didn't say anything more.

The judge addressed the jury at large. "I will admonish the jury—that is, all the prospective jurors—that they should not discuss or draw any conclusions until the evidentiary part of the trial is over, and furthermore, what conclusions you do draw should be based upon the evidence presented at trial and nothing else. Mrs. McKensie's remarks should be disregarded in their entirety." She turned back to Ben, a weary expression on her face. "All right, counsel?"

Ben nodded. "Thank you, your honor." He could read what was in her eyes quite clearly; he was thinking the same thing himself. If they couldn't get past the first voir dire question without a prejudicial incident, what hope did they have of actually completing a fair and unbiased trial?

Mrs. McKensie was excused and replaced, and Bullock continued with his questions, carefully but systematically probing the venirepersons about their jobs, their significant others, their habits and hobbies. Most of his questions did not bear a direct relationship to the case. Many followed up on seemingly trivial matters that had been mentioned in answers to the written interrogatories. Most were easily answered questions. Bullock never pressed anyone or embarrassed them.

And Ben knew why, too. He could still remember the advice Bullock had given him so many years ago. "People think the main point of voir dire is to find out about the jury," he had said, "but they're wrong. That's okay if you happen to be able to read minds. But the realistic best thing you can do during voir dire is let the jury find out about you. Let them learn to like you, to trust you. If you can get that, then later in your closing argument when you tell them to convict, they will. They'll do whatever you want. Fact is, trials are long and complicated, and the jurors have a hard time following everything. Most of their decisions are based principally on who the jurors think they can trust, not on the evidence. Once they figure out who they can trust, they do whatever that person tells them to do."

And Bullock was a master at earning jurors' trust. Ben knew that by the time Bullock was done, the jurors would have nothing but respect for the assistant district attorney. Ben would have to be just as good, and to have better evidence, if he expected to win them over.

As he watched Bullock examine the jury, Ben made two distinct observations, both disturbing. First, he noticed that the jury seemed uncommonly cooperative, even eager. Jurors were usually indifferent as to whether they were chosen. These people, however, seemed to want to be chosen. Ben supposed that was only natural. It was a big trial; it was something you could tell your grandchildren about.

The other thing Ben noticed was the serious, probing, nonhyperbolic nature of the questions Bullock was asking. The prosecutor seemed to want a smart jury.

Now that was a frightening thought.

Ben's opportunity to examine the jurors did not arrive until mid-afternoon. He straightened his tie, put on his most earnest expression, approached the jury box and introduced himself.

"All we are interested in is fairness," Ben told them, and he hoped they believed it. "As I'm sure you've gathered from Mr. Bullock's remarks, the charges against my client, Wallace Barrett, are very serious, so we want him to have the most fair hearing possible."

He glanced back at Barrett and smiled. "That's why I'll be asking you these questions. Please don't feel like I'm trying to pry into your personal life. I'm not. I'm just trying to learn as much as possible so that we can choose the fairest jury possible."

With that, Ben launched into a harmless series of questions designed to elicit the most obvious kinds of bias. Do you know the mayor personally? Did you ever work for him or his staff? Were you involved in the mayoral campaign? Ben knew the answers would be no, but he needed something safe and nonconfrontational to get the ball rolling.

The next level of scrutiny was considerably more complicated. Normally Ben would begin by asking if anyone knew the defendant. The problem here was everyone knew the defendant. Everyone had seen him on television. Everyone had voted for or against him. And everyone knew what he was accused of doing.

"I know you all know who Mr. Barrett is. You've already told Mr. Bullock about that. But are there any of you who have some personal or private information that might affect your deliberations?"

A middle-aged man on the second row raised his hand.

"Mr. Torres," Ben asked, "do you think you might have some preconceptions or ideas that might affect your serving on this jury?"

"I do," the man said firmly. "I don't like what he done. Not one bit."

Ben proceeded cautiously. "You must realize, sir, that we are gathered here to determine what, if anything, he has done."

"I ain't talkin' about no murder. I'm talkin' about that pension plan for sanitation workers."

Ben did a double take. "That what?"

"The pension plan. He cut back the pension plan. Said he had to cut the sales tax. Fools like me that's worked for the city for twenty years, we were depending on that money."

"Sir, you must realize that that is not what this trial is about."

"I know that. I ain't no fool. Jus' the same, I'm gonna have a hard time forgettin' that he's the man who screwed up my retirement. I bet a lot of other folks feel the same way."

Ben took a deep breath. This was a wrinkle he had not anticipated. Barrett had told Ben he tried to get raises for city employees; he hadn't said anything about cutting the pension plan. At least four of the jurors worked for the city in one capacity or another, as well as two of the jurors' spouses. "Sir, this trial is being convened to consider whether Mr. Barrett has committed a crime. It is not a referendum on his political positions."

"That may be, Mr. Defense Attorney," Torres snapped back. "But I still don't have my pension plan."

Ben glanced back at Barrett. He was tugging his left earlobe, their pre-arranged signal for "get this man off the jury!" Unfortunately, Torres had said nothing that would absolutely indicate that he was unable to evaluate innocence or guilt and thus would mandate dismissal for cause. Ben would have to wait and use one of his preemptories.

"Is there anyone else who feels that their political differences might make it difficult to consider the accusations against Mr. Barrett fairly?"

Ben detected a few tiny movements, but no hands rose. But of course not. He had asked the question wrong, had asked them to draw the conclusion.

"Well, is there anyone in the jury who particularly dislikes a political decision my client has made?"

Six hands shot into the air. Add that to the six jurors connected to city employees, and Ben realized he was going to be discussing this subject for a good long time.

TWO HOURS LATER, Ben decided that he had learned all he could possibly know, and far more than he had wanted to know. The truth was, his client was a celebrity, and whether anyone cared to admit it or not, celebrities were treated differently in this country, including in the justice system. The idea that he could select a panel of jurors who would not bring any preconceived notions to the trial was laughable.

The next topic on Ben's agenda was even more delicate than the previous one. Racism. The problem here was that no one was going to admit to being a racist, not even the Grand Dragon of the Ku Klux Klan. Ben knew—he'd tried it before. If he was going to make any headway, he was going to have to try a subtler approach.

"As you're all aware, my client is a black man. As I gaze out in the jury box, though, I see that only two of you are black, and one Hispanic. Is this a problem?"

Ben knew he wasn't going to get an answer to a question like that. He just wanted to put the topic on the table and let them think about it.

"Don't get the wrong idea. I'm not accusing anybody of anything. But I know very well, from the work I've done on previous cases, that some people harbor less than charitable feelings about members of other races. Maybe you had a bad experience when you were young. Maybe your parents told you things that you accepted without questioning. It doesn't matter how it happens, but sometimes it does happen. It's nothing we like to admit. But it's there."

There was a long pause. Ben walked to the opposite end of the jury box. "I'm not going to put anyone on the spot. I'm not going to try to trick you into confessing your sins in public. I'm just going to do this. I'm going to ask you all to close your eyes."

Out the corner of his eye, Ben saw Bullock twitch and half rise to his feet. Then he stopped. Ben could imagine the thoughts racing through his head. Yes, this was certainly irregular. But what exactly would your objection be? Bullock settled back into his chair.

Ben returned his attention to the jury box. "All right, all eyes closed? Fine. Now I want anyone who thinks they may have some biases or prejudices that might prevent them from being absolutely fair in this trial to raise their hand. No one will know. Just raise your hand. I won't identify you. I will see that you're removed from the jury, but I won't say why. You'll just be one of many who end up not serving. Okay? Look deep into your heart. Be honest with me. Be honest with yourself. If you can't be a fair and impartial juror, raise your hand. Please."

Ben waited a full ten seconds. No one raised a hand. Well, it was a nice try.

And then, to his astonishment, a hand inched into the air. Mrs. Applebee, an older woman in the middle row, slowly hoisted her hand.

"All right," Ben said, "all hands down. And you may open your eyes. Thank you for your cooperation."

After that, Ben ran through a myriad of questions on a myriad of topics, trying to learn more about the jurors, trying to unearth random bits of information that might be more telling than anything he could discover through direct questioning.

The responses he got were straightforward, reflective, and occasionally surprising. Christina jotted down some of the highlights:

"Criminals have too many rights. What about the victims?"

"I like to unwind at night with a frozen margarita, *The New York Times* crossword puzzle, and Regis and Kathie Lee. I tape the show every day. I love that man."

"I just don't understand people today. Sex, sex, sex—it seems like that's all anyone cares about. Personally, I don't see what the big fuss is."

"Corporations control America. Everyone's just in it for a buck."

"Did you ever wonder—when you're smelling a flower, is it smelling you?"

"I believe that key personnel in our government have been abducted and replaced by alien beings."

"My brother-in-law Harold was the second gunman on the grassy knoll."

"Counsel, do you mind if I ask where you got that tie?"

"I can't stand lawyers. Nothing personal."

AFTER VOIR DIRE was finally completed, Ben huddled in a side room with his client, Christina, and of course, Harold Sacks, the juror consultant.

"All right," Ben said, "let's start with the foregone conclusions. Mrs. McKensie is removed, preferably to another county. Torres obviously can't stand you, Wallace."

"Agreed," Barrett said.

"So he's out. What else?"

"I think the alien abduction lady has to go," Christina offered.

"Really?" Ben raised an eyebrow. "I figured you'd want to make her the foreperson."

Christina offered an extremely thin smile.

"All right, enough fun. Now let's do the serious work." Sacks shoved his way into the middle of the huddle. He was holding a clipboard with charts and diagrams showing the position of each prospective juror. He had also worked up brief Jungian personality profiles of each, indicating whether they were an ESTJ personality type, or INFP, or whatever. Finally he had rated their likely compatability to Wallace Barrett on a scale from one to one hundred. "One thing is obvious. That old woman in the back, Donnelly, has to go."

Ben's head tilted to one side. "Really?"

"Oh, yeah. She's exactly our worst statistical, demographic and personality type."

"I thought she seemed sympathetic when I hammered on the 'presumed innocent' standard."

"She was just being polite."

"And I thought she seemed skeptical of some of the stuff Bullock was trying to ram down their throats."

"How would you know what she's thinking?"

"I used my eyes."

"Look, Kincaid, have you done a statistical workup?"

"No."

"Then shut up and let me do my job." He flipped a page on his clipboard. "Now, needless to say, both of the black men stay."

"Wait a minute," Ben said. "One of them, Jeffers, has a daughter who works at the sheriff's office."

"Yeah. So?"

"So?" Ben stared at the man. "So, first, he's probably got a huge law enforcement bias. And second, he's probably sitting there stewing about how Wallace Barrett ruined his daughter's pension, especially now that Torres has reminded him about it."

"You're just guessing, Kincaid."

"True, but—"

"What I have here are facts. Data. Analysis. You can guess all you want about what he's thinking, but I know for a fact that he's black, and that gives us an edge."

"You don't know that. You're just guessing, too. You stick an equation on top of it to make it seem more reliable, but you're still just guessing."

"It's not a guess, it's a fact." He nudged Barrett in the side. "All you black boys stick together, right?"

Barrett stared at him wordlessly.

"Your statistics don't mean a damn thing," Ben said. "All that matters is what those twelve people in the box think. They might be a demographically representative group, or then again, they might not be."

"I've already made up my mind, Kincaid. He stays."

Ben imagined he could feel the steam rising off the top of his head. He gave Barrett a sharp look. "Wallace, I think it's fairly clear at this point that the two of us cannot work together. So make a decision. Is he picking this jury, or am I?"

Barrett was still staring at Sacks. His eyes narrowed. Finally he spoke. "You are, Ben."

Sacks threw his hands into the air. "You stupid—" He pounded his fist on his clipboard. "Do you know what you're doing? You're throwing sixty thousand dollars down the drain."

"Actually," Barrett said, "I think I already did that. Now I'm trying to prevent that mistake from costing me my life."

Sacks's face turned a vivid red. He threw his clipboard down on the floor and stomped out of the room.

"Thank you," Ben said.

Barrett nodded in acknowledgment.

"Okay," Ben said, "let's get on with this. Christina, what do you think of the woman on the end of the second row?"

"The anti-sex maniac?"

"Right . . ."

36

"I'M AFRAID WE haven't made much progress," Mike explained. He was sitting on the edge of the desk in his office, thumbing through the contents of a tan file folder. "Your mad bomber didn't leave us much to go on."

"I'm sorry to hear that." After the jury had been selected and Judge Hart recessed the trial for the day, Ben had stopped in at Mike's office to check the progress of the investigation into the bombing of his office. So far he hadn't heard much he liked. "No clues in the wreckage?"

"Clues to how it was done, yes. Clues to the identity of the culprit, no."

Ben pressed his hand against his forehead. He had been hoping for better news. "Are you sure they've tried everything?"

"Ben, I've been involved in this investigation personally. As you know, I worked arson cases for several years. I know how to roll up my sleeves and root around in the ashes. There just wasn't anything there."

Ben nodded grimly. "Say, while you were rooting around in the ashes, you didn't happen to see my opening statement, did you? In all the excitement, I've forgotten what I was planning to say."

Mike smirked. "I expect you'll think of something. Lawyers always do." Mike walked behind his desk where he kept a small compact refrigerator, opened it, and pulled out a Red Dog. "Care for a beer?"

"Thanks, no. Have to deal with Joey."

"And I'm on duty. But why be a stickler about details?" He screwed off the top and took a long draw. "Are you sure you don't have any idea who's gunning for you, Ben?"

"I'm sure. Who would do something like this?"

"I don't know." He paused. "Unless he's someone you really pissed off."

"I don't think so. I think it's someone who's been drinking in the endless press coverage of this trial. Someone who believes this really is the trial of the century."

Mike smiled. "Have you noticed how one of those comes along about every two or three years?"

"I suppose if someone listened to that media crap long enough, and watched it often enough, defense attorney Ben Kincaid might start to seem like a celebrity worth stalking. I've been more visible on television during the last two weeks than Heather Locklear."

"Not in nearly as good shape, though." Mike took another swallow. "You can't fault the press for covering the story. It's a matter of public interest."

"Bull. This is a private tragedy that the press has latched onto because a celebrity is involved. Worse crimes occur every day. But the press loves celebrity stories. They sell papers; they boost ratings."

"I think you're wrong, Ben. This case raises a lot of serious issues."

"That's the excuse the press always uses. If they want to publicize some lurid statutory rape, well, it's a child-abuse issue. If they want to dig up trivial mistakes a candidate made thirty years ago, it's a trust issue. If they want to pry into someone's sex life, it's a character issue. What it really is, is a tawdry effort to pander to our worst instincts by sensationalizing the news and turning reporters into gossip columnists."

"Well, if you went a little easier on the press, this case might go better for you."

"True. And isn't that a pathetic statement? If I play up to the media—not the jury, not the judge, but the *media*—my client might have a better shot at acquittal. Tell me who's running the justice system now."

"Speaking of which." Mike reached behind his desk and lifted a hardcover book with a glossy photo dust jacket. "Have you seen this?"

Ben took the book from him. It was titled *The Whole Truth, and Nothing But.* It was written by Cynthia Taylor, Caroline's sister. On the cover was a photo of Wallace Barrett, obviously taken during an off moment when he was not aware he was being photographed. His eyes were hooded; he seemed to be looking deviously out of their corners. He was wearing a tank top. His fists were pressed together in such a way that his biceps bulged. He looked like a thug. At the top left, about where his brain should be, were fuzzy, spectral images of the murder victims.

"Cynthia probably snapped the main photo at that gym where she works," Ben commented. "Of course, it presents Wallace in a distorted manner."

"Distorted or not, that book had an initial hardcover print run of three hundred thousand copies. She's been on all the talk shows promoting it. Even Oprah!"

"Why would television shows participate in this obvious attempt to influence—"

"They don't see it that way. It's supposedly a serious discussion of a serious issue—domestic abuse. You need to get out more, Ben. This book is everywhere. It's in bookstores, drugstores, groceries." He paused. "Everywhere your jurors shop."

"Great." He thumbed through the relatively short book. "Man, she must've written this practically overnight."

"I expect she had some help, don't you?"

Ben tossed the book back on Mike's desk. "Surely no one will read this obviously biased crap."

"Obviously biased sells, Ben. People want the dirt. This is a very effective bit of propaganda. Nothing the prosecution has done or probably will do will influence as many people's opinions as this book does."

"I can't believe people would support such an unmitigated attempt to get rich quick on her sister's murder."

"Ah, but you see, she's donating all the profits to various women's shelters across the country. At least that's what she's saying on the talk shows."

"Great."

"Don't worry. I understand Barrett's supporters are preparing an instant book for him. That's going to be a fund-raiser, too. To help that multi-millionaire cope with the backbreaking burden of paying your legal fees."

"Are you serious? He hasn't mentioned this to me."

"Well, you're not exactly likely to be supportive, are you? He'll probably fill you in sometime after the Dove audiobook hits the stands."

Ben frowned. "He probably thinks a sympathetic book will improve his image. And he's probably right. There are already four books on the market that paint him as some demented demon from hell, not counting Cynthia's. So long before I can call witnesses to tell the jury what really happened, the media will be leaking the allegations from these books and treating them as fact. By the time I get a chance to tell people what really happened, no one will believe it. Another example of how the media distort the trial process."

Mike hoisted his bottle and polished off the rest of his beer. "Well, I'm not as concerned about the distorted trial process as I am about this distorted wacko who seems determined to distort you. I've already got a man at your apartment, and I'm posting one at your hotel, too. If you hear anything more from Sick Heart, I want to know about it immediately."

"Don't worry. You will."

"And I mean anything, Ben. Don't hold out on me."

Ben had to smile. The concern on Mike's face was evident and genuine. It was comforting to think that even as a grumpy grown-up, he still had a few friends in the world. "Thanks, I won't."

"And good luck at the trial tomorrow." He propped his feet on his desk and pointed at the nine-inch television on the corner of his desk. "I'll be watching."

Ben frowned. "I know. You and everyone else."

"I DON'T MIND staying," Joni was saying as she scurried through Ben's apartment gathering her belongings. "I know you've got that big trial tomorrow. I mean, who doesn't, right? If you want me to hang around so you can prepare, that's fine."

"Thanks, no." He glanced down at Joey, who was silently playing with a set of dinosaur figures Joni had picked up at Imaginarium. "I want to spend some time with Joey. Then I want to hit the sack."

"Okay. Well, I fixed his dinner, it's in the refrigerator—macaroni and cheese—so he should eat it. His crib has clean sheets and there's a clean pair of pajamas draped across the sofa."

"Thanks." He walked her to the door. "Good night."

A man who was obviously a plainclothes policeman sat at a small desk at the top of the stairs. He rose to his feet when Ben opened the door.

"Tomlinson!" Ben said. "I thought you were working homicide now. What are you doing on this security detail?"

Tomlinson grinned amiably. "Personal favor to Mike. He's really worried about you, you know. I think he'd be here himself, except he knows you'd tell him to get lost."

"He's right." Ben stepped back inside the doorway. "Well, I suppose I'd better lock the door. But if you need anything, just holler."

"Will do."

"I'll make a duplicate key for you tomorrow. I'm going to put this kid to bed now and hit the sack."

"That'll be fine. You take care of yourself in that courtroom tomorrow."

Ben smiled. "I'll be fine. 'Night."

Ben closed the door. I'll be fine. That was what he kept saying, anyway. He wondered if he could possibly make anyone believe it.

He swooped Joey up in the air and held him above his head. "Look, it's Super-Joey! Faster than a speeding bullet, more powerful than a locomotive . . ." He laughed, then brought the child down and gave him a tremendous bear hug. Did Joey laugh, too? Ben checked his face. There was definitely some sort of gurgling noise. Gas, perhaps? Or had he maybe decided being stuck with Uncle Ben wasn't such a bad thing after all? Maybe he was going to say a few words, crack a few jokes.

Well, no. Joey seemed as impassive as ever. There was no sign of a smile, much less a laugh. Just the same barren expression that told Ben nothing.

"What's going on in there?" Ben said, squeezing the boy gently. "I wish you would talk to me."

But he didn't. Ben sighed, then lowered Joey to the ground. Joey crawled back to his dinosaur figures and began arranging them in a long orderly line.

Ben knew he probably should prepare for trial, but he was too beat. Maybe just a song or two on the piano, or maybe he could spin that new Janis Ian CD. Then bed. He'd get up early tomorrow and do whatever needed to be done. Who knew? With any luck, by that time Christina might've already done it for him.

Ben crawled across the carpet and peered into Joey's eyes. "I wish you would talk to me," he repeated. "Or just make a noise. A sound. Anything."

But there was no response. A wave of guilt and suppressed depression flooded over Ben. He'd been holding it back, trying not to think about it while he dealt with the more pressing crises. The trial. The maniac.

He stared at his front door. The unknown monster lurking somewhere on the other side of that door. How had he let this happen?

Ben closed his eyes. He couldn't deal with it all at once. He hoisted Joey into the air. "What would you say to some macaroni and cheese, pal? Probably not much, huh?"

He pushed the swinging door and entered the kitchen. Small wonder I do such a wretched job of taking care of you, Joey, he thought to himself. I can't even take care of myself.

37

BEN WAS AMAZED at the speed at which the trial cruised into first gear the next morning. Given the intense scrutiny given every word, every minor action or ruling, the trial made astounding progress. Or perhaps it only seemed that way because he was dreading every minute of it.

All the preliminary matters were dispensed with in less than half an hour. By nine-thirty, Judge Hart called for opening statements. Jack Bullock was standing before the jury again, assuring them in his calm, trustworthy manner that everything he said was correct.

"I'm not here to put on a show," he told the jury, one hand in his pocket and one hand on the railing. "I won't patronize you. I won't humor you. I won't try to win you over with courtroom tricks or flashy flourishes. I will let the facts speak for themselves. And believe me, they speak volumes."

He paused, then walked thoughtfully to the opposite side of the jury box. "You already know what happened. I won't melodramatize it." He stopped again, and his face screwed up slightly. "The facts are horrible enough as they are."

He walked to an easel, where several enlarged photos rested face down. "These are the photos taken at the crime scene. I won't show them to you now. I wouldn't do that to you. I wouldn't be that . . . cruel."

Ben suppressed a smile. In fact, Bullock had wanted to use the photos in his opening, but the judge wouldn't permit it.

"You will, unfortunately, have to look at them later in this trial. This is what you will see." He held his hands up chest-high, as if creating an imaginary television screen for them. "The defendant's wife and the mother of his children—lifeless, draped backward over a dining room chair, almost every inch of her skin and clothes soaked and smeared with coagulated blood. Knife punctures in over twenty different places. She died, although the coroner's testimony will reveal that she died neither quickly nor painlessly."

Bullock removed the second of the still facedown photos. "In the upstairs bedroom, the defendant's four-year-old daughter lying on her bed, a fatal puncture wound through her heart. Her hands folded across her chest in a grotesque parody of sleep."

Bullock withdrew the third photo in the stack. Ben could only admire Bullock's brilliant presentation. He was using the photos without showing them. In fact, this was better. He was creating an enormous sense of anticipation, causing the jury to hang on his every word and to wait breathlessly for the evidence he had to share with them.

"And finally," Bullock continued, "in the bathroom, the defendant's eight-year-old daughter. Dead—stabbed. Many times. And once again— blood everywhere."

Bullock stepped away from the exhibits and rubbed his hands, as if washing away the blood and horror. "The crime scene alone tells us much about the person who committed these horrors. Obviously it was someone strong, someone . . . physical. Someone with access to the Barretts' home. Someone consumed with hate. Not just a random grudge but a personal and specific enmity."

Slowly and deliberately, Bullock moved back toward the prosecution table. "There has never been much doubt in the minds of the law enforcement community who committed this crime. The Barretts' next-door neighbor saw Wallace Barrett flee from his home at the approximate time of the murders. Barrett then led several police officers on a high-speed chase down the Indian Nation Turnpike, a chase many of you watched on television. Was there any doubt in the minds of those who watched that chase why Wallace Barrett was running? I don't think so. Common sense will answer that question for you. And if common sense isn't enough, the witnesses we call to the stand, experts in their field, will give you rock-solid scientific evidence that will establish his guilt beyond question. Fingerprints. Blood analysis. DNA evidence. All pointing to the same culprit." He turned and pointed. "Wallace Barrett."

"The defense will undoubtedly expend all their energy trying to convince you that what is obvious is not true. I don't know what their story will be. You see, in our criminal justice system, the prosecution has to give the defendant everything they've got, but the defendant doesn't have to give the prosecution anything. So I can only guess. Maybe they'll tell you it was all a mistake. Maybe they'll tell you it was an accident. Maybe they'll tell you it was drug dealers or Middle Eastern terrorists or some supernatural refugee from a Stephen King novel. Who knows? With some lawyers, the bigger the lie, the more convincing it seems. I can only ask that you disregard the theatrics, that you not be swayed by fancy footwork. Remember the evidence. Remember the facts. Listen to what common sense tells you. Listen to your heart. And do the right thing."

Bullock paused. For a moment, Ben thought he might be finished. Then he raised a finger. "As you weigh the gamut of *what ifs* the defense offers to you, you may wish to keep one telling fact in your mind. When the police arrived after the fact in the living room of the Barrett home, they found a framed photo of Caroline Barrett that had been thrown against the wall and smashed. Ask yourself this question: Would a burglar stop to destroy Mrs. Barrett's photo? Would a terrorist? Would a hit man? I will suggest to you that no one would smash that photo—except someone who knew her personally . . . and hated her. Someone who had decided that he couldn't live with her any longer. That he *wouldn't* live with her any longer."

Bullock laid his hands gently on the rail. "By the time this trial is completed, I believe you will know not only who committed this crime, but why. At that time, I will ask you to do what must be done, even though some of you may find it personally unpleasant, even painful. Perhaps some of you recall the defendant from his football days or his press conferences and think of him as an amiable, good-natured fellow. Well, the Wallace Barrett you will meet in this courtroom—the real Wallace Barrett—is an entirely different person. A harder, more evil, more . . . malevolent man. A man who beat and tortured his wife. A man who terrorized his children. A man who used brute force to achieve his every petty desire. A man with a temper, a temper that, when it exploded, made him capable of anything. Absolutely anything." He gestured toward the downturned photographs. "Even this."

He turned back and looked each of them in the eyes. "Once you have met that man, I believe you will be able, will perhaps even be anxious, to do what must be done. To do the right thing."

He glanced up at the bench. "Thank you, your honor."

Judge Hart leaned forward. "Thank you, counsel. Mr. Kincaid, do you wish to make your opening remarks at this time?"

"I do." Ben gathered his notes and moved toward the jury box. He had not expected to be called so soon. In your average big murder case, opening statements often went on for hours. But, Ben realized, Jack Bullock was not your average prosecutor. He was much smarter. He knew he didn't need to give the jury every little detail about this case. They already knew what it was about. He just needed to tell them enough to get them to trust him, to believe him, and to make them eager to hear what he would have to say next. And at that he had succeeded.

"Ladies and gentlemen of the jury." Ben cleared his throat awkwardly. He wished again, for about the millionth time, that he had some of the finesse that Bullock brought so masterfully to the courtroom. "Ladies and gentlemen, Wallace Barrett did not commit this crime. Let me say it again." Ben paused to give each word its own punch. "Wallace Barrett did not commit this crime.

Now I know you will hear people say that he did; you have already heard people say that he did. But he didn't. *I* know that. And by the end of this trial, you will know it, too."

"I am about to offer you two words, the two most important words you will hear during the entire course of this trial. Reasonable doubt." He smiled, hoping perhaps just one of the jurors would smile back. They didn't. "As the judge will instruct you later, you cannot convict this man of this crime if you have a reasonable doubt about whether he committed it. That's the standard. Not more likely than not. Not a seventy-five percent chance or better. *No* reasonable doubt. Doesn't even have to be a great big doubt. If you have a reasonable doubt, you must bring back a verdict of not guilty. That's the law."

Ben dropped his notes and legal pads on the table and returned to the jury box. He didn't need them; they were just a crutch. Bullock didn't use notes, and he knew that the jury was subtly comparing the two of them, trying to decide whether Ben measured up. He needed to seem as if he was speaking from the heart, not from a prepared text.

"I'm sure you remember everything the prosecution has told you about their evidence. Let's talk about everything they didn't tell you. Let's talk about everything they don't have or won't show you. They'll tell you they are certain that Wallace Barrett committed this crime, but did anyone see him commit this crime? No. Did anyone hear the crime being committed? No. There are no eyewitnesses, no earwitnesses. The closest they come is one neighbor who saw Barrett at his home at the approximate time of the murder. But why shouldn't he have been there? He lived there! That proves nothing.

"The evidence will show that when Barrett left his home that day, his children and wife were alive and well, and that no one was more shocked than he to later find they had been killed. He was shocked and devastated. Emotionally confused. He didn't know what to do. So he got in the car and drove. Didn't even know where he was going. He just knew he had to get away from there. The prosecution would have you believe that this was some high-speed flight from justice. It was nothing of the sort. As the evidence will show, Barrett didn't even see any policemen chasing him until just shortly before he crashed into the tollbooth.

"This need to run, to get away, may seem strange, even irrational, to you, but ask yourself this question: if you came home and found your entire family had been slaughtered, mightn't you be just a bit irrational? Mightn't you make a mistake or two?"

"Your honor." Bullock had risen to his feet. "I'm sorry to interrupt, but I have to interpose an objection. This is becoming quite argumentative."

"I'll sustain that objection," Judge Hart said. "Counsel, please stick to the preview of the evidence that will be presented. Save the argument for later."

"Yes, your honor." Ben had known full well that this portion of his remarks might draw an objection. But the specter of this high-speed chase that had been witnessed by virtually everyone was so damning he knew he had to try to dismantle it as soon as possible, whether it drew an objection or not. And it was rather difficult for him to stick strictly to a preview of the evidence he would put on, since he was still uncertain what in the world he would be putting on. In fact, there was only one witness he could count on for certain.

"Some of you may be wondering—will Wallace Barrett take the stand? This is often a point of great curiosity and suspense throughout a trial. Well, let me see if I can alleviate some of the suspense. Wallace Barrett will take the stand. Does he have to? Of course not. The Fifth Amendment provides that he doesn't have to say a word. Frankly, I usually advise my clients not to. But Wallace Barrett wants to take the stand. He wants to talk to you, he wants to tell you his story. Because he's an innocent man. And he wants you to know it."

Ben racked his brain for another subject that should be broached on opening. Nothing leaped to mind. He thought he'd covered most of the high points. He decided to move to the wrap-up.

"Before I sit down, I would like to leave you with one question. This is a question I would like you to keep inside your head, to ask yourself throughout the course of the prosecution's case. Mr. Bullock has told you that the police pursued Wallace Barrett as their suspect from the very beginning, and that's true. They never considered any other suspect. They never investigated any other suspect. Never even questioned another suspect. So as you listen to the testimony, ask yourself this: Are they going after Wallace Barrett because he is the only possibility—or because he was the easiest possibility?"

Ben glanced up at the judge. "That's all I have, your honor."

Judge Hart swiveled to face the courtroom. "Very well, opening statements being completed, and since there is still ample time before lunch, the prosecution may call its first witness."

Ben nodded at his client, clapped him on the shoulder, sat down, and gripped the edges of his table.

It had begun.

38

THE PRESS HAD been speculating for days as to who would be the first witness the prosecution called to the stand. Would they try to hit a home run first time at the plate, or would they build slow and easy, starting with the dullish forensic evidence and saving the high drama for later? When the announcement was finally made, it was almost anticlimactic.

"The State calls Cynthia Taylor, your honor."

Well, Ben mused, she was a natural choice. Everyone knew the victim's sister; she had, after all, been on magazine covers and television talk shows throughout the preceding month. She was an appealing witness, personally attractive, well-spoken. She was someone the jury would take seriously, would be sure to listen to carefully. She was in a position to comment and reflect on almost every aspect of the case. And she could be counted on to help the prosecution in any way she possibly could to see Wallace Barrett convicted of her sister's murder.

She was wearing a black pantsuit, stylish, although it tended to obscure her trim, athletic figure. Probably a smart strategy; they didn't want the jury writing her off as a self-absorbed pretty face. She spoke in a clear yet fragile voice, like thin glass, crystal clear for now, but capable of shattering at the slightest pressure. She introduced herself, explained her relationship to the key players, and told the jury that she taught aerobics part-time at a local gym and was also the president of the local chapter of Domestic Violence Intervention Services.

"Would you say you were close to your sister, the late Caroline Taylor Barrett?"

"We were best friends. It was always that way. We're only two years apart in age. We grew up together. We wore the same clothes, had the same friends. We took vacations together. We told each other everything." She smiled bitterly. "She was the best friend I ever had."

"Did you spend a lot of time together?"

"Oh, yes. As much as we possibly could. We loved to talk. We would stay up all night sometimes, just sitting around the kitchen table talking to one another, sharing secrets and favorite things. She was a lot smarter than I was. I remember, the last time we vacationed together, she was reading some Greek tragedy. *Medea*, I think. I was reading Michael Crichton. But she never lorded it over me. She never made me feel stupid."

"Have you always lived in Tulsa?" Bullock asked.

"No. We grew up in Crescent, a much smaller town north of Oklahoma City. We both went to nursing school here in Tulsa. Then I moved away about two and a half years ago."

"Why?"

"Well, I married, and my husband took a job in Chicago. Unfortunately, the marriage broke up about seven months ago. After the divorce was final, I returned to Tulsa."

"Did you see your sister when you returned?"

"Of course I did. In fact, she met me at the airport. She knew I'd been through a . . . difficult time, and she wanted to be there for me." She paused, and her eyes lowered. "She was always there for me."

Bullock also paused, allowing silence to heighten the drama of the moment. "Was she alone when she met you?"

"Oh no. She had—had—" Cynthia's head suddenly dropped, and her hand rushed up to meet it. Her face twisted in the picture of sadness. "She brought her two girls," she said, first whispering, then crying. "My nieces." Tears began to flow from her eyes.

"I'm so sorry," Bullock said solemnly. "I know how hard this must be for you. Your honor, may I approach?"

The judge nodded, and Bullock stepped forward and handed her a tissue which he just happened to have in his coat pocket. She dabbed her eyes, but the tears continued to trickle forth.

"It's all right," she said, whispering again. "They were just so . . . so young and pretty and . . ." She turned abruptly and looked up at the judge. "I'm sorry, your honor. I can go on." She dabbed her eyes again and tried to compose herself.

Bullock gave her plenty of time. He seemed to be in no hurry, or perhaps more accurately, recognized that this emotional display would have more impact on the jury than any number of questions.

"What did you do that day? After she met you."

"Oh . . . I hardly remember." She forced a smile and tried to bravely carry on. "Nothing unusual. Shopping, eating. Just girl stuff. You know."

"Do you recall anything unusual that occurred that day?"

"Oh, yes. It was—" She stopped. "I hardly know what to say. She was wearing sunglasses."

"Was that unusual?"

"Well, yes. I had never seen her wear sunglasses before, and the sun wasn't that bright. And then when we got back to her house, she still wore the glasses."

"Inside?"

"Right. I pointed this out to her, but she just laughed and shrugged it off."

"What did you do then?"

"Well, I became very suspicious. At that time, I'd been associated with DVIS for several years, and I knew that when a woman starts wearing sunglasses she doesn't need to shield her eyes from the sun, it can mean trouble."

"So what did you do?"

"Well, I couldn't get any sort of straight answer out of her, so finally I just reached up and yanked the glasses off her face."

"And what did you see?"

Cynthia hesitated, then turned her head to face the jurors. "Her left eye had a huge black bruise around it. Black and blue and red. I'm not exaggerating when I say it was the ugliest black eye I've ever seen, and I've seen some doozies. It was horrifying."

"What did you say?"

"Well, of course I asked her how this happened. Who did this to you?"

"And what did she say?"

"Objection." Ben jumped to his feet. "Hearsay." Ben knew he would win few points with the jury by preventing them from getting an answer they were dying to hear, but given the circumstances, he had to try.

Bullock barely batted his eyelids. "Of course I think an argument can fairly be made that the declarant is unavailable. Since she's been murdered."

Judge Hart nodded. "And moreover, I find that the circumstances surrounding this testimony suggest unusual trustworthiness. I'm going to allow the testimony."

Ben retook his seat. That was two for Bullock, zip for him.

"Please answer my question," Bullock said, nudging her along. "What did your sister say?"

"Well, at first she told me some cockamamie story about falling down the stairs, but I let her know in no uncertain terms that I wasn't having any of it. So then she told me the truth."

"Which was?"

"He hit her."

"Who?"

"Him." She pointed across the courtroom. "The defendant. Wallace Barrett." She paused. "Her husband."

The courtroom acquired an audible buzz, whispers and scribbling pencils.

It was the first nail in the prosecution's case, the first nail in Wallace Barrett's coffin.

Cynthia continued. "Apparently they'd been to some party, some mayoral function. She didn't even want to go, but he forced her, and then complained that she had had the audacity to actually speak to another man while she was there. He's a very jealous man. Crazy jealous. Irrational. Mean."

"Was this the first time he'd struck her?"

"Objection," Ben said. "Lack of personal knowledge."

Judge Hart nodded. The objection was proper, although given that she had already permitted the hearsay testimony, it was largely a question of semantics. "Counsel, rephrase."

"Certainly," Bullock said. "Anything to please defense counsel. Cynthia, did your sister tell you anything else?"

"Yes. She said this was not the first time her husband had hit her. In fact she told me that on two occasions she'd had to call the police. She hadn't wanted to, she said, but he was out of control. She was afraid—well, she was afraid he might hurt the girls. Or even kill them."

The buzz following that tidbit was even louder. Ben could already hear the sound bite replaying on the six o'clock news.

Bullock continued as if nothing unusual had occurred. "Do you know what caused these incidents?"

"What caused them is Wallace Barrett's insane jealousy and uncontrolled temper."

"Objection!"

Bullock held up his hands. "We'll withdraw that, your honor. I believe the witness misunderstood my question. Cynthia, what I meant was, do you know what provoked the incidents that led to the violence and the police being called?"

"I know about one of them. It was another typical Wallace Barrett fight. Apparently he was laying his clothes out for the next day and he couldn't find the tie he wanted. I mean, can you imagine? Just a stupid tie, that was all. He blew his top because he couldn't find a tie. And of course he blamed her."

"What did your sister say that he did?"

"He beat the hell out of her, that's what he did. And I've seen the pictures, so I know it's true. She had bruises on her face, arms, legs, breasts . . . everywhere." She inhaled and her voice lowered. "That son of a bitch hit her everywhere there was to hit."

"And then?"

"And then he threw her out of the house. I mean he picked her up and bodily threw her out of the house. She wasn't even dressed; she didn't have anything on but her bra and panties. So here she is, practically naked, banging on the front door of her own home, begging him to let her in. But does he? No, he's upstairs watching television or something while she's outside being humiliated. Such a cruel man. Heartless."

"Your honor, I have to object." Ben knew this was probably hopeless, but if nothing else, he could remind the jury that this was grade-A hearsay they were listening to, not an eyewitness account. "The witness is describing this incident as if she was there. She was not. She is simply recounting what she was told in a conversation."

Judge Hart tapped her pencil on her desk. "I understand your concerns, counsel. But the jury has been informed of the circumstances surrounding this testimony. I believe they are in a position to evaluate its credibility for themselves. Overruled."

Something about the judge's even, flat tone bothered Ben. She made every response sound as if she was being scrupulously fair. But the result was always the same. Ben was overruled; Bullock got whatever he wanted.

"What did your sister do?"

"Eventually she went next door and asked a neighbor to take her in. He gave her some clothes and let her stay there till Wallace calmed down. I think his name was Harvey. He's an actor."

Bullock turned to address the court. "The prosecution will be calling Harvey Sanders later to testify about these and other relevant matters." Back to the witness. "Did you ever try to . . . counsel your sister with regard to this repeated violence from her husband?"

"Of course. This was what I did, after all. Working with battered women was second nature to me. What a crushing blow that I couldn't help my own sister. I tried to talk to her, or I offered to have someone else from the shelter come talk to her. She would never agree."

"Why? What explanation did she give?"

"Oh, different things. She said she was taking care of it, or that she could handle it. She said she had to think of her girls first."

"Meaning?"

"Meaning she wouldn't get a divorce and destroy the family. She'd just go on being his personal punching bag." Her hand darted back to her face. "I pleaded with her. Pleaded with her to leave that man. But she wouldn't do it."

"Did that ever change?"

Ben's ears pricked up. He knew Bullock wouldn't ask the question if he didn't know—and like—the answer.

"Yes. She called me on the phone. She said that something had happened—she didn't say what—and she realized she couldn't go on living with this man any longer. She was ready to leave him."

"What did you do?"

"I offered to drive over that very second and pick up her and the girls."

"Did she agree?"

"No. She said she had to tell Wallace first. I tried to talk her out of it. He would only become mad, I told her. Probably violent. He'd try to stop her from leaving. I told her to just go and send a letter later. But she wouldn't. She said fair was fair, or something like that. She was going to confront him."

Bullock took a deep and slow breath. "Cynthia, when was this telephone conversation with your sister? When she said she was going to leave her husband."

"That was the morning of March eleventh. The day she was killed."

Bullock rushed right into the next question. "Cynthia, do you think telling Barrett she was leaving him could have provoked the violence that led to her death and the death of her children?"

"Objection!" Ben shouted, drowning out the answer, but he knew the damage had already been done. The point of Bullock's question was not to elicit an answer. The point was to suggest a rationale, an explanation for this horrible crime. At long last the prosecution had a motive.

"Sustained," Judge Hart said. "Anything more from this witness?"

"Just one more question. Did your sister tell you anything else during that . . . final phone call?"

Cynthia's eyes seemed to blur. "Only about her plans. Our plans. Once she was free from him, we were going to take a trip together, just us and the girls, taking it easy, really getting to know each other. I can't tell you what that meant to me, how much I looked forward to it. Now, it will never . . ." Her hand covered her face. Tears streamed through her fingers. "Now it will never . . . never happen."

Bullock lowered his head sadly and turned away. "Nothing more, your honor."

CHAPTER

39

"WILL THERE BE any cross?" the judge asked.

Ben tried to imagine whether there was anything he would like to do less than cross-examining this tear-stained, grief-stricken witness. Nothing came to mind.

Jeez. No wonder people hated lawyers.

"Yes, your honor." Ben grabbed his notes and strode dutifully to the podium, contemplating his approach. Obviously, trying to come on like the tough guy would be a mistake. He wouldn't get anything out of the witness and the jury would despise him.

He gave her a few more moments to collect herself before he started. "Ms. Taylor, my name is Ben Kincaid, and I'm counsel for the defendant, Wallace Barrett."

"I know," she whispered. "I remember."

"Ms. Taylor, I have a few questions to ask you. Not all that many. I feel I already know most of what you have to say. You see . . . I read your book."

Her head lifted. "What?"

"Your book. *The Whole Truth, and Nothing But.* That is your book, isn't it? It has your name on it."

Cynthia smiled but did not speak.

Ben held up the copy of the book that Mike had given him, with its lurid cover and unflattering photograph. "That's your name on the cover, isn't it?"

She licked her lips. "Yes. That's my name."

"So you wrote this."

"I—uh—well, no."

"No?"

"I told my story to someone else. A professional writer. He wrote it."

"Is there some reason why you used an uncredited ghostwriter?"

She crossed and recrossed her legs. "My publisher felt that . . . time was of the essence."

"Meaning they wanted to get the book on the street fast, while the story was hot, before the trial was over."

"I suppose that's correct."

"You've been very busy since this book came out, right? Even been on some of the national talk shows, I understand."

"That's . . . true."

"Sales good?"

"I . . . don't know any actual figures, but . . . I understand sales are healthy."

Bullock rose wearily to his feet. "Your honor, I fail to see the relevance of this testimony, unless perhaps Mr. Kincaid is hoping to write a book himself. If so, I can give him the name of Ms. Taylor's literary agent and save the court a great deal of time."

Judge Hart tried not to smile. "I think we'll give Mr. Kincaid some leeway here, counsel. This may turn out to have some bearing on the matters at issue."

Ben continued. "Ms. Taylor, did you receive an advance from your publisher?"

"Uh, yes. That's standard procedure, I believe."

"How much did you get?"

Bullock was on his feet again. "Objection! Your honor, this is not relevant. He's just trying to embarrass her."

Judge Hart shook her head. "The witness will answer the question."

Cynthia licked her lips again. "Two hundred and fifty thousand dollars."

Ben's eyes widened. "A quarter of a million bucks?" It was more than even he had imagined. "That's a pretty unstandard advance."

Cynthia shrugged. "I guess they had a lot of confidence in the book."

"I guess so. I would have to imagine, though—for that kind of money, they're going to expect a very good book."

"I'd imagine."

"They're going to want you to tell some juicy stories. Something that will sell that three-hundred-thousand-copy initial print run."

Cynthia's eyes lowered. "What are you suggesting?"

"Well, ma'am, did you ever tell anyone about this alleged abuse to your sister prior to her death?"

"Not that I recall."

"You didn't call the police?"

"I didn't feel it was my place."

"And you didn't report it to any social services agencies. Including the one for which you are president."

"I tried to get Caroline to do that."

"So the whole time your sister was alive, you didn't say a word, but as soon as she's dead, and there are book publishers offering you a quarter of a million bucks, then suddenly you've got a story to tell."

"That's all wrong."

"What did I say that was wrong?"

"It wasn't what you said. It was . . . the way you made it sound. It wasn't like that at all."

"It wasn't?"

"Besides, I'm giving the money to DVIS and several battered women's shelters."

"All of it?"

"Well . . . no, not all of it. I have to live."

Ben nodded. "I'm sure. And I bet you're living a lot better now than you were before this book deal, huh?"

"Objection! Argumentative."

"Sustained." Judge Hart gave Ben a stern look. "Counsel, you know what is and isn't permissible. Don't cross the line again."

"Yes, your honor." Ben glanced down at his notes. Personally, he hated this, but Cynthia and others like her had turned this into a showbiz trial, not him. The jury had to realize the extent to which showbiz was coloring what they saw and heard. "Let me put it this way. If you hadn't had anything interesting to say, the publisher probably wouldn't have paid you all that money for your book, would they?"

"Obviously not."

"Thank you." He'd made his point as clearly as he could. It was time to move on. "Now, Ms. Taylor, you're not exactly an unbiased witness, are you?"

Tiny tendrils of irritation were beginning to crease her eyes and lips. "I don't know what you mean."

"Well, you yourself said you were very close to your sister, right?"

"Right. Absolutely."

"You want to see her murder avenged, right?"

"That's . . . right."

"And you've never liked Wallace Barrett, have you? Not from the start."

Her head bobbed slightly as she considered her response. "No, I've never liked him."

"And your testimony today hasn't done him much good, has it?"

"That's not for me to say."

"Basically, you've come in and trashed a man you admit you don't like, even though you in fact never witnessed any of the incidents to which you testified, correct?"

"That's not correct."

"Did you ever *see* Wallace Barrett strike your sister?"

"Well—no."

"Did you ever see him strike either of the children?"

"No, I—"

"Did you ever see him hug, or kiss, or show affection to his wife or children?"

"Well, yes, of course, but—"

"Nonetheless, you've sat before this jury and painted him as a cold, uncaring monster, based on incidents you never saw, and totally ignoring the many loving moments that you did see."

"He's a mean, cruel bastard!" Her sudden cry echoed through the courtroom. "She knew it and so did I. She was going to leave him."

"But we have only your testimony to that, right?"

"Perhaps so. But it's true. She told me she was going to leave him."

"But she didn't, did she?"

"No. He never gave her a chance."

Ben bit his tongue. Left himself wide open for that one. Best to just ignore it and move on. "Did you perhaps . . . encourage her to leave her husband?"

"I told you I tried to get her to leave. I wanted her out of there before he killed her."

"Your own marriage had broken up."

"So?"

"What was the cause of your divorce?"

Bullock was back on his feet. "Your honor, I protest. This is—"

"I'll allow it," the judge said, cutting him off. "Proceed."

"What caused your divorce, ma'am?"

Her head lowered until nothing was visible but a shadow. "My husband . . . drank. Not too much. But when he did . . . well, he changed. One day he came home and . . . hit me. That's when I left."

Ben nodded soberly. He had suspected as much. "You were a victim of spousal abuse yourself."

"Yes. I've never told anyone, but—yes."

Ben paused, asking the next question as gently as he could. "Ms. Taylor, is it possible that you, having had this horrible experience, *assumed* that your sister was having the same problem?"

"No."

"It's quite a coincidence."

"It's not a coincidence. Wife beating is an epidemic."

"Still, after the murders, when you were looking for answers, perhaps you invented one that seemed . . . appropriate."

"That's not true. I had proof. I saw her black eye."

"You had facts which you interpreted to prove what you wanted to prove."

"My sister told me!" Cynthia leaned forward, almost tipping out of the box. "I know what I heard. Don't try to"—her voice had a catch in it—"don't try to make her life a lie."

"Ma'am, I'm just trying to determine what happened."

"I told you what happened!"

"After you made your two-hundred-and-fifty-thousand-dollar book deal."

"That had nothing to do with it."

"Perhaps you wanted a dramatic story to dramatize the cause of battered women. After all, it's not as if it could do Caroline any harm now if you . . . exaggerated a few details."

"I'm telling the truth!" Her voice screeched out and filled the courtroom. "The man beat her! He's a maniac! She was going to leave him!"

"And if she did," Ben said, "then she'd be free to spend more time with you, right?"

"What?"

"You wanted her to spend more time with you, didn't you?"

"Well . . . yes."

"You encouraged her to leave her husband."

"Damn right I did."

"Where were you all going? Hawaii? I suppose Caroline would have paid your way."

"So? That was her decision."

"Was it?" Ben turned just enough to check the jury. "First you encouraged her to tell you a grossly exaggerated story of spousal abuse that you wanted to hear; then you talked her into leaving her husband, which freed her up to take you to Hawaii."

"That's not true!"

"Your honor, I object." Bullock had positioned himself so that he could make eye contact with both the judge and the television cameras. "This is the most outrageous, cruel abuse of cross-examination I have seen in my entire career. He's not uncovering any new information. He's just torturing a woman who has lost her sister. This is inhuman!"

Judge Hart seemed to think carefully before responding. "Mr. Kincaid, I do have the sense that we have explored this area about long enough. Can we move on?"

"Certainly, your honor." Ben hadn't enjoyed this any more than anyone else. He was more than happy to skip to the next subject. "I just have a few more questions. Ms. Taylor, you spent a great deal of time with your sister, both before and after you were in Chicago, right?"

Cynthia's jaw was tight and grim. "That's right," she said curtly.

"As a result, you must have spent a great deal of time in the company of her husband, Wallace Barrett."

"That's true."

"Ms. Taylor, in the entire twelve-year history of their marriage, did you ever hear Wallace Barrett threaten his wife?"

"She told me—"

"That wasn't my question, ma'am. Please listen carefully and answer the question put to you. Did you ever hear Wallace Barrett threaten his wife?"

Her eyes narrowed. "No."

"Never even once?"

"No."

"Did you ever hear him threaten his children?"

"No."

"In fact, he was very loving toward his children, wasn't he?"

"He . . ." She exhaled heavily. "Yes. He treated his girls very well."

"Did you yourself ever see Wallace Barrett strike his wife or children?"

"No, I did not."

"And you certainly never heard him say he was going to kill them."

She folded her hands in her lap. "No, I did not."

"Thank you. I appreciate your honesty." Ben started away, then, as if in afterthought, turned back to the podium. He knew he'd already gotten everything useful out of this witness he was ever likely to get. But there was one more matter he wanted to inquire about, for his own curiosity's sake, if nothing else. "I just have one more question, Ms. Taylor. Why did you call the city office building?"

The question obviously took her by surprise. "What? What are you talking about?"

"You remember when I came to interview you at your place of work?"

"I remember you were a fairly sad excuse for an aerobicizer."

Ben smiled. "After I left your office, you called the city office building. Where the city council meets and most of the members have offices. Why?"

Her eyes widened. "How do you know who I called?"

"Please answer the question."

"But—"

Judge Hart intervened. "The witness will answer the question."

For the first time, Cynthia seemed flustered. "Well, I don't—I mean—I can't imagine. I don't think . . . oh yes. It must have been DVIS business. That's right. I was working with the city council to toughen the laws on mandatory police investigation of domestic abuse calls. That must have been it."

"I see. So you did call the city council offices, after all."

"Yes, I guess I must have."

"Did you talk to any particular city council member?"

"No, no one in particular."

"Who in general?"

"Well, Loretta Walker was the one who sponsored the ordinance. Brian Erickson has been very supportive."

"Bailey Whitman?"

She looked up at him quickly. "Yes, of course. He's the head of the council."

"Have you had many occasions to talk to Mr. Whitman?"

"Well, I don't— Many? A few. I wouldn't say many."

"But you were in communication with him during the time of the murder and the subsequent investigation."

"Uh, yes. I suppose I was."

"Thank you. No more questions."

Bullock waived redirect, and Cynthia, obviously shaken, stepped down. Ben avoided her eyes as she passed by his table. He felt certain that whatever small affection or respect he had earned by rescuing her from the reporters was now totally eradicated. It was a shame, but unavoidable.

"Very well," Judge Hart said. "We've still got some time before lunch. Mr. Bullock, please call your next witness."

CHAPTER

40

"THE STATE CALLS Mr. Arthur Prentiss to the stand."

As Mr. Prentiss strode forward and was sworn in and introduced, Ben made a silent prayer of thanks to the great gods of the judiciary for pretrial discovery and *Grady v. Wisconsin*. If the prosecution hadn't been required to identify their witnesses in advance of trial, he wouldn't've had a clue who this witness was or what he was about to say.

"Mr. Prentiss," Bullock asked, after the witness was settled, "where do you work?"

Prentiss was a tall thin man with a scraggly black mustache and beard. He was in his mid-thirties, although he looked younger. Despite the beard, he had a clean, fresh-faced look. Basically, he looked like an honest man, which worried Ben no end.

"I work at the Baskin-Robbins over on Fifty-first, near Harvard. You know, next to Novel Idea."

"What do you do there?"

"Well, I scoop ice cream, for the most part." He grinned. "I'm the assistant manager, but we have a very small staff. There's never more than two of us on-site at once. So I usually end up doing a little of everything. Stocking, scooping. Ringing up the cash register."

"I see." Bullock turned a page in his trial notebook, usually his subconscious signal to the jury that he was about to get to the good parts. "Let me ask you, Mr. Prentiss, if you've ever had occasion to know the defendant, Wallace Barrett."

"Sure. Of course." He shrugged. "He's the mayor. I've seen him in the papers, on TV. And he used to come into the store."

"Really. That's interesting. I'd like to talk about that." Ben knew better than to trust Bullock's feigned surprise. Something was in the offing. "Did he by any chance come into the store on the afternoon of March 11?"

As if you didn't know. "Yes, he did."

"Was he alone?"

"No, he was with his wife and kids." He glanced awkwardly at Barrett. "Er . . . late wife and kids."

"Would you please describe that encounter for the jury in your own words?"

Prentiss shifted his angle slightly so that he faced the jury and could speak directly to them. "Well, at first it was no different from any other visit. Mayor Barrett greeted me by name, asked about my kids. He was that kind of guy, you know—always remembered your wife's and children's names and always remembered to ask after them. A good politician, I guess. We shot the breeze a little bit, like we always did. They'd just come from that press conference he gave. Where he announced he was running for reelection."

Bullock nodded. "What was different about their visit on this particular occasion?"

"Well, it's hard to describe. There was some kind of tension in the air, particularly between Wallace and his wife. Something was going on between them, but I wasn't sure what."

"What was the first . . . manifestation of this tension you're describing?"

"It was the strangest thing. Those two little girls of his had their noses pressed up against the glass counter—you know, picking out their flavors. Mayor Barrett asked them what they wanted, and told them they could have any kind they wanted. And—"

Bullock leaned forward. "Yes?"

"And . . . " Prentiss seemed to be struggling for words. "And . . . the tension was so thick you could cut it with a knife. So thick I thought it was going to strangle them. Or her, anyway."

"Her being?"

"Mrs. Barrett. Caroline. She told the girls they couldn't have chocolate. The mayor apparently disapproved of this limitation. They started to argue."

"Did the defendant become . . . angry? Agitated?"

"Actually, I thought he showed a remarkable amount of self-control. She was coming on pretty strong, but he kept calm. He told her she was creating a scene, and he was right, she was. Everyone in the store was watching them."

"Did the defendant's attitude ever change?"

"Unfortunately, yes. I don't know what triggered it. I don't think it was anything she said. It was just as if something inside of him snapped, as if he decided he'd had enough—"

"Objection." Ben decided to interject. This account was becoming a bit too colorful. "The witness has gone beyond recounting what he saw and heard and is . . . interpreting."

Judge Hart nodded. "Sustained. I'll caution the witness to stick to what he saw and heard."

Bullock stepped in to retake control. "You were telling the jury when the defendant's attitude changed."

Prentiss nodded. "Right, right. All of a sudden, his face got real solid and serious, and his eyes shrunk down to two tiny little slits. And he told her to shut up."

"How did he say it?"

"The first time, he whispered it. Unfortunately, she kept right on talking. That's when he went into a rage."

"What did he do?"

Prentiss looked directly into the jurors' eyes. "This time he shouted it: 'Shut up!' After that, the whole place got real quiet. I think we were all holding our breath, afraid of what might happen next. He snapped his arm back like this"—Prentiss demonstrated—"like he was getting ready to throw a forward pass. Then, like a rocket, he brought his clenched first forward. Toward his wife's face."

There was an audible gasp from the courtroom gallery. The cynic in Ben wanted to imagine that Bullock had planted someone to do it, but he knew that even Bullock was probably not that shabby. The truth was, Prentiss was doing a good job of recreating a horrific incident.

"And did Mr. Barrett strike his wife?"

"No," Prentiss said. "Well, not then, anyway. His fist stopped maybe half an inch from her face. I was amazed he could stop in time."

"And what was Mrs. Barrett's reaction?"

"Well, she was horrified, of course. Her eyes were wide as moons. And the funny thing was, she hadn't had that much time to react. It was as if she instantly realized what was about to happen." He paused. "I had the distinct impression that this had happened before."

"Objection," Ben said. "Speculation."

"Sustained."

Ben sat back down, unable to savor this Pyrrhic victory. It was a petty objection in the face of devastating testimony, and he knew it. He wanted to turn to Barrett and shake him by the shoulders, to say What the hell did you think you were doing? But he knew he couldn't. He couldn't even risk turning to look at his client. The slightest glance might be misinterpreted by a juror as concern over the testimony or, worse, an admission of its truth.

"Did the Barretts get their ice cream?" Bullock asked, breaking the silence.

"No. He told the girls they were leaving."

"Did they comply?"

"The little one, Annabelle, the four-year-old, whined. She wanted her ice cream."

"So what did the defendant do?"

"He . . . swatted her. On the backside."

Bullock blinked twice. "Do I understand you correctly? He hit his daughter?"

"Yes."

"Hard?"

"Oh, I don't know. Hard enough that she didn't give him any more trouble."

Ben simply closed his eyes. It was just too much. All through Cynthia's testimony, in fact, all through the case, he'd told himself, Yeah, but there's no proof that he would ever harm his daughters. If nothing else, I can convince the jury that he would never harm them. Except now that was all ruined. Shattered. An eyewitness who had no reason to lie told the jury that Barrett hit his daughter. And Ben knew they would believe him.

He knew they would because he knew he did.

"Did anything else unusual occur?"

"No. Barrett gathered together his family and they left hurriedly. Believe me, I was relieved."

"Did he say anything else before he left?"

"Yes." Prentiss's voice lowered. "Just after he almost hit her. He dropped his hands, but his eyes were still glaring at her, still drilling her so hard I thought they'd leave a mark. He looked at her like that and he said, in a low, growling voice, 'You'll regret this.' "

Bullock paused to let the import of that statement sink in. "And this was on the afternoon of March 11? About two-thirty in the afternoon?"

"Right."

Bullock nodded. "Four hours later, all three of them would be dead."

There was a great and heavy sense of weight in the courtroom. Heads turned and nodded, eyes widened. And for good reason. Now the prosecution had established not only a motive, but an expression of intent. And all of that before the first lunch break.

Bullock glanced up at the judge. "No more questions."

ORDINARILY, BEN WOULD'VE preferred to start with t
build to the hard, but in this instance, he knew he had to go strai
of the matter, to undermine the impact of that last bit of testimon
a chance to make a permanent impression on the jurors' perception

"Let's talk about Wallace's last statement, Mr. Prentiss. He s
regret this.' Did he explain what he meant?"

"Well, no, but I had the definite impression—"

Ben stopped him cold. "Mr. Prentiss, I didn't ask for your impre
The judge has instructed you to stick to the facts. Please do so."

Prentiss took in a deep breath. "All right. No, he didn't explain wha
meant."

"So, he could've meant, say, 'You'll be sorry you didn't get the girls i
cream, 'cause now they'll be whiny all afternoon.' "

"I suppose that's possible."

"Or he could've meant, 'You'll be sorry you raised your voice in public,
because now your approval rating will go down in the polls.' "

"If you say so."

"The truth is, sir, you don't know what he meant."

Prentiss chose his words carefully. "Based upon everything I witnessed, I
had the definite impression that he was threatening her."

"Threatening what?"

"Threatening bodily harm."

"That's your guess, and I emphasize the word *guess*, based on what you
know or think you know happened later. But in fact, as you testified, he had a
chance to hit her—and he didn't."

"Well . . . not in public, no."

"You don't know for a fact whether he ever hit her at all, do you?"

"I heard the—"

again, sir, I must ask you to stick to the things you have actually
...rd. Did you ever see Wallace Barrett strike his wife?"

...'ll regret this.' Did your *guess* about what this remark meant occur
...ne, or only after you'd read in the papers that Barrett's family had
...led?"

...ell, after I read what happened it seemed clear—"

...fter you read the incredibly biased reportage suggesting that Wallace
...t was guilty, which came before any evidence had been gathered or pre-
...d, you decided to jump on the bandwagon and reinterpret what you saw
...st him as a killer making a threat."

"That's not true. I saw what I saw."

"The truth is, sir, you saw next to nothing. But to listen to you testify,
...u'd think you'd witnessed the murders themselves."

"Objection!" Bullock shouted.

"Sustained. Mr. Kincaid, please control yourself."

"Sorry, your honor." Ben flipped to the next page of his notes. He was
getting carried away, and he knew that always led to sloppy lawyering. It was
just so frustrating. Barrett was being hung on a circumstantial mass of innu-
endo, supposition, and media bias. "Let's talk about the incident you
described involving Wallace's daughter Annabelle."

"All right."

"Despite your best efforts to turn it into some hideous public child abuse,
basically, what you witnessed was a mild spanking, right?"

"I wouldn't use those words."

"Well, was the contact intended as a punishment?"

Prentiss tossed his head to one side. "I suppose it was."

"And where did he touch her?"

"On her little bottom."

"Sounds like a spanking to me."

Prentiss straightened in his chair. "Look, I don't think you can write
something like this off by calling it a spanking. When you hit a kid, it's abuse,
whatever your supposed motivation."

"That's your opinion."

"Damn straight."

"You don't believe in corporal punishment."

"No, I don't."

"But you must realize that many people, particularly people older than
you, do. They believe it's necessary to discipline a child."

"Discipline." He snorted. "That's what parents always say to justify hitting their kids. Most of the time it's just plain uncontrolled anger. Venting
their temper on their children."

"Still, there are times—"

"Look, mister, I've got two kids of my own, and I've been able to discipline them just fine, but I've never hit them. Never once."

Ben swallowed hard. What a position he'd gotten himself into. He'd sooner die than strike Joey. But here he was coming off as the defender of corporal punishment. He could see the headlines: BARRETT ATTY FAVORS CHILD BEATING. "Mr. Prentiss, this is a murder trial, not a referendum on the propriety of spankings. I realize there are television cameras in the room and that creates a temptation to pontificate on important issues, but I'll have to ask you to stop trying to promote causes and to limit yourself to answering my questions."

"Fine."

"When Wallace administered this disciplinary blow to his daughter's bottom, did he appear to be acting out of anger?"

"Well, no, not particularly."

"Did he appear to do any serious harm to her?"

"No, no."

"After the spanking, did he continue to show hostility to her?"

"No. In fact, he picked her up and carried her to the car."

"So your portrait of a man abusing his family really comes down to a man raising his voice and giving his daughter a mild swat on the backside."

"I wouldn't—"

"Thank you, sir. No more questions."

Ben sat down quickly, hoping they could move to the next witness. To his dismay, the instant he sat, he saw Bullock rise to redirect.

"May I approach the witness?" The judge nodded, and Bullock handed what appeared to be a videotape to Prentiss. "Have you seen this before?"

"Yes."

"What is it?"

"It's a tape made in the ice cream parlor on March 11. We have a security camera behind the counter that tapes everything that goes on in the store. This particular tape displays the encounter with the defendant and his family that I just described."

"Your honor, I move that this tape be admitted—"

Ben shot to his feet. "Objection, your honor! This is redirect. He can't bring in new evidence."

"This is in the nature of rebuttal," Bullock explained. "I had hoped to avoid showing this to the jury"—I'll just bet, Ben thought—"but now Mr. Kincaid has called into question Mr. Prentiss's testimony. Was it a threat or a joke? Was it a spanking or a beating? The best way for the jury to determine the answers to these questions is to let them see what happened for themselves."

"But your honor," Ben protested, "this is duplicative. Prentiss has already testified to all this."

"And the defense has disputed it," Bullock answered calmly. "We now wish the opportunity to demonstrate that everything Mr. Prentiss has said is true and is in no way exaggerated."

The judge nodded. "It's a bit irregular, but given the circumstances, I'll allow it. Have you got the proper equipment ready?"

Bullock nodded, and began setting up his VCR and television monitor in front of the jury box.

Ben collapsed into his seat. Damn! He'd been totally set up. Bullock had held back the tape, hoping to have a second shot, and Ben had given him his opportunity on a silver platter. Even if the tape showed nothing more than what Prentiss had already said, the jury would now hear it twice, instead of just once. It would be indelibly imprinted on their brains.

Ben sat down glumly as the lights dimmed and watched the grainy security video that was now being presented to the jury. He tried to focus, but one grim truth kept reasserting itself in his brain.

The first morning of trial had been a disaster for the defense. Or more to the point, for Wallace Barrett.

CHAPTER

42

As it turned out, the videotape didn't impart any more information than Prentiss had already done. In fact, in many ways, the tape was an inferior means of conveying the information, which explained why Bullock had decided to lead with his live witness and to save the tape for redirect. The graininess of the tape, coupled with the poor audio, undermined the impact of some of the events, plus the shots of the spanking made it clear that it was a spanking, and a rather lighthearted one at that.

After the tape, Judge Hart called for a late lunch break. Ben ate with Barrett in his holding cell, but neither had much to say. What could he ask the man? Why the hell did you hit your kid in public? Why did you throw your wife out on the front porch half naked? All these questions would have to be asked before Barrett took the stand, but somehow, Ben just couldn't bring himself to ask them now.

After lunch, Judge Hart reconvened the trial and instructed the prosecution to call its next witness. Ben tried to cheer himself. After all, the worst was surely over now. Who could they possibly call who could make Barrett look worse than he already did?

"The State calls Karen Gleason." There was a mild stir, and then, from the back of the courtroom, a tiny eight-year-old girl slid off the bench and started timidly toward the front escorted by the sergeant at arms.

Ben's head fell to the table. Just when you think it can't get any worse . . .

Bullock boosted the child into the large chair in the witness box, putting a thick pillow beneath her so she could be seen over the rail. She had a small face with large brown eyes, pretty in an innocent, prepubescent way. Her black hair was braided back in matched pigtails on either side of her head.

Judge Hart swore in the witness, being particularly careful to speak clearly and to keep a pleasant expression on her face. Whatever it took to make this experience less of a nightmare for her than it would likely be anyway. Studies had shown that testifying in court was one of the most traumatic experiences a small child could undergo. It was worst, of course, when the case centered around child abuse or charges against the child's parents. Nonetheless, the murder of your best friend was not a piece of cake.

"Karen, there are a few questions I need to ask you before you answer the lawyers' questions. You understand that the lawyers are going to ask you some questions, don't you?"

Karen's small oval face turned up at the cheekbones. "Yes, ma'am."

"And you understand that you've promised to tell the truth, don't you?"

"Mm-hmm."

"You need to say yes or no, Karen. So the court reporter can take it down."

"Oh. Sorry." A flush of embarrassment colored her face. "Yes, I promised."

"And you're how old?"

"I'm eight, ma'am."

"Eight. So you're old enough to know the difference between the truth and a lie, aren't you?"

"Oh yes. My mama has been real strict on that."

Judge Hart beamed a smile that was one part judicial and two parts maternal. "Good. Then just answer these questions truthfully and we shouldn't have any problems. If you don't understand their questions, you just tell them so." She glanced up. "And I can assure you the lawyers will make themselves clear and won't try to be tricky or to upset you in any way whatsoever."

Message received and understood, Ben thought.

"Counsel, you may proceed."

"Thank you, your honor." Bullock squared himself behind the podium and borrowed the friendly smile the judge had been using. "Karen, you know why you're here today, don't you?"

Karen's head bobbed gravely. " 'Cause Alysha got killed. With her mama and sister."

"That's right, honey." Ben felt a catch in his throat, and he knew the other jurors were feeling it as well. Not as if they didn't all know what the crime was. But somehow, hearing it come from the lips of an eight-year-old girl made it all the more heartbreaking. "You knew Alysha, didn't you?"

She nodded. "We went to school together. At Forestview."

"What grade are you in?"

"Third. We're both in Ms. Holman's class." Her head drooped. "Were."

"I see. Was Alysha your friend?"

"Yes. We were best friends."

"Did you play together?"

"Uh-huh."

"Did you ever go over to her house?"

"Uh-huh."

"Did you know her sister Annabelle and her mother?"

Her voice became quiet. "Yeah. I liked them."

Some time passed before Bullock asked his next question. Just this once, Ben thought that perhaps his hesitation was genuine. "Karen, I know this will be uncomfortable for you, but I'm afraid I have to ask you to tell us what you know. Do you recall any time when Alysha appeared to have been . . . hurt?"

Ben considered objecting on grounds of vagueness, but decided not to. What would it accomplish? Everyone knew where this was headed.

"Yeah," Karen said quietly. "I do."

"What do you know?"

"She had . . . bruises on her."

"Bruises? Where?"

"All up and down her legs. On her arms, too."

"When was this?"

"Last December. We went swimming together. Janie Pearson invited us. She has an indoor swimming pool," she added. Obviously, Janie's indoor pool had made a great impression on her. "Normally, like when she had her clothes on, you wouldn't see the bruises. But when she changed into her swimsuit . . . they were all over her."

"How many bruises did she have?"

Karen shook her head. "Lots. Higher than I can count."

Ben knew he shouldn't, but found himself unable to resist. He leaned over into Barrett's ear and whispered, "Is she telling the truth?"

Barely perceptibly, Barrett nodded his head in the affirmative. Yes.

"Did you ask Alysha about the bruises?"

"Oh, yeah. I said, like, wow, Alysha. What happened to you?"

"And what did she say?"

Karen frowned. "She said she had an accident."

"Really." Bullock looked down at his papers. "Perhaps she fell down the stairs also. Did she say anything more?"

"No. She started getting real embarrassed about it. I guess she thought, like, maybe no one would notice or something. But once I did, she got upset and started trying to cover them up."

"Did she go swimming with you?"

"No. Like I said, she acted real embarrassed. She put her clothes back on and wouldn't swim. Called her mom to come pick her up."

"I see. And this was about three months before the . . . the . . . end?"

"Right. Around Christmas."

Bullock turned a page in his notebook. "Karen, when was the last time you talked to your friend Alysha?"

"On the day . . . the . . ." Her voice dropped. "The last day."

"You talked to her on the day she was killed?"

Ben sensed everyone in the courtroom inching forward with interest. Another detail that had not been reported in the press.

Karen nodded her head. "Sure. We talked almost every day. We were best friends."

"What time of day was it?"

"About five in the afternoon. I remember 'cause I had just finished watching Power Rangers."

"What did you talk about?"

"Oh, nothing special. Just the usual stuff. School. Homework." Her face flushed again. "Boys."

"Did Alysha seem . . . upset?"

"No. Well, not at first."

"Not at first? What happened later?"

"Well, there was like some . . . screaming in the background. I couldn't hear the words. I asked Alysha, but she just said, 'It's them again,' and tried to ignore it like."

"Was she able to ignore it?"

"No. About a minute or so later, someone shouted out her name. I wasn't sure who it was, but it was a real loud voice. Yelling at her."

"And then what happened?"

"Alysha screamed. I mean, like, real loud screamed. It was scary. Then I heard this loud thunking in my ear, like she'd dropped the phone."

"Did you hear anything else after she dropped the phone?"

"Yes. Her voice was fainter, like she'd moved away, but I could still hear what she was saying."

Bullock took a deep breath. "Karen, would you please tell the jury what were those last words you heard Alysha saying."

She looked down at her hands. "Yes, sir. She was crying and shouting and she was saying, 'Daddy! Daddy!' "

Bullock paused, obviously moved. "Did you hear anything else?"

"No. That was all. The line buzzed and the operator came on."

Bullock nodded. "Judging by the time, those were probably her last words." He lowered his head and quietly closed his notebook. "Thank you, Karen. I have no more questions."

Ben saw Judge Hart check her watch. Apparently she was deciding whether to proceed or to take a break. He was hoping for the latter; after that, he thought everyone needed a breather. But unfortunately, she opted for the former. "Mr. Kincaid? Have you any cross for this witness?"

Ben nodded and slowly walked to the podium. This was a true no-win scenario. If he did nothing on cross, the jury would be left with a nightmarish mental image—Wallace Barrett dragging Alysha from the phone to her death.

On the other hand, if he did cross and tried to challenge or impeach her or otherwise give her a bad time, the jury would hate him, the judge would hate him, and he'd probably be lynched on his way out of the courtroom.

Well, he had to cross. He would just give her the kid-gloves treatment. "Karen, my name is Ben Kincaid. I represent the defendant. Do you know what that means?"

She nodded. "You're helping the bad man."

Ben drew in his breath. It's a wonderful life. "No, Karen. I'm helping your friend's father. Did he ever do anything bad to you?"

"Well . . . no."

"Then why do you call him a bad man?"

"My momma said—"

"Karen, I'm going to have to ask you to put aside anything you were told by other people. Even your mother. All we want to hear about is what you actually saw or heard. Okay?"

Karen frowned, obviously displeased to have her mother's opinions so ruthlessly cast aside. "All right."

"Now then." He pointed to his client. "Did Alysha's daddy—Mr. Barrett—ever do anything bad to you?"

She shrugged. "No."

"Did you ever see him do anything bad to Alysha?"

"Mmm, no."

"Did she ever tell you that her father had done anything bad to her?"

Karen thought for a moment. "Alysha told me he wouldn't buy her the new Nintendo GamePro even though she really wanted it and all the other kids had them."

Ben tried not to smile. "Anything else?"

Karen shook her head. "No, sir."

"And you don't know how she got those bruises, do you?"

"Well . . . no . . ."

"And you don't know who killed your friend or her sister or her mother, do you?"

"No, sir."

"Thank you, Karen. That's all I have."

It wasn't much, but there wasn't much you could do with a witness like this. At least he'd managed to remind the jury that, as bad as it was looking, all of this evidence was still purely circumstantial. Karen Gleason didn't know who committed the murder any more than the man at the ice-cream store.

Ben took his place beside his client. Barrett was still in his chair, still staring straight ahead, but his attitude, his demeanor had changed in some barely perceptible way Ben couldn't quite identify. It must be hard, he realized, hearing those horrid things said about you, realizing that almost everyone probably believed them. That would be a difficult burden to bear. And then, just to top it all off, you learn that your deceased little girl's eight-year-old friend thinks you're guilty, too. That you're a bad man.

Ben looked deeply into Barrett's eyes. He had hoped, although the odds were looking slimmer by the minute, that he would be able to prevent Barrett from being convicted. But even if he did, how could he prevent Barrett from being convicted in the court of public opinion? What could he ever do to prevent the world from thinking of him as . . . a bad man?

He knew the answer before he had finished asking himself the question.

Absolutely nothing.

43

THE NEXT WITNESS was Harvey Sanders, who Ben knew from pretrial discovery and Christina's briefing notes lived in the house next door to the Barrett family. Ben could only surmise what the nature of his testimony might be. Living in such close conjunction to this house of turmoil, he might be able to say anything—all of it bad.

"What do you do for a living, Mr. Sanders?" Bullock asked.

Sanders was a slim, reasonably handsome man who looked like he was somewhere in his thirties or early forties. He was wearing a collarless shirt with a scarf draped artfully around his neck. "I'm an actor. And I'm also an assistant curator at the Gilcrease Museum. Have been for eight years."

"You're an actor?"

"Right. Between jobs at the moment. That's why I'm working at the Gilcrease."

"I see. An odd combination."

"I haven't quite gotten my big break yet, you know? Once that comes, I'll drop the day job and devote myself to my art. It's just a matter of time."

"Of course. Where do you live, sir?"

"Sixteen twenty-two Terwilliger."

"Do you know the defendant?"

"Of course I do. He's my next-door neighbor."

"And how long have you lived next door to the defendant and his family?"

"Gosh, let me think. More than three years now."

"So you must have known his two children. And his wife."

"Caroline. Yes, I knew Caroline. And the children."

Ben listened carefully to Sanders' words. There was something about the way he said *Caroline* . . .

"Were the Barretts good neighbors?"

Sanders grinned. He did have a rather charismatic air about him, Ben thought. Maybe he could be a successful actor at that. "Well, they kept the lawn mowed, if that's what you mean."

Bullock tried it a different way. "Did you have much opportunity to see the family interact? To see Mr. and Mrs. Barrett together?"

"Oh, yes. Scads. I saw them practically every day. And I frequently went over to their house."

"Why?"

"Well, sometimes I'd help with some little household chore. Faulty plumbing or what have you. Wally—excuse me, the defendant—was so busy, you know, sometimes he didn't have the opportunity to keep up with these things. And sometimes I'd go over to show off a new museum acquisition, some piece of pottery or something. Caroline was a great admirer of antiquities."

There it was again. Caroline. Ben made a few notes on the cross-ex side of his legal pad.

"Based on what you saw and heard," Bullock carefully asked, "would you say the Barretts had a happy marriage?"

"Objection," Ben said. "He's asking the witness to form an opinion."

Judge Hart drummed her fingers thoughtfully. "I'll allow it in this instance. So long as the witness bases his testimony on what he has personally observed, I think it's permissible."

Sanders didn't wait for the question to be reasked. "They had their pleasant moments, like anyone else, but no, I wouldn't call it a happy marriage. In fact, I'd call it a decidedly unhappy marriage."

"Upon what do you base that opinion?"

Sanders shifted to face the jury. He seemed perfectly relaxed and at ease, more like a man chatting with his friends than a man testifying in court. "Well, a lot of things. They fought constantly. Loud fights, like cats and dogs. I mean, I lived in the house next door, for Pete's sake, and I could usually follow the combat like I had a ringside seat."

"What kind of things did they say?"

"Mean things. I mean, really awful. Things I wouldn't want to repeat in court. Particularly Wa—er, the defendant. He has a real vicious streak in him when he loses his temper. Really perverse. You wouldn't believe some of the things he called Caroline. And this was his wife. The mother of his children." He shook his head. "Caroline deserved a lot better than that."

"Mr. Sanders, let me direct your attention to March 11. Were you at home that day?"

"I got home around four o'clock, like usual."

"Did you see or hear any member of the Barrett family after you arrived at your home?"

"I didn't see them, at least not at first, but man-oh-man did I hear them."

There was a spattering of smiles and chuckles from the gallery. Sanders's exuberance and amiability were charming the masses.

"They were fighting?"

"Oh yeah. Like nobody's business. I don't know what started it. Usually it wouldn't take much, and these things would just get blown all out of proportion."

"Whose voices did you hear?"

"Mostly the defendant's. He has that deep, booming voice, you know. It really carries."

"Do you remember what he said?"

"I don't remember all of it. But I remember the highlights. I remember he called her a stupid cow. I remember he called her—excuse me, Judge—a fucking whore. And"—his eyes dropped, and his voice took on a note of sorrow—"and I remember he said she didn't deserve to live."

The reaction from the reporters and spectators in the gallery was immediate. Pages and pencils flew; many people whispered at once.

"Did you hear anyone else?"

"Yes. The two girls. That was the worst of it. Not only was this horrendous fight going on, but those poor little sweethearts were getting every word of it. I could hear them screaming and crying. It just broke my heart."

"What else happened?" Bullock asked.

"Well, frankly, it got to the point where I just couldn't stand it anymore. I closed my window and turned on the television. Watched *Little House on the Prairie*. I know it's corny, but I really like that show. May sound stupid to you, but after hearing all that hatred, I needed a dose of innocent family drama."

"Doesn't sound stupid to me at all," Bullock commented. "Did you hear anything further from your neighbors?"

"Amazingly enough, yes. About halfway through the show, I heard a tremendous crashing noise from next door. I still don't know what that was, but man alive, it was loud! I mean, I was next door, for cryin' out loud. I had the windows shut and the television on. And I still heard it."

"Did you take any action?"

"Yes. I went to my kitchen and reopened the window. That's the room closest to the Barretts' house. I heard one of those girls crying out."

"Did you hear what she said?"

"Yeah. Clear as a bell. She cried out, 'Daddy! Daddy!' "

Ben knew how devastating this was going to be. Sanders was confirming Karen Gleason's testimony about what she heard on the phone. And if that part was true, the jury would reason, everything else she said must've been true as well.

"What did you do next?" Bullock asked.

"Well, I closed the window again and went back to my television show. I know that may seem strange in retrospect, but you have to realize—this sort of thing happened all the time. What was I supposed to do? March over there and tell the defendant to straighten up? Of course, if I had known what was going to happen, I would've called the police, but at that time, who knew? Who could have dreamed?"

Who, indeed? The question hung heavily in the courtroom. Who could have dreamed?

"Did you have any further contact with the Barrett family?"

"Yeah. About half an hour later, after I finished watching *Little House*. That fight I'd heard next door was still weighing heavily on my mind. I thought by then, though, they might've cooled down a bit and I could go over and make sure things were okay, you know?"

"So what did you do?"

"I stepped outside my front door and started toward their house."

"And what happened?"

"Well, the strangest thing. Before I got five footsteps out the door, I saw Wallace Barrett tearing out of his house. Fast. I mean, those quarterback thighs were pumping like pistons. In nothing flat he crossed his front lawn and jumped into that red sports car of his that was parked on the street."

"Did you speak to him?"

"I shouted at him. 'Wally! Hey, Wally!' But he didn't hear me. Man, he didn't hear nothin'. He was the wind. He was out of there."

"And what did you do next?"

"That was pretty much it. Since he was gone, I figured there was no reason to go over. Still, something about the whole situation bothered me. I argued with myself for a while, then ultimately called the police. Reported a domestic disturbance. Let them go in and make sure everything's hunky-dory, you know. And then I turned the tube back on and vegged out for a bit. Imagine my surprise when, maybe a couple hours later, the news guys broke in with some special report, and it was Wally! In that same red sports car, doin' the blitz down the Indian Nation Turnpike."

Bullock took a videotape from his legal assistant. "Your honor, I have a videotape recording of a special report that aired on most stations the night of March 11. With your permission, I'd like to play it and to ask the witness to identify it."

So this was how Bullock planned to get it in, Ben realized. Well, he had to try to stop it. "Objection. The witness was not responsible for the creation of this exhibit. He can't authenticate it."

"Your honor," Bullock replied, "all I'm asking the witness to do is tell us whether this is what he saw on television the day of the murder and to tell us whether the man and car in the tape are the man and car he saw at the crime scene."

How convenient. Under the simple rubric of identification, he would give the jury a chance to watch a tape that was not at all probative but massively prejudicial. "Your honor," Ben said, "I don't believe this tape has any value—"

Judge Hart waived his objections aside. "You've already raised these issues in your pretrial motions in limine, counsel. I overruled them then and I will do so again. Please do not continue asking the court to revisit matters that have already been resolved."

And so the tape got to the jury. Bullock already had the equipment set up from the last videotape. All he had to do was slide it in and watch the jurors go into their video-drone modes. Bullock showed almost twenty minutes of frenzied flight, from the moment the minicams in the helicopters first picked up Barrett's car to the moment he crashed into the tollbooth. They saw the copters swirl over the speeding sports car; they saw the police broadcast commands that were ignored. They saw Barrett's car swerve erratically all over the road, like a man who was drunk, or crazed, or desperate to get south of the border. Ben knew the questions that had to be racing through the jurors' brains. Why would Barrett desert his family in this moment of crisis? Why was he heading south in such a hurry? Why would an innocent man flee?

After the tape was completed, Bullock shut off the VCR and took his place behind the podium. "Mr. Sanders, was the man you saw in that videotape the same man you saw bolt out the front door of the Barrett home a few hours before?"

"Yes, sir. It was."

"Any doubt in your mind about that?"

"No. None whatsoever."

"Was he wearing the same clothes?"

"Yes. And driving the same car. It was him." Sanders shifted his gaze, turning to look for the first time directly at his friend and neighbor. "Sorry, Wally, but I gotta tell the truth. It was you."

Bullock closed his notebook. "Thank you, Mr. Sanders. I have no more questions for you at this time."

44

AFTER A BRIEF break, Ben began his cross-examination. He knew he had to be careful with this witness. Sanders was articulate, smart, and appealing. The jury was responding positively to him. Ben had to find a way to poke holes in his testimony without suggesting that he was a bad person.

"Mr. Sanders," Ben began, "you seem to have been very fond of the Barrett family. True?"

"Oh yes. I liked them all. Even Wally—sometimes. I didn't particularly want to testify here but—you know—a man has a duty."

"I'm sure. But you seem to have been particularly fond of Wally's wife, Caroline."

A frown line appeared above Sanders' eyes. "I'm not sure what you mean."

"I mean you seem to have been very fond of my client's wife, Caroline Barrett. Is that true?"

"What are you trying to suggest?"

"I'm not trying to suggest anything, Mr. Sanders. Why are you being so defensive?"

"Well, I just don't like you casting aspersions—"

"And I assure you I'm not casting aspersions, sir, but I must insist that you answer my question. Were you very fond of Caroline Barrett?"

"I don't see what this has to do with anything."

"So are you saying you didn't like her?"

"No, of course not."

"Then you did like her?"

Sanders pursed his lips. "Yes, I liked her."

"Very much?"

Sanders spoke slowly through tight lips. "Yes, very much."

"You know what, Mr. Sanders?" Ben kept his voice even and calm. "I think maybe you loved Caroline Barrett."

"This is outrageous. I would never do anything improper."

"I'm not suggesting that you did. It's not a crime to love someone, is it?"

"Of course not."

"But you did love Caroline Barrett. Didn't you?"

Sanders glanced down at his hands. "Suppose I did. So?"

"You thought Wallace Barrett was . . . mistreating her, didn't you? That she deserved better."

"That's certainly true."

"And that leads me to think that, well, if you loved her, and thought he wasn't very nice to her—you probably wouldn't like him very much."

"I had no axe to grind against Wally."

"Are you sure?"

"Absolutely."

"So it didn't bother you when he called the woman you loved those awful names?"

"Well . . ." Sanders began fidgeting with his hands.

"Mr. Sanders, why don't you just tell the jury the truth? You hated Wallace Barrett, didn't you?"

His chin lowered, and his voice became quiet. "Yes, I suppose I did."

"It wouldn't break your heart at all to see him locked away in jail, would it?"

"No. But if you're suggesting—"

"Thank you, Mr. Sanders. I think you've answered my question." Ben moved quickly to his next subject, not wanting to give Sanders a chance to rationalize his answer. "Now, you testified that during the fight that preceeded the deaths, you heard Wallace Barrett's voice but did not hear his wife. Is that right?"

"That's right."

"Well, now, it takes two to fight, doesn't it?"

"Yes, but that doesn't mean they're both aggressors. One can be the attacker and one can be the victim."

"Mr. Sanders, is it possible you just didn't hear what the woman you loved—Caroline Barrett—had to say?"

"I heard a lot."

"A lot of Wallace, yes. But as you said yourself, he had a loud, booming voice. What was Caroline's voice like?"

"Soft. Gentle."

"Not the kind of voice that would likely carry all the way next door, right?"

Sanders's lips pursed in irritation. "Perhaps not."

"So for all you know, she could have said things that were far more horrible than what Wallace said. You just didn't hear them."

"That's right. I didn't hear them."

"Thank you, Mr. Sanders. I wanted to ask you about one other matter—something I noticed you failed to mention in your testimony."

Sanders looked startled, as did Bullock.

"In the newspapers, and when you spoke to my investigator, you mentioned that you had seen two strangers prowling around the neighborhood about the time of the murders. Why didn't you tell the jury about that?"

"Well, it didn't seem relevant since . . . since . . ."

"Since you wanted the jury to pin the rap on my client."

"No, but—I mean, the evidence is clear."

"Mr. Sanders, let's let the jury evaluate the evidence. You just tell us what you saw."

Sanders sighed heavily. "I saw two people. A tall young man, early twenties probably. Thin, scraggly. Wore fatigues. Had a goatee. Sometimes he carried a black bag over his shoulder. Once or twice I saw him with a younger girl—teenager, I'd guess. That's it."

"You didn't think this was unusual? Two strangers in your high-dollar neighborhood?"

"I did think it was unusual, but I didn't have any reason to believe they committed murder."

"When you were initially interviewed by the police, almost the first thing you told them about was these strangers who were, in your words, casing the neighborhood."

"That's true . . . but at that time, I didn't know . . ."

"You didn't know the police were going to pin it on my client, right?"

"Well—"

"In fact, despite having witnessed this big fight, the first suspects you offered the police were these two unidentified strangers."

"The police asked me if I had seen anything unusual in the neighborhood. So I told them."

"Told them about the strangers. Not the fight. Not Barrett rushing out of his house."

"I told them about everything. I just happened to mention the strangers first."

"Indeed you did. The rest was practically an afterthought."

Bullock sprang up. "Your honor, I object!"

"Sustained. Counsel, watch yourself."

"Sorry, your honor." But not very. "Mr. Sanders, did you ever see either of these strangers in the company of anyone else?"

Sanders started to shake his head, then stopped. "You know, now that you mention it, I do recall a time when the tall guy talked to someone else. Someone drove up in a car, leaned out the window, and talked with him. It was very quick. Not really a conversation. More like he barked out a few orders and then drove on. Very strange."

"Did you recognize the man in the car?"

"No, sorry."

"And you don't recall anything else about these two strangers?"

"No. Nothing."

"Thank you, sir. I have nothing more."

The instant Ben had taken his seat, Bullock was back on his feet. "Just a short redirect, your honor."

Judge Hart nodded.

"Let me ask you just a few questions about these spectral assassins defense counsel is trying to use to confuse the issues. I'm sure we'd all like to believe these horrible crimes were committed by some unknown, unnamed strangers. But, Mr. Sanders, did you ever observe these two doing anything that suggested they meant to harm anyone in the Barrett home?"

"No, I did not."

"Did they seem to show unusual interest in the Barrett home?"

"Not that I saw."

"Did they do anything that suggested they were dangerous?"

"No. I never saw them do anything but walk down the street. They were just strangers, that's all."

"You certainly didn't see them fighting with Mrs. Barrett or her children."

"No."

"You didn't see them hit or beat Mrs. Barrett or her children?"

"No."

"And you didn't see them dash out of the Barrett home minutes after the murders took place."

"No, I didn't."

"Thank you, Mr. Sanders. I just wanted to put this ghost to rest. That's all."

Ben's jaw clenched tightly together. Bullock had put that ghost to rest, at least for now. If he was ever going to convince the jury there was another assailant, he was going to have to do a lot better than that.

CHAPTER

45

THE LAST WITNESS of the day was Officer Kevin Calley, the first police-man at the scene of the crime. Calley was a baby-faced officer with curly brown hair and a smooth, somewhat chubby face. He looked younger than he probably was. Ben wondered if this was his first time to testify. He was obvi-ously nervous, although, given the general clamor and hubbub in the court-room, who wouldn't be?

"What were your duties on the day of March 11, Officer?" Bullock remained crisp and professional, despite the fact that he was on his fifth wit-ness of the day and had to be tired.

"I was on patrol duty in one of the downtown districts. We call it the Utica beat." Because it was in the vicinity of Utica Square, Tulsa's shopping haven for those who don't look at price tags before buying.

"Do you recall receiving a call on your car radio at approximately five forty-five in the afternoon?"

Calley nodded. "I do."

"What were your instructions?"

"I was told to proceed to a residence on Terwilliger not far from Philbrook Museum."

"And did you?"

"Yes."

"Whose residence was it?"

"Well, as I saw upon arrival, it was the home of the defendant. The mayor." He nodded toward the defense table. "Mr. Barrett."

"What was the nature of the call?"

"I was told that an anonymous caller had reported a domestic disturbance."

"Domestic disturbance being a euphemism for what?"

"Violence. Wife beating, usually."

"I see." Bullock folded his hands on his notebook. "Tell us what happened next."

"When I arrived at the Barrett home, I exited my vehicle and approached the front door."

"Did you see or hear anything unusual?"

"Well, what was unusual was that I didn't hear anything. Usually, on these domestic abuse calls, you can hear the couples going at it a mile away. I didn't hear a thing."

"Did that concern you?"

"Yes, it did. It was possible that the parties involved had simply cooled down on their own, but that would be quite unusual. Therefore, I became concerned that the incident may have escalated into something more serious."

Ben knew perfectly well why Bullock was dragging the officer through all this testimony about his concerns. Ben had made a pretrial motion to exclude evidence based on Calley's unwarranted entry and search of the home. Bullock was trying to show that Calley had ample justification for entering the premises.

"What did you do?"

"I rang the doorbell, but there was no answer. I knocked on the door, but again there was no answer. While I was knocking, however, the door swung partly open."

"What did you do then?"

"Well, since whoever left the door open obviously wasn't too concerned about privacy"—a quick glance at the judge—"and since I was concerned that some violent activity might be occurring inside, possibly involving children, I decided to enter the premises."

Ben saw Bullock check him quickly out the corner of his eye to see if he was going to object. Forget it. Ben knew this was a loser.

"What did you see inside?" Bullock continued.

"At first, nothing. Then I passed through the entryway into the dining room."

"And what did you see there?"

Calley frowned. His respiration seemed to quicken.

"Officer Calley," Bullock said sympathetically, "I know this is probably difficult for you. These are unpleasant details, to be sure. But I must ask you to describe for the jury what you saw."

Calley spoke in measured, even tones. "In the living room, draped across a dining room chair, I found the body of Caroline Barrett. She was dead."

"Could you tell how she had been killed?"

"Not specifically, but she was covered with blood. Some of it was already dried and caked. It covered her face and her hands and her clothes and—" He stopped himself, shaking his head. "Everywhere."

Bullock strolled over to the podium and reversed the first enlarged photo. It was every bit as hideous as every juror had imagined it might be. Red was the dominant color—bright, vivid, sickly red. It covered almost every inch of her face and hands, every inch of her clothing.

"Officer, can you identify this photograph?"

"Yes," he said, only looking at it for the briefest of moments. "That's Mrs. Barrett. That's how she looked when I found her."

Bullock asked a few more procedural questions to fulfill the authentication requirements. "Your honor, I move that this photograph be admitted into evidence." Ben did not object. The photo was admitted. Bullock returned to his podium, leaving the photo exposed and facing the jury. "What did you do next?"

"After I confirmed that she was dead, I began searching the rest of the house. Obviously, at this point, I felt it was urgent that I determine whether there were any more victims in the house, anyone who might require emergency medical assistance. I toured the rest of the downstairs, but I didn't find anyone. I then proceeded upstairs."

"Did you find anything unusual there?"

"Yes." His voice cracked. Ben looked up and saw, to his surprise, a tear creeping out the corner of Calley's eye. Police officers were usually coached to remain stoic and nothing-but-the-facts when testifying. Ben had never seen anything like this before.

Bullock cleared his throat. "And . . . what did you find?"

"In one of the upstairs bedrooms, the one on the far left, I found the Barretts' younger daughter. She was lying on her bed, her arms folded across her chest—" Calley choked—literally choked. He could not complete the sentence.

Bullock didn't press him. "Was she alive?"

Calley shook his head. "No. I could tell at a glance, although I confirmed it by searching unsuccessfully for a pulse. Her face and body were an almost . . . unnatural white, a ghostly pale. I guess." Once again, Calley did not manage to finish his sentence.

Bullock flipped over the next enlarged photo. If anything, this one was even worse than the one before. It had an unholy calm about it; it at first suggested that she was simply resting on her bed, a suggestion soon shattered upon closer inspection by the realization that she had been murdered.

"Officer Calley, is this the scene you witnessed in Annabelle Barrett's bedroom?"

"Yes. That's it."

Bullock moved that the photo be admitted into evidence, and it was.

"Officer Calley, where did you go next?"

Calley seemed flushed and embarrassed, both sickened by the memory and upset that he wasn't handling himself in a more professional manner. As if anyone could. "To tell you the truth, sir, I . . . uh . . . wasn't feeling very good at that point. I had noticed that there was a bathroom near the bedroom so I ran in there thinking that, um . . ." He swept his hand across his face. "Well, I thought I was going to be sick."

"And what happened?"

"I ran to the bathroom, pushed wide the door, and was instantly confronted with . . . the other daughter."

Bullock paused to give Calley a few moments to gather himself. "Could you tell the jury precisely what you saw?"

"The older Barrett girl—Alysha—was lying in the bathtub. There was no water in it, and she was still in her clothes."

"Was she dead?"

"Yes, of course she was dead." Calley pressed his hand against his forehead. "She was very dead."

Bullock flipped over the third of the grisly enlarged photos, revealing a bathtub streaked with blood and the lifeless body inside, one arm draped over the edge, like a pathetic parody of the famous painting of Marat. "Does this photo accurately represent what you saw?"

"Yes."

Bullock had the third photo admitted into evidence. He allowed another respectful silence, then continued. "Did you do anything else in the Barrett home?"

"No," Calley whispered. "I left the house. I called for an ambulance, although I knew they were all dead. And I called homicide."

"Thank you, Officer Calley. I have nothing more."

CHAPTER

46

BEN GLANCED OVER at his client. He was not in good shape. The pain in his face was evident. Ben had to remind himself that Barrett had come home and seen these horrible images, too. His experience was much like Calley's, only earlier. Reliving it in this manner, being reminded of the hideous demise of his entire family, had to be awful for him, and the strain was showing in his face.

With all the enthusiasm of a corpse, Ben strode to the podium. He decided to keep the cross short and sweet. After all, the man had simply testified to what he saw at the crime scene, and none of it was in dispute. The main point of his testimony had been to shock and horrify the jury, which he had certainly done. The sooner they moved on to someone else the better.

"Officer Calley, at the time of this incident, March 11, you were rather new on the force, weren't you?"

"Uh . . . yes." Ben noticed that as soon as the testimony shifted to cross-examination, he adopted the flat, unembroidered voice police officers are trained to use in court.

"How new?"

Calley thought for a moment. "I'm not sure I remember exactly."

"Isn't it true that this incident occurred on the Friday of your first week?"

"Uh . . . yes, I believe that's correct."

A few eyebrows in the jury box raised.

"Obviously, then, you hadn't had much experience with domestic disturbances."

"No. Only discussions while I was at the academy."

"And you probably hadn't had any experience with homicides."

"No."

"Well, I appreciate your honesty. This may help explain some of the . . . irregularities at the crime scene."

Ben could see Calley's eyes narrow. He was on his guard now.

"For instance," Ben continued, "it isn't really standard police procedure to enter a home uninvited just because they don't answer the doorbell, is it?"

"I felt that there was a great potential—"

"Yes, yes, I'm familiar with your justifications. But that isn't exactly what they taught you back at the academy, is it?"

"I suppose not."

"And I'm curious—when you found the first body, why didn't you immediately call for medical assistance?"

"Well, she was dead."

"Officer Calley, are you a doctor?"

He frowned. "No."

"Have you taken classes in emergency medicine?"

"No. Just the fundamentals at the academy."

"You know, sometimes experienced doctors are fooled about whether a patient is dead when they have to make a field diagnosis without instruments. Is it possible you made a mistake?"

"She was dead. It was later confirmed—"

"Later, yes, but at the time you were there, is it possible she was alive?"

"I don't think so . . ."

"Officer, my question was—is it possible?"

He sighed heavily. "I suppose it's possible."

"And if an officer finds an injured person and there is a possibility that the victim is still alive, the proper police procedure is to immediately summon medical aid, correct?"

"That's correct," Calley said resignedly.

"Your honor, I object," Bullock said. "What's the point of this? Officer Calley is not on trial."

"I'm testing the credibility of his testimony," Ben told the judge. "That's the main point of cross-ex."

Judge Hart nodded wearily. "I'm going to allow a little more of this. I would appreciate it, however, counsel, if you could bring the discussion a little closer to the matters at issue."

"Very well, your honor." He turned his attention back to the witness. "My point is, this was not a perfect, by-the-book initial investigation, was it?"

"There were many variables—"

"Sir, please answer the question."

"No, it was not."

"Please understand, I'm not trying to blame or incriminate you. But the jury needs to know the facts. And the facts are—you were a brand-new officer on your own and you made mistakes, right?"

"That's true." His shoulders sagged. "I made mistakes."

"Did you ever see my client during your initial tour of the house?"

"No, he had already—"

"Did . . . you . . . see . . . him . . . there?"

Calley swallowed his words. "No."

"Did you see anything that indicated who had committed these crimes?"

"Not specifically, no."

"Not specifically or generally, right?"

Calley almost smiled. "Right."

"There is one other matter I'd like to ask you about. You've admitted this initial investigation was flawed and that you made mistakes. You also said that after you found the third victim, you left the premises. Right?"

"Right."

"At what speed did you depart?"

"Speed? I don't follow."

"Well, did you saunter? Stroll? Walk briskly?"

Calley seemed to struggle for the correct word. "I . . . believe I moved downstairs and out with all deliberate speed."

"Meaning fast, right?"

He shrugged. "I guess you could say that."

"Were you running?"

"I don't know if I was running . . ."

"But you were moving very rapidly."

"I suppose so."

"And on your way out, you had to pass through the living room. Right?"

"Uh, yes. That's right."

"Officer, in his opening statement, the prosecutor made much of a photograph that was found on the floor in the living room. Did you see that photo?"

"As I recall, there were many photographs in the home."

"Ah, but this one was on the floor. Surely you would have noticed. If it was there."

"I . . . There was a lot going on . . . I had a lot on my mind . . ."

"Officer Calley, did you see a smashed photograph of Caroline Barrett on the floor?"

"I . . . don't recall it, but as I say, I was moving quickly. It was probably there and I didn't notice."

"Officer Calley, in your haste to leave the Barrett home, is it possible that *you* knocked over the photo?"

Calley appeared momentarily stunned. "I—what?"

"You heard me. Did you?"

"Did I—no, I most certainly did not."

"It would have been an easy thing to do. No one would blame you. But we need to know the truth. Did you knock over that photograph?"

"No!"

"You were running—or moving very rapidly—through the living room. Very upset. You would have had to run right by the coffee table where the photo normally rested. Tell us the truth, sir. You knocked it over, didn't you?"

"No!"

"And that's how the frame glass was broken."

"No! Absolutely not!"

"I'm sure it was an accident. But you did it, didn't you?"

"I—" His head began to tremble. "No! I did not knock over the picture!"

"That's your story and you're sticking to it."

"I did not knock the damn thing over!"

"Your honor," Bullock shouted, "we apologize for that outburst, but this question has been asked and answered. Several times now."

Judge Hart did not look happy. "I will excuse the outburst—just this once. The question has been asked and answered. If you have nothing more, Mr. Kincaid, sit down."

"Nothing more," Ben said. There was no point in pushing any longer. If Calley was responsible for breaking that picture, he sure wasn't going to admit it now.

"Very well. Court is recessed for the day." Judge Hart gave the jury the usual end-of-the-day instructions, particularly complicated in this instance since the jury had been sequestered. "We'll resume tomorrow morning at nine o'clock sharp." She banged her gavel, and the courtroom exploded.

Ben could see the reporters surging up the aisle. As soon as the jury was escorted out, he pointed Barrett toward a door at the back of the courtroom.

"Wait a minute," Barrett said. "I want to make a statement."

"That's an incredibly stupid idea."

"I don't care. People have been lying about me all day. Why should I sit there and take that silently?"

"Well, at least let's talk—"

"There's no time. The marshals will come for me any moment." Barrett pushed forward to meet the reporters. In a matter of moments, a multitude of cameras and lights and microphones were working.

Ben listened as Barrett did his best to put a positive spin on the day's testimony, which was nearly impossible, since almost all of it had gone against them. For the most part, Barrett avoided the specifics of the evidence and statements, and simply reiterated his innocence in strong and impassioned tones.

Which was well and good for the six o'clock news, Ben thought, but the jury would require something more. If he was going to turn them around, he would have to give them something concrete, something that seemed at least as plausible as the evidence the prosecution had put on, and would continue to put on tomorrow.

This was one election Wallace Barrett couldn't win with a press conference. Barrett might win over thousands of viewers, but the only twelve votes that counted would not be watching. They were the ones who would determine his fate. And they were the ones, Ben knew, who at that point had been given no reason to doubt that Wallace Barrett was guilty.

CHAPTER

47

BEN AND CHRISTINA headed back from the courthouse to the Adam's Mark in silence. Ben knew he was being sullen and uncompanionable, but he couldn't help himself. It all seemed too grim and hopeless.

Finally, Christina broke the silence. "Ben, I know things look gloomy at the moment, but I think you're doing a great job in there. *Sans pareil.*"

"Thanks for the kind words, but we're losing, and you know it."

"You've been losing from the second you accepted this loser case. Any little thing you can do to improve the situation—and you've done several already—is pure gravy. And a testament to what a fine trial attorney you're becoming. You shouldn't get so upset about every single unfavorable ruling. You know how trials go. *Comme çi comme ça.*" She poked him in the side. "Look, when this is all over, let's go camping again, okay? You and me, back-packing in Heavener State Park. I'll show you the runestone left by the Nordic discoverers of this continent."

Ben smiled faintly. "Deal."

Despite the late hour, Ben found both Jones and Loving working at their desks at the hotel room. They took no particular notice when he walked in.

"I'm back," Ben said.

Jones glanced up quickly. "Hi, Boss."

Loving echoed with a grunt.

Ben was perplexed by their marked lack of interest. "Is something wrong?"

"Nope." Jones continued typing away.

"Well . . . have I done something to offend you?"

Jones frowned, still typing. "Not that I'm aware of. Have you done something that you feel guilty about?"

"No, but . . ." He dropped his briefcase. "Normally when I come back from court, you two are hanging by the door like vultures, pumping me for information about what happened. Now I'm handling the trial of the century, and you guys act as if you're not even interested."

Jones pivoted around in his chair on wheels. "But, Boss—" He pointed to the television in the corner of the room. "We saw it all as it happened. Court TV, remember?"

Of course. "You watched the whole first day?"

"Right." He stopped momentarily. "Don't worry. I still got my work done."

"Oh, no doubt." Ben craned his neck awkwardly. "So . . . how'd I look?"

Jones smiled. "You really want to know?"

Good question. "I suppose."

Jones sprang out of his chair. "First of all, ditch the suit."

"Huh?"

"That gray pinstripe. Lose it. The stripes show up wavy and blurred on television. It's very distracting. Gray isn't good for color television, anyway. Makes you look evil, like a Mob lawyer or something. Stick to the Reagan ensemble—blue suit, red tie. It's a winning combination."

"I see." Ben tugged at his tie. "Anything else?"

"Well, yes, now that you mention it. Stop doing that."

Ben froze. "Doing what?"

"That thing you do with your tie. Adjusting it. Whatever."

Ben slowly lowered his hands. "It's just a nervous habit."

"Exactly. And it makes you look nervous. Not exactly the message you want coming from the defense lawyer."

"Hmm. I'll see what I can do."

"And while you're at it, don't move your head around so much."

"Huh?"

"Your head. It bobs when you talk."

"That's because my words carry great conviction."

"Well, whatever it is, stop it. It's very distracting on television. It makes you look like one of those plastic birds that dips its beak down into a glass of water."

"I'm trying to impress a jury, not the folks back home."

"Hey, you're the one who asked." He turned back to his work. "Other than that, you're not bad. You've even got some camera appeal. Boyish charm and all that. Maybe you could get one of those news show jobs commenting on legal issues. Sort of a Geraldo Rivera gig."

"How wonderful. Anything else I should know about?"

"Nothing comes to—oh, there is this one thing."

"Yes?"

"You're being sued by Channel Eight."

"What, for not giving interviews?"

"Nooo." Jones tossed him the pleadings. "For smashing their minicam against the courthouse wall."

"Oh, that."

"I was hoping maybe if you offered them an exclusive interview, they'd settle for costs."

"I can't do that."

"Whatever. It's your funeral."

Truer words were never spoken, Ben thought. It still embarrassed and terrified him. He'd never even thought he had a temper, much less one that could get so incredibly out of control. But he knew now that he did.

He knew now that he truly was his father's son.

He turned his attention to Loving. "How's the investigation going?"

"It ain't," Loving groused. "I ain't got a thing."

"I'm sorry to hear that."

"You and me both." He stood and shoved his enormous hands in his pockets. "I haven't been able to find a trace of that weasel I saw at O'Brien Park, much less link him to Whitman."

"Mmm. Well, keep trying."

Loving pounded a ham-fist down on the desk. "Damn. I never should have let that creep get the drop on me."

"You couldn't help that."

"I could've. And I should've. I screwed up."

Ben gave him a friendly slap on the back. "Cut yourself some slack. You did the best you could."

"Yeah. But it wasn't good enough."

Ben tried to sound optimistic. "I'm sure you'll turn something up soon." It'll have to be soon, he thought. Because if it's late, Wallace Barrett is going up the river, maybe on a one-way trip.

Loving glanced down at the stack of mail on his desk. "Oh yeah. You got a package." He tossed a medium-size padded folder to Ben. "I already sent it through an x-ray machine. It ain't a bomb."

"I'm sure the owners of the Adam's Mark will be glad to hear that." Ben took the package and pulled open the staples sealing it shut. He reached in and withdrew . . .

A videotape.

All at once, Ben's blood ran cold. He held the tape between two fingers, like a bomb. Despite the fact that the tape barely weighed a pound, his arm trembled.

He checked inside the folder. No letter, no words of explanation or description. No label on the tape itself.

Just like before.

"Have we got a VCR in here?" Ben asked quietly.

"In the bedroom." Jones pointed without looking up.

Ben entered the bedroom, flipped on the TV, and plugged the tape into the VCR. A few moments later, the machine whirred to life.

This time, there was no mystery about the image that filled the television screen. It was an outside view of Ben's office—Ben's former office.

Before the explosion.

The camera was hand-held, or perhaps shoulder-held, and the shots were taken from the opposite side of the street. Ben could just make out the reflection on glass; the cameraman must have shot through a pane of glass. He had probably broken into the empty space that used to be the bar.

About thirty seconds after the tape began, Ben saw three figures emerge from the front door of his former office. It was him. Just behind and on either side of him were Christina and Jones. He was pulling them out the door. The expressions on their faces were wild, panic-stricken. They raced across the street and out of the range of the camera.

Barely a second later, Ben saw his office burst into flames. The noise of the explosion was just as deafening as it had been in real life. Ben found himself reliving the horror of the moment, the flying debris, the smoke, the collapsing infrastructure. It was horrible, nightmarish. But the most nightmarish part of it all . . .

Ben's knees sagged. He dropped down onto the edge of the hotel room bed.

He had been there. The maniac had been there.

He was there with his camera, taking pictures, recording the whole hideous incident for posterity. He had been ten, maybe twenty feet away from them when it happened.

He could've killed Ben if he had wanted to. But he didn't. Not then, anyway. He wanted to play with him first. He wanted to torture him. He wanted him to suffer.

He had been there.

Jones entered the bedroom. "So what's the—" His eyes darted to the television screen, and his voice disappeared. "Oh my God." Jones dropped onto the side of the bed beside Ben and stared slack-jawed at the flickering image on the television screen. "I don't believe it."

The smoke cloud on the television screen billowed out, almost obscuring the office ruins.

And then they heard the laugh.

It started soft, then grew louder, larger and louder, strong in its undisguised malevolence. In its hatred.

It was him. *He had been there.*

After what seemed an eternity, the horrible laughter faded, replaced by a voice that was both threatening and merry.

"Sick heart," the voice said over and over again. "Sick heart. Sick heart. Sick heart."

48

AFTER A LONG and mostly sleepless night, Ben dragged himself back into the courtroom. The scene was much as it had been the day before. Reporters and sightseers crowded the aisles and offered their opinions to anyone who would listen. There were several familiar faces in the courtroom, and several city council members, including Whitman.

Despite her traumatic experience the day before, Cynthia Taylor was back, sitting silently in one of the front rows where the jury couldn't miss her, where she had undoubtedly been strategically placed by the prosecution. There were several other people he couldn't identify but recognized from the day before; the fact that they seemed to have reserved seats told Ben they must have some importance. Potential witnesses, perhaps, or maybe writers taking notes for their forthcoming best-sellers.

Wallace Barrett was already in his seat at the defendant's table, with three men from the sheriff's office standing discreetly in the background. Ben slid into the chair beside him.

"How're you holding up?"

Barrett shrugged. "Doing the best I can. Under the circumstances."

Ben nodded. If he thought he was having a bad time, imagine what it must be like for the man on trial.

Barrett coughed once, then spoke. "It's . . . not going too well, is it?"

Ben hesitated before answering. He made it a policy to tell his clients the truth, no matter how grim it looked. But he knew Barrett needed some sort of boost if he was going to get through another day like the last. "It always looks dismal when the prosecution is putting on their case. Our prospects will improve once we get our turn at bat." Ben smiled and tried to sound convincing. "You'll see."

Barrett gave Ben a quick nod. He probably didn't believe it, but it was a nice thought, anyway.

Barrett's eyes turned toward the jury box. The jury was filing in, taking their seats. As they did every day, they gazed across the courtroom and looked into the defendant's eyes, trying to see what there was to see. Barrett met their eyes, giving them a practiced smile and a look of total confidence. Ben just hoped it was enough.

Ben pulled his notebook out of his briefcase and prepared for the day's trial. Despite his wretched night, he felt much sounder than he had the day before. It always took at least a day before he found his footing in the courtroom. At least. Surely the worst of the prosecution's case was over. It had been tough, but they'd survived. Now, Ben felt like he was ready for anything.

He was wrong.

"The State calls Lieutenant Michaelangelo Morelli to the stand."

Ben's eyes went wide as cantaloupes. *Mike?*

Sure enough, Mike pushed himself out of his seat in the back of the courtroom, shrugged off his trenchcoat, and pushed his way into the aisle. He was wearing a suit and tie, a phenomenon Ben didn't think he'd observed since Mike's wedding.

This had to be some last-minute decision. When he had last talked to Mike, he hadn't said anything about testifying, and Ben felt certain he would have if he'd known. It must've been a recent decision by Bullock, probably made last night as the prosecution forces evaluated the first day's trial. But why?

He watched as Mike trudged up to the witness stand and took the oath. He didn't look at all pleased about being there. That, at least, gave Ben some small measure of comfort.

Mike introduced himself and briefly outlined his position, his duties, and his years of service leading to his current position as one of the chief homicide detectives on the Tulsa police force.

If anything, Bullock seemed even more confident than usual. Perhaps the delight of putting a close personal friend of the defense counsel on the witness stand was giving him an extra charge. "Lieutenant Morelli, did you have any connection with the investigation of the murder of Caroline Barrett and her two children?"

"Yes I did."

"What exactly was your role?"

"I was the homicide officer assigned to the crime scene."

"What are your duties as homicide officer at the crime scene?"

"Basically, to take charge and secure the area, protect the integrity of the evidence, and collect whatever clues or witnesses we could find."

"And did you perform these duties?"

"I did. To the best of my ability."

Wait a minute, Ben thought. Aren't we leaving out a few steps here? He began scribbling notes furiously on the left side of his legal pad.

"What did you do when you arrived at the crime scene?"

"I cordoned off the area and posted a sentry to ensure that no unauthorized personnel were allowed inside the house. Entrance was restricted to those who had to be inside and could follow evidence purity procedures."

"I see. Then what did you do?"

"We laid butcher paper down on the floor to cover the main walkways and to protect any evidence that might be there."

"I see. And after that?"

"Then I allowed in members of the police staff who were trained to gather evidence. First, the photographers and videographers, so they could make a record of the scene of the crime exactly as it appeared when I arrived. Then we sent in representatives from the hair and fiber department. Then the blood specialists. And finally, the DNA experts."

Ben stared deeply into his friend's eyes. Granted, a general sense of unease was part of Mike's makeup on a day-to-day basis. But this time there was something more. He simply did not want to be here. There had to be some reason.

"Please explain to the jury what the photographers do."

"They make a visual record of the crime scene. Principally, the three corpses, although in this case I had every square inch of the house photographed."

"Why did you do that?"

"Well, given the nature of the case and the . . . er . . ." Ben watched Mike squirm for the right word. "Well, since there were no eyewitnesses and the crime involved prominent members of the city, I thought it best to take every possible precaution."

"I see. What does the hair and fiber team do?"

"They look for trace evidence. Hairs, obviously, bits of clothing, fabric. Anything that might help identify the perpetrator."

"Were they successful in finding any such trace evidence?"

"Sure, lots of it."

"Any fibers that matched clothes belonging to the defendant?"

"Of course. Lots. He did live there, after all."

"Thank you, Lieutenant." Bullock's thin smile could've cut glass. "Just answer the questions, if you would."

Mike almost grinned. "Whatever you say."

"Tell us about the blood team. What did they do?"

"They searched and scraped for traces of blood. All over the house, but particularly near the bodies."

"Lieutenant, I won't ask you about their results, because we'll have a member of that team testify shortly. But let me ask you this. Had you allowed any disturbance of the crime scene before or during the blood team's sampling?"

At last Ben saw the light. That was why Bullock had dragged Mike to the stand. He was laying the foundation for the credibility and purity of the forensic evidence yet to come. The lab experts wouldn't be able to fend off Ben's questions about chain of custody. So Bullock was using Mike to establish it in advance.

"No," Mike answered. "I made sure all blood splatters, drops, and traces were undisturbed from the moment I arrived until well after the blood team had completed their work."

"And what about the DNA experts?"

"Same thing. I believe they removed skin tracings from under the fingernails of one of the victims. I didn't allow anyone near those fingernails before the DNA experts were able to do their work."

"Thank you, Lieutenant. No more questions."

Bullock sat down, and Ben took his position behind the podium.

"Good morning, Lieutenant," Ben said.

"Morning to you, counsel."

Ben tried not to smile. He felt ridiculous, standing here pretending to cross-examine his old college roommate. Like two little boys playing Perry Mason.

"I heard you tell the prosecutor that you were the homicide officer in charge at the Barrett home after the tragedy occurred."

"That's right."

"And I heard you say that once you arrived you secured the crime scene."

"That's also correct."

"Funny thing, though. I didn't hear you say exactly when you arrived at the crime scene."

Mike smoothed his lips with his tongue. "I arrived on the morning of March 12. Just after sunrise. About six-thirty A.M."

Ben put on his puzzled expression. "But I thought the murders occurred in the late afternoon of the previous day."

"That's correct."

"Well, were you delayed?"

"Yes. I was investigating the murder of a homeless person on the north side of town."

"So you were not in fact securing the crime scene from about six P.M. on Sunday night—after the murders—till about six-thirty the next morning. Correct?"

Mike tried to look nonchalant. "There was another officer in charge at that time."

"Who was that?"

"That was my colleague, Lieutenant Prescott."

"I see. Would he be the one the men call Pigpen Prescott?"

Mike had to close his eyes and bite his bottom lip. "I wouldn't know, sir."

"Uh-huh." Ben leaned against the jury rail. "So for over twelve hours following the murders, Prescott—not you—was in charge of the crime scene."

"Right."

"Did he secure the crime scene?"

Mike hesitated for only the barest of seconds. "He did."

"To your satisfaction?"

The hesitation was a bit longer this time. "I'm not his superior, so my satisfaction is irrelevant."

"Did he do things the way you would have done them?"

Mike's eyes focused on Bullock for a moment, then darted away. "No." Then he added: "But every officer has a different style—"

"Was it Lieutenant Prescott's style to allow a lot of unnecessary personnel to tromp through the Barrett home?"

Mike licked his lips again. Ben knew Mike well enough to know that, however uncomfortable this made him, he was an honest man. He wouldn't lie. "There were a number of persons in the home when I arrived that morning."

"Were these all police officers?"

"Uh, no."

"Well, then who were they?"

"For the most part, they were . . . sightseers."

Ben blinked, giving the jury a moment to absorb it all. "I beg your pardon?"

"Curiosity seekers. People who heard about the killings on TV or radio and decided to take a look."

"How many?"

"I'm not sure. Ten or fifteen."

"And these people were able to get inside the house?"

Mike nodded. "True."

"Was butcher paper on the floor?"

"Not yet."

"Photographs taken?"

"Not yet."

"Forensic teams been through?"

Mike shook his head. "Not yet."

"So none of that happened until *after* you chased these ten or fifteen people out of the house."

"You got it."

"Thank you." Ben allowed himself a small smile. "Just a few more questions. After the preliminary investigation, did you continue to work on the Barrett case?"

"No."

"Why not?"

"The feeling of my superiors in the department was that there was no need for further investigation. The case was assigned to another officer who specializes in pretrial preparation."

"I see. And when was that decision made?"

"I believe it was March 12."

Ben blinked. "The day after the murders?"

"That's correct."

"Lieutenant Morelli." Ben spoke slowly and carefully. He wanted the jury to absorb every word. "To your knowledge, did any member of the police department ever investigate the possibility that someone other than my client might have committed these horrible crimes?"

Mike's answer was firm. "Not to my knowledge."

Ben smiled. "Thank you, sir. No more questions." And, Mr. Bullock, let that be a lesson in the dangers of putting an honest man on the stand. Ben had assumed he would have to wait until he was putting on the defense case to introduce his main theme—police mishandling of evidence. Instead, he'd been given a brilliant opportunity to do it during the prosecution's main case.

Bullock rose more slowly than usual this time, a rare sight that cheered Ben's heart. He stood as close to Mike as he could and began his redirect. "Lieutenant Morelli, I just want to ask you a few more questions. It's unfortunate, but sometimes lawyers couch their cross-ex questions in ways that can mislead the jury." Ben noted that Bullock's voice had acquired just the tiniest edge. "Lieutenant, you didn't mean to suggest that the crime scene was contaminated during the time that Lieutenant Prescott was in charge, did you?"

"Objection," Ben said. "Leading."

Judge Hart nodded, but said, "I'll allow it."

Mike eased forward in his seat. "I was not present at the time Lieutenant Prescott was in charge, so I can't possibly testify as to what happened then."

Bullock spoke in soft, even tones. "But, Lieutenant, I know you've been working in Homicide for some time and undoubtedly hope to continue to do so in the future, so let me ask my question again. I'm asking, did you see any evidence that the crime scene was contaminated?"

Mike leaned forward, his jaw tightening. "Let me make myself clear. I took an oath to tell the truth, and that's what I'm going to do, and there isn't anybody or any threat that can make me do differently." He paused. "Now, having said that, let me answer your question. No, I did not see any evidence that the crime scene was contaminated."

"Thank you, sir. You may—"

"At the same time, I know there's no way in hell that ten or fifteen rubber-neckers could stomp through a house without disturbing things. I don't know of any specific item that was altered, but I can't dismiss the possibility."

Bullock's voice was cold as ice. "Thank you, Lieutenant."

Mike smiled congenially. "My pleasure."

"The witness may be dismissed."

Mike stepped down from the stand and hurried to the back of the court-room, but not so fast that Ben didn't notice a definite bounce in his step that hadn't been there before. He didn't miss the wink Mike gave him on the way out, either.

49

AFTER A MID-MORNING break, Bullock called his next witness, a Dr. Albert Camilieri. Ben knew from the prosecution's witness list that he was their blood expert.

Bullock began the witness examination in the traditional fashion, trying to wow the jury with a seemingly endless recitation of the witness's qualifications, recommendations, degrees, professional memberships, and the like. The strategy was simple. For most of his testimony, he would likely be talking way over their heads. They wouldn't be able to follow the analysis, much less duplicate the procedure. They simply had to take his word for it. To make sure that happened, Bullock had to make the man more than just a run-of-the-mill police lab tech. Albert Camilieri wasn't enough. He had to be the Albert Einstein of the blood world.

For more than half an hour, Bullock dwelt on the man's professional credentials, including a review of prestigious cases he had worked on—indeed, had practically solved single-handedly, if you believed Bullock.

Finally he brought the witness around to the case at hand.

"Dr. Camilieri, have you had any connection with the case that is presently before the court?"

The doctor was a thin man wearing a tweedy coat that seemed about two sizes too big for him. "Yes, I have."

"How were you involved?"

"I was the blood expert called to the scene by Sergeant Tomlinson."

"And who is Sergeant Tomlinson?"

"He's Lieutenant Morelli's assistant."

"And, as we've previously been told, Lieutenant Morelli was the investigating homicide officer in charge at the scene, correct?"

"That's correct."

Bullock paused and did a little pirouette around the podium. "Now, before you tell us what you did, I'd like to ask you what you saw. When you arrived at the scene, what did you see?"

Camilieri shrugged. "It . . . seemed like a standard crime scene."

"Were there hordes of gawking tourists?"

"No. No one but authorized police personnel."

"Had the blood evidence been contaminated?"

"Not in any way that I was aware of."

"Very good. Now, please tell us what you did."

Camilieri took a deep breath. Recalling this job probably wasn't any more pleasant for him than it was for anyone else. "I was shown to the three areas of the house where the bodies were found. I then removed representative blood traces from those areas, including from the bodies themselves."

"What did you do with these blood traces?"

"I placed them on individually labeled glass slides and placed those inside individually labeled petri dishes, then sealed the dishes in individually labeled paper bags."

"Is there any chance that the various samples could have been switched or mislabeled?" A leading question, but Ben let it pass.

"No, none. I was very careful."

"We appreciate your professionalism, doctor." Well, Ben thought, Bullock does, anyway. "What did you do with the samples next?"

"I took them to our central police lab for examination. I did this work in the presence of at least two witnesses at all times. These witnesses took notes on exactly what samples were being scrutinized and exactly what results were discovered."

Ben had to admit to being impressed. Camilieri seemed to have covered every base in the chain-of-custody ballpark. He was leaving no room for a clever cross-examining defense attorney to wriggle in some reasonable doubt.

"Dr. Camilieri, would you please tell us what those results were?"

"Of course." He inched forward a bit in his chair. This, of course, was the part everyone had been waiting for, and he knew it. "In most cases, the blood found at the scene of the crime belonged to the victim. The blood surrounding Alysha belonged to Alysha; the blood surrounding Caroline belonged to Caroline. There was one exception, however."

He paused, giving Bullock a marvelous opportunity to draw out the suspense. "Really? An exception? What was that?"

"The blood surrounding the corpse of Caroline Barrett for the most part did belong to Caroline Barrett. But I found a few traces of blood from another source. A splatter on the bodice of the dress she was wearing, plus some smeared on her hand."

Bullock nodded. "And did you perform an analysis of this unmatched blood?"

"I did."

"Were you able to identify it?"

Camilieri ran a finger down the side of his nose. "Well, as I'm sure you know, it's impossible to make an absolutely positive identification of a blood source. It isn't like fingerprints; it isn't that unique. What we can do, however, is identify various blood characteristics, such as type, constituency, secretions, white blood cell counts, and so forth, and determine whether the characteristics in the sample match those found in a given individual's blood."

"I see. And did you perform such an analysis on the unmatched blood found on the body of Caroline Barrett?"

"I did."

"Good." Bullock paused again, and this time he allowed his eyes to drift across the courtroom until they rested on Wallace Barrett. "Dr. Camilieri, did you ever have an opportunity to examine the blood of the defendant?"

"I did. I took a blood sample from him after he was incarcerated."

"And did you analyze his blood for those distinguishing characteristics you described earlier?"

"I did."

"And did you have an opportunity to match the results you received from the unidentified blood found on Caroline Barrett's body with the blood taken from Wallace Barrett?"

"I did."

"And what was the result of that comparison?"

Camilieri held his breath for a few moments before answering. "It was an almost perfect match."

Bullock nodded his head grimly. "I see." He cast a gravely disapproving glance toward Barrett, then continued his questioning. "Dr. Camilieri, have any studies been performed of these blood characteristics as they pertain to the general public?"

"Yes, the blood traits of the population have been categorized and mapped. Of course, I can't identify the specific blood characteristics of any given individual, but I can determine the statistical likelihood of any combination occurring in the general populace."

Ben sat up straight. Any time the prosecution started talking statistics, it was time for the defense to watch its backside.

"Did you have an opportunity to compare your findings from the unmatched blood found on the body of Caroline Barrett with the population at large?"

"I did."

"And what did you find?"

"Objection!" Ben said. "This is not relevant. Statistical probabilities can in no way tell this jury whether the defendant committed this particular crime."

Judge Hart removed her glasses and tapped them against the bench. "I'm familiar with those arguments, counsel, and I'm not unsympathetic to them. But I'm going to allow this."

Ben gritted his teeth and sat back down. He knew this was going to be bad.

"Please answer the question," Bullock said.

Camilieri nodded. "Statistically speaking, the chances of another person having exactly the same blood characteristics as Wallace Barrett are almost one in one hundred thousand. Given that the population of the Tulsa metropolitan area is only about half a million, that means there are only about five people who would make a positive match with that blood."

Bullock pondered that information with his soberest expression. "Five people." Once again his eyes turned toward the defendant, and this time the eyes of the jury turned with him. "And one of them is Wallace Barrett."

"That's correct."

"Thank you, Doctor. I have no more questions for you."

50

BEN HAD CROSS-EXAMINED expert witnesses before, and often enough to know that trying to attack their credentials was a fool's game. Better to go after the statistics, to try to expose them for the intellectual game-players they were.

"Dr. Camilieri," Ben said, "if I understood your testimony correctly, you said that there are only five people in the Tulsa area whose blood characteristics would match the blood you found near the body of Caroline Barrett."

"That's correct. Statistically speaking."

"Ah. Statistically speaking. And those statistics are based on the population of the entire country, right?"

"That's right."

"That's a national average."

"Right."

"But that doesn't tell you how many people with those characteristics live in the state of Oklahoma, does it?"

"Not specifically, no."

"And it certainly doesn't tell you how many people with those characteristics live in the Tulsa area, does it?"

"Using the national statistical map as a guide, I can—"

"Doctor, please answer the question. Your national statistics cannot tell us with any certainty how many people with these blood characteristics live in the Tulsa area. Right?"

"That is correct."

"There may be five, or there may be fifty. You just don't know."

"Well, I haven't taken a census, if that's what you mean."

"What I mean, sir, is that you don't know. You're just guessing."

"On a large-scale sampling, the statistical probabilities will come out correct."

"On a large scale, yes, but on a small scale, say, a single city, the statistics may be totally skewed, right?"

"Well . . . it's possible."

"In actual practice, statistics don't always play out the way they're supposed to, right?"

"If the sampling is small, it's possible—"

"Possible? Anybody who's ever been to Las Vegas knows that statistical probabilities don't always play out according to the book."

"Yes, but the point—"

"The point, sir, is that you've told this jury there are only five people in town whose blood matches the sample you found, but the truth is, you don't know how many possible matches there are. Right?"

"I can perform a probability analysis—"

"Answer the question, sir. The truth is, you don't know how many people in this city have blood that matches your sample. Correct?"

Camilieri's lips pursed tightly together. "That's correct."

"Thank you, sir. I appreciate your candor." Ben flipped a page in his notebook. "For that matter, there's no reason to assume that the killer resides in the Tulsa metropolitan area, is there?"

Camilieri glanced up at Barrett. "Well . . ."

"Doctor, do you know who the killer was?"

"Well, not from my own personal knowledge, no."

"So therefore, you don't know where the killer lives, either."

"I suppose."

"So there was no reason to limit your blood analysis to Tulsa. You just did that as a means of justifying a smaller statistical base."

"I did that because it seemed probable."

"Are you a detective, sir?"

"No, of course not."

"Is it your job to detect?"

"No."

"Then don't." Ben quickly checked the judge. He was getting a bit rowdy even by defense attorney standards. "Did you uncover any evidence that suggested where the murderer lived?"

"No."

"Then please don't suggest to the jury that you did. The decision to limit your statistical base to the Tulsa area was an arbitrary decision on your part, right?"

Camilieri seemed resigned to the inevitable. "That's correct."

"Thank you." Ben knew that was as good as it was going to get. Time to move on.

"Did you find any other traces of blood anywhere in the Barrett home other than those you've mentioned?"

"I found blood on or near each corpse, and some mixed with smeared footprints in the front hallway."

"Anything else?"

"Well, there was one small sample in Mrs. Barrett's bed, but I hardly thought that relevant, since none of the murders occurred there."

"Now, you admitted yourself that it was not possible to make a positive identification of any particular suspect simply by comparing blood samples."

"That's true."

"So even with all your statistics, you cannot say with certainty that the blood you found on Caroline Barrett came from her husband, correct?"

It seemed Camilieri had had enough. "Well, given the circumstances, it seems damned likely."

"Ah. So you, like everyone else on the police force, went into your analysis assuming my client was guilty and looking for ways to prove it."

"I wouldn't put it like that."

"In fact, all you can say for certain is that the blood came from someone other than Caroline Barrett, right?"

Camilieri sighed heavily. "Yes. That's what I said."

"But you did consider the circumstances when you made your analysis. You said so yourself."

"Right."

"As to any other conclusion, even you must admit there is some element of . . . doubt."

"Objection!" Bullock rose to the occasion. "This is improper."

Judge Hart nodded. "I believe I will ask you to rephrase that question, counsel. This isn't closing argument."

"That's all right, your honor." The point was already made, as well as it was likely to be made with this witness, anyway. "Doctor, I believe your exact testimony was that the blood samples taken from Caroline Barrett and my client were an almost perfect match."

"That's correct."

"Not a perfect match, but an almost perfect match."

Camilieri spread his hands wide. "Well, you have to be realistic. Blood is not static. Minute changes occur every second it pulses through your veins. If I took two samples from you today, one now and one half an hour later, they would not match each other perfectly."

"Did you figure these . . . imperfections into your statistical analysis?"

"How do you mean?"

"Well, you told the jury that only five people in Tulsa could make a perfect match with the blood taken from Caroline Barrett. How many could make imperfect matches?"

"That's an absurd question."

"Is it? What's the degree of variation between the sample taken from the crime scene and the sample taken from my client?"

Camilieri twitched. "About six percent."

"Six percent!" Ben said it as if it was enormous, although he had been hoping for a larger number. "How many people in Tulsa have blood that would come within six percent of matching the sample you found at the scene of the crime?"

"I don't know."

"But it would be more than five."

"Ye-es."

"Substantially more."

Camilieri took another deep unhappy breath. "Yes. Substantially more."

"In the hundreds?"

"I . . . suppose."

"In the thousands?"

"It's . . . possible. I'd have to run an analysis."

"Thank you, Doctor. I believe I see the suspect pool expanding right before my eyes." Ben flipped another page in his notebook. He'd done enough on statistics. Surely the jury had some idea now how misleading they could be. Time to hammer again on his main theme. "Doctor, you said there were no spectators at the crime scene when you arrived, correct?"

Camilieri seized the opportunity to try to do the prosecution some good. "That is absolutely correct."

"But in fact you did not arrive until after Lieutenant Morelli did. Right?"

"That's . . . right."

"And as he told us, he chased off the spectators when he got there."

"I wouldn't know."

"Well, now, that's the truth of the situation, isn't it? You don't know whether unauthorized personnel were at the crime scene before you. Right?"

"I don't know what occurred before I got there, no."

"Similarly, you don't know whether there was any contamination of the blood evidence—before you got there."

"I saw no evidence of it."

"But you wouldn't, would you? Because you arrived after the damage was already done."

"I—still—"

"You don't know whether some blood evidence was trampled away before you got there, do you?"

"No."

"You don't know whether one of the spectators bled on the bodies before you got there."

"I think that's highly unlikely."

"But the fact is, you don't know."

"I don't know what happened before I arrived, no."

"So it's possible that the blood evidence was contaminated before you arrived."

"Objection!" Bullock said. "Anything's possible. This doesn't aid the jury."

"Your honor," Ben said, "this witness's entire testimony is just a tissue of possibilities. I'm trying to make sure the jury understands all the possibilities he didn't tell them about."

Judge Hart's eyes lit up. "I think he's got you there, Mister Prosecutor. I'll allow the question."

Ben re-asked it. "Is it possible the blood evidence was contaminated before you arrived?"

Camilieri frowned. "I can't rule it out."

"Thank you. No more questions."

For once, Ben sat down happy. Two witnesses in a row had gone well for him, or so it seemed. But he knew he couldn't let himself rest easy. Yes, two witnesses had gone well, he told himself, but for all he knew, the next one could be a disaster.

As it turned out, he was right.

51

BULLOCK AND THE rest of the prosecution team were late returning from lunch. Apparently a big strategy powwow had taken place, a development that Ben found distinctly heartening. Normally Bullock coasted through a trial with an unruffled sense of aplomb; this development suggested that just this once he was a tiny bit worried. Like Ben, he must've felt that the defense had effectively dealt with the first two prosecution witnesses of the day, and he was concerned.

Good.

On the other hand, of course, as Ben knew quite well, when Bullock felt it was time to pour on the pressure, he knew how to do it. But there was no way to anticipate that. All he could do was stay alert and wait for the other shoe to drop.

"The State calls Dr. Stafford K. Regan to the stand."

Goodness, Ben thought. Not only an honorific but a middle initial. He must be an important witness indeed.

Dr. Regan took the stand. He was younger than one might guess, trim and handsome and athletic. Obviously not someone who had spent his entire life gazing out from behind the test tubes. In fact, as Ben already knew, Regan's specialty was DNA analysis. Ben supposed it was only natural that the DNA expert would be on the young side. As in the case of computers or any other emerging science, it was the next generation that took the lead.

Bullock led Regan through a succinct accounting of his background and credentials. He was in fact a medical doctor, but had chosen to pursue research rather than practice. For the last four years, he had been at the Cellmark facility in Dallas, where he not only received a salary but had a small ownership interest. His current title was vice president of research and analysis.

"Dr. Regan," Bullock asked, "how did you become involved in the present case?"

"I was contacted by a member of the Tulsa County district attorney's office," he answered. He seemed calm and self-assured. Someone you'd want your daughter to marry. And, Ben thought, unfortunately, not someone who was likely to crumble under cross-examination. "A woman named Myrna Adams."

"Why did Ms. Adams contact you?"

"She was working on the prosecution team for this case, investigating the murders of the three Barrett family members. They had a few unmatched blood traces, and also, the coroner had found some skin tissue that they believed might be susceptible to genetic testing."

"Do you know where this skin tissue came from?"

"Yes. The coroner found it under Mrs. Barrett's fingernails."

"How did you respond to this inquiry?"

"Well, I was concerned about whether they would have sufficient material to conduct accurate testing. So I asked her to have the genetic materials forwarded to my office."

Bullock paused, glanced up at the jury. "Before we go any further, Doctor, perhaps I should ask you to explain to the jury just what DNA is."

Regan nodded, and following his cue, turned to face the jury. "Human chromosomes are made up of deoxyribonucleic acid—what we call DNA. It's found in the nucleus of human cells. DNA is a highly complex, two-stranded molecule wound into a double helix—sort of like a spiral staircase." He wove his hands around one another in demonstration. "These strands are made up of some three billion chemical units, each of them representing one of the four letters in the genetic code. The chemical components of the DNA strand have a certain sequencing, sort of like if you threw letters of the alphabet up in the air and watched them fall back into place. Most of the sequence is the same in all humans, but there are variations, particularly in what we call the 'junk' stretches of DNA between the genes, where triplets of code letters are repeated over and over again. It is the sequence and number of these components that becomes a blueprint for the inherited traits that make each of us what we are."

"Thank you, Doctor." Bullock made a small, probably meaningless notation on his outline. As he had told Ben many times, when the experts go into their lecture mode, it was best to take things slow and easy. The last thing you wanted was a panel of confused, glassy-eyed jurors. "Where can this DNA be found?"

"DNA can be extracted from almost any living tissue. Blood, semen, saliva, hair. And as I mentioned, skin."

"And what is the value of this DNA analysis?"

"Well, that's probably already obvious." He smiled slightly. Never hurts to flatter the jurors. "Once you've determined a DNA sequence from trace evidence found at a crime scene, you can compare it against a sample taken from a suspect to see if it matches."

"Thank you, Doctor. Now let's return to the case at hand." Ben saw the jurors almost imperceptibly inch forward as the conversation moved from incomprehensible genetic science to very understandable high-gloss murder trial. "Did you in fact do any DNA analysis of the samples found at the Barrett crime scene?"

"Yes. There was sufficient material in the blood samples for what we call RFLP testing, and although the skin traces were very small, there was enough to conduct what we call PCR tests. They are both highly reliable DNA tests."

Uh-huh. Ben started making notes. He knew this would be important later.

"What's the difference between the two, Doctor?"

"Well, without getting overcomplicated, the RFLP stands for restriction fragment length polymorphism."

Oh, well, Ben thought, thank you for not getting overcomplicated.

"This test requires more genetic material, which is why we used it only on the blood. It involves a complicated process of radioactively photographing the DNA bands on X-ray film."

"And the other test procedure?"

"That's the PCR—for polymerase chain reaction. For that, we don't need any more genetic material than would fit on the head of a pin. It's a sort of genetic Xeroxing. Individual genes are copied millions of times to form a composite picture—a series of blue dots, actually—that can then be tested for common chemical sequences."

"Would you explain just how these tests are conducted, Doctor?"

"Certainly." Regan turned toward the easel as Bullock mounted several more enlarged charts illustrating the DNA analysis process for the doctor to use as visual aids. "I'll use the RFLP procedure by way of example. First, we extract the DNA from the sample, in this case the blood. Then we expose the DNA to enzymes that recognize certain sequences of code letters and snip the strand at those sequences, thus cutting the DNA into fragments of varying lengths."

Regan pulled out his next chart, then continued his explanation. "These segments are placed in a gel and are subjected to an electrical charge that pulls them down into the gel. The critical factor here is that the short pieces move faster than the longer ones. Therefore, the fragments are separated into a pattern of bands that can then be recorded on X-ray film."

"Thank you, Doctor. Once you have recorded these patterns on X-ray film, what do you do with them?"

"Then we can make comparisons, such as the comparison I made between the patterns derived from the DNA found at the crime scene and the DNA taken from the defendant. The comparison is actually quite simple; you can literally lay the two X-ray films on top of each other." Regan moved to the next chart, which was an enlarged photo of him doing just that. "In this manner, it is easy to determine whether there is a match between samples."

Bullock laid his hands down on the podium. "Dr. Regan, I thank you for making this complicated process understandable. What we all really want to know about, of course, are the results of the tests you made in this case."

"Certainly." Regan exposed the final exhibit in his stack. "We compared the DNA samples taken from the defendant while he was incarcerated to both samples taken from the crime scene, using both tests. The blood was subjected to RFLP testing, and the skin was subjected to PCR testing."

"And?"

Regan looked directly at the jurors. "And in both cases, the DNA from the crime scene matched the DNA taken from Wallace Barrett."

"In both cases? Both the skin and the blood?"

Regan nodded solemnly. "That's correct."

There was an audible stir in the jury box. This was perhaps the most incriminating evidence yet. After all, witnesses could make mistakes, but science never makes mistakes. Or so the prosecution would have them believe.

"Dr. Regan," Bullock said slowly, "I don't want to make you repeat yourself, but you have to understand—this is a very important piece of evidence. Is there any possibility that you or your staff could have made an error?"

"None. I either did or supervised the work at every step. We double-checked and triple-checked everything. There was no mistake. The DNA samples match."

"Very well then. Thank you, Doctor." Bullock hung his head low and wore a grave expression. "I guess that's all there is to say."

CHAPTER

52

BEN PLANNED HIS cross as he walked to the podium. Obviously he would have to attack the methodology and the purported certainty of these DNA techniques, but there was another point to make that was probably even more important. Throughout the direct examination, Bullock had treated Dr. Regan like a member of his staff, like a police lab tech, which of course he wasn't, by a long shot. That was something that needed to be set straight right off the bat.

"Good afternoon, Dr. Regan," Ben said.

Regan looked at him warily. Was this a trick question? "Afternoon."

"Dr. Regan, how much has the State paid you to testify today?"

There was a stir in the courtroom. Ben was pleased to find that Bullock was not the only one who had the ability to do that.

"I . . . I haven't been paid for my testimony," Regan protested.

"But you have been paid."

"Ye-es."

"And you are testifying."

"Ye-es . . . but I—or rather, my firm was paid for its scientific expertise and professional services."

"Which include providing a jury-and-camera-friendly witness to testify in court."

"Objection!" Bullock said.

"Sustained." Judge Hart looked at Ben sternly. "Counsel, restrict yourself to the relevant matters at hand."

"Yes, your honor." He looked back at Dr. Regan. "You're not a member of the police force or the district attorney's office, right?"

"That's correct."

"You wouldn't be here, except that they needed a DNA expert, so they paid you to be their expert."

"Counsel, these scientific procedures are very expensive. The bills have to be paid."

"I understand that. But when a witness is being paid to testify, I think the jury has a right to know it, don't you?"

Regan began to get his dander up. "For the last time, I was not paid to testify. We receive a flat fee up front. That fee does not change, regardless of what our findings are."

Ben continued to push. "So you think the prosecutor's office would be happy to pay you thousands of dollars even if you couldn't help their case."

It was the classic one question too many, as Ben immediately recognized just as soon as it was too late to take it back. "In fact, our DNA analysis more often excludes suspects than it positively identifies them. DNA is a brilliant tool for eliminating suspects. Numerous people in the past few years have been released, even after conviction, when DNA evidence proved they could not have committed the crime."

Swell, Ben thought. That's what he gets for talking faster than he could think. "Let's talk about these purported matches, sir. Are you saying that you examined every single chemical unit of the DNA found at the crime scene and found that they matched every single chemical unit of the DNA taken from Wallace Barrett?"

"No, of course not."

"No?" Ben turned toward the jury box. "But you told these jurors that they were a perfect match."

"Matching here is a term of art. You have to understand—a human DNA molecule contains over three billion chemical units. Even if we had the scientific capability of examining every one of those—which we don't—it would take forever. Instead, we scan a representative sample. If there are no deviations in those samples, we call it a match."

"Even though it may not be."

Regan's face flushed with irritation. "It is a match, counsel. Given the impossibility of examining every single chemical unit."

Ben continued to push. "But it's still possible that some of the other chemical units—the ones you did not scrutinize—might not match."

"It is theoretically possible, yes, but the odds against that happening are astronomical."

"How astronomical?"

"It's ridiculous to even contemplate these numbers. The odds of an RFLP DNA match between samples from two different people are one in ten million."

"Ah, another oddsmaker. The prosecutor should be Jimmy the Greek." Ben glanced at his notes. "Of course, you only conducted the RFLP test on the blood. The presence of Barrett's blood doesn't necessarily make him the murderer."

"There was also the skin beneath his wife's fingernails—"

"Yes, but you conducted only the PCR test on the skin samples, right?"

"That's true. There wasn't enough material for a RFLP."

Ben's eyes raced through his notes. Thank goodness, Jones's pretrial research had made him something of a DNA expert himself. Otherwise, an effective cross would be impossible. Unless the lawyer educates himself, there is no hope of a successful cross. That's why scientific experts were so often able to bamboozle lawyers. "And the chances of a match between samples from two different people are much greater on the PCR test, aren't they?"

"It's still about four thousand to one."

"Is that all?" Ben tried to sound incredulous. "Then you could have a false positive."

"It is theoretically possible. But highly unlikely."

"Four thousand to one doesn't sound impossible to me, Doctor. And you haven't even accounted for statistical skewering due to subpopulations, have you?"

Regan tugged at his tie. "Well, no."

"Certain subpopulations will have DNA that is more similar than others, thus increasing the chances of a match. True?"

"That's true."

"If you consider the genetic differences of the entire world, you can get long statistical odds. But if you limit your comparison to certain subpopulations, the chance of a false positive is much greater, right?"

Regan took a deep breath. "That's true. But there's no evidence—"

"One example of such a subpopulation would be the black race, wouldn't it?"

"Yes."

All eyes darted to Wallace Barrett.

"Another would be members of the same family."

"That's also true."

"Among these groups, the chances of a false DNA match are much greater, correct?"

"I can't deny it."

Ben smiled. "We appreciate your honesty." He walked back to counsel table and retrieved an exhibit Christina had found for him a few days before, careful to keep it hidden from the witness. "Dr. Regan, would you say your business has been a success?"

He folded his hands across his lap. "I like to think so."

"Get a lot of business?"

"Yes, our clients seem to be very pleased with our work—regardless of the result," he added hastily.

"I'm sure. Just how much business do you have?"

"We're now processing over six hundred samples a month."

"Six hundred a month! By a staff of how many?"

Regan was a bit slower to answer this time. He was beginning to realize where this was going. "There are ten of us in the lab."

"Wow," Ben murmured. "Ten people handling six hundred samples every twenty or so working days. Must get very hectic."

"Nothing we can't handle."

"Confusing, too. All those different samples flying about."

"I assure you our labeling protocols are very reliable."

"Still, Doctor, with all those different samples rushing through the lab—some mistakes must occur."

Regan ruffled a bit. "Not that I'm aware of."

Ben looked at him sternly. "Doctor, isn't it a fact of forensic life that every lab has an error rate?"

"Most government-affiliated forensic labs handle a much higher volume of samples. At our lab, we can pick and choose what to handle. We don't let ourselves get swamped. Each sample is handled individually and is read by two different analysts for confirmation."

"Still, Doctor—"

"I assure you, counsel, we are quite careful."

"Perhaps so, Doctor—but you're not perfect, are you?"

"I beg your pardon?"

Not really a fair question, but it would get him where he wanted to go. "My mother always told me that no one was perfect, but I don't know, maybe she was wrong. Are you perfect, Doctor?"

He gazed at Ben wearily. "No, I would not say that I was perfect. Although—"

"You do occasionally make mistakes."

"I suppose. But even if I erred in the lab, the confirmation procedure—"

"No confirmation procedure is flawless, is it, Doctor?"

He stuttered a bit. "I suppose I could conceive of a situation—"

"And every lab has an error rate, right?"

"If indeed we have an error rate, it would be negligible. Barely worth mentioning."

"But you did mention it, didn't you, Doctor?" Ben held up his exhibit, a magazine-size color brochure. "This is the Cellmark annual report, isn't it?"

Regan's eyes widened. "It . . . seems to be."

"Being a publicly held corporation, you have to file these things, don't you?"

"I'm . . . not really sure of the legalities."

"You'd be committing a securities violation if you didn't, right?"

"Right."

"And the SEC demands scrupulous honesty in these things, doesn't it?"

He folded his arms. "I'm sure you know more about that than I do."

"Well, Doctor, according to this report, your lab has an error rate of about two percent. Right?"

"If that's what it says, then that's what it says."

"Well, that's what it says. Is it true?"

There was a long pause before Regan finally answered. "I suppose it must be."

"Thank you. Now, as this report points out, two percent is quite low, and you should be commended for your high standards of excellence. But the fact remains—two percent is two percent. Right?"

Regan pursed his lips. "Yes, two percent is two percent. I can't argue with that."

"So it is in fact possible that your lab made an error when analyzing the Barrett DNA samples, right?"

"It is theoretically possible."

"Because, in fact, no one is perfect. Not even DNA analysts."

"That's correct, counsel. No one is perfect."

Ben beamed. "Well, my mother will be pleased to learn that she was right after all. So, Doctor, if we may, let's summarize what we've learned. First of all, despite what the prosecution would have this jury believe, DNA analysis is not a perfect science, at least not yet, is it?"

"N-no, it isn't perfect."

"What's more, the chances of making a false identification using DNA analysis are in fact much greater than you first suggested, right?"

"Arguably."

"And besides which, none of these results are valid if the samples provided are tainted or handled improperly."

"That's certainly true."

"Thank you, sir." He closed his notebook. "I have no more questions."

53

THREE FOR THREE, Ben kept muttering to himself on his way back to his table. Three witnesses up, three witnesses down, and each time he thought he'd managed to do a reasonably effective job of undermining their testimony on cross. True, he couldn't totally undo what they had to say—some of that forensic testimony was still keenly damning. But he had managed to do what every defense attorney hopes to do during the prosecution's case. Sow the seeds of reasonable doubt.

The next witness up to bat was the medical examiner, Dr. Hikaru Koregai. Ben had crossed him several times before, so he knew what to expect. Koregai was gruff, self-important, and most of all, a team player. He was on the prosecution's side, and he never forgot that.

Koregai took the stand in his usual dignified, deliberate manner. Ben thought he detected some uncertainty in his gait, a barely visible trembling in his step. He had heard that Koregai was having some heart problems.

After the introductions and the credentials—Koregai's thousands of autopsies, his numerous articles for medical journals—were out of the way, Bullock asked the witness about the present case. "Did you perform the autopsies on the Barrett family members?"

"Yes." As always, Koregai's answers were crisp and direct. "I performed the autopsies on the mother, Caroline Barrett, as well as her two small children, Alysha and Annabelle Barrett."

Ben saw several members of the jury wincing. It was gruesome just to think about autopsies being performed on those two tiny, beautiful girls. He hoped to God Bullock wouldn't be dragging out any pictures.

"Let's begin with the children," Bullock said. His expression was grim and humorless, as befitted the topic at hand. "Based on your examinations, can you identify the cause of death?"

Koregai nodded. "Both children died as a result of an attack by a sharp instrument, probably a knife."

"And what was the cause of Caroline Barrett's death?"

"She was also injured by wounds inflicted by a sharp instrument, probably a knife, and probably the same knife that killed her daughters. But she suffered numerous wounds, over twenty by my count."

There was an audible gasp from the jury box and the gallery.

"The worst was a slash that proceeded halfway across her throat. At one point, this slash was so deep it touched her spinal column. There was also a gash four and a half by two and a half inches running from left to right on the side of her face."

"Was that . . . all?"

"No. There were numerous wounds on the right side of her face and several punctures at the back of her head. It was as if the assailant had been trying to eliminate her face. To erase her existence."

"Any other wounds, Doctor?"

"Yes. She also suffered several slashes to her hands. The wounds went vertically down her palms"—he held up his hands to demonstrate—"suggesting that she was trying to defend herself."

"But not very effectively."

"No," Koregai echoed. "Flesh is a poor defense against a knife."

"I assume then that these wounds were the cause of Caroline Barrett's death?"

Koregai concurred. "No single one of these blows would necessarily have been fatal, not even the one to the throat. But the cumulative effect of the massive hemorrhaging was deadly."

"Would that have been a sudden death, Doctor?"

"No," he replied solemnly. "It would have been a slow death. Slow and painful."

Several jurors lowered their eyes or clutched their stomachs. In his own emotionless way, Koregai was painting a picture more horrifying than the crime-scene photographs.

"Can you tell us the time of death, Doctor?"

"I cannot say with absolute certainty—" He glanced quickly at Ben. Experience had taught him not to presume to know things he really couldn't prove. "I can narrow the time of death to between four and six o'clock on the afternoon of March 11."

"I think that's good enough," Bullock said, reminding the jury in his own way that Barrett's neighbor saw him racing out of the house just before six. "Thank you for your help. I have nothing more."

Ben approached the podium in a quiet, almost reverent manner. He would have to be respectful and serious with this witness. There was no way he could seriously impeach any of Koregai's conclusions. His best shot was to hammer on all the things Koregai didn't say.

"Dr. Koregai, I'm surprised you weren't able to identify the time of death more accurately. Why is that?"

"Unfortunately, in this instance, the forensic indicators necessary to ascertain the time of death with a greater degree of accuracy were not available."

What goobledygook, Ben thought. He's hiding something. "Dr. Koregai, didn't you preserve the contents of the victims' stomachs?"

"Uh . . . no."

"No?" Ben was genuinely surprised. "If you had, wouldn't you have been able to more narrowly nail down the time of death?"

"It is . . . possible, yes."

"Well then, why didn't you?"

"At the time, that was believed to be an unnecessary procedure."

"Because the police had already decided who they thought did it. And since they knew when he left the house, and weren't planning to consider any other suspects, there was no reason to preserve the contents of the stomach."

"I wouldn't put it that way," Koregai said, but his discomfort was clearly growing. "However, it is true that the prevailing feeling at the time was that there was no need to take extraordinary investigative measures, as the case was already considered to be solved."

"In other words, they already had someone to pin it on, and they didn't want a bunch of extraneous evidence messing up their case."

"Objection!" Bullock said with a decided air of contempt.

"Sustained." Judge Hart removed her glasses and stared at Ben sternly. "Counsel, I've already warned you about these kinds of remarks. Do it again and you'll be in contempt of court."

"Sorry, your honor." Ben glanced down at his notes. "I also noticed, Doctor, that you did not identify a murder weapon."

Koregai bowed his head slightly. "Since no murder weapon has been discovered, it would be impossible for me to identify it as the actual weapon used."

"So in fact you cannot say with certainty what the cause of death was."

"I can say that the cause of death was a thin instrument with a single sharp cutting edge. That description could fit innumerable knives or, for that matter, other sharp instruments. Every home has knives in it. Why must I point to the specific one that was used?"

"And besides, knowing the specific murder weapon might eliminate suspects, including the one on trial, which is exactly what the prosecution doesn't want."

Judge Hart didn't wait for an objection. "Mr. Kincaid!"

"I'm sorry, your honor. But it's frustrating to see time and time again that the prosecution and police failed to follow up leads or even to investigate possible alternatives because they were so determined to put one man behind bars."

"Counsel, this is cross-examination, not closing argument. Either ask your questions or sit down!"

"Right, right." Ben pulled out his copy of Koregai's autopsy report. "Speaking of not pursuing possibilities, you didn't perform a rape test on Caroline Barrett, did you?"

Koregai looked up suddenly. "What?"

"Isn't it standard procedure in cases of murder involving women to perform a rape test?"

Koregai looked slightly puzzled. "But there was clear evidence of sexual congress."

Ben was caught totally flat-footed. His eyes widened. "There—there was?"

"Indeed. Whether it was a forcible assault I cannot say, because of the great amount of damage resulting from wounds inflicted after the sexual contact. But the witness had engaged in sexual intercourse prior to her death."

"How soon?"

"That is impossible for me to say with precision. Within twenty-four hours."

"But she—" Ben struggled to get a grip. He knew what everyone would assume from this. That she must've been with her husband. "But you don't know who her partner was?"

"No. I found no traces of semen or other trace evidence from which I might make an identification."

"And I suppose you did nothing to follow up this lead, either."

"Actually, I did." Ben suddenly felt a cold clutching at his heart. What had Bullock told him so many times? If you don't know the answer, don't ask the question. "I performed a pregnancy test."

Ben's brain was racing. The case seemed to be spiraling out of his reach. "And—the result?"

"Caroline Barrett was pregnant."

The reaction in the courtroom was like none before. First, there was a harsh, almost unnatural silence, followed by a sudden eruption so loud Judge Hart was forced to resort to the gavel.

"Order! Order!" Reporters jumped out of their seats and raced for the back. All three cameras zoomed in for closeups.

"She was pregnant?" Ben repeated. "You mean from—"

"No, not from the recent incidence of sexual activity. The embryo was almost two months old."

Ben knew he shouldn't, but he couldn't help himself. His eyes twisted round to look at Wallace Barrett, just as every other eye in the courtroom did. As it happened, Barrett seemed just as stunned as everyone else. His lips parted; his eyes went wide, then blank. His lips moved slightly, but no sound came out.

Pregnant?

"She was carrying a child," Koregai stated flatly. "A boy."

Barrett's head dropped to the table. Judge Hart continued pounding her gavel. The courtroom was in an uproar.

"Your honor," Bullock shouted above the hubbub, "this is a truly startling development." So he said, but Ben noted he didn't seem all that startled. "The State moves for an immediate amendment of the indictment. The defendant should be tried for *four* murders, not just three."

Judge Hart continued pounding her gavel. "Counsel, you know perfectly well you cannot alter the charges in midtrial. If you want to try the fourth murder, you'll have to file another indictment."

Bullock nodded, acquiescing. He turned just enough to face the cameras, giving them a silent look of grim sadness, followed by steely resolve.

Ben felt a cold shiver running up and down his spine. An unborn baby. Murdered. This changed everything. Everything. The worst crime of the century just got worse still.

"Do you have any more questions, counsel?" Judge Hart asked.

"No, your honor. I guess not." Ben hated to leave his cross on this abysmal note, but he had no idea what to ask next. He simply had no idea.

He took his seat beside Wallace Barrett. "How're you doing, man?"

Barrett turned his head to the side, just enough for Ben and every juror in the box to see his tear-streaked face. "She never told me, Ben," he said, barely in a whisper. "A boy. I always wanted a boy."

Tears streamed out of his eyes; his face returned to the makeshift privacy of his hands.

Ben felt a hollowness in his heart that was almost unbearable. He knew Barrett must feel horrible; his agony was almost palpable. But at the same time, he knew that the jury, depending on which way they were leaning, could see an entirely different motivation for the scene at the defense table.

Where Ben saw tears of grief, they would see tears of guilt.

CHAPTER

54

MERCIFULLY, JUDGE HART called a recess so the reporters could file their reports and some semblance of order could be restored before hearing the final witness of the day.

Ben's aching had transmuted itself into a numbness, an emptiness he could hardly describe. He tried to put it out of his mind. They had one more witness to deal with, and it was important that this one go better for Barrett than the last had gone.

"The State calls Dr. Herbert Fisher to the stand."

Ben shot a quick, puzzled look back at Christina. Weren't they done with the forensic testimony?

He flipped quickly through his trial notebook to the witness list. That's right—Fisher was a fact witness, not an expert. He was a friend and doctor to Caroline Barrett. Why on earth would they be calling him now?

Fisher took the stand. He was a tall man about Barrett's age. Obviously a professional. He was handsome—so handsome, in fact, that it dominated all first impressions and obscured any lesser facts that might otherwise have been gathered. As Joni would say, he was a hunk.

Ben almost immediately noticed the difference in his client when Fisher took the stand. He became stiff and cold; his eyes burned across the courtroom to the witness stand. It was clear to Ben that there was no love lost between these two men.

Despite the lateness of the day, Bullock spent a fair amount of time delving into the witness's educational background, his medical practice, his home in South Tulsa near Southern Hills. Almost half an hour passed before he asked, "Doctor, did you ever have occasion to meet a woman named Caroline Barrett?"

"Yes, sir."

"And when did you meet her?"

"Six or seven months ago."

"Can you please describe the circumstances?"

Dr. Fisher folded his hands and nodded. "At that time, I was a general practice physician at Springer Clinic. Caroline was referred to me one day when her usual physician was unavailable."

"Why did she need a doctor?"

"She had a bruised eye, as well as some damage to her nose."

"Do you know what caused the injuries?"

Dr. Fisher paused, looked at the jury. "She told me she fell. But it didn't take a rocket scientist to see that she was lying."

"Lying? Why would she lie?"

Fisher frowned. "It was obvious to me that she had been punched. Probably several times, given the extent of the injuries."

"And do you know who struck her?"

"Objection," Ben said. "Lack of personal knowledge. He wasn't there."

"Sustained," the judge said.

"Very well," Bullock said, "did she tell you who struck her?"

"I still object," Ben said. "That's hearsay."

"But your honor," Bullock said, "the declarant is dead. She's obviously unavailable."

Judge Hart nodded. "I don't like this sort of evidence, Mr. Bullock. I don't think it's the most reliable evidence to give the jury. But given the circumstances, I'm going to allow it once again. Just don't take it too far."

Bullock nodded. "Of course not." He returned his attention to the witness. "Did she tell you who struck her?"

"Yes. Not that first day, but later, as we got to know each other better." He turned his head to stare directly at Wallace Barrett. "She told me her husband beat her up."

The murmur from the courtroom was somber and low. Ben immediately saw the plan behind Bullock's seemingly erratic ordering of his witnesses. Now that he had nailed down the DNA identification, assuring everyone at the very least that Barrett was at the scene of the crime, he reconjured the specters of wife beating and domestic abuse. It was all the jury needed to understand the how and the why of the murder.

It was all they needed to convict.

"Did you believe her?" Bullock asked.

"Of course I did. The truth had been evident to me all along."

Bullock pivoted around his podium. "You've said that you later got to know Caroline Barrett better. How did that occur?"

Fisher waved a hand casually. "Oh, in the same manner that all friendships do, I suppose. I saw her a few more times after that initial consultation. We met at a party. We had lunch together. We came to be close friends."

"Did you continue to act as her physician?"

"No. After it became apparent that we were going to be close personal friends, I thought it was inappropriate for me to act as her doctor, so I referred her to someone else, although of course, just by seeing her as often as I did, I was aware of her continual injuries on an informal basis."

Bullock pulled himself erect. "Let me apologize in advance, Doctor, but I'm afraid I have to ask you a personal question. Were you and Caroline Barrett intimate?"

"Intimate? What do you mean?"

"Was it a romantic relationship?"

"Certainly not." Fisher spoke as if the very notion was absurd. "She was still married to the defendant, even though he made her life miserable. No, it was purely friendship. Nothing more."

"Thank you, Doctor. Did you see Caroline Barrett during the month before she was so brutally killed?"

"Yes, I did."

"How would you describe her state of mind at that time?"

"Not good." Fisher frowned. "During that last month, I probably saw her almost every day. Certainly never more than a day or two passed that I didn't see her. And she was miserable. Unhappy, depressed, despondent."

"Why was she unhappy?"

"In a nutshell? Because she was afraid of her husband."

"Why?"

"Because he had beat her up so many times before, and there was no telling when he would hit her next. She lived in fear—I mean, absolute fear—on a daily basis. The most innocent remark might set him off. There was just no way of knowing. And when those rages came over him, he was uncontrollable. Mean, violent, and uncontrollable." He paused again, then made eye contact with the jurors. "She was afraid he'd kill her."

Ben watched the jurors' faces grow still and grim. Many of them looked over at Wallace Barrett, who was looking away, avoiding eye contact.

The testimony was having its intended impact. Slowly but surely the jury was seeing Barrett less as the sports hero/mayor and more as the abusive, wife-beating maniac.

"Why would she be afraid he would kill her?"

"He'd come close several times already. Beating her into unconsciousness, till she had to go to the hospital for emergency treatment. Or humiliating her in public, like the time he locked her out of the house in her underwear. Things that made her want to die. He was destroying her. Bit by bit he was draining everything away from her, including her will to live."

"Did you report any of these incidents to the police?"

"No. I wish to God I had. But she begged me not to, for the sake of the children, she said, and I didn't. I was a fool. I might've . . . might've . . ."

"Don't blame yourself, Doctor. We all understand the circumstances. Tell me, given the enormous abuse Caroline Barrett was suffering, why didn't she leave him?"

Fisher grimaced. "It's the classic battered-woman syndrome. She hated the man but she couldn't separate herself. Plus there were the children to think about. How would she care for them without him? How would she live? Certainly not in the manner to which she had become accustomed. She'd signed a prenuptial agreement before marrying Barrett. In the event of divorce or separation, she got nothing." He shook his head gravely. "She often said the children were all she had, the only weapon she could use against him. If it hadn't been for them, she was sure she would've been dead already."

Bullock moved through his questions slow and easily, letting these devastating words hang heavy in the hearts of the jurors. "What would trigger these irrational bursts of fury?"

Fisher shrugged. "It varied. Sometimes it was his chauvinistic, piggish attitudes about what a wife should do. Sometimes it was his irrational jealousy. She couldn't breathe on another man without him going ballistic."

"How did this affect her?"

"I'm sure you can imagine. What would be the effect of living in constant fear for yourself and your children? Of being constantly battered and abused, verbally and physically? She was on the edge, if she hadn't gone over already. I have to say, I was afraid for her mental health. I tried to get her to seek professional help, or better yet, to get away from him. But she never did. I mean, when she told me about her pregnancy, she was practically in hysterics."

Ben sensed Barrett straightening beside him. "That son of a bitch knew," Barrett muttered under his breath. "I didn't know, but he did."

Bullock raised an eyebrow. "Dr. Fisher, you knew about her pregnancy?"

"Of course. As I've said, we saw each other frequently."

"Do you know if she told her husband she was pregnant?"

"I know that she did not, unless perhaps she did it on the day she died, which might in fact explain what happened."

The hubbub in the courtroom swelled. "What do you mean?" Bullock asked.

"Your honor," Ben said, "I'm going to object to any speculation by the witness."

Judge Hart nodded. "Dr. Fisher, you may tell the jury what you know, but please refrain from speculating about what you do not know but think might have happened."

Dr. Fisher nodded his understanding. "Caroline told me on several occasions that her husband hated her when she was pregnant. He belittled her and made fun of her, told her she was an ugly pig—charming statements like that. He flew off the handle once and hit her. Can you imagine? Punching a pregnant woman? Your own wife? She'd been pregnant three times—for their two children and one miscarriage, which may have been induced by violence from her husband—and he had made her life a misery each time. She knew as soon as she told him she was pregnant again, the abuse would escalate. That's why she refrained from telling him."

"But she had to tell him sometime."

"Yes," Fisher agreed, "she did. Which makes me wonder if she didn't tell him the night he killed—I mean, the night she was killed."

"I would've thought she might've thought the pregnancy was a blessing. Surely the man wouldn't intentionally kill his own child. So long as she carried the child, she would be safe."

Fisher shook his head grimly. "Nothing could make her think she was safe from him. Not after the incident with the baseball bat."

A deadly hush fell over the courtroom. No one twitched; no lips moved.

"The incident with the baseball bat?" Bullock asked finally.

"You heard right." Fisher shifted uncomfortably in his chair.

"When was this?"

"Two days before she was killed. Another one of his jealous fits. He ran into the house, screaming at the top of his lungs, calling her a bitch, a whore. Accusing her of things"—he shook his head—"horrible things. Unmentionable. Of course, both children were at home the whole time this was going on. She tried to protect them, but—"

He brushed his hand across his face, then continued. "The worst of it, she told me the next day, was that she realized how powerless she was against him. Powerless to help herself or her children."

"You mentioned . . . a baseball bat?"

"That's right. According to Caroline, he was swinging a baseball bat, one of those modern aluminum jobs. And he had a mean swing, too. He kept swishing that thing through the air at deadly speeds, shouting at the top of his lungs, 'I'm gonna kill you, you fucking bitch! I'm gonna kill you, you filthy whore!' Over and over again. 'I'm gonna kill you!' "

Bullock spoke softly but audibly. "And two days later . . ."

Fisher nodded. "Two days later, she was dead. Killed. In a horrible, violent, brutal way."

Bullock closed his notebook and turned slowly to face the bench. "No more questions, your honor."

Judge Hart turned toward Ben. "Cross-examination?"

Ben nodded, then leaned into his client's ear. "Wallace, tell me about this guy."

"Tell you about what?"

"About what he said! All those stories about you beating and mistreating your wife! Tell me how to prove he's lying."

Barrett's voice seemed broken and emotionless. "I . . . can't."

"Mr. Kincaid, do you intend to cross-examine?"

Ben's brain kicked into warp drive. He hated to leave the jury with this image of Wallace Barrett swinging a baseball bat through the air like a crazed maniac. But there wasn't much to cross-examine Fisher about. None of his testimony actually went toward proving Barrett was the murderer. But the overall effect left by this testimony, on top of all that went before, was devastating.

"No questions, your honor."

She did not look surprised. Apparently she saw the difficulties as clearly as Ben did.

"The prosecution rests," Bullock said, wearing his usual graveside countenance. He must be relishing it—going out on a bang, letting the jurors return to their rooms with the image of Mayor Wallace Barrett and his baseball bat, swinging at his pregnant wife, to haunt their sleep.

Judge Hart pounded her gavel, gave the jury the usual instructions, and recessed the court for the day.

Ben made his way toward the judge's chambers. He had to make the usual motions that came at the conclusion of the prosecution's case—motions to dismiss, motions for mistrial, reurging motions in limine. But he knew it was futile. The prosecution had done its job. They had made the jury believe that this respected, educated, prosperous member of the community could be the coldhearted murderer of his own family. He knew it, and he could see it— could see it in the expression of each and every juror as they filed out of the courtroom.

The prosecution had done its job, all right. And unless he did his, unless he did something extraordinary when the defense put on its case, Wallace Barrett was going to get the death sentence.

CHAPTER

55

BACK AT THEIR hotel-room headquarters, Jones and Loving were waiting for Ben and Christina. To Ben's surprise, his friend, former brother-in-law, and recent prosecution witness Mike Morelli was there as well.

As Ben came through the door, Mike spread open his hands and smiled. "No hard feelings?"

Ben returned the smile. "None. Personally, I think you did more good for our side than you did for the prosecution."

"So does Bullock. And boy, is he pissed. He's been stomping all over the station, griping to Chief Blackwell, threatening to yank my badge. All the usual DA histrionics."

Ben threw down his briefcase and grabbed a chair. "When did you find out you were going to testify?"

"Just found out for sure this morning. Called me in on my day off, no less. Which is a good sign for you."

"Oh, yeah? How so?"

Mike's head cocked to one side. "Ben, Bullock knows you and I are friends. He wouldn't have called me in a million years unless he was worried."

Ben shook his head grimly. "Maybe he had some doubts yesterday, but not today. He hurt us today."

Jones chimed in with his color commentary. "I thought you did a great job of taking apart those high-priced so-called experts, Boss."

"Ditto," Christina offered.

Ben shrugged. "But when all is said and done, juries don't make up their minds based on what experts say. They might use the testimony of experts to reinforce their impressions, but their minds are made up by the fact witnesses. Hearing what people have seen and heard. And what that last witness had seen and heard was devastating. Can you imagine? The mayor of the city swinging a baseball bat through the air and threatening to smash his wife's head? How is the jury ever going to get that picture out of their heads long enough to even consider another suspect?"

"Don't look to me for help," Mike said. "I told you this was a loser when you took it. Is there any way you can dispute Dr. Fisher's testimony?"

Ben shook his head. "No one was there except Caroline and the children. And they're all dead."

"Except," Loving added, "for Wallace Barrett."

Ben nodded. "He's going to take the stand. I know there are risks. Bullock will get a chance to cross. But Barrett's used to handling himself in public, facing tough questioning."

"Ben," Mike said, "I'm not revealing any secrets by telling you that this is exactly what Bullock is hoping for. A chance to take Barrett apart on national television."

"I know. But no one else can dispute that baseball bat testimony, not to mention the alleged incidents of abuse Cynthia Taylor testified about. He's the only one who can do it." Ben kept his own private doubts to himself. Yes, Barrett was the only one who could do it, but given his behavior in the courtroom—would he do it? "The jury won't believe he isn't an irrational maniac until they hear it from his mouth."

"And maybe not then," Mike added.

Ben nodded. "Christina and I are going to his cell tonight to prep him. And speaking of which, Loving—"

Loving's head snapped up. "Yes, Skipper?"

"Any luck tracking down the man you saw at O'Brien Park?"

"Sorry, Skipper. This is the most frustratin' investigation I've handled in my entire life. I come smack up against a stone wall every step I take. I just can't find the creep."

"Well, that settles it, then. We're putting you on the stand."

Loving looked horrified. "*Me?* On the—"

"You got it. I don't like it much either. The jury will know you work for me and will weigh your testimony with that in mind. But we don't have any other choice. You're the only link we have between Whitman and the hit man."

Loving swallowed. "When do you think I'll go on?"

Ben shrugged. "It's impossible to predict these things with certainty. Maybe tomorrow, although Judge Hart isn't resuming the trial till afternoon. So probably the day after."

Loving looked as if he might be sick. "Tomorrow? Or the day after?"

Ben tried to be reassuring. "Relax, Loving. Christina and I will prepare you. By the time you're on the stand, you'll be able to do it in your sleep."

"You know," Loving said, "I was supposed to testify once before. I . . . kinda sorta didn't show up."

Loving was supposed to testify? Of course, Ben remembered. During his divorce. Ben had represented his ex-wife and Loving didn't show up for the trial. And now he knew why. Loving wasn't the first person who'd tanked a lawsuit because he couldn't cope with cross-ex. "There's no need to worry, Loving. I know everything Bullock will ask, and we'll think out all your responses in advance. Christina will help. She's the best witness preparer I've ever known. She thinks of everything. Seriously. You have nothing to worry about."

It was amazing to see such a tiny voice come out of that hulking frame. "If you say so."

"I do. You'll see. You'll come out smelling like a rose."

Loving nodded, but it wasn't hard to detect that he was somewhat less than convinced.

"The truth is," Ben said, "the trial isn't going very well for us just at the moment. The jury has heard a truckload of damaging evidence against our client. More than enough to convict him, frankly. If we're going to prevent that, to prevent an innocent man from going to prison or being executed for a hideous crime he didn't commit—we're going to have to pull out all the stops. I need everyone to do everything they can to make our part of the case as good as it can possibly be. Understood?"

All heads nodded. Understood.

"By the way, Mike, any luck catching the creep who blew our office to smithereens?"

"Not yet. Sorry."

Christina jumped in. "What's taking so long?" The concern in her face was evident. "We can't just sit around on our hands until this creep kills Ben."

"The psych guys say he doesn't want to kill Ben, at least not right away. He wants Ben to suffer."

"Based on what?"

"Based on the facts. Think about it. Most of the bomber's hijinks have been designed to torment, not to exterminate. Even when he blew up your office, he used a bomb with a detectable—and, I might add, totally unnecessary—ticking noise that could tip Ben off just in the nick of time. There are plenty of silent bomb trigger mechanisms around these days. Plenty of instantaneous, radio-signal remote-control detonators. He didn't have to tip you off. But he did."

"If I'd been half a minute slower," Ben said, "we would've all died."

Mike held up his hands. "Look, I'm not saying he's a nice guy. And I'm not saying killing you wouldn't necessarily make his day. I'm just saying it hasn't been his immediate goal." He paused. "Yet."

"Yet?"

Mike's teeth set together in a grim expression. "That's the typical psychological profile. Eventually they get tired of toying with you."

"And then?"

"And then they try to kill you."

"Oh." Ben sank back into his chair. "Any new leads? Any hope of finding this maniac?"

"The bomb ingredients were so common they were impossible to trace. We've got video experts going over and over the tapes he sent, but so far they haven't uncovered any identifying features. We're also cataloging all the nuts who have sent hate mail about the Barrett case to the courts or any of the participants. I'm hoping they'll lead us to something."

"What if this particular nut isn't the letter writing type? What if he's just the bombing-killing type?"

"We're doing everything we can, kemo sabe."

Ben nodded. He knew they were. It was just too frustrating, trying to conduct a murder trial while some maniac was determined to make your life a misery. Or end it.

Ben glanced at his watch. "Well, Christina and I need to head back to the jailhouse."

"Can you give me a lift?" Mike asked. "I need to go back to my office and do some paperwork."

Ben raised an eyebrow. "Trans Am in the shop again?"

"No, I walked over here. Thought I needed some exercise."

"You? Why?"

"If you must know, since I quit smoking, I've put on a pound or two. So I try to get some exercise whenever this impossible job of mine allows."

"I see." Ben smiled. "Well, I'd be happy to give you a ride back. I think my Honda can still carry three people. Can't it, Christina?"

Christina wavered her hand in the air. "Close call."

BEN LED MIKE and Christina out to the street where he had parked his Honda Accord. Mike grimaced when he saw the dented, rust-encrusted silver frame, the dragging muffler, the crushed grille. Mike took the front seat; Christina took the back.

Mike crawled into the bucket seat and slammed the door closed. The entire frame seemed to shudder and shake. "Good grief, Ben. When are you going to get a new car?"

"When I'm rich and famous."

"Hell, you're already famous, thanks to this case. And I assume Barrett is paying you."

"True. But holing up in the Adam's Mark isn't exactly cheap. Neither is finding new office space."

"Well, whatever it takes, do it. Riding around in this bucket of bolts is embarrassing."

Christina piped up from the back. "Agreed."

Mike continued. "You don't see me driving a heap like this, do you?"

"No, I see you driving a Trans Am, like some teenager on his way to peel out at the drag races with Betty Lou."

"A Trans Am is not a teenager car. It's for all ages. Cool people of all ages, that is."

"Look," Ben said, "I don't have my ego wrapped up in my car. It's not a status symbol. It's a way to get from Point A to Point B."

"If you say so."

Ben turned the key and started the engine.

Mike grimaced. "Listen to that. That's pathetic." He paused for a moment so they could all appreciate the clanging and rattling. "Sounds like your carburetor is gasping for air. And I can hear the brakes grinding. Your pads are probably worn down to nothing. And listen to that exhaust! And—"

He paused. There was something else, but he couldn't quite place it.

"What's that other noise? The high-pitched one."

"Don't ask me," Ben said. "I don't know beans about cars."

"Well, I do, and I've never heard—"

He quieted again, tried to block everything else out and focus on the mysterious noise. It was high-pitched and rhythmic, a back-and-forth sound, a sort of sonic—

Ticktock. Ticktock. Ticktock.

A cold chill gripped everyone in the car.

"Get out!" Mike shouted.

Christina leaned forward. "Our stuff is in the trunk—"

"I said, *get out!*" Mike dove out his side door, then whipped around and hauled Christina out of the back. Ben opened his door and hit the pavement. All three scrambled to their feet and ran.

They had barely made it to the other side of the street when the bomb detonated. The force of the explosion knocked Ben facedown onto the sidewalk. The hood of his car flew up and a red fireball leapt out of the charred engine. Safety glass flew everywhere. The sound of the explosion reverberated off the buildings on either side of the street. It was earsplitting, Ben thought. And disturbingly familiar.

The frame of the car disintegrated, like a clown car in the circus, falling outward onto the concrete.

Ben scrambled back onto his feet, then looked frantically for Christina and Mike.

They, too, were a safe distance from the car. As far as he could tell, they were fine. Ben cautiously made his way to them.

"Like I said," Mike offered, "I think you should consider getting a new car."

"Everyone okay?" Ben asked.

Christina and Mike nodded. "Just a little shaken up," Christina said weakly. "This is becoming monotonous."

"Right. My thought exactly."

"Fact is, Ben," Mike said, "you're becoming a pretty damn dangerous guy to know."

"Yeah." Ben steered them down the street, away from the smoke clouds. "Well, maybe now that this sadist has had his fun, he'll lay off."

"If you think that, you're kidding yourself," Mike said. "It's obvious this creep enjoys tormenting you, and it's obvious he wants you to suffer. But he's not going to be happy with that. He's not going to be happy until you're dead."

Ben continued walking down the street, eyes straight ahead, not saying a word.

CHAPTER

56

DEANNA COLLAPSED INTO her hotel room, kicked off her heels, threw herself down on the bed, and cried.

My God, my God—what was she doing here? She had never meant to mislead anyone, never meant to be a fraud. And now, here she was on the jury of the Wallace Barrett case, probably the most publicized murder trial in the history of the state. The cameras were rolling, the prosecution was piling on evidence, and all she could think about was her daughter. Her own daughter.

My God, Martha. What have you done?

Voir dire turned out to be a breeze. She hadn't even had to lie, not really. No one ever came close to the truth. True, she had blanched a bit at the end of the jury examination when that young attorney, the one representing the mayor, asked if anyone knew of any other reason not already discussed that might prevent anyone from serving as an impartial juror. It was a vague, broad question. Easily ignored. And yet she knew why he had asked it. He had asked it in an attempt to root out people like her, people who might be biased one way or another by factors he couldn't even imagine, much less ask about.

But she had not raised her hand. She had remained painfully silent.

After that, she had become a full-fledged member of the Wallace Barrett jury. She'd had to get her friend Suzanne to stay with Martha while the jury was sequestered at the Downtown Doubletree Hotel. Sequestered—that was a laugh. It felt more like they'd been indicted. The whole *juror compound*, as they called it, was run like a prison camp. The jurors had had to meet in secret, at the fairgrounds, before the trial started. They were searched, first by hand, then by metal detectors. Their luggage was searched as well. Then they were herded onto a bus and, escorted by six men from the sheriff's office, taken to their hotel.

Security was no less tight at the hotel. Everyone had their own room, but none of the rooms had locks on the doors. Officers from the sheriff's office were posted in the hallway outside, not to keep them safe, but to keep them from meeting and talking about the case. No one said that the rooms would be searched while the jurors were out, but it was obvious to Deanna that they were. When she returned to her room each evening, personal belongings had been moved slightly from where they had been left that morning.

No juror was allowed to go to any other juror's room—ever. There was one communal meeting room, which was the only place two or more jurors were allowed to gather. Again, deputies were posted in the room at all times, to make sure no one talked about the case. Meals were served in the same room, and under the same scrutiny.

The jurors were getting along well enough for the most part, but there was no denying the fact that tempers were fraying. The isolation was causing irritation, and irritation was always dangerous when people were in such close quarters. If for nothing else, Deanna was grateful that the lawyers and the judge seemed to be moving the trial along in an expeditious fashion. She couldn't imagine living in these subhuman conditions for months on end. She was sure it would drive her mad. It would drive anyone mad.

The jurors had all sworn not to expose themselves to media accounts of the trial or to discuss the case amongst themselves before the time for deliberation. They had given their word. You would think that would be enough. But instead, the jurors were restricted and monitored constantly. They were treated like children, children who had to be surrounded at all times by hall monitors to prevent them from talking. It was insulting and degrading. Clearly the judicial system did not trust them. A woman giving up her time, separated from her loved ones, ought to be entitled to better treatment.

And in the midst of all these miserable living conditions, all Deanna could think about was her Martha. She felt certain that Martha would not intentionally participate in any murders. But Martha had a huge blind spot where Buck was concerned; she had proven that many times over. She might have done something unwittingly, might've helped in the tiniest way. Tiny, but still enough to get her a felony conviction. And jail time. Enough to ruin her life.

If Wallace Barrett went free.

That was the rub. She was convinced that Barrett was innocent. Maybe no one else on the jury believed it, but she did. She had believed it from the instant she'd heard his neighbor describe the strangers he'd seen casing Barrett's home. The tall man with the goatee wearing fatigues. The shorter, younger, dark-haired girl with the blue headband.

How could she doubt that Buck was involved? She had seen his camera; she had developed the pictures herself. Pictures of Barrett's house taken from every possible angle. The work of a hit man planning his crime. Indeed, she could believe a monster like Buck could commit this crime a good deal more easily than she could believe Wallace Barrett did it.

But what if Barrett was acquitted? What if, in the jury room, she argued her heart out and convinced the rest of the jury to acquit? Barrett would go free, and the DA, feeling pressure from all sides, would start looking for a new suspect. He would follow the only other real lead they had—the tall stranger casing the neighborhood. If they worked hard enough at it, in time they would eventually find Buck.

And Buck would lead them to Martha.

Deanna couldn't let that happen. She couldn't let her little girl's life be ruined before it had really begun.

But the alternative was watching an innocent man go to prison. Or worse.

Even if he avoided the death penalty, Barrett would have to live the rest of his life with the shame and despair of knowing that the world believed he had killed his own wife. His own two small children.

When he hadn't.

The defense case was not expected to take more than a day or two. If she hadn't spoken up by then, it would be too late.

Deanna buried her face in the pillow. There had to be some way out, some solution, some compromise. Some way to prevent this great injustice without destroying her little girl's life.

But she was damned if she could think of it.

She rolled over onto her back, wiping the tears from her eyes. She was damned, all right. Either way she went, any way she turned, she was damned.

57

THERE ARE MOMENTS in every trial when time stands still. Even in the most ordinary exercises in judicial fact finding, there are unexpected moments, moments of upset or revelation or salvation or despair. A trial is simply too huge, too complicated; even the best attorney on earth cannot anticipate everything. It is during these breakthrough moments that the true character of the jury trial system is revealed.

The trial of Wallace Barrett was far from ordinary. But its breakthrough moment was close at hand.

"Your honor," Ben said, "I call Wallace Barrett to the stand."

It was the announcement everyone had waited for, hoped for, speculated about. Everyone knew that a criminal defendant was not required to testify; the Fifth Amendment protects the innocent as well as the guilty. Everyone knew all the perfectly sound reasons why even the most innocent of defendants often opt not to take the stand. But at the same time, everyone hopes that they will. There's no substitute for hearing the story from the defendant's own lips. There's nothing quite as telling as being able to look into the man's eyes as he tells it.

O. J. Simpson never took the stand. Lee Harvey Oswald never took the stand. James Earl Ray never took the stand.

But on this day, Wallace Barrett did.

FLASHBULBS, SUPPOSEDLY BARRED from the courtroom, erupted like lightning. Minicam operators climbed onto seats and chairs, craning for a better view. The courtroom was pandemonium, a loud roar punctuated by the judge's futile pounding of her gavel. Despite what Ben had said in opening statement, everyone had expected the defense to begin with its less important witnesses, evaluating as they went the need for placing Wallace Barrett in the witness stand, making him subject to scrutiny by God, his country, and cross-examination.

But on this point, the defense had fooled them all.

And for about the ten millionth time, Ben wondered if he had done the right thing.

They had been over and over it, almost throughout the entire night. After the explosion, Mike had insisted that he and Christina go to the police station to file reports and provide any information that might possibly allow them to track down the bomber who was stalking Ben. It was after eleven before they got out of there. And then they had to return to Barrett's jail cell and prepare him to testify.

To his credit, Barrett had come through all the pretrial rehearsals with flying colors. And why not? He was a seasoned media veteran. Barrett had insisted on testifying, had demanded his chance to confront his accusers and to tell his faithful followers the truth. Given his insistence on testifying, the only decision left to Ben was when. And he had decided to put Wallace on first.

There were a few other possibilities for lead witnesses. Jones had lined up a crime reconstructionist, a man who used computer graphic reenactments to show the jury how a crime was committed even when there were no eye-witnesses. His presentations suggested for a variety of reasons that it was unlikely (though not impossible) that one assailant committed all three murders. But his testimony was founded on a host of likely but unprovable assumptions, assumptions Ben knew Bullock would tear apart on cross. Besides, all the prosecution had to prove was that Barrett had committed one of the murders. Any one of them would be sufficient to strap him down on the lethal injection table.

Jones had also found some forensic experts who were willing to testify for the defense, assuming Barrett would pay their not insignificant fees. There might have been some value in calling their own experts on blood or DNA. But the bottom line was that these witnesses would only reiterate the issues Ben had already introduced during his cross-examination of the prosecution's witnesses. The points had already been made, and they had not been sufficient to overcome the presumption of guilt created by the prosecution's mountain of evidence. If he was going to win this trial, he needed something more.

He needed Wallace Barrett. On the witness stand.

Barrett took the stand with his usual deliberative, confident manner. Ben had coached him to be careful not to seem in any way smug or overbearing. He should at all times seem helpful, even deferential, to the judge and jury. And without being indignant or melodramatic, he must make it clear that he did not enjoy this. After all, a tragedy had occurred, a tragedy that had struck him personally. He had to make sure the jury never forgot that.

As Ben elicited the introductory information, Barrett performed flawlessly. He was striking exactly the right chord, making exactly the right impression. At this stage, the information being conveyed didn't much matter. Everyone already knew who he was, what he did for a living, why he was here. What mattered was the impression he made on the jury while he was saying it.

They were watching him.

Ben was also riding a perceptual tightrope, vacillating between the formality required by the court and the casual friendliness necessary to show the jury that Ben liked the man. "Wallace, how long had you and Caroline been married?"

"Twelve years."

"And how would you describe your marriage?"

"I would describe it as being very happy, for the most part. Sure, we had fights now and again, like any other couple. But the bottom line was I loved her, and she loved me. And we both loved the kids."

The kids, the kids, the kids. The specter of those poor horribly murdered children hung over this trial like a thundercloud. "Some of the prosecution's witnesses have suggested that your marriage was an unhappy one."

"They're wrong." Barrett seemed firm, not pushy, but certain. "Believe me, I'm the one in the position to know. We had a very loving marriage. The fact is, Caroline's sister never liked me from day one. I don't know why. But she's never made any bones about it. This is not the first time she's tried to embarrass me publicly. And now that she's got this six-figure book deal—well, she's not going to do me any favors, put it that way."

"We've also heard testimony from your neighbor, Mr. Sanders, and Caroline's . . . friend Dr. Fisher."

"They were both in love with her," Barrett said flatly. "I don't think anything ever came of it. I don't think Caroline would've allowed anything to come of it. I think she loved me too much. But that didn't stop them from trying. Sanders was constantly at our house on the feeblest of excuses. He wasn't protecting Caroline; he was trying to get close to her. And Dr. Fisher was just the same."

"That seems a bit . . . unusual."

Barrett shook his head. "It wouldn't if you knew my wife. She was beautiful. More than beautiful . . . breathtaking. And she was smart and funny and fun to be with. She was the perfect companion. Of course everyone wanted her. Who wouldn't?"

"So it was not true that your marriage was unhappy?"

"No, it was not. That was a figment of their imagination. That was the way they wanted it to be, not the way it was."

"Wallace, some of these witnesses have suggested that you . . . physically hurt your wife."

"Absolutely one hundred percent not true." He leaned forward in his chair, still remaining calm, but making it clear that he did not like or appreciate these vile accusations. "I did not. Never."

"You didn't fight with her?"

"Fight, yes. We fought verbally. But I wouldn't hurt her, not physically. I'd rather have died first. Really. I'd rather have died."

"We've heard intimations that the police were called out to your home."

"The police came twice. That's it. I'm sure Harvey Sanders, our resident nosy neighbor, called them both times. They came out, saw that nothing serious was going on, and left. Although they stopped once to lecture Sanders on misuse of police resources on their way out. I guess he forgot to mention that part. And that's it. That's the only time police ever stepped inside my home until . . . until . . . well, you know."

Ben did know. They all knew. Ben paused, swallowed, then continued. "We've also been told that on one occasion after a fight you locked Caroline out of the house wearing nothing but her underwear."

"Again, that's a major distortion. She locked herself out of the house. She ran out for the mail in her underwear, the wind blew the door shut, and she was trapped. The doorbell was broken and I was sleeping, so I didn't hear her pounding on the door. Eventually she went next door to see Sanders, which I'm sure was the cheap thrill of his life. She called from his place and I let her in. That's all there was to it. Sanders imagined the rest. It was no great big deal."

"So you did not lock her out of the house to punish her?"

"Of course not. That's nuts. Why would I want to do that, even if I was the maniac Sanders wants you to think I am? Do you think I liked having my wife running around the neighborhood in her underwear? Believe me, I didn't."

Ben made a quick and unobtrusive visual survey of the jury. They seemed to be going along with him, following with him, maybe even believing him. At any rate, they were definitely paying attention.

"Wallace, we've also heard about an alleged incident with a baseball bat—"

"That was a lie."

"But Dr. Fisher—"

"I don't care what he said. That was just a bald-faced lie. I never did anything like that. I never would. I guess Fisher thinks that"—his voice quietened—"now that Caroline is dead he can claim she told him anything. That simply never happened."

"You never aimed a baseball bat at your wife's head?"

"Of course not. Think about it. If I had done a thing like that, do you think Caroline would've stayed in the house with me? Do you think she would have left the kids in the house with me? Despite this battered-woman stereotype her sister is determined to force on her, the fact is, Caroline wasn't stupid, and she wasn't weak, either. If something like that had happened, she'd have been out of the house in a heartbeat, with the kids, and she would've never returned."

Again, Ben checked the jury, and to his delight saw a few heads subtly nodding. Barrett was winning them back with his calm, logical presentation. He was making them believe.

"One last question about your wife, Wallace. Did you know she was pregnant?"

"No, I did not. I don't think she did, either, at least not for long, or she would've told me. I loved our kids, and despite the lies her would-be Romeo told you, I wanted more. Specifically, I wanted a son. Not that I didn't love my daughters, but you know how it is. I guess every guy wants a son, someone to carry on after he's gone. We'd been trying for some years, without any luck. We'd been to all the doctors, and they were telling us it probably wouldn't happen. They were telling us Caroline wouldn't have any more children. This baby boy"—he raised his hands to his face—"he must've been a godsend. I mean, a miracle. And now—" His voice cracked. He shielded his face with his hand and didn't make a great show, but it was clear he was crying.

Ben noticed a few moist eyes in the jury box as well. He waited several moments till Barrett collected himself.

"You had no idea your wife was pregnant?"

"I did not. And what's more—" His head raised, and he stared down at the prosecution table. "I am revolted by the thought that the police and prosecutors have known for weeks, and not one of them ever saw fit to tell me. Apparently they saw no reason why the father—the father!—had any right to know. They preferred to keep it quiet so they could use it for shock value in the courtroom. That sickens me."

There was another long pause. For once, the eyes in the jury box turned to do a careful scrutiny of Jack Bullock.

"What about your children, Wallace? How was your relationship with them?"

"The best. Absolutely the best. They were great kids and I loved them. Yes, I did spank them, but believe me, I got no pleasure from it. I'm talking about real spankings, not little love pats like the one I gave Annabelle at the ice-cream parlor. Sometimes children do have to be punished, but we never hit hard enough to leave a mark. Caroline and I used spankings only for extreme cases—life-and-death issues, like playing in the street, getting in a car with strangers. I know it's fashionable now to say you never spank your kids, but let me tell you something. I could live a lot easier with the knowledge that I gave my girls a little spanking now and again than I could live with knowing they'd been hit by a car because I failed to apply the appropriate discipline."

"Punishment aside, Wallace, did you ever strike your children in anger?"

"Never. Never once. And I defy anyone to come up here and say anything different. I have never, never hurt my children. Never!"

"Alysha was reported to have bruises—"

"Alysha was accident-prone. That's a fact. No one ever suspected anything until after this tragedy occurred and I became the scapegoat for every false accusation in the book. Ask yourself this. If she was showing up at school looking like she'd been beaten, why didn't her teachers report it? Why didn't the other parents? Because it wasn't true. It didn't happen."

Ben turned a page in his trial notebook. "Wallace, I know this will be extremely unpleasant for you, but I'm going to have to ask you now to return to the day your family was killed."

His face became set and grim. "All right."

"Could you tell us what happened that day?"

Barrett took a deep breath and released it slowly. "We all got up, ate breakfast, got dressed. Everyone was in good spirits—no squabbling, no problems. I kept the kids out of school because I wanted my family with me at the press conference, when I announced my decision to run for reelection. After the conference, we had a quick lunch, then I took the kids to Baskin-Robbins for ice cream."

"The prosecution witness who worked at the ice-cream parlor said that you and your wife were fighting there."

"Well, you saw the tape. I would not say we were fighting, but we were having a somewhat agitated discussion. And it was hardly over a life-and-death issue. It was about whether Annabelle got chocolate ice cream."

"Could you explain?"

He nodded. "It's pretty simple. Annabelle wanted chocolate ice cream. It's her favorite. I thought we ought to let her get what she wanted, but Caroline didn't want her to have chocolate, because she was still wearing her fancy clothes, and as you undoubtedly know, chocolate stains. It wouldn't be the first time chocolate ice cream had ruined one of her outfits. So that's what we were talking about. That's it. There was no shouting, no threatening, no hitting. Nothing about other men or the baby I didn't know about. Just a normal discussion like all parents everywhere in the galaxy have on a daily basis. It was only after the . . . the tragedy . . . that someone got the idea of saying that this stupid discussion at Baskin-Robbins proved that I was some kind of monster."

"The man at the register said you almost hit Caroline."

"I talk with my hands, and I can see how he might be confused, if he didn't know me well. I always talk with my hands. I'm just that kind of guy. I'd be doing it now, Mr. Kincaid, if you hadn't told me not to."

There was a pleasant tittering of laughter from the jury box.

"The man at the parlor also said that you threatened her. Something about the children."

"The man is confused. Caroline was the one who talked about using the kids as a weapon. But she wasn't threatening me any more than I was threatening her. She was just saying that we had to be careful about arguing around the kids, dragging them into it, trying to use them against one another."

"So you were not fighting the day of the murder?"

Barrett frowned slightly. "Actually we were, but not yet. The real fight came later that afternoon, after we got home."

"What were you fighting about?"

Barrett glanced out into the gallery. "Him." All heads turned to see who Barrett was singling out. "Fisher—excuse me, *Dr.* Fisher. It was obvious to me that he was in love with Caroline and was trying to get her to go to bed with him. He'd propositioned her on more than one occasion, and was constantly dropping by when he knew I wouldn't be at home. I knew Caroline would never sleep with him, but just the same, I didn't want the creep around. I didn't want him bothering Caroline or the children."

"And what was Caroline's response to this request?"

"She refused. She insisted that he was just a friend, and she needed friends. I disagreed. I had no problem with her having friends, but I thought having this lecherous pervert around was not good for our marriage or our family. I admit I got pretty heated and did some shouting. I assume that's what our ever-alert neighbor Mr. Sanders overheard, once he flung open all his windows and craned his head out as far as it would go."

Again, some of the jurors laughed. With him, Ben noted.

"We went back and forth for probably fifteen, twenty minutes. I shouted, Caroline shouted. She actually threw a few plates and knocked over a table. Made a huge crashing noise, but it didn't hurt anything. Then I got really steamed. I knew arguing wasn't going to make things any better, so I decided it would be best if I just left for a while and cooled off. I ran out of the house."

"About what time of day was this?"

"I'm not certain, but I think it was around four forty-five."

"So this is not when your neighbor saw you run to the car?"

"No. That came later."

"What did you do after you left the house?"

"I just got in my car and drove. Nowhere in particular. Just drove. Tell you the truth, I just needed to let off some steam. I crossed town on the Broken Arrow Expressway, shot back on I-44. Crossed over the river and went away up I-75. Drove for about an hour. Maybe an hour and fifteen minutes."

"And then what did you do?"

"Then I came home."

"And what happened?"

"Then . . ." His voice suddenly broke off. When it returned, it was barely a whisper. "That's when I found them."

Ben tried to go easy. Barrett was doing wonderfully; he didn't want him to break down before the examination was over. "I'm sorry, Wallace, but I'm afraid I'm going to have to ask you to go through what happened step-by-step so the jury can understand all the details. Please tell us what happened, beginning when you returned to your home."

Barrett took a deep breath and steeled himself. "I parked on the street. I was anxious to get in and apologize. I still didn't want Fisher around, but after thinking about it a while, I realized I didn't have the right to dictate who her friends were. So I wanted to apologize before any more damage was done."

"What did you do after you parked on the street?"

"I walked to the house. The front door was open. And before you ask, no, I don't remember whether I closed the door on my way out when I left. I was mad and I was in a hurry. I'm sure I meant to close it, but it's possible I didn't. I just don't know."

"What did you do next?"

"I stepped inside. Everything was very quiet. That was the first thing that bothered me. That sent a chill right up my spine. We have two young girls, after all. The house just isn't quiet in the middle of the day. I thought maybe they had all gone somewhere."

"What did you think about that?"

"Well, it made me want to kick myself. If I had stayed home, instead of running off like an idiot, I could've spent some time with them. Instead, I was going to spend the evening alone. Or so I thought."

"What did you do next?"

"Well, since it looked like Caroline wouldn't be making dinner, I decided to go fix myself a sandwich. But on my way to the kitchen, I had to pass through the dining room—"

"And?"

Barrett swallowed. "That's when I saw her," he whispered.

"That's when you saw who?" Ben urged.

"Caroline," he said. "Sprawled across a dining room chair."

"Could you please describe her condition when you found her?"

"She was . . . red . . . and . . ." He struggled to force the words out. "There was blood, all over her body. Her face was . . . mutilated."

"What did you do?"

"I shouted out to her. But she didn't answer. I tried to pick her up. I remember, I cut myself—maybe on her ring? I don't know. Whatever it was, I guess it bled. I didn't notice; I had a lot more on my mind at the time. I tried to move her, but she was so limp, and I was so upset. My eyes blurred, and I just kept shouting, 'Caroline! Caroline!' "

Ben looked away. This was the hardest witness examination he had ever done, ever. He just hoped it was affecting the jury as strongly as it was affecting him. "Then what did you do?"

"I couldn't move her, and I couldn't get her to respond. I tried to take her pulse. Got her blood all over me. And the smell! It was so sickening, I just—" He shook his head. "There was no pulse. I knew she was dead."

"Then what did you do?"

"I panicked. Just panicked. Started running through the house, shouting for the kids. Of course they didn't answer. Finally I ran upstairs. And then I found them. Annabelle on the bed, Alysha in the bathtub."

"Would you please describe the condition in which you found them?"

Barrett was shaking. His eyes were beginning to water. "It was just like the police officer who found them said. Annabelle was lying still, her hands folded, like she was sleeping. But I knew she wasn't just sleeping. And then I found Alysha—my poor precious Alysha—in the tub with all that blood dripping and splattered and—"

His face fell into his hands, and he was consumed by weeping. Tears streamed through his fingers. The jurors watched, then eventually looked away. No matter what they believed, at that moment in time, no one doubted the depth of the grief Barrett was experiencing.

Several moments passed before Ben asked the next question. "Wallace, would you please tell the jury what you did after you found the last body?"

"I fled," he said. "I ran. Bolted out of the house. That's when Sanders saw me—it would have been six or so by then. I'm not proud of it. But I just panicked. My whole family had been killed. I didn't know what to do. I couldn't think straight. For all I knew, the killer was still on the premises. For all I knew, I was the one he wanted. I don't know what all I thought, really. I just ran to my car and drove."

"Where were you going?"

"I didn't know. Nowhere, really. Just driving. Just putting as much distance as I could between myself and that . . . atrocity. I couldn't deal with it. I think I thought that maybe if I could put enough distance between myself and all that blood, then it wouldn't be real. It would all disappear and everything would be normal again."

"You were headed south."

"Yeah, I know. I don't know why. I have a sister in Dallas—she's my only living relative. I think maybe some part of me was trying to get to her, trying to find the comfort and easy acceptance that only a family member can provide."

"You did not call the police."

"No. I should have, I know that. But they couldn't have helped. They couldn't have given my family back to me. I can't explain how I felt. I just . . . wasn't thinking in any sane, logical manner. I had just witnessed the most hellish nightmare that I could ever imagine. I wasn't thinking straight."

"And what happened after that?"

Barrett shrugged wearily. "You've seen the tape. The police cars and copters found me. I knew they were there, but some part of me just wasn't processing information properly. I felt like I had to keep on driving, that if I stopped, it would be like admitting they were dead, that my whole family had been taken away from me. I just couldn't make myself do it." He wiped the tears from his eyes. "Then I got the searchlight from one of those helicopters in my eyes. It blinded me, I lost control, and I hit that tollbooth. I woke up in the hospital, and I've been in police custody ever since."

"Have you cooperated with the police?"

"Absolutely. I've told them everything I know, tried to help them in every way possible. You got to understand—I thought the police would try to find the monster who committed these crimes. Imagine my shock and"—his teeth clenched together—"*anger* when I realized they were trying to pin it on me! Trying to accuse me of killing my own wife and children!"

"How did you respond when you heard the charges?"

"With outrage. But even then I didn't understand the truth. I thought they'd follow up all the leads, whether they thought I did it or not. But they didn't. Once they had me behind bars, they called the case closed and stopped looking. Why hasn't anyone found those strangers who were seen casing my home? I get death threats every month. Why hasn't anyone followed up on any of those? Every time I turn around I find out my opponents on the city council have been butting into this investigation—illegally. Why hasn't anyone investigated that? The police don't care about the truth. They just wanted a scapegoat, someone to save their butts and make it look like they'd done their jobs. I was the easiest scapegoat available, so they've tried to pin it on me and never even considered any other possibilities. Hell, they botched the evidence collection and let thrill-seekers trample through my house. People I don't even know were barging through my home hoping to get a cheap thrill by seeing the dead bodies of my family!"

"Your honor, I must object," Bullock said. "The witness is no longer being responsive."

"Overruled," she said curtly.

"All my life," Barrett continued, "I've tried to work with the system, tried to do things the right way. That was true when I was growing up in the ghettos of North Tulsa, and it was still true when I was elected mayor. But I must tell you, this case shames me. This case has exposed our system for how fallible, how prejudiced it really is. How easily it can be manipulated. How much evil there is in the world. First they took my family away from me, then my freedom, then my dignity, then my good name. And as if that wasn't enough, now they're trying to take everything else."

"Wallace," Ben said evenly, "did you kill your wife?"

Barrett looked him straight in the eyes. "No, sir."

"Did you kill your daughter Alysha Barrett?"

"No, sir."

"Did you kill your other daughter, Annabelle Barrett?"

"No, sir. I did not." He turned to face the jury. "I did not kill any of them. I would not—I could not commit these horrible crimes."

"Thank you, Wallace. That's all."

Judge Hart, to the relief of everyone, called for a blissful thirty-minute recess.

CHAPTER

58

AFTER THE BREAK, a refreshed jury retook its seats and Bullock began his cross-examination. His jaw was set; his eyes had a steely cast to them. Ben knew he had spent the whole recess staring at his legal pad, furiously scribbling notes. Obviously, he planned to give this cross his best. Bullock, no less than Ben, had to be aware of the impact Barrett had made on the jury. Now Bullock would try to undo that good, to reestablish his portrait of Barrett as a cold-blooded killer.

"Mr. Barrett," Bullock began, pointedly not calling him "Mayor," "do you feel able to proceed now?"

"Sure," Barrett replied. The break had done him some good, too. He'd regained his equilibrium; his voice had refound its strength. "Whenever you're ready."

"Thank you. If you feel you need another break at any time, just let me know, okay?"

"Okay," Barrett said. "Thanks."

Bullock's lips turned up into a smile more enigmatic than the Mona Lisa's. "That was quite a performance you just gave."

Barrett blinked. "I beg your pardon?"

"Quite a performance. But, I'm sure, no great trick for an old media hound like you."

"I'm not following you."

"Of course you're used to being grilled. Press conferences, debates. You're used to being sent out to pitch a story to the audience."

"Your honor, I object," Ben said. He preferred to let Barrett take care of himself; it would look better to the jury than having Ben come to his rescue. But this was beyond the pale. "This is offensive and argumentative, and as far as I can tell, Mr. Bullock hasn't even asked a question yet."

Judge Hart pushed her glasses up her nose. "I would prefer if you used your cross-examination time to ask questions, counsel. You can save the color commentary for closing argument."

"Very well, your honor. I'll ask questions." He stared back at Barrett. "You're accustomed to handling yourself in front of an audience, aren't you, sir?"

"I suppose."

"In fact, you've done quite a bit of . . . acting, haven't you?"

Barrett's teeth set together. "You mean, ever? Or here in the courtroom?"

"You have a fairly extensive acting background, don't you?"

"I made a few films. Low-budget action pictures. After I got out of college."

"They didn't do too well, did they, sir?"

"Well, I didn't give Denzel Washington anything to worry about, let's put it that way."

"But people did compliment you on your ability to . . . play a part convincingly, didn't they?"

Barrett leaned forward. "Mr. Bullock, have you got some kind of point to make? 'Cause if you do, I'd rather you just made it, and stopped all this weasely beating around the bush."

Judge Hart pounded her gavel. "I will direct the witness to restrain himself. Just answer the questions." Then she looked at Ben. "Counsel, you're responsible for your witness."

"Yes, your honor. I'm sure it won't happen again." Although if it did, he wouldn't complain. Personally, he'd enjoyed it, and he hoped some of the jurors did as well.

"My problem is this, Mr. Barrett," Bullock continued. "How do we know whether you're telling the truth now, or just giving another brilliant performance?"

"I'm telling the truth." Barrett's voice was low and flat.

"Are you? Are you really? You claim you never physically hurt your wife. Is that correct?"

"That's correct."

"Yes, and cleverly phrased, too. Your lawyer asked if you hurt her, and you said no. But I notice he never asked if you've ever hit her." There was a stir in the gallery. "What about it, Mr. Barrett. Did you ever hit your wife?"

"I—" Barrett's shoulders rose, then sank. "I—never meant to hit her."

"You're very clever with words, aren't you, Mr. Barrett? And very careful. I suppose your lawyer has taught you that. My question was whether you ever hit her, and I want an answer. *Did you ever hit your wife?*"

The disparity between the bellowing by Bullock and Barrett's quiet answer was jarring. "I—did hit her once. It was an accident."

"An accidental hitting?"

Barrett shrugged. "We were arguing. I was talking with my hands, as usual. Flinging them around. Her face got in the way."

"Her face got in the way? Mr. Barrett, please."

Barrett almost rose out of his chair. "It's what happened!"

Ben's brain raced, trying to come up with some objection, some excuse to interrupt.

"Was that the time you blackened her eye," Bullock asked, "or the time you pushed her down the stairs?"

"That's not true!"

"We have witnesses who say it is."

"Your witnesses are full of—" Barrett caught himself just in time. His fists were clenched; veins were protruding in his neck.

Ben tried to make eye contact, tried to send him mental messages. Stay calm, Wallace! Ride it out!

"And what about your daughters?" Barrett continued, not missing a beat. "Did you ever hit them?"

"I've already said I gave them spankings."

"How?"

"How?" Barrett shrugged. "On their bottoms."

"Through their clothes. Or did you pull the clothes down?"

Barrett frowned. "I pulled the clothes down."

"Of course. It hurts more that way, doesn't it?"

Ben jumped up. "Your honor!"

Judge Hart didn't wait for the objection. "Counsel, you will discontinue your comments and side remarks immediately, do you understand me? This is not a request."

Bullock bowed his head. "Yes, your honor." He went right back at Barrett. "And what did you use to administer these punishments? A stick? A paddle?"

"My hand."

"Your bare hand. I think we have the idea now, sir. You pulled down their little panties and applied your bare hand to their bare bottoms. Did you enjoy that?"

Barrett boiled. "You son of a—"

Judge Hart pounded her gavel. "Counsel, you are treading on very thin ice!"

Bullock spread his hands. "Your honor, I'm demonstrating that the man has a propensity for violence."

"Then do it! And stop these offensive insinuations!"

Bullock turned back to the witness. "Mr. Barrett, how often did you administer these punishments?"

"I don't know. Once or twice a month."

"Once or twice a month! Meaning, twenty or thirty times a year!"

"If you say so."

"So. Twenty or thirty times a year, you applied your bare hand to your young daughters' bare bottoms."

"If they needed it!"

Bullock clamped up, letting Barrett's words reverberate through the courtroom. Ben checked the jurors. Bullock's cross was indeed beginning to have its intended effect.

They were losing them.

"Tell me," Bullock continued in a soft, precise voice, "did they need punishment on the day they were murdered?"

Barrett was so close to the explosion point Ben was afraid they would never make it. "What are you trying to say?"

"I'm just wondering if you punished them on that day. Their last day."

Barrett's head lowered. "I . . . did have to spank Annabelle. I don't mean that little nothing at the ice-cream parlor. I mean later. I didn't want to, but after the disappointment of not getting any ice cream, she started getting out of hand." He raised his head. "Sometimes children need discipline. In fact, they want it. They expect it."

"I don't think your daughters wanted what they got that day, sir. Although I wonder if they didn't expect it."

"Your honor!" Ben shouted across the courtroom.

Judge Hart pounded her gavel. "That's it, Mr. Bullock. This is over. I'm instructing the jury to disregard this entire cross-examination thus far. It will be stricken from the record. And I will be strongly considering disciplinary action when this case is completed. Now move on."

"Very well, your honor." He flipped over another page of notes. The judge's words, of course, had been utterly ineffective. Instructing the jury to disregard something was like cementing it into their memories. And Bullock could care less about the judge's threats. Like always, he was playing to win. As long as he won, what did he care if she sanctioned him later? She would just be helping to make him a hero. A martyr, even.

"Mr. Barrett, your performance—excuse me—your story is that you and your wife had a big fight on the day she was killed and you ran out of the house and missed all three murders, right?"

"That's right."

"How convenient. So you didn't see anything. One minute, everyone's fine, and the next, everyone's dead."

"That's . . . right." His voice cracked slightly.

Bullock's voice boomed out. "Can you explain how traces of your blood were found on your wife's body?"

"No," he whispered. "Unless, when I cut myself—"

"Mr. Barrett, the forensic team found a significant quantity of your blood. How much did this cut bleed?"

"I—I don't really know . . ."

"And what about the DNA test? How did your skin get under her fingernails?"

"I—I don't know . . . Unless maybe, when we were fighting earlier—"

"Mr. Barrett, how much do you expect this jury to believe?"

"I—I don't know all the answers. I don't remember everything—"

"Mr. Barrett!" Bullock boomed out at the top of his lungs. "If you didn't kill your family, who did?"

"I don't *know*—"

"Who had the opportunity? Who had the motive? Who could've done it?"

"I—I just—"

"I repeat, sir. If you didn't kill them, who did?"

Barrett held up his hands helplessly. "I don't know."

Bullock turned away, shaking his head with disbelief and disgust. "I have no more questions for this witness."

"Any redirect?" Judge Hart asked.

Ben shook his head no. He wanted Barrett off the stand, the sooner, the better.

As Barrett returned to the table, Ben scanned the eyes of the jurors. If he had learned anything in the time he had been trying cases, it was to watch the jury. Their faces could usually tell you which way the wind was blowing.

But not this time. This time Ben saw faces in turmoil, confusion. Barrett had made a good initial impression, but Bullock had put on an effective cross, raising all sorts of doubts with his insinuations and accusations. The jury didn't know what to believe. They were troubled.

And Ben knew what was troubling them, too. Bullock had hit the nail on the head, had known exactly how to finish. With the one question that no one could answer. The one question that cut the heart out of all Barrett's protestations of innocence.

If you didn't kill them, who did?

Ben knew that if he wanted to have any hope of winning this case, he would have to provide the jury with an answer to that question. And he would have to make them believe it.

59

THERE WAS NO longer the slightest doubt in Deanna's mind. Wallace Barrett was innocent.

She knew it. She felt it in her head, her heart, and her gut.

The question was: What was she going to do about it?

She'd been dwelling on this ever since she left the courtroom and got back to her hotel room, retracing the same thoughts, running the same futile arguments over and over in her brain.

Wallace Barrett's reputation was already shot, she rationalized to herself. His life was irrevocably ruined. Even if he beat this rap, he could never again run for public office, could never again live in the public spotlight, and probably wouldn't want to.

But Martha still had her whole life before her. All her opportunities were still possible; all the doors were still open.

Unless Deanna closed them.

Could she do that? Could she do it to her own flesh and blood? Even to save an innocent man?

It would be so much easier if she could just talk this out with Martha, discuss it, plan what to do together. But that was no longer a possibility. She was sequestered now, and there was no way the deputies were going to let her talk to Martha just so she could ease her conscience. Whatever decision she reached, she would have to reach on her own.

She would have to shoulder all the responsibility.

And all the blame.

She rolled over on her hotel-room bed, cradling the pillow in her arms. How had she gotten into this situation? She'd been a fool to let herself be put on this jury. She should have told them something, anything, to make sure she would be removed. But she had thought she was doing what was best for her daughter, trying to protect her.

What she'd forgotten was to protect herself. Now, as a result, she'd been forced to go into that courtroom every day. Been forced to stare out at that man sitting at the defense table, stricken, scared, on trial for his life. Been forced to harden her heart and to try not to think about what this must be doing to a man accused of committing a nightmarish crime she was almost certain he had not committed.

Because she was almost certain she knew who had.

It was just too much to be a coincidence. The camera, the photos. Buck's constant flow of unearned wealth. His presence in the neighborhood at the time of the killings. He may not have acted alone; in fact he almost certainly was acting at the instruction of some other, richer person. But he was definitely involved.

It had been painful sitting in the courtroom today, watching that man plead to be believed. Watching the prosecution cut him and hurt him in all the most vulnerable, most personal ways. Despite the way the prosecutor battered him, she thought he did an amazing job of maintaining his dignity, of refusing to play the prosecutor's games. He was a noble, honorable man. Surely that would be enough, surely the tide would turn and the other jurors would see him as she did.

But she knew that was not the case. She had heard two of the jurors whispering in the elevator, had heard a telling remark from another in the food line. They thought Barrett was guilty. They were leaning toward conviction.

And she knew why, too.

Bullock had brought all their reasonable doubts to a standstill by asking that one overwhelming question.

If you didn't kill your wife and children, Mr. Barrett, who did? Who could have?

That was the question that dominated the trial now. And that was a question that she could answer.

She could remain quiet. She could say nothing, but refuse to join in a guilty verdict, hanging the jury. But what would that accomplish? Everyone would still believe he was guilty, just as they did now, conviction or not. He would always live with the stain, and eventually they would retry him and get a conviction, and he'd be executed or spend the rest of his life in jail. She wasn't sure which would be worse. Put the man out of his misery, or let him live fifty or sixty more years with the knowledge that the world believed he had killed his own wife and children.

And if by some miracle they didn't convict him? Then the investigation would continue, they would find Buck, and then Martha. And for that matter, they'd find Deanna, and they'd realize why she had refused to convict Barrett when she'd been on the jury. That she'd been withholding information.

Great. Maybe she could share a cell with her daughter.

If she went to the judge and told her what she knew, she didn't know what would happen. Maybe a mistrial. Maybe some criminal charge. And there would certainly be an investigation of Buck.

And Martha.

But if she didn't . . .

She kept thinking of that man, that face, those two brown eyes peering out from the witness stand, begging people to believe him, to believe that he did not and could not have committed this hideous crime.

And no one believing him. Not because of anything he had failed to do, but because she had failed to tell them what she knew.

Deanna threw the pillow down on the floor. She still wished she could talk to Martha first. She wished she could consult a lawyer, or at least a friend. But as she had told her daughter so many times before, if wishes were horses . . .

She cracked open her hotel-room door. A deputy was posted in the corridor outside, just a few feet from her door.

"Is something wrong, Ms. Meanders?"

"No. Well, yes. I mean—"

He stepped toward her. "What do you need?"

She lifted her chin and squared her shoulders. "I need to see the judge."

The deputy frowned. "Now?"

She nodded. "Right now."

CHAPTER

60

BEN ARRIVED AT his apartment just before nine, late, although the earliest he had made it back since the trial began. Joni was sitting on the floor in the living room with Joey, who was arranging irregularly shaped puzzle pieces to make a perfect square, over and over again.

"The warrior returns from the battlefield," Joni said as he stepped through the door. "Look, Joey, it's Uncle Ben."

Joey continued putting the pieces into his puzzle.

"How's the trial going?" Joni asked. "I didn't have time to watch it on television today."

"Not good," Ben replied. He flung his coat and briefcase onto the sofa.

"Barrett flopped on the stand?"

"No, he was actually very good, for the most part. Problem is, he's all we've got. And it wasn't enough."

"You know, Ben," Joni said gently, "all you can do is your best. The facts are what they are."

Ben shook his head. "Wallace Barrett is innocent. He may not be a perfect human being, but he didn't commit those murders. If I can't convince the jury of that, I've failed."

Joni changed the subject. "I took Joey to Woodland Hills Mall again today. He rode the carousel."

Ben half smiled. "Yeah? How'd he like it?"

"Well, you know, it's always hard to tell with Joey. But I think he enjoyed it."

Ben stared down at his taciturn, emotionless nephew, obsessively putting the puzzle pieces into their slots. What was going on in that mind, anyway? Surely there was some way to break through. "He's up kind of late, isn't he?"

"Yeah. But I thought you might want to spend some time with him, since you've been so busy all week. I hope you're not upset."

"Of course not. You've been a lifesaver, Joni. I don't know how I can thank you."

"Well, since you brought it up . . ."

"Yes?"

"Do you suppose you could get Wallace Barrett's autograph for me?"

"You want his autograph?"

"Yeah. And maybe your buddy Jack Bullock's?"

"Bullock? What do you want with his autograph? He's just a lawyer."

"Just a lawyer? Ben, where have you been? He's a celebrity now. You're all celebrities."

"That's ridiculous."

"It's not ridiculous. Who's had more television time lately than you guys? Good grief, Kato Kaelin was only on the stand for a few days, and he became a celebrity—for a little while, anyway. You guys are on every day."

"Celebrity should be based on merit, not exposure."

"Maybe that's the way it should be, Ben, but that's not the way it is. You should give some thought to how to make the most of this."

"What do you mean?"

"You ought to get, you know, an agent."

"An agent? Lawyers don't have agents."

"*You* should. You might get some talk shows, a legal commentary spot on the news, maybe a contract for a book of trial memoirs. Who knows—you might even get on one of the daytime talk shows."

"Great. Me and the transsexual hermaphroditic Siamese twins who love too much."

"Seriously, Ben. You could make a lot of money."

"What would I do with a lot of money?"

"Well, for starters, you could give me a raise." She beamed.

"I'll take that under consideration."

"And you could buy Joey some of those classy Little Tikes toys. And you could get a new, better office. And you and Christina could get serious and settle down."

"*What?*"

She looked down sheepishly. "Just a suggestion."

"I think you have the wrong idea."

"Uh-huh." She pushed herself off the sofa. "Still, Ben, opportunity is knocking. Don't forget to open the door."

"Open the door? I think I'm going to put in a dead bolt."

AFTER JONI LEFT, Ben gathered all the toys and books and games and everything else he could muster that might possibly capture Joey's attention.

He was resolved; one way or another, he was going to get a reaction out of that kid.

"Look, Joey, puppets!" He put his hand up a green frog which played a computer chip version of "Over the Rainbow" that seemed to go on forever.

Joey did not appear remotely interested.

"Hello, Joey," Ben said, using a deep, croaking voice that he imagined was something like the way a frog would talk. "Would you like to play with me? *Ribit.*"

Joey pushed the puppet out of his face and reached for his puzzle.

Well, Ben reasoned, that's sort of a response. Not the one I was hoping for, but . . .

He turned on the Smart Little Driver, a noisy computer toy shaped like a plastic dashboard that played songs. "Look at this, Joey. It talks!"

Joey did not look.

Ben pushed a button, treating them to another burst of computer chip "music," this time playing "Pease Porridge Hot."

"Isn't that neat, Joey? Look, I can sing along! Pease porridge hot, pease porridge cold . . ."

Ben proceeded to sing along with the Smart Little Driver, not that Joey appeared to care.

"What about this?" Ben said, pulling out two Bert and Ernie dolls. "Remember these?" He dangled the dolls in front of the boy's face. "Remember? These used to be your favorite toys!"

Of course, he thought to himself, that was before your mother abandoned you. That was before she dumped you on Uncle Ben, who in turn dumped you in a preschool and dumped you with a nanny so he could continue his brilliant legal career. That was before you shut yourself inside and refused to come out.

Ben stood up and went to the piano. "Look, Joey. I can make music, too." He wanted to play a Dar Williams tune he'd been trying to teach himself, but decided that Mother Goose was probably more Joey's speed. He banged out "Yankee Doodle," giving an extra boost to the chorus: "Yankee Doodle, keep it up, Yankee Doodle Dan-dy . . ."

It was as if Joey was in another room, or perhaps another world. He continued working the puzzle. Trapezoid in the trapezoid space, semicircle in the semicircle space . . .

"Look," Ben said, "you've played with that long enough." He snatched the puzzle away, pieces and all.

Joey did not look at Ben, but he certainly reacted. He looked all around, as if searching for the puzzle. A panicked expression washed across his face. He began to bawl.

"Joey, stop that!"

Joey did not stop that.

"You can have the puzzle back later. We're going to do something else now."

Joey continued wailing at the top of his lungs.

"Joey, look." Ben began desperately running about, grasping at toys. "Look, it's a Magna-Doodle. See, I wrote your name!"

Joey sat with his hands in his lap, wailing. His face flushed beet red. Tears dribbled down his chin.

"Okay," Ben said, "how about a talking clown?" He desperately grabbed the doll and pulled its talk string. " 'It's time to have fun, kiddies! Hoo-hoo-hoo-hoo!' "

Joey was oblivious. He screamed like he'd lost everything, like there was no reason to go on living. Worst of all, he had not come out of his shell. He was still isolated, unresponsive, self-absorbed. He was just miserable as well.

Ben began to feel seriously guilt-ridden. What right did he have to demand that the child react to him, anyway? Still, he tried to maintain his resolve. "Look, how about card tricks?"

He reached down furiously for a deck of cards on the floor, but slipped on the area rug and fell into the nearby armchair. He hit the chair sideways, face first, rolled off it, and tumbled down on the hardwood floor.

Ben lay flat on his back on the floor. As soon as his head cleared, he began taking a mental inventory. Everything seemed to still be attached, no major spinal damage, although he definitely had a sore spot on his backside. But something had changed. It took him a moment to realize what it was.

Joey had stopped crying.

Ben pushed up off the floor. Joey was looking at him.

It took a moment to register. Wait a minute . . .

Joey was looking at him!

This was something he hadn't seen in months. The boy was looking straight at him, and . . . and . . .

And he was beginning to smile.

"Gin," Joey gurgled.

Ben looked at him in amazement. "What? Did you say something? You did! You said something!" He paused suddenly. "What did you say?"

"Gin," Joey repeated, followed by something that sounded a lot like laughter.

"Joey!" Ben said. "I can't believe it! You're—" He tried to listen closer. "But what are you saying?"

"Gin!" Joey insisted.

"Gin? You mean again? Do it again?" Joey's pronunciation was far from perfect, but not bad considering that he had barely made a peep for the last six months. "But what do you mean?"

Joey looked up at the armchair. "Gin."

"You mean, you want me to do it again? But, Joey, that was an accident."
Joey looked away. His smile faded.

"But that's okay!" Ben leaped to his feet. "If you want it 'gin, I'll do it 'gin.
I knew you'd like that. I meant to do it. Yeah, that's my story. I'm a whiz with
kids. Look, Joey, I'll do it again."

Joey did look up. And Ben flopped forward, first into the armchair, then
down onto the floor. Doing it on purpose, of course, made it a good deal less
graceful than when he had fallen by accident, and he hit the floor a good deal
harder, too. *"Owww!"*

Joey giggled. His face lit up a like a candle. He clapped his hands together.

"Joey!" Ben crawled up and swept Joey up his arms. "You're paying attention! You know who I am! Don't you? Say 'Uncle Ben.' Can you? Say 'Uncle
Ben.' "

Joey giggled even more. "UngaBen."

"I knew you did! I knew if I could just get through to you—" Ben stopped
talking and pressed the child close to him. "Thank you, Joey!"

Joey smiled back at him. "Gin."

"Again? Oh, right. Whatever you say." Ben got into position and took
another swan dive into the armchair. He hit the floor like a sack of potatoes.
His back was beginning to ache, but he barely noticed.

Because Joey was laughing. Happy, hysterical laughter.

Ben smiled his biggest smile. His eyes were starting to water. "This is
ridiculous," he said. "It's just—it's not—oh, hell." He stopped fighting and
let the tears fall. "Joey," he said, crawling close to him, "you're the best little
boy in the world, you know that? The best little boy who ever was." He gave
Joey another bear hug. "By God, if I can bring you around, I can bring that
jury around, too."

Joey smiled back at him and clapped his little hands together. "Gin."

CHAPTER

61

SOMEHOW BEN MANAGED to avoid the now-permanent camp of reporters on the plaza outside the courthouse. They had erected a large tent to protect themselves and their equipment from the erratic Oklahoma weather. Wally-World, the local wags were calling it.

The reporters shouted out questions as he passed through.

"Do you think anyone believed your client's story?"

"What about the blood and the DNA?"

"Is it true Barrett gave you his bloodstained clothes and they're hidden in a safe in your office?"

Ben's jaw tightened. "No comment."

"What are you going to do with yourself when this trial is finally over?"

Ben stopped, then pivoted. "Actually," he said, "I'm planning to go back-packing. I need to exercise something other than my lips."

He rode to the seventh floor and entered Judge Hart's courtroom. As he walked to the front, he spotted a female network anchorperson sitting on the defense table. He recognized her—CNN, he thought—but couldn't come up with her name. Her cameraman and his assistant were in front of her; obviously they were preparing to broadcast.

Ben tried to contain his irritation. After all, court was not in session and he didn't own the courtroom. He just walked quietly behind her and started setting up.

The anchorwoman whirled around. "Excuse me. You're in my key light."

"Excuse me," Ben shot back. "You're on my table."

She did not appear to be amused. "Couldn't you stand back long enough for me to tape this intro?"

"Sorry, I have work to do." He continued taking papers out of his briefcase.

She placed her hands on her hips. "How am I going to tape this lead-in with you making that racket?"

"Life's hell sometimes, isn't it?"

"Look, can't you give me five minutes?"

"Sorry. This trial could start at any moment."

She looked perplexed. "Haven't they told you yet?"

"Told me what?" Ben did a quick scan of the courtroom. It did seem unusually empty. Bullock wasn't here, nor any other member of the prosecution team, much less the judge. "What's going on?"

"I wish I knew. All I know is that the judge's bailiff read a prepared statement explaining that the trial was on hold indefinitely, and that he would be meeting with all counsel in chambers as soon as they arrived."

Ben sprang out of his seat. "I've got to get in there."

"Thank goodness." The anchorwoman turned back toward the camera and smiled. "Roll 'em."

WHEN BEN BURST into Judge Hart's chambers, he found the judge at her desk and Bullock and his assistants sitting in chairs surrounding a brunette middle-aged woman. He couldn't remember her name, but he knew who she was.

Juror number twelve.

"We've been waiting for you, Mr. Kincaid," the judge said. "Have a seat and we'll get started." She cocked her head to one side. "You're walking a bit stiffly this morning. Did you hurt your back?"

"Uh . . . yeah . . ." Ben said as he angled into the nearest available chair. "Several times."

Judge Hart appeared mystified, but didn't pursue it. "Gentlemen, we have a problem."

Ben eyed the juror carefully. She was sitting with her hands in her lap, kneading them with such force that it was painful to watch.

"Juror Number Twelve"—she glanced at her legal pad—"Deanna Meanders was brought to my chambers first thing this morning. At her request."

"Why?" Bullock's eyes seemed sunken and uneasy. Did he fear some juror misconduct might spoil his imminent victory?

Deanna began to speak. "I just—"

Judge Hart stopped her. "Let me handle this. It seems Ms. Meanders should never have been placed on this jury. She has some personal knowledge relevant to the case that she believes might potentially influence the jury's deliberation, if revealed. Having discussed this matter with her in camera, I have to agree."

Bullock seemed almost as nervous as Deanna. No one had spoken the word yet, but it was foremost in everyone's mind. *Mistrial.* "Well," he said, "we have two alternate jurors. Can't we just replace her?"

Judge Hart held up her hands. "I'd prefer to have the concurrence of counsel before I take that step."

"The prosecution consents," Bullock said immediately.

Judge Hart nodded. "Mr. Kincaid?"

Ben leaned forward. "Can I voir dire her first? Find out what she knows?"

Judge Hart shook her head. "Not while she's a juror."

Ben sat back. The dilemma was becoming clear to him. "Okay, I consent."

"Very well. Juror Number Twelve, you are hereby relieved of duty. Bailiff, please notify the first alternate that she is now a member of the primary panel." She glanced toward Deanna. "You're free to go."

"Wait," Ben said. "I want to talk to you."

"Your honor, I object." Bullock leaned against the edge of the judge's desk. "We're in the middle of the trial. The defense is putting on its case."

Ben shrugged. "So?"

"If he's allowed to quiz this woman, he might be able to use her information during his case. This gives him an advantage—since our case is completed, we *won't* have a chance to use her. It's unfair."

"Unfair?" Ben's face tightened. "If I'm not given every possible opportunity to clear my client, that's unfair."

Judge Hart held up her hands. "Calm down, gentlemen. I know argument is your life, but there's no need for it here. I understand your position, Mr. Bullock, but I can't agree. Mr. Barrett is, after all, literally on trial for his life. We cannot withhold any arguably relevant evidence from the defense, even under these unique circumstances. But to make sure this development is not exploited improperly, the interrogation will take place right here, in my chambers, with both sides present, not to mention me. You'll know as much as defense counsel does, Mr. Bullock, even before you read about it in the *Enquirer*. And if Mr. Kincaid uses this witness and you want to respond, you'll have cross-ex and closing. You may even be able to call rebuttal witnesses, depending upon the circumstances. However it plays out, it will play out fair. I guarantee it." She looked up at Deanna. "Does that sound satisfactory to you?"

Deanna nodded.

"Good. Mr. Kincaid, would you like to begin the questioning of this witness?"

"I certainly would. Ms. Meanders, do you know who killed Caroline Barrett and her two children?"

Deanna twisted her fingers around themselves. "No. I mean, I'm not sure. Maybe."

Ben whipped out his legal pad and started taking notes. "Tell me everything you know."

* * *

ABOUT AN HOUR later, Ben left the conference in Judge Hart's chambers. He motioned to Christina, Jones, and Loving, who were waiting in the back of the courtroom.

"Team meeting," he said. "Now."

They found a private nook in the foyer outside the courtroom and huddled. "You're not going to believe this one," he warned them in advance. "This case gets weirder by the minute."

As quickly as possible, Ben told them everything he had learned from Deanna Meanders.

"We have to get a hold of this Buck character," Ben said firmly. "And we don't have much time. Loving, are you prepared to give this your full-court press?"

"You bet, Skipper. I just wish I knew where to start."

"Even if you find him," Ben said, "he probably won't talk to you, much less come to court voluntarily and testify. We'll need a subpoena. Christina, can you work that up?"

"*Tout de suite.*"

"Good. Judge Hart has agreed to stay in chambers today and make herself available. Given the way this mess has unfolded, I'm sure she'll sign the subpoena. If we find him. Any other suggestions?"

Jones chimed in. "Maybe we should drag in Whitman, too. He's been coming to the trial, but there's no guarantee he won't disappear, especially if Buck tells him he's been subpoenaed."

"Good thinking," Ben said. "If Buck is the punk Loving saw at O'Brien Park, then he's contacted Whitman at least once before. The day Christina and I went to Whitman's office."

"No, that's wrong." Christina snapped her fingers. "Don't you remember? When we were listening in on Whitman, after we left his office. There was silence, then clicking noises. About a minute later, Buck called him."

"It could just be a coincidence," Ben murmured.

"That Buck calls Whitman moments after we've stirred up the hornet's nest and Whitman is desperate to talk to him? No way. Somehow Whitman got a message to him."

"But how?" Ben asked. "Whitman was in his office the whole time. He didn't pick up the phone till Buck called him. He didn't have time to send a letter or fax. How could he have contacted him?"

"E-mail," Jones said. "That has to be it. Those clicking noises you heard— he must've been typing at the keyboard of his desktop computer. Whitman sent an e-mail message to Buck, telling him to contact him."

That would explain the almost-immediate call from Buck, Ben thought. "Why not just call Buck directly?"

"I don't know. Maybe Buck works near a computer terminal but not near a phone. Or maybe Whitman didn't want a record of the contact."

"Listen, Jones, you're our computer expert. Are you familiar with the computer system they use at the city office building?"

"Sure. I'm over there all the time."

"Okay, narrow the field for us. Who could Whitman have e-mailed?"

"Well, if you're on the Net, you can e-mail anyone else on the Net, assuming you know their address. Thing is, the city office building isn't on the Net. All they have is an intranet connection with an internal e-mail system."

"Meaning what?"

"Meaning city employees can e-mail each other." His eyes widened. "Buck works for the city."

"Of course," Ben echoed. "He probably works in the same building. That would explain how he and Whitman were able to work so closely together. Loving, we just narrowed the field for you."

"Roger. I'm out of here."

"All right. But be back by two, when the judge calls the court back in session. I'm probably going to have to put you on the stand, no matter what happens."

Loving looked as if he might be sick to his stomach. "I'll try not to think about it." He hustled through the back doors and disappeared.

"We still have a problem, though," Christina said, "even if we do find Buck. We have nothing to link him to Whitman other than Loving's testimony. Even if we prove Buck was the guy casing Barrett's neighborhood, Whitman will deny that he knew him."

Ben nodded grimly. "We need some sure way of tying the two men together. That's the problem with e-mail. Once you've sent the message or read it, you click on the delete button and it's gone forever."

"Don't you ever listen to anything I tell you?" Jones said, raising a finger.

"I beg your pardon?"

"Remember what I told you in the office the very first day we started working on this case?"

"Actually . . . no," Ben admitted.

"Well then," Jones said, a slow smile creeping across his face, "listen up."

62

COURT DID NOT resume until shortly after two in the afternoon. By that time, each of Ben's staff members had reported back, Ben had made the necessary motions, and the judge had issued the necessary subpoenas. Bullock was being quiet, but Ben could see that his eyes were alert and he was riding wary, ready to pounce as soon as he had the opportunity. He knew something was up. He just wasn't sure what it was.

Which was fair enough, since Ben wasn't entirely sure himself.

"The defense calls Mr. Aloysius J. Loving."

Loving took the stand and growled and mumbled his way through Ben's preliminary questions. He did not appear at all comfortable; he slouched, he shifted his weight, he talked through his hands. In a way, though, Ben thought that might actually work in their favor. After so many media-savvy witnesses and high-dollar experts, the jury might be relieved to see someone who was, well, just as they would be.

Loving related the story of how Ben had asked him to stake out O'Brien Park (without revealing the means by which Ben acquired his suspicion that a meeting would take place). Loving described how he saw two men meet and argue. How the first man had beaten the second and then given him cash to "take care of business." Finally Loving described, to his obvious mortification, getting conked over the head and losing his camera. "If it hadn't been for that," he explained, "I'd have pictures here today to prove what I saw. But the chump that got the drop on me swiped the film. And my only camera."

"Do you know who the men you saw were?" Ben asked.

"Yeah. I only learned who one of them was this morning. The younger guy, with the long hair and goatee. I tracked him to his office just across the plaza in the city office building. He works as a data processor in the mail room. His name is Bradley Conners." He glanced at the jury. "He goes by Buck."

"And do you know who the other man was?"

"Oh, yeah. I knew who he was the second I saw him. I've seen him on TV, and I saw him a few weeks ago at a city council meeting. He's in the gallery today." Loving lifted a hand and pointed. "It was Councilman Bailey Whitman. Excuse me. Interim Mayor Whitman."

Murmurs and whispers blanketed the courtroom. No one was clear yet what was the significance of this testimony, but it was definitely interesting.

After Ben sat down, Bullock began his cross. "Now let's play straight with the jury," Bullock said. "The fact is, you're currently employed by the lawyer for the defense, right?"

"Right," Loving said, without blinking an eye. "I told you that already."

"He pays you a regular salary."

A quick glance at Ben. "Well . . . sorta regular."

Bullock lowered his chin, his eyes making a beeline for Loving's. "Well, sir, how much is he paying you today?"

Loving chuckled. "A hell of a lot less than you're payin' those fancy experts of yours."

Several jurors burst out laughing.

"Be honest, sir," Bullock continued, trying to maintain control. "Don't you think the fact that you work for Mr. Kincaid has influenced your testimony?"

"No, sir. It didn't influence what I saw in the least. I saw what I saw."

"Uh-huh. And what would've happened if you'd come back to your boss and told him that you came up with nothing?"

Loving shrugged. "Happens all the time. He ain't fired me yet."

A few more chuckles from the gallery. Ben marveled. And he had been worried that Loving would be a flop. He should put him on the stand in every case.

Obviously irritated, Bullock tried a new tack. "Mr. Loving, isn't it true that you were divorced about three years ago?"

Loving seemed understandably puzzled. "Ye-es."

"And isn't it true that your wife's suit against you was based on claims of moral indecency?"

"Your honor," Ben said. "This is not relevant. We all know people say extreme things when they're going through a divorce. This is cheap and petty."

"True, but I'm afraid I'll have to allow it." Judge Hart looked up at Bullock, telling him in no uncertain terms what she thought of this line of questioning without actually overruling him. "You may proceed."

Bullock looked sternly at Loving. "Please answer the question."

Loving shot Ben a quick, piercing look. "I don't personally know what the lawyer said about me at the trial. I wasn't there."

Bullock continued. "Isn't it also true that you were once arrested on charges of solicitation?"

"That was a farce! I picked up this gal at Orpha's Bar. How did I know she was a hooker? I thought she was just overcome by my manly charm."

"Nonetheless, you were arrested, correct?"

"Yeah. And the charges were dropped almost immediately. I didn't even spend a night in jail."

"Still, if someone sat and watched you and your female companion in . . . that bar you mentioned, they might well come away with the impression that you had done something illegal, even though you hadn't, wouldn't you agree?"

"I suppose."

"So in other words, sometimes, even when you see what you see, it isn't what you thought you saw. Correct?"

"I think I'm confused."

"The fact is, Mr. Loving, you don't know what the two men you observed in the park were talking about, do you?"

"Well, not for certain."

"And you don't know why the man you claim was Bailey Whitman gave money to the other man, do you?"

"Not for certain."

"And you don't know who hit you over the head, do you?"

"No," he said, pounding a fist into his hand. "Wish I did."

"All you know is that two men met in a public park and talked. And that's hardly illegal, is it?"

"No."

"Thank you, Mr. Loving. Nothing more."

Ben thought about redirecting, but innuendos aside, Bullock really hadn't done that much damage to Loving, and he was anxious to get on with the next witness.

"The defense recalls Harvey Sanders to the stand."

Ben had made sure Barrett's now-famous neighbor was in the courtroom. Happily, despite the hard time Ben had given him on cross two days before, he had agreed to come when Ben called him. If anything, he seemed eager to take the stand again.

"How's the acting career coming?" Ben asked, smiling, as soon as Sanders was ensconced in the witness stand again.

"Much better, actually." Sanders flashed his grin, the one that had been featured on front pages from coast to coast the day before. "It's amazing what a few hours in court can do to jump-start a career."

"I can imagine. Sir, I've called you back to the stand to ask you a single question. Earlier, you testified that you saw two strangers casing your neighborhood, and in particular, the home of Mayor Wallace Barrett."

"That's correct."

"And you described one of those two people to the police as male, tall, lanky, wearing green fatigues and sporting a goatee." Ben was careful to use the same words Loving had used to describe the man he saw meet Whitman in the park.

Sanders grinned. "That's what I said, counsel. Sounds like you've done your homework."

"You also testified that on one occasion, you saw the tall young man talking to another man in a brown sedan-type car, right?"

"Still correct."

"But you didn't recognize that man."

" 'Fraid not."

Ben sidled toward the jury box. "Mr. Sanders, do you read the daily paper?"

"Only the horoscopes."

"Watch TV news?"

"Never."

"Keep up with local current events?"

"Can't say that I do."

"Do you think you could identify the members of Tulsa's city council?"

"I couldn't even name one."

"Well, let me ask you this. Is the man you saw sitting in that brown sedan in this courtroom?"

Sanders seemed surprised, taken aback. His eyes began scanning the packed courtroom. "I don't know."

"Let me make it easier for you." He walked over to the prosecution table and asked Bullock to stand. Bullock grudgingly complied. "Is this the man you saw in the brown sedan?"

Sanders shook his head. "No. Definitely not."

Ben gave Bullock a gentle pat. "Looks like you're off the hook this time, Mr. Prosecutor." The jurors, as well as most of the courtroom, laughed.

Ben passed through the swinging doors into the gallery. He approached Brian Erickson, the city councilman from the far south district, and asked him to stand. "What about him, Mr. Sanders? Is he the one you saw in the car?"

Sanders stared at him carefully, then answered decisively. "No."

Ben crossed the nave of the courtroom and stood beside Interim Mayor Whitman. "Would you please stand, sir?"

Whitman glared up at Ben with a look that could turn Kool-Aid to Popsicles. Wordlessly he pushed himself to his feet.

"I object," Bullock said. "Is counsel planning to go through the entire courtroom one at a time? This is nothing but a fishing expedition."

"Maybe so," Judge Hart said, "but I gave you plenty of leeway when you were putting on your case, and I intend to give the defense the same latitude. Overruled." Ben couldn't be sure, but he thought the judge had definitely chilled toward Bullock.

"What about this one, Mr. Sanders? Is he the man you saw in the brown sedan?"

Sanders stared intensely across the courtroom. His eyes locked onto Whitman. For the longest time, no one in the courtroom stirred.

Finally Sanders turned toward the judge. "Your honor, may I take a closer look?"

"Of course. You may step down from the stand. Get as close as you like."

Sanders moved off the witness stand and slowly, almost timorously crossed the courtroom. It was a dramatic moment, and he seemed to be playing it to the hilt. He didn't stop until he was only a foot away.

Sanders's eyes slowly widened; his lips eventually parted. "It *is* him," he whispered.

The courtroom roared. The television cameras whirled around to monitor Whitman's reaction. Spectators stood in their pews, trying to get a closer look.

"Take a close, careful look," Ben urged him. "Make certain. This is very important. Are you absolutely sure that this is the man you saw in the brown sedan on the street outside Wallace Barrett's house?"

Sanders's face became set and resolute. "I'm certain," he said firmly. "It's him."

The rumble in the courtroom continued unabated. Judge Hart pounded her gavel, fighting it back.

"It's a lie," Whitman spat out.

"I know what I saw," Sanders shot back. "It was *you!*"

Judge Hart pounded even harder. "That's enough. The witness will return to the stand. Everyone else will sit down and be quiet or you will be escorted out of the courtroom."

The room gradually quieted, but most eyes were still focused on the interim mayor, whose face was a rapidly fluctuating mix of surprise and rage.

"Anything more?" Judge Hart asked.

Ben knew how to quit when he was ahead. "No, your honor."

Bullock jumped to his feet. "Your honor, I move that this entire examination be stricken from the record. It is grossly misleading, prejudicial, and irrelevant. Even if this dubious testimony is believed, and Mr. Whitman was driving a car on the street outside the defendant's house, does that make him an accomplice to murder? It doesn't prove anything."

"Mr. Kincaid hasn't rested his case yet, counsel." Judge Hart's voice was cold. She seemed to have little patience for Bullock. "We'll see where it goes. Overruled. Would you care to cross?"

Bullock sat down sullenly. "No." Apparently, the prospect of impugning the testimony of a witness he had first called to the stand himself didn't much appeal to him.

"Very well," the judge said. "We're certainly making good time today. Mr. Kincaid, call your next witness."

Ben rose to his feet. "First, your honor, I have a special request—that Interim Mayor Bailey Whitman not be permitted to leave the courtroom until court is recessed for the day."

"Granted," Judge Hart said instantly. "The sergeant at arms is so instructed."

"Thank you. Now, your honor, we call Bradley 'Buck' Conners to the stand. He's waiting outside."

CHAPTER

63

NORMALLY, EVEN THE sleaziest swine in the universe dress up for court. Buck Conners, alas, had never had a chance. Ben had managed to get Judge Hart to issue an emergency subpoena and warrant; the second the server laid the paper in Buck's hands, two men from the sheriff's office escorted him across the plaza to the courthouse. He had had no opportunity to upgrade his attire. More important, he had had no opportunity to call Whitman, or anyone else for that matter, other than an attorney, which he declined.

He was not, as Ben had hoped, wearing the now-famous green fatigues, but his tattered blue jeans and black T-shirt didn't seem far from the mark. He had shaved off the goatee, however, and his hair seemed significantly shorter than it had been when Loving saw him at O'Brien Park.

"Would you state your name, please?"

Buck cleared his throat. "Uhh . . . that's, um, Bradley Conners. My buds call me, uh, Buck."

Ben nodded. "You'll excuse me if I call you Mr. Conners."

"Whatever."

"Mr. Conners, what do you do for a living?"

A small crease slithered down the center of his forehead. His concern was understandable; he had no way of anticipating what question would come next. He didn't even know why he had been dragged to court. Not for certain, anyway. "I'm a data processor. In the mail room. In the city building." He pointed. "You know. Just across the way." He shrugged. "Sometimes when they get busy I help sort the mail."

Ben suppressed a smile. Buck had given him twenty-eight words in response to a question he could've answered with four. Just the kind of witness lawyers liked. "How long have you worked there?"

" 'Bout six months."

"Do you use a computer?"

"It'd be pretty hard to data-process without one."

"Does your computer have e-mail capability?" Ben briefly explained what that was for the benefit of the non-computer-literate jurors.

"Yeah. Sure."

"Who can you get e-mail from?"

He shrugged. "I think anyone in the building who's got a computer."

"Good." Ben was trying to lay all the necessary groundwork before he asked the questions that were likely to make Buck balk. "Do you have a girlfriend?"

Buck grinned. "Several."

Ben did not grin back. "Do you know a sixteen-year-old girl named Martha Meanders?"

Buck's face paled. "Yeah," he said finally. "I know her."

"Spend a lot of time with her?"

He did his best to appear indifferent. "Some."

"Hang out together?"

"Whatever."

"Go for walks?"

"Right, right."

"If I'm not mistaken, you particularly like to go for walks on Terwilliger Avenue. Where Wallace Barrett and his family lived."

Bullock jumped up. "Objection, your honor! He's leading, plus this entire examination is a ridiculous fishing expedition. Are we going to hear from everyone who ever walked down this street—"

"Counsel, sit down." Judge Hart pivoted her chair decisively away from Bullock. "As for the leading, I will declare Mr. Conners to be a hostile witness. As for the objection, it's overruled. Mr. Kincaid, you may proceed."

"Thank you, your honor." Ben tried not to stare. What on earth had happened? Somehow Bullock had definitely found his way onto Judge Hart's mad list. "What about it, Buck? Ever take a stroll down Terwilliger?"

"I might've. Is that against the law?"

"Nope. Why did you carry the camera?"

Buck was slow to answer. Ben could almost see the wheels turning as Buck tried to decide how big a lie he could get away with. "I'm an amateur shutterbug. It's my hobby."

"Uh-huh." Ben decided to back off for the moment. In all likelihood, the man was not going to confess to murder. It would be best to get as much as he could out of him as possible before pressing him to the breaking point. "Mr. Conners, do you know the members of the city council?"

"Oh, I see some of them come through the office sometimes, on meeting days."

"Ever do any business with any of them?"

Another thoughtful pause. "Like who?"

"Mr. Conners, let's not beat around the bush. I'm talking about Councilman

Whitman, who I guess is now Interim Mayor Whitman. You and he have been . . . well, working together, haven't you?"

"I'm . . . not sure I know what you mean."

"Don't know, Mr. Conners, or don't want to know?" Ben inched forward, laying on the pressure. "It's an easy question. Have you ever done business with Councilman Whitman?"

"We've talked a few times."

"About what?"

"Objection." Bullock had mustered enough courage to attempt another objection. "Calls for hearsay."

Judge Hart frowned. "I suppose I'll have to sustain that objection as to what Mr. Whitman may have said. For now, anyway. Until an acceptable foundation for an exception is laid."

She couldn't have told Ben what to do more clearly if she'd given him a road map. "What was the nature of the relationship between you and Councilman Whitman?"

Buck propped himself up with one arm. "He's asked me to take care of a few things for him."

"So you were in business together."

Buck shrugged. "I guess you could say that."

"And what was the nature of the business?"

Buck's answers came slower and slower. "It varied. Different stuff."

"Mr. Conners, you are being uncommonly evasive. Why don't you just come clean and tell the jury what it was you were doing for Councilman Whitman?"

Several seconds ticked by. Finally Buck answered. "Yard work."

"Yard work?" Ben's eyes ballooned. "You were helping him do yard work?"

"Well, he's a busy man, and he has a big yard."

"Is that right. Tell me, Mr. Conners, when you met with Councilman Whitman in the middle of the night out at O'Brien Park, was that to discuss yard work?"

Buck clenched his jaw.

"Don't bother denying it. I can have Mr. Loving back on the stand in a heartbeat, not to mention Mr. Sanders. They both can and will identify you."

Buck clenched his jaw all the tighter, but did not answer.

"Mr. Conners, do you understand that perjury is a criminal offense? I want an answer, and I want the truth! Were you meeting our city councilman in the middle of the night in secret to discuss yard work?"

"Well . . . no."

"Then what was it? Why were you meeting a city councilman in secret in the middle of the night?"

Buck looked up at the judge. "May I have a lawyer?"

"If you wanted a lawyer present, you should have arranged it before you took the stand," she said firmly. "You will answer the question or I'll find you in contempt of court."

Buck turned slowly back toward Ben. "I'm not gonna answer that."

"Didn't you hear the judge?"

"I'm taking—whaddaya call it?—I'm taking the Fifth."

Ben took a step back. Damn. This was an obstacle that would be difficult to overcome. "Are you refusing to answer my question?"

"I ain't refusing. I'm just taking the Fifth." He looked up at the judge again. "Don't I have the right to do that?"

Judge Hart nodded. "That you do. If you believe answering the question might tend to incriminate you. But you should be aware that any refusal to answer will result in your testimony being brought to the immediate attention of the district attorney's office."

Some threat that was, Ben thought, since the district attorney's office probably preferred that he not answer. "So," Ben asked, "you admit that you met Whitman for some illegal purpose." With luck, maybe he could bully the witness into answering.

"I ain't admittin' or denyin'," Buck said flatly. "I just ain't answerin'."

"But you admit that you met Whitman in the park. That you were the man my investigator saw."

Buck shrugged. "I suppose."

"And you were the man Mr. Sanders saw in his neighborhood. The man with the camera who was seen near the Barrett home."

"It's possible."

"Why were you casing the Barrett home, Mr. Bradley?"

Buck looked away. "I'm takin' the Fifth on that one, too."

"But you were there."

"I'm not answerin' any more."

"I'm not asking you why you were there. But you were there, right? *You were there!*"

Buck's teeth locked; he frowned. "Right. I was there."

"Thank you." Ben knew that was the most he could get out of this witness, now, anyway. Best to quit while he was arguably ahead. "That's all."

Judge Hart cocked an eyebrow. "Cross?"

Bullock waved a flat hand. "None, your honor. I'm going to wait until counsel has a witness say something that relates to this case."

"Fine. Then the witness is dismissed."

"Your honor," Ben said, "I may need to recall this witness." And then again, I may not. How was he supposed to know? He was making this up as he went along. "I request that he be required to remain in the courtroom till the close of trial today."

"Granted. The sergeant at arms is so instructed. Call your next witness."

Ben took a deep breath. Had he created a reasonable doubt? Buck had certainly suggested that something improper was going on, but had he suggested enough to dissuade the jury from finding Barrett guilty? He couldn't be sure.

Like it or not, Ben had to try to get more. "The defense calls Bailey Whitman to the stand."

64

BACK IN THE gallery, Interim Mayor Whitman slowly rose to his feet. He was wearing a bright yellowish red shirt—alizarin crimson, Ben supposed. The only color Whitman could see.

"Step forward, please," Judge Hart said.

Whitman hesitated. "Your honor, I just came in today to watch. No one told me I was going to have to testify."

She smiled. "Life is full of little surprises, isn't it? Step forward."

Whitman moved to the front of the courtroom, muttering. "Don't know what you want from me. I don't know anything about it."

A good sign, Ben thought. Most witnesses wait till they're accused before they start denying.

The judge swore him in and Whitman grudgingly settled himself into the witness chair. He touched the mike, then gave his name and address.

"Permission to treat Mr. Whitman as a hostile witness," Ben requested.

"Well," Judge Hart said, "he certainly doesn't look too happy to be here. Granted."

Ben grasped the podium and began. "Mr. Whitman, you've known Wallace Barrett for many years, haven't you?"

"Seems like forever."

"You both went to college at the University of Oklahoma, didn't you?"

"We did."

"And of course, football is very important at OU, isn't it?"

Whitman shrugged. "I'd say it's their main claim to fame."

"Wallace Barrett got a full sports scholarship. Did you?"

"No," Whitman said flatly. "I paid my own way. Always have."

"You did play football at OU, though, right?"

"Right."

"Wallace Barrett was the star quarterback. Um . . . what were you?"

Whitman's lips pursed together. "Second-string tight end. For a while. I quit my sophomore year."

"Couldn't take it anymore?"

"Didn't see the point in getting my brains beat out for second-string tight end."

"So you quit, and Wallace Barrett rode on to fame and fortune. Right?"

Bullock pushed himself out of his chair. "Your honor, this is a marvelously nostalgic interlude, but it isn't very relevant to the case."

Judge Hart spoke crisply and without even looking at him. "I'm sure Mr. Kincaid will link it up in time. If that was an objection, it's overruled."

Whitman leaned forward and answered. "You're right, counsel. Barrett did a lot better than me on the college football team. Happy now?"

"The question," Ben shot back, "is whether *you* were happy. I suspect you were very unhappy."

"I had hoped to do better, sure. Things don't always go the way you wish they would. What of it?"

"You and Barrett both moved to Tulsa after college, right?"

"Well, not together."

"But this is where you both ended up."

"True enough."

"Barrett made a few movies, then went into business and became a big success." Ben glanced at the notes he had made from Jones's report. "Your first three business ventures flopped, didn't they?"

"They were speculative ventures, and they failed. There's no shame in that. Everyone knows what the economy has been like in the Southwest since the oil bust. All my creditors were paid."

"Must've been embarrassing to tell your father, though. The successful oil tycoon. And you couldn't even drill a well without losing your shirt."

Whitman's teeth clamped down on his lower lip. "Is there some point to these questions, Mr. Kincaid?"

"There certainly is."

"Well, I don't see it."

"You don't have to. All you have to do is answer the questions."

"Your honor," Bullock said, "I protest. Mr. Kincaid is being abusive."

"To the contrary," Judge Hart said, not missing a beat, "I think he has summarized the witness's role admirably. I only hope the witness will take his words to heart. Proceed, counsel."

"So," Ben continued, "your businesses flopped, while Barrett's flourished."

"I did all right in time. I'm the president and owner of Whitman Oil Corporation."

"Actually," Ben said, referring to his notes, "you inherited that business, correct?"

"Well . . . yes, but still, I've been making money with it ever since I got it."

"Your biggest accomplishment, if I'm not mistaken, was the hostile takeover of the Apollo Corporation."

"That's probably true." Whitman folded his hands proudly across his chest. "That shook the business world up. Got coverage on business pages all across the country. Doubled the value of my stock."

"Put a lot of people out of work, too," Ben noted. "The Apollo Corporation had been the city's leading employer. You bought them out, cannibalized the resources, and sold off the assets piece by piece."

"That's just good business. And for the record, my corporation employs people, too."

"Your honor!" Bullock just couldn't stay down, even when he was striking out every time. "What is this? A referendum on sound business practices?"

Judge Hart turned her attention to Ben. "Are you going to be bringing this back to the case at hand soon, counsel?"

"Yes, your honor. Very soon."

"Fine. Proceed." Bullock sat down in a huff of moral outrage obviously intended for the cameras, but unfortunately for him detected by the judge. She peered down at him with a look that could melt steel. "Mr. Bullock, do you have a problem with my ruling?"

"But I—it's just—" Bullock swallowed. "No, ma'am."

"Good." She turned back toward Ben. "Please proceed, counsel."

"So," Ben continued, "you're not denying that the success of your company is founded on the demise of another."

Whitman edged forward. "Look, counsel, that's the reality of business. Apollo was our leading competitor, so we bought them out. Not only did we acquire some valuable assets, we garnered a larger market share. The fact is, Apollo had been a thorn in my side for years. I know how to deal with my enemies. They don't last long."

"Shortly after the takeover, you ran for city council and were elected. True?"

"That's true."

"Of course, Wallace Barrett had leapfrogged right past the city council and become mayor."

"Yes, he became the mayor. Of sorts." Whitman's patience seemed to be fraying.

"You have ambitions to be mayor, don't you, sir?"

Whitman squared his shoulders. "I don't know why I should deny it. Yes, I do. I plan to run this next term."

"In truth, you've been planning your campaign for some time, haven't you?"

"True. These days, you have to start early if you hope to make a serious bid."

"That includes fund-raising, speechmaking, poll taking—right?"

"Right, right."

"The only problem is, according to your campaign manager, another council member, every poll you took showed you being beaten by Wallace Barrett. By a substantial margin." Ben stared down at him. "Isn't that true?"

He hesitated.

"My investigator met with Loretta Walker for some time. I have her affidavit right here, if you'd like to see it."

Whitman stared back emotionlessly. "That's quite all right. It's true."

"It must have seemed like, no matter where you turned, Wallace Barrett was there doing just a little bit better than you were."

"I don't measure my worth against"—his teeth clenched—"him."

"Don't you, though? Sure looks that way to me. You wanted to be mayor, and that was impossible, because once again, Wallace Barrett was in the way. You must've hated him, didn't you?"

Whitman turned toward the jury. "Again, I see no reason why I should lie. Relations between Barrett and me were not good. That's hardly a secret."

Ben closed his notebook and put away his notes. It was time to take the plunge. Off the script, into never-never land. "And that's when you decided to get in touch with Buck Conners, isn't it?"

"What?"

"Buck Conners. Our last witness. Surely you recall."

"Right. I know who he is."

"You work together at the city building."

"Right."

"And according to him, before he crouched behind the Fifth Amendment, you and he had some business dealings together."

Ben could see the same analytical clockwork going on in Whitman's brain that he had earlier seen in Buck's. How much could he get away with? "That's true."

"According to Mr. Conners, you employed him to do some . . . yard work."

A slow smile tickled the edges of Whitman's lips. "Actually, Buck is probably being modest. He has done yard work for me. But at the time of the murders, he was working on a different project."

Ben could see the jury subtly leaning forward. "And what project was that?"

Whitman smiled. "A marketing brochure."

Ben nearly tripped over his podium. *"What?"*

"A marketing brochure. Something to help the council market Tulsa to major corporations looking for a place to locate. It's a common practice. As you mentioned yourself, Tulsa needs new job opportunities. I was trying to create some."

Ben tried to get his bearings. How did he take this lie apart? "Did Mayor Barrett know about this project of yours?"

"No. I was hoping to surprise him. I wanted to wait until I had a completed prototype. Thought it would make it easier to push the project past the council."

"And you expect us to take this story seriously?"

Whitman remained calm. "It was a serious project."

"If it was so serious, why on earth would you use Buck Conners?" Ben pointed dramatically with his finger, forcing the jury to turn to scrutinize the scruffy, ill-clad, ill-groomed data processor.

"Simple," Whitman replied. "I needed a good photographer, and I knew he was good and wouldn't charge me as much as a professional. It's his hobby, you know."

"What did you tell him to photograph?"

"I left it at his discretion. To be honest, I'm not very artistically inclined. I don't have a good eye for that sort of thing."

"Why was he hanging around the mayor's house?"

"I can't say for sure, but I assume he thought a photo of the mayor's home would be a nice addition to the brochure. It's a logical choice."

Ben gripped the edges of his podium. Somehow this thing was slipping away from him. He had to get it back before it was too late. "If your joint project with Buck really was this perfectly respectable marketing brochure, as you would have this jury believe, why did you meet Buck in the dead of night in a North Side park?"

Whitman shrugged. "It was a convenient halfway point between our homes. I live on the North Side, Mr. Kincaid, near Gilcrease Museum. I don't have the prejudice against the North Side some people do."

Ooh. Nice zinger. About half the jury lived on the North Side. "And what about Mr. Sanders? He saw you in a car talking to Buck near the mayor's home."

Whitman shook his head. "He's mistaken. I've never been there."

"He said he saw you."

"He saw a car. Lots of people have brown cars. That doesn't mean it was me."

Ben's voice rose. "And so you're telling this jury that it's just a coincidence that he was hanging around the neighborhood, working for you, at the same time that someone else committed the murders? That's pretty convenient, isn't it?"

"No," Whitman said calmly, "I don't find it convenient at all. I find it very inconvenient. I find it very inconvenient for me, and very tragic for the Barrett family."

"Your honor," Bullock said, "I must object to this rude and abusive questioning of the city's acting mayor. Mr. Whitman is not on trial."

"That distinction didn't stop you from doing your best to smear Mr. Kincaid's investigator," Judge Hart said curtly. "Overruled."

Ben switched gears. "If you didn't direct Buck's work, Mr. Whitman, why were you communicating with him constantly at work?"

A small furrow crossed Whitman's brow. "I think you're mistaken."

"In the two weeks prior to the murders, you probably communicated with Buck a dozen times during office hours."

"That's simply incorrect. I never went to his station. I never called him on the phone."

"Are you denying that you communicated with him regularly during the weeks prior to the murders?"

Whitman's eyes flickered for a moment. "Yes, I am. It's simply untrue. I had no reason to talk with him."

At last! Finally Whitman had given Ben enough rope to hang him. "Do you have a computer in your office, Mr. Whitman?"

He looked distinctly bored. "You know I do. You've been there."

"And according to Mr. Conners, the city offices have e-mail capability. Is that true?"

"I suppose so. To tell you the truth, I don't use those machines much." He chuckled. "Don't understand them, don't trust them."

"Are you claiming you don't use e-mail?"

"I may have once or twice. Not often. And never to Buck."

Ben started walking back toward counsel table. "You wouldn't object if we examined your computer to verify that, would you?"

He spread wide his hands. "Of course not. But I'm afraid I always delete my messages at the end of the day. So there would be nothing for you to see. Once it's gone, it's gone."

Now it was Ben's turn to smile. "You know, that's what I thought, too. I thought that once an e-mail message was deleted from the hard drive on your desktop computer, it was gone. Vanished into the ether. But my office assistant, who's a computer whiz, told me otherwise. He explained that although pushing the delete button will delete the copy of the message that has been stored on the hard drive of your individual computer, the mainframe or server—the central computer that routes the e-mail from one machine to another—retains a copy. And those copies remain in the central computer system until they are actively deleted, which is usually done only once or twice a year. Did you know that, Mr. Whitman?"

Whitman's response was slow and brief. "No."

"Well, turns out it's true. It also turns out you can hire a computer expert to hack into the central computer and extract all the messages that have gone to or from a particular terminal. Isn't that amazing?"

Whitman didn't appear amazed. "Indeed."

"Now, you wouldn't object if we took a look at the messages that went to and from your terminal during the two weeks before the murders, would you? Well, you've already said that you wouldn't. You're not going to revoke your permission now, are you?"

Whitman's voice was considerably quieter. "I . . . suppose not."

Good. That helped Ben past a major evidentiary obstacle. "Thank you, sir."

"We'll have to go back to the office. I don't know how long it will take—"

"Fret not, Mr. Whitman." Ben popped open his briefcase and withdrew a stack of letter-size papers. "I've already done it."

He stopped at Bullock's table and dropped a certified document in his lap. "Here's the subpoena the judge issued for the documents themselves. Here's an affidavit from the computer supervisor at the city office building who actually extracted the messages." He approached the witness stand and forced the papers into Whitman's hands. "And here are the messages."

Ben returned to the podium with his copy of the messages. "Feel free to sort through them, Mr. Whitman. I'm sure they'll all be very familiar to you. Those are your messages, aren't they?"

Whitman glanced down at the papers in his hands. "I suppose."

"By my count, sir, you communicated with Mr. Conners a total of eleven times by e-mail during the two weeks prior to the murders."

Whitman fumbled through the papers. His manner and voice seemed disjointed, lost. He was scrambling. "I guess there were more details to work out than I recalled."

"I guess so. Some of those details really intrigued me. Like the one mentioned in message six." Whitman thumbed to the document while Ben held it up and read it out loud. " 'Meet me on Terwilliger at six.' " Ben looked up. "Just in case anyone has forgotten, Terwilliger Avenue is the street the Barrett family lives on, isn't it, sir?"

Whitman's eyes darted from side to side. "I . . . believe that's correct."

"Mr. Sanders lives there, too. I wonder if this is the day he saw you there? When you met Buck at six."

Whitman did not respond.

"And then there's message eight," Ben continued. "That's an interesting one. 'Barrett will be home early this afternoon.' " Ben put down the paper. "Now, that's an interesting bit of information to be conveying to your photographer, especially since you didn't know he would be photographing the Barrett home. Why would he want to know this?"

Out the corner of his eye, Ben saw the jurors carefully scrutinizing Whitman. They wanted to know the answer to that question, too.

Whitman stumbled, stuttered. "I . . . don't recall . . . It's been a long time."

"But this is probably my favorite of the messages," Ben continued. He held it high in the air so the jury could see. "Number eleven. This one was sent on the very same day the murders occurred. I admire brevity in a writer, and this message is the very soul of brevity. Only five words, in fact." Ben faced the jury and read. "It says, 'Did you get the nigger?' "

The courtroom went crazy. The roar was loud enough to cause feedback on the television mikes. People stood on the pews, craning their necks for a better view. The cameras swirled around, trying to catch everyone's reaction. Reporters threw messages to runners, while the rest of the gallery stared forward in stunned silence.

Judge Hart pounded the courtroom back into order, and Ben asked his next question. "Mr. Whitman, what exactly were you trying to find out when you asked Buck Conners 'Did you get the nigger?' "

Whitman's hands were pressed against the edges of the witness box. He blinked, twitched, rubbed his finger against the side of his nose. He looked up at the jury, then over at the judge, as if searching for some recourse, some place of appeal. "I don't believe I want to do this anymore. This is an outrage. I am not the defendant."

"No," Ben said, "but you should be. Answer my question."

"I won't. I want a lawyer."

Judge Hart leaned down from the bench. "Excuse me, sir. You will answer the question. That is an order."

"I will not." Whitman folded his hands across his chest. "I'm taking the Fifth."

"That again?" Ben turned wide-eyed toward the jury. "There seems to be an epidemic of this today." He took a step toward the witness. "Tell us the truth. You hated Barrett. You've hated him for years. You couldn't be mayor as long as he was around. You had to get him out of the way. He was your enemy."

"Yeah? What of it?"

"As you said yourself, Mr. Whitman. You know how to deal with your enemies, don't you? Those were your own words!"

Whitman's lips parted wordlessly.

"That's why you hired Buck, isn't it? You didn't hire him for any phony photography job. You hired him to 'get the nigger'!"

The clamor rose, this time even louder than before. Judge Hart pounded her gavel futilely.

Ben shouted above the tumult. "Answer my question! Isn't it true? You engineered these murders, didn't you? *It was you!*"

"It was not! I—" Whitman stared back at Ben with unmasked hatred. "I'm not saying another word till I see my attorney. You're wasting your time."

Ben threw his hands down in disgust. "That's just fine, Mr. Whitman. I think we all know what happened, whether you care to admit it or not."

"Objection!" Bullock shouted.

"Never mind," Ben said. "I'm finished with this witness."

Judge Hart leaned across the bench. "Do you care to cross-examine, Mr. Prosecutor?"

Bullock frowned. If he thought he could do himself any good, Ben knew he would. But it was hopeless. Whitman had taken the Fifth. And even with a friendly questioner, Whitman couldn't explain away Ben's evidence without risking a waiver of his Fifth Amendment right of silence. "No."

"Very well. Anything else, Mr. Kincaid?"

"I see no need," Ben said. He placed his documents back on the table and firmly placed his hands on his client's shoulders. "Wallace Barrett did not commit these crimes. We rest our case."

65

As it turned out, there was no rebuttal testimony, so Ben got to go out on a high note. That was good, but the critical question was—how good? Whitman had been proved a liar, but had he been proved a murderer? There was no doubt in Ben's mind, but he knew it was pointless to try to predict what the jurors were thinking. All they could do was wait and hope for the best.

After the tumult of the last witness, closing arguments were almost an anticlimax. Ben wondered what approach Bullock would take. He remembered that old trial lawyer's canard: When you have the facts on your side, argue the facts. When you have the law on your side, argue the law. When you have neither, holler.

As it happened, Bullock did very little hollering. He had plenty of compelling evidence to wield, and he reintroduced every bit of it.

"I'm reminded of a story my father told me once," Bullock began. He leaned his hands against the rail and edged toward the jurors. "Seemed a married man had been out all night, drinking and carousing and carrying on, and he didn't get back until the wee hours of the morning. He knew his wife would be angry, so he took off his shoes and tiptoed into the kitchen. To his surprise, he found his wife was already up and sitting at the kitchen table, with a very angry expression on her face.

" 'Where have you been?' she asked.

" 'Well,' he said, thinking quickly, 'I woke early this morning, so I thought I'd go out for a jog.'

"His wife stared back at him. 'I woke several times during the night,' she said. 'You were never there.'

" 'Well,' he said, thinking at lightning speed, 'I didn't come to bed because I knew you were already asleep and I didn't want to wake you.'

" 'I dead bolted the doors last night,' his wife replied. 'You were never inside.'

" 'Well,' he said, 'I didn't want to disturb you, so I slept outside in the hammock.'

"His wife shook her head. 'I sold the hammock last week at a garage sale.'

"The man took a deep breath, folded his arms, and said, 'That's my story, and I'm sticking to it.' "

Bullock pushed himself away from the railing. "For some reason, I kept thinking of that story the whole time the defense put on its case. That's my story and I'm sticking to it. That was more or less the main theme of the entire defense. Wallace Barrett has his little story about how he was conveniently not at the scene of the crime at the exact time of the murder, even though he was seen there throughout the afternoon. It's illogical. It's preposterously contrived. It conflicts with the evidence. But that's his story, and he's sticking to it."

Bullock sauntered into the center of the courtroom, gesturing toward the defense table. "They would have you forget all about the mountain of evidence we have laid before you, all of which points to one man. Wallace Barrett. They have even attempted to tarnish the reputation of one of the leading citizens of this community in their desperate attempt to break the strong arm of justice. They want you to forget everything, but I want you to *remember* everything—*all* the facts, *all* the evidence."

Bullock then proceeded to catalogue in detail the considerable evidence the prosecution had put before the jury. He covered it all—the eye- and ear-witnesses to Barrett's violent episodes and his threats—Cynthia Taylor, Dr. Fisher, the man at the ice-cream shop. And perhaps most poignantly, Karen Gleason, the little girl who had the misfortune to hear her eight-year-old playmate being murdered on the other end of the phone.

And then he started on the forensic evidence. Ben could see the jurors' eyes dart, their heads nod, as he reminded them of some of the most compelling, seemingly unrefutable points. The blood traces—could anyone deny that Wallace Barrett's blood was on his wife's body? DNA blood typing might not be precise, but the odds against that blood coming from anyone else were enormous. And then there was the skin sample found under his wife's fingernail, the sample that DNA testing proved had almost certainly come from Barrett. How could he possibly explain that? And then, of course, there was the devastating testimony of the coroner—that Caroline Barrett was pregnant at the time of her death, a two-month-old fetus who had died with her.

"In the light of such overwhelming evidence," Bullock said, "how can you possibly be misled by a few trivial inconsistencies, by some unconvincing speculations about cameras and e-mail and a secret rendezvous in the park? Ladies and gentlemen, conspiracy theories are always appealing. It's more comforting to believe that great acts of evil are committed by vast unseen forces than to believe that one man—a husband and father—could be so evil, so cruel. We would rather believe in unknown bogeymen than believe in a real-life monster who could kill his own wife, his own children. But that's what happened."

He walked to the easel and retrieved the three enlargements. "I could try to melodramatize the horror of the crime that this man committed. I could go on and on, I could rant and rave. But what would be the point? A picture is worth a thousand words. And ladies and gentlemen, these pictures say it all."

Wordlessly, he held up the exhibits: first the enlargement of the crime-scene shot of Caroline Barrett, soaked with blood and draped over a dining room chair, then the picture of Annabelle Barrett, lying mummy-like on her bed, then Alysha Barrett, lying dead in a bathtub awash in blood.

"Ladies and gentlemen," he said, in a voice barely more than a whisper, "I ask you to do your duty as responsible citizens and jurors. I ask you to find Wallace Barrett guilty of first-degree murder. *Please.*"

He folded up the exhibits and returned to his seat.

Judge Hart gave Ben the nod, and he took his place before the jury. How could he follow a presentation like that one?

Slowly Ben made eye contact with each of the jurors. "This is not a game. It is not a contest. It is not a duel between Mr. Bullock and me. It is not a horse race, where you try to bet on the winner. And it is not a circus, media or otherwise. This is a murder trial. A man is on trial, and make no mistake, the action you take today will irrevocably change the course of his life, and the lives of others, for all time. In your entire lives, you may never again do anything as important as what you do today. I do not want to make your job any harder than it already is. But given the gravity of the situation, you must be certain that you have considered all the facts. You must be certain that you have considered all the evidence. And you must be certain that you are right."

Ben pressed his hands together. "What is it the prosecution would have you believe? First, that Wallace Barrett, successful athlete, businessman, and politician, is really a heartless, twisted, violent man with a temper he can't control. Well, I don't doubt that Wallace has a temper. We all do. He's probably even lost it once or twice. I know I have. In fact, I've lost my temper once or twice since this trial began." The jury smiled appreciatively. "But, ladies and gentlemen, this crime required far more than a temper. This crime required a callous, cold-hearted disregard for human life, even children. Have you heard or seen anything that suggested that this man was capable of destroying his entire family? I don't think so.

"And even assuming that he could commit this crime, why would he? Just because he got mad one day? Because he was jealous? Because they had an argument at an ice-cream parlor? I find that impossible to believe. This man loved his children. You can hear it in his voice, see it in his eyes. He wouldn't hurt them for any reason, much less a trivial one. The prosecution would have you believe he was furious because his wife was pregnant, a fact he didn't even know, because being pregnant would make her ugly. Is that credible? He loved his children, and he has always wanted a son. They'd been trying to have another child for years. Bizarrely enough, the prosecution would twist what should have been a blessed event into a motive for murder. Does that even make sense?"

Ben nodded toward the prosecution table. "Now, Mr. Bullock has made much of the fact that Wallace Barrett told you he was at home the afternoon of the murders, but left after an argument and was gone when the murders took place. Isn't that convenient? they say. Well, I say, convenient for whom? For Wallace? Or for the man who had been stalking his family, the man who we know was in the neighborhood watching, waiting for his opportunity. When he saw Wallace Barrett leave the home, right after a noisy argument, he saw the chance he had been waiting for, not only to commit the murders, but to guarantee that Wallace would be blamed. That was part of the plan, after all. They didn't just want him dead. They wanted him to suffer. They wanted him destroyed."

Ben gestured toward the prosecution exhibits, still leaning against the central podium. "The prosecution has made much of the forensic evidence in this case, because that's really all they have. But let's face it. It's all circumstantial. At best, some of it proves that Wallace Barrett was at his home the day of the murders, a fact he has never denied. None of it proves that he was the one who killed his wife and children. Moreover, you've heard from the lips of the prosecution's own witnesses how tainted the crime scene was. Dozens of people tramped through that house, touching things, leaving tracks, covering others. These shoddy police procedures call into question the credibility of any evidence taken from the crime scene. And ask yourselves this: If proper procedures had been followed, what other evidence might have been discovered? Evidence pointing to Buck Conners, perhaps? Or even Councilman Bailey Whitman?

"The prosecution has suggested that this trail of evidence pointing to the city council is speculative and unconvincing. Can you say the same? It doesn't matter, actually, because that is not the question the judge will put before you. The important question is: Can you say that this evidence does not create a reasonable doubt in your mind? You've seen the evidence. Buck Conners admitted he was in the neighborhood at the time of the murders. He admitted that he worked with Councilman Whitman. He admitted their secret rendezvous at a secluded park in the middle of the night. Then he clammed up—because he didn't want to incriminate himself.

"What about Councilman Whitman himself? He admitted hiring

Conners, he admitted meeting him in the park, he admitted Conners was in Barrett's neighborhood. He gave you some cock-and-bull story about a marketing brochure. Ask yourselves this: If that's true, where's the brochure? It's been weeks since the murders took place. Shouldn't it be done by now? The truth is there was never any brochure. There was only this—a cold-blooded plan to eliminate a political opponent, engineered by a man who has admitted that he hated Barrett, admitted that he has hated Barrett for years. Now that, ladies and gentlemen, is a motive you can believe.

"The proof of the pudding is in the documents. Whitman took the Fifth—so as not to incriminate himself—but he couldn't deny the truth spelled out by his own e-mail messages. Those messages prove he was plotting with Conners, prove he met Conners on the street where Barrett lived. If there is any doubt whatsoever in your mind about the complicity of Conners and Whitman, ask yourselves this question: What did he mean when he asked Buck Conners on the day of the murder—'Did you get the nigger?' What did he mean? What else *could* he have meant?"

Ben lowered his hands and took a step back from the jury box. "Ultimately, you do not have to determine who committed this crime. You do not even have to determine whether you think the defendant committed this crime. The question before you as jurors is simply this: Is there a reasonable doubt? Regardless of what you think likely or probable—is there a reasonable doubt? Given all that you have seen, all the lies and deceit, sloppy police work and Fifth Amendment cover-ups and secret e-mail messages that drip with hatred, can you honestly say that there is no reasonable doubt? And if you cannot, if you are willing to admit that there *is* a reasonable doubt, then, as the judge will instruct you, you have only one choice. You must find the defendant not guilty. If you are not absolutely certain, if there is a reasonable doubt in your minds, you must agree with what Wallace Barrett said the day he was indicted for this horrible crime. He said that this monstrous crime made him sick at heart. But he was absolutely not guilty.

"Ladies and gentlemen, I ask you to follow the facts, follow the evidence, follow the judge's instructions, and follow your hearts. This man would not commit this crime. He could not commit this crime. I ask you to return a verdict of not guilty."

Bullock's rebuttal was brief, to everyone's relief. He did not attempt to rehash the whole trial, nor did he directly refute anything Ben had said in his closing. Instead, he approached the jurors holding a smashed picture frame in a plastic evidence bag.

"Like I mentioned before," he said quietly, "a picture is worth a thousand words. Here's one more picture I wanted to show you." He held it up so the jury could see. "This is the smashed framed photograph of Caroline Barrett found at the scene of the crime. It must've been smashed by the murderer. Certainly, neither Wallace Barrett nor any other defense witness has ever suggested otherwise."

He paused, took a deep breath. "Ask yourselves this question, ladies and gentlemen of the jury. Would a hit man have any reason to smash Caroline's picture? Would Councilman Whitman have any reason to smash her picture? Would anyone—other than *him*?" Bullock whirled around and pointed directly at Wallace Barrett. "Only one man would have smashed her picture. The man who hated her, the man who was so overcome by jealousy and rage that he lashed out and destroyed everything in sight. Forget these fairy tales and contrived fantasies. We all know who killed the Barrett family. *We all know! He's sitting right over there!*"

Bullock turned back around and closed his eyes. "Ladies and gentlemen, do the right thing. Find this man guilty. Not because you have to. Certainly not because you want to. Because he is."

When Bullock took his seat, the courtroom was still, but for the barely audible whirring of cameras and the soft intake of breath. The trial, everyone realized, was finally over. All except for the final act.

AFTER CLOSINGS, ALL that was left was the part of the trial that Ben hated most. Waiting. Judge Hart calmly and deliberately read the instructions to the jury. It was one of those irrational, unfathomable eccentricities of the jury system that the instructions—which basically told the jury what was important and what they should be listening for—were read only after all the evidence was completed. The sun was just beginning to set when the bailiff escorted the jury into the deliberation room.

Ben sat in the courtroom with Wallace Barrett while Christina and Jones made a run to Coney Island for dinner. It was a tradition of sorts for the lawyers to go into the judge's chambers while the jury deliberated and to swap war stories, but Ben wasn't in the mood. And he thought Wallace might prefer to have some company.

"So," Barrett said, with a painfully unconvincing smile on his face, "what do you think?"

Ben shook his head. "I never try to predict what a jury will do." Especially not this time.

Barrett nodded. "Sure. I understand." He pressed his hands together. "Well, however it turns out, I want you to know—you did a good job. No matter what happens, I've got no complaints. I'll pay your fee in full, as promised."

Ben smiled. "Well, that will make my creditors happy, anyway. Not to mention my staff. Who knows? Maybe I'll even be able to get a new Honda."

Barrett grimaced. "Honda? Ben, think big. You're a celebrity now, man. How about a BMW? Better yet, a Jag."

"I don't think so. I'm not the type."

"So you say. Try driving my XJS convertible for a week. You'll never go back to Hondas, believe me."

Ben leaned back in his chair. "Well, we'll see."

There was a long pause. Barrett stared at his hands for a long time.

"Ben," he said quietly, "do you think they believed me?"

Ben closed his eyes. "I hope so, Wallace. I really hope so."

IT WAS BARELY two hours later when they got the word that the jury was returning.

"Wow," Barrett said. "I thought we'd be here all night. At least."

"So did I," Ben echoed.

"How did they make up their minds so quickly? What does it mean?"

Ben didn't answer. The O. J. Simpson case aside, traditional trial lawyer wisdom was that a speedy return meant a guilty verdict. He opted not to share that nugget of wisdom with Barrett.

The jurors took their places. The television cameras came on and white-hot lights burned across the courtroom. The tension and suspense in the room were almost unbearable.

Just get it over with, Ben thought. Just get it done.

The piece of paper went from the foreman of the jury to the bailiff to the judge. Unfortunately, Judge Hart did not use color-coded jury forms; Ben had no way of knowing what it said till it was read aloud. He tried to scan the jurors' faces, hoping to pick up a clue. But every face was set and solemn. No one was telling. And, he noticed, no one was making eye contact with Wallace Barrett, either.

Judge Hart's eyes scanned the verdict form. The judge then returned it to the bailiff, who passed it back to the foreman.

"Madame Foreperson, have you reached a verdict?"

Juror Number Six rose. "Yes, your honor. We have."

Judge Hart nodded. "The defendant will rise and face the jury."

Wallace Barrett did as instructed, Ben at his side.

"Well," the judge said, turning back toward the jury, "the whole world is waiting. Give us your verdict."

CHAPTER

66

THE FOREWOMAN CLEARED her throat, and her hands began to tremble, as if, given the judge's instruction to proceed, she suddenly became aware of the enormous number of people listening to her words, breathlessly awaiting what she had to say.

"We the jury, duly formed and constituted pursuant to the laws of the great state of Oklahoma, having heard the evidence set forth against the defendant, who has been charged with murder in the first degree of Caroline Barrett, Alysha Barrett, and Annabelle Barrett, three human beings and citizens of this state, do hereby find and declare the defendant to be—"

She paused, catching her breath, while everyone in the courtroom held theirs in suspense.

"Not guilty!"

Ben gripped Barrett by the shoulders. Barrett slapped Ben's hands, his eyes closed, and his face relaxed for the first time since the trial had begun. "Thank you," he said, just under his breath. "Thank you for believing me. Thank you so much."

The courtroom went totally out of control. Pandemonium ensued— a flurry of shouts, cries, and rushing feet. The gallery was blanketed by a blinding glare of flashbulbs and key lights.

Judge Hart pounded the gavel, trying to reestablish control. "Is that your verdict?" she shouted.

The jurors nodded.

"So say you one, so say you all?"

Again, there was no dissent.

"Marvelous." She thanked them, then dismissed them, warning them that they were not required to speak to the press, the lawyers, or the parties unless they chose to do so. Finally she looked down at Barrett, smiled, and said the magic words. "Mr. Barrett, you have been found not guilty of the charges against you. You are free to go."

There were cheers from the back of the courtroom. Judge Hart dropped her gavel and stepped down from the bench.

Barrett embraced Ben, his face overcome with relief and joy. "Did you hear that? Did you *hear* it?"

Ben smiled and clasped his shoulder. "I heard it. Congratulations!"

"Congratulate me? Hell, you did all the work. I oughta carry you outta here on my shoulders!"

"A handshake will be fine, thanks."

Ben held out his hand, but Barrett gave it a yank, pulled Ben close, and gave him a huge bear hug. "I can't thank you enough, Ben. I really can't. You've saved my life. I owe everything to you."

"Nonsense. You were innocent, so you weren't convicted. It's that simple. Despite what some people think, the justice system does work. At least most of the time."

Barrett pulled away, wiped his eyes, and straightened his tie. "Well, if you'll excuse me, I believe I'll have a few words with the press."

Ben nodded. He supposed Barrett had earned that right. For weeks now, he'd been living with biased reports that implied, if not declared, his guilt. How could he possibly resist the opportunity to ram all those words down their throats?

Ben heard a voice, barely discernible above the clamor. "So you got another one off."

Ben closed his eyes. "Bullock, I've had about as much of you—"

He whirled around. It wasn't Bullock. It was Judge Hart. And she was smiling. "Just teasing," she said.

"Oh. Right." Ben tried not to appear puzzled. The joking judge? "Is there . . . something I can do for you?"

"No." She seemed hesitant, as if unsure herself what exactly she was going to say. "I just wanted to . . . congratulate you."

Ben blinked. What? Since when? "Thank you, your honor." Congratulations from the judge? What on earth was going on?

"There was something else . . ." She glanced over her shoulder, obviously making sure none of the media reps were listening in. "When we were in chambers this morning . . . you remember?"

Ben nodded. He did, although it was hard to believe that it was only this morning. It seemed like a million years ago.

"When that juror—Ms. Meanders—told us what she knew, gave us the names of her daughter and her boyfriend, Buck . . . I noticed how astonished and surprised you were."

"Yes," Ben agreed. "I was." His forehead creased. "If my behavior was inappropriate, I apologize."

"No, no, it was entirely natural, given the circumstances. What was unnatural was"—she glanced over her shoulder again—"your worthy opponent. Mr. Bullock. Did you notice him?"

Ben shook his head. "I guess I didn't."

She nodded. "As I said, you were astonished. But he was . . . not. Which seemed very odd to me. And the other odd thing was that, when your investigator tracked Buck down and brought me his full name so I could issue the subpoena, I was almost certain I had heard it before."

"Really? Where?"

"That's what I wondered. It took me a while, digging through the file, before I figured it out." She paused, frowned. "It was on the prosecutor's preliminary witness list. You've never seen it. It was something they filed with the court in camera to get warrants and subpoenae issued. I checked it myself. Sure enough, Bradley J. 'Buck' Conners's name was on it."

Ben's eyes narrowed. "He knew."

Judge Hart nodded. "He did. I don't know how exactly, but somehow in the course of the investigation, after Bullock had already charged Barrett, he tumbled onto Buck. Brought him in. Interviewed him. And did nothing."

"He knew Barrett was innocent?"

"I don't know about that," the judge said. "It's possible he thought the Buck connection was unimportant, that he couldn't get Buck to admit he'd been out to the mayor's home, and that he still thought Barrett was guilty. Probable, in fact. But what's unforgivable is that he withheld Buck's name from you—the defense. Buck's testimony clearly would tend to exculpate Barrett. He had a duty to inform you. But he didn't."

"He wanted to win that bad."

Judge Hart agreed. "So you can understand why I've been somewhat . . . well, less than charitable to Mr. Prosecutor today. I considered calling a mistrial, but since the information had come out, and we were so close to a resolution, I decided against it. If the jury had voted to convict, I would've declared a mistrial *sua sponte*, but since the man has been acquitted, and since the eyes of the entire world are upon us . . ."

"I understand," Ben said.

"Still, I wanted you to know. And I wanted to congratulate you. Sincerely. This business of treating trials like they're intramural scrimmages—us against them, shirts against skins, anything to win—it's just repugnant to me. Practicing law is not about winning. It's about justice. Simple, naked justice. It's about finding the truth. People like Bullock and his police cronies who disregard leads that don't point the way they want them to seem to have forgotten that"—her eyes met Ben's—"but you haven't." She extended her hand. "Thanks, Ben."

"My pleasure, your honor."

Judge Hart returned to chambers, and Ben was confronted by a barrage of reporters shouting questions. He tried to be cooperative, for his client's sake, but his heart wasn't in it. These people had made it virtually impossible for his client to get a fair and impartial trial. He wasn't going to play nice-nice now.

Ben pushed his way through the reporters to the back of the courtroom. Christina was waiting for him; when he approached, she threw her arms around his neck. "Congratulations, champ. I knew you'd come through."

Ben grinned. "Thanks. Couldn't have done it without your help." He noted the many boxes of files and documents beside her. "Let me help you with some of that."

She held up her hands. "No way, hero. Jones and I can manage. You deserve a rest."

"Well, if you insist." He grabbed his coat. "I'll meet everyone back at the hotel room in half an hour, okay? We should celebrate. Room service, maybe even. I'm buying."

"You're on."

Ben pushed through the remainder of the courtroom into the hallway. He managed to clear a path to the elevators, waited the usual interminable length of time for one to come, then stepped inside.

Just as the elevator doors were about to close, a tall young man Ben didn't recognize darted between the doors.

"Just made it," the man said. The doors closed behind him. "Going down?"

"All the way." The man punched one.

Conforming with usual elevator etiquette, they stood on opposite sides, folded their arms, and didn't speak. Until, as they dropped below the fourth floor, the other man said, "Bet you're glad that's over."

"Definitely." Ben smiled politely. Who . . . ? Must've been in the courtroom, although Ben didn't recall seeing him. A journalist, perhaps? He hoped not.

"I have to say, I was surprised. I thought your client was guilty as sin."

"A lot of people made that mistake."

"In fact, I would've bet on it."

"Well," Ben said cheerily, "you would've lost your money. Barrett isn't a killer. He isn't the type."

The elevator glided past the third, then the second floor. "Isn't he?"

Ben turned his head slowly. "No, he isn't. He doesn't have the killer instinct."

"Oh, I never thought he had that," the other man said, just as the elevator touched down on the first floor. "I just thought he had a . . . sick heart."

CHAPTER

67

BEN FELT THE hairs prick up on the back of his neck. "What did you say?" he whispered hoarsely.

"I think you heard me."

The bell rang and the elevator doors began to part. Ben threw himself toward the doors, but he was too late. The other man knocked him to the side and hit the close button.

Ben scrambled up and found himself face-to-face with a pistol. "Don't think I won't shoot," the man said. "I will. I want to. I've been dreaming about it for weeks."

"What is it you want?" Ben asked, gasping.

"For the moment, I want you to walk out of this building, without attracting any attention, and to get in your car. Your rental car. I'll be your passenger. Do it right, and I won't shoot you or anyone else. Do something stupid and I'll shoot you and everyone else in sight. And there are a lot of people in this courthouse right now."

Ben eyed the young man carefully. He didn't doubt for a moment that he was capable of carrying out his threat. "I'm parked downstairs. Near the city building."

"I know."

The man holding the gun released the close button, and the doors slid open. A crowd was waiting to get on. One of them, a reporter probably, recognized Ben and shouted something at him. Ben ignored him and walked on by.

"That's it," the man said. He had concealed his gun in his coat pocket, but Ben knew it was still trained on him. "Just stay quiet and keep walking."

Ben walked through the doors onto the plaza outside the courthouse. It was dark now. They walked to his rental car without passing anyone Ben knew. He had secretly harbored hopes that they would meet someone who would realize something was wrong—Mike, perhaps, or Sergeant Tomlinson. But it didn't happen.

Ben slid into the driver's seat and started the car. The man with the gun in his pocket took the passenger side. "Good so far," he said. "Now drive to the River Parks. And don't try to be clever, understand? Don't wave at a cop car or drive into a telephone pole. Try anything like that and you'll find a bullet in your brain. And then I'll take out your friends back in the hotel room and everyone in that goddamn boardinghouse of yours. Understand?"

Ben's lips thinned. "I understand."

"Good. Drive."

Ben pulled out of the parking garage onto Fifth Street. His brain was racing. What was he going to do? There must be some way out of this, but for the life of him—literally—he couldn't think what it was. What would Mike do? he wondered. Mike would probably refuse to cooperate, would throw himself at the man. Mike might get away with it, too. But Ben knew perfectly well that if he tried it, he would just end up a bloody blot in a Thrifty rental car.

"You know you've had it wrong from the start," Ben said easily, never taking his eyes from the road. "Barrett isn't guilty. He never was. There was no chicanery or deceit in that courtroom, at least not by me. Barrett was acquitted because he was not guilty."

"I don't give a damn about the Barrett case," the younger man spat out. "I'll leave that to the tabloids and housewives. The world obsesses on some stupid celebrity trial while important trials, things that matter, are totally forgotten."

What? Ben was confused. If Sick Heart wasn't stalking him because of the Barrett case, then what the hell was it?

"I don't understand," Ben said as he pulled onto Riverside Drive. "Why me? Why are you doing this?"

The young man's eyes glistened. They seemed detached, manic. Ben had the unsettling feeling that his companion might not be entirely together. As if that should come as a surprise.

"I don't have to explain myself to you," the man said.

"No, but don't you want to? Don't you want me to know what I'm being punished for?"

"Pull over here." With his gun hand, the stranger motioned toward a sloping driveway down into the River Parks. The River Parks were one of the loveliest parts of Tulsa—miles and miles of unspoiled land on the east bank of the Arkansas River. Jogging and bike trails lined the area between the river and Riverside Drive, as well as parks and band shells and exercise parcourses.

Ben parked a few slots down from another car; it was dark, but he saw two heads inside, both facing away. Making out? Whatever it was, they seemed to take no notice of him.

"Get out of the car."

Ben obeyed. He stepped out, eyeing Riverside Drive. It was only a few feet away. If he made a run for it—

He'd be shot dead. It was that simple.

He followed the man with the gun to the bank of the river. They stood in the middle of a jogging trail. Unfortunately, at this time of night, there were no joggers. Even in a relatively safe city like Tulsa, smart people didn't jog at night. The area was deserted.

"I still don't understand why you're doing this," Ben said. "Can't you even give me a hint?"

The young man brushed his dark, curly hair out of his eyes. "Don't you recognize me?"

Ben peered at the face, the wavy hair, the cold, bitter eyes. There was something about them . . . but what was it? He couldn't make the connection.

"Think back," the man said. "Think back a long time ago. Eight years ago, to be precise. Think back to another controversial trial in which you played a pivotal role. Another time justice was thwarted."

"Eight years ago?" Ben said. "But I wasn't even out of law school then."

"That's right," the man said coldly. "You weren't."

The truth struck him like a thunderbolt. "You're talking about my father's trial."

"Damn straight. Don't act as if you don't remember it. I know you do. I know you were there. I saw you."

"You—but—" Ben stared into that face, trying to make a connection. He was sure he had never seen this face before. Maybe not this face exactly. But that would have been eight years ago . . .

"You're the little boy," Ben said, the light slowly dawning. "The little boy at the courthouse." The one who spat in Ben's face. The one who swore he would never forget. "Your father died."

"My father was murdered!" His hand clenched tighter on the pistol. "Murdered by that defective cardiac valve. That sick heart that was sewn into his chest."

Ben felt his knees sag. Sick heart. The clues had been right in front of him all along. And he had been too stupid to see them.

"My dad was wonderful," the young man said, his voice trembling. "The best man I ever knew. The only one who ever really gave a damn about me. Was it his fault his heart was bad, that he hoped for a miracle cure? Did he deserve what happened to him?"

"No, of course not," Ben said. "But if his heart failed—"

"He should've gone to Houston. They do heart transplants fairly regularly now. They have a success rate better than fifty percent. He would've lived. I would've had a father." A dark cloud covered his eyes. "But no. Instead, he let those doctors convince him to go with the EKCV. The Kincaid special. And it killed him."

"That's horrible," Ben said. "But surely you realize that no one intended to kill your father."

"Of course they didn't intend to!" He was shouting now, screaming. Ben could only hope he would attract some attention, even though he knew the odds were long. "They just didn't care! They didn't give a damn!" He swung his pistol wildly through the air, gasping, crying out. "They were more concerned about getting rich than they were about my daddy!"

Ben took a deep breath and tentatively extended his hand. "Look, I know how you must feel. It was a terrible thing. But it has nothing to do with me."

The young man glared at him, eyes cold. "It was the Kincaid valve."

"That was my father. He—"

"You were all in it together."

"I wasn't in it at all. Hell, I worked for the prosecutors."

"You've lived off it. You've wallowed in the profits."

"I haven't wallowed in anything. I've never accepted a cent of my father's money, from this project or anything else."

"Don't make your stupid excuses to me!" His eyes were blazing, wide as they could possibly be. "You killed my father!"

"It wasn't *me*!" Ben screamed back. "It was *my* father! It was your father and my father. It doesn't have anything to do with us!"

He placed the barrel of the gun against Ben's chest. "The sins of the fathers are visited on the sons." His hand was trembling, including the finger curled around the trigger. "Your father escaped the hands of justice. You won't."

Ben stared down at the cold steel pressed against his chest. "Why now? After all these years."

"I didn't know where you were!" Ben knew the man was losing control. The only question was whether he could stay alive long enough to take advantage. "After your father died, I looked for you. But I couldn't find you. You left the DA's office, disappeared from Oklahoma City. It seemed I had been robbed again, or so I thought. I grew up, I joined the army, but I never forgot. And then one day, I turned on the television and there you were. God had delivered you to me. The coverage of this Barrett case was everywhere; you were on almost every day. How could I miss it?" His voice dropped; his eyes narrowed. "So I came to Tulsa. And I started laying my plans."

"Your plans have caused me a lot of grief. And my friends as well."

"Good. That makes me happy." He smiled. "The grief is about to intensify."

With his free hand, he reached into his coat pocket and withdrew a small, hand-sized black box with an antenna extending from it. There was a red light on the top, not currently illuminated, above two red buttons. "Do you know what this is?"

Ben shook his head. "Some sort of radio signal transmitter."

"Right the first time. As you may have gathered, I have a certain facility with explosives. A gift from Uncle Sam, courtesy of my army days, before I departed prematurely from my distinguished career of service." He paused. "I know where you live. You and the kid."

"You son of a bitch," Ben muttered.

"And that whore babysitter, and the landlady, and everyone else in your happy little extended family. Guess what? The building is wired. Plastic explosives." He looked down at his box. "This is a very good transmitter. Even though the house is almost a quarter of a mile away, this will trigger the detonation almost instantaneously."

"Don't do it," Ben said. "It isn't worth it."

The man ignored him. "I think you're familiar with some of my previous work, so you know I'm not bluffing. I can do this. I have done this. All I have to do is push this button. And they all die."

Ben carefully eyed the distance between his hand and the transmitter. Could he knock the thing out of this lunatic's hands before he could push the button?

Probably not.

Was he going to throw dice with the lives of everyone in the house?

"What is it you want?" Ben said evenly.

"I read in the paper that you were hoping to get some exercise when the trial was over. So I'm going to accommodate you. That's why we're here, in the park. On the jogging trail. You're going to run."

"In my street shoes?"

"Already making excuses? I wouldn't. My fingers are very antsy tonight." He placed his gun in his coat pocket, keeping his left thumb poised over the deadly red button. Then he gripped the transmitter with both hands. "There's another device like this one, a transmitter, taped to the side of the bridge, about a mile south on this trail. If you get there and push the button, the little light on my transmitter will light and I'll know you made it. I'll give you five minutes."

"What? I don't get it."

"What do you say, Kincaid? Think you can run a five-minute mile?"

"No!"

"Pity. If this light doesn't shine inside of five minutes, I'm pushing the big red button. And they'll all die." He withdrew a stopwatch, keeping his thumb poised over the red button. He clicked the top of the stopwatch. "Go."

"This is crazy. I can't—"

"Your time is ticking, Kincaid. Your friends and your nephew are five minutes from doomsday. Less now."

Ben ran. He barreled down the jogging path, the wind whistling in his face. He wasn't a particularly fast runner, especially in a suit, tie, and street shoes. But he couldn't think about that. He had to run; he had to make it. One thing he was absolutely sure of—this maniac meant what he said. He would push the button if Ben failed. What's more, he was hoping Ben would fail.

Ben blitzed down the path into the darkness. It was hard running at top speed when he could barely see two feet in front of himself, but he pressed on. He glanced back over his shoulder; the crazy was behind him, keeping him in sight. Ben knew if he detoured from the path or tried to run for help, he'd push the button.

Suddenly Ben's foot hit something—he never knew what—and he went tumbling to the ground. He hit shoulder first, smack on the gravel. It stung like hell; his shoulder felt wrenched.

It didn't matter. This was costing him time. He pushed himself to his feet, forcing his limbs to work. He had to keep running. He *had* to.

The stitch in his side felt like a knife. He wasn't used to this sort of exertion; usually, about the most exercise he got was chasing his cat. His chest was aching and he could barely breathe.

Didn't matter. He had to keep running. He had to keep running.

Up ahead, he saw the Fifteenth Street Bridge that crossed over to the west bank of the river. He scanned as best he could, never breaking his speed. Finally he saw it, near the bottom.

The transmitter.

He had no idea what his time was, but he knew it was close. He dove toward the little black box, crashing down onto the pavement, punching the button.

He lay on the ground, panting, aching, trying to catch his breath. A few moments later, the man trotted up beside him. "Not bad, Kincaid. Not bad." He glanced at the stopwatch. "Four minutes and forty-six seconds. Who'd have thought you had it in you? Not bad at all."

He kicked Ben in the side, just below the ribs. "Get up."

Ben grabbed his aching side. "Give me a minute."

"I said, get up." He kicked Ben again, this time even harder.

Gritting his teeth, Ben pushed himself to his feet. "All right," he said. His chest ached with each syllable. "You've had your fun. I've played your game. Can we all go home now?"

The young man's face was split by a smile so cold, so eerie it illuminated the darkness. "Hell no, Kincaid. We're just beginning. That was just a warm-up. Now you're going to do it again."

CHAPTER

68

CHRISTINA GLANCED UNHAPPILY at her watch. "This isn't like Ben."

Jones shrugged his shoulders. "He's probably exhausted. Wouldn't you be?"

"But that doesn't explain why he didn't come back to the hotel room. He told me to meet him here."

"Maybe he saw a bar on the way and decided he needed a couple of quick shots."

Loving chuckled. "The Skipper? More likely he stopped at Quick Trip for a quart of chocolate milk."

"Guys, this isn't funny. I'm worried." Christina paced around the hotel room. "He tells us to meet him in the hotel room, and then he doesn't show up. It isn't like him."

"Give him a little more time," Jones said, trying to relax her. "He'll show. Don't you think, Loving?"

Loving slowly moved his head to one side. "I dunno. It is strange. And Christina's instincts are usually pretty darn good." He pushed himself off the sofa. "You want I should go look around at the courthouse?"

Christina shook her head. "He wasn't there when I left. Why would he be there now? No, he must've been waylaid somewhere after he left." She paused for a moment, thinking about what she had said. *Waylaid.* The word echoed in her brain. "Oh, my God. You don't think—"

"Think?" Jones jumped to his feet. "What? What are *you* thinking?"

"Sick heart," she said succinctly.

Their eyes moved from one to another. "But how?"

"I don't know," Christina said. "And we won't find out sitting here." She grabbed the phone and punched nine for an outside line. "I'm calling Mike."

* * *

THE MAN HOLDING the transmitter was still laughing.

"Surely you didn't think we were done. Oh, no, Kincaid. We're just beginning! After all, we have to get you in shape."

Ben leaned heavily against the bridge. "What do you want now?"

"Same drill, but this time we'll go back up the trail. I left another transmitter on the pavement."

"Look," Ben said breathlessly, "I'm totally winded. I don't think I can do this again in five minutes."

"Can't do it in five? Very well. I'll give you four minutes and thirty seconds."

"That's impossible!"

The man clicked the top of the stopwatch. "Go."

"But—"

"Four minutes and twenty-five seconds. And counting."

Ben shoved himself away from the bridge and started barreling down the jogging path. It was harder this time. Much harder. His side already hurt from the last desperate run, and the two kicks in the stomach hadn't helped any. And he had to be faster this time. Much faster.

He was running against the wind now. It braced his face, chilling him, numbing him. Just as well. He had to ignore the pain. He had to focus on the goal. To break through the wall, as the runners said. To be faster than he had ever been before.

As he ran, he ticked through a mental checklist of everyone who would surely be in his boardinghouse right now. Mrs. Marmelstein. Mr. Perry, who he had still never met. Joni and Jami, their twin brothers, their parents. Giselle. And Joey.

Joey.

His teeth clenched tightly together. He had just made a small inroad, just broken through to the boy. It was finally looking as if they might be able to make a life together, that Ben might not be the miserable substitute parent he had thought he was. He was looking forward to seeing him at the end of each day. He was learning to love the kid, just as if he were his own son.

He wasn't going to let this son of a bitch take him away now.

Ben forced his legs through the motions, willing them to move. They were aching, erring. His gait was slowing, and he knew it. He tried to make them go faster, but they weren't responding. He clenched his fists and poured out everything he had. He had to make it. He had to!

He saw the transmitter up ahead of him. The bastard had stuck it on the back bumper of Ben's rental car. Ben raced toward it, hands extended. Squeezing every last erg of energy out of his body, he threw himself forward and pushed the button.

He collapsed on the pavement, beneath the car bumper, panting for air. A few short moments later, the man with the stopwatch ran up behind him.

"Well, well," he said, grinning. "What a performance." He looked down at Ben, sprawled on the ground. "Get up."

"I—I can't—"

"I told you to get up!"

Ben's voice was barely a whisper. "I can't move," he lied.

"What a wimp. Pathetic. And here I was about to compliment you. Your time was good." He checked the stopwatch. "But, alas, not quite good enough. Four minutes and thirty-four seconds. A valiant effort. But not successful." His eyes diverted to the transmitter. His thumb twitched. "So now I'm afraid I have no choice—"

Ben sprang forward, fist extended. Before the man could react, Ben knocked the transmitter out of his hand. It flew up into the air in a concentric arc, then plummeted downward and splashed into the water of the Arkansas River.

"You stupid little—"

Ben didn't wait to hear what name he came up with. He sprinted into his rental car, shoved in the key, and started the engine.

"You can't do this!"

Just watch me, Ben thought. He threw the car into reverse, aiming straight for the creep, who was fumbling to get his gun out of his coat pocket. He leaped out of the way, barely in time. Ben threw the car into drive and floored it.

Maybe a second later, Ben heard the first gunshot, but it went wild. In his rearview mirror, Ben saw the man run up to the other car in the parking lot, gun in hand. He dragged two men out of the front seat and started their car.

Damn! He was after him.

Ben pulled onto Riverside Drive, hoping to lose him in the darkness. It was no good. The man was too fast; he pulled onto the street bare seconds after Ben did. Worse, Ben soon saw that he was in some kind of souped-up sports car, while Ben was stuck in a Chrysler sedan. Nice car, but not one you'd pick for a high-speed chase.

He was gaining on him.

Ben tried to think what to do. Go to the police. For help? The problem was, this maniac was right behind him, and Ben knew if he stopped anywhere, much less stepped out of the car—

A bullet struck the back window. It shattered, flinging bits of safety glass in all directions. Ben clenched the wheel tightly, trying to maintain control. He couldn't risk stopping anywhere. He couldn't even slow down.

The light was with him, which was fortunate, because Ben knew if he had to stop at a light he was history. At the end of Riverside, he swerved onto Seventy-first Street and barreled past the neon lights of every fast-food chain known to man. He could see his friend pulling up right behind him, his headlights getting closer by the second. The glare practically blinded Ben; he looked away and concentrated on the road ahead.

What the hell was he going to do? He needed a plan. He couldn't just keep driving; eventually that creep would catch up to him and one of his bullets would connect. But he couldn't stop, either. And even if he were lucky enough to lose this nut, Ben knew what he would do. He'd head back to Ben's boardinghouse and try to kill Joey or Joni or Mrs. Marmelstein. Or he'd get another transmitter, tune it to the right frequency, and detonate the explosives.

It wasn't enough to just get away, even assuming that was possible, which at the moment, it wasn't. He had to stop this man. Quickly.

Ben jerked the car to the right and hit Lewis doing almost eighty miles an hour. He cruised past Oral Roberts University. Maybe if he closed his eyes and said a prayer by the giant praying hands . . . or maybe not. The light in front of him turned yellow. Didn't matter; he sailed through just as the light changed. He checked his rearview; Sick Heart was still behind him, but he'd had to apply his brakes and swerve a bit to avoid a collision in the intersection. Ben had gained a few feet and a few seconds.

Maybe even more. He saw his pursuer apply his brakes and hesitate momentarily before following. Ben had to think a minute. Why—

But of course. He wasn't from Tulsa. He didn't know his way around, at least not well. He might have the gun and the faster car, but he didn't know where he was going.

That was the key.

Ben swerved onto Eighty-first Street and made a beeline for Yale. He had a plan now, but he had to bring it off before that clown put a bullet through one of his tires. Or his head. They were deep in south Tulsa now. Even if this maniac had been staying in Tulsa since his campaign of terror began, which Ben doubted, there was no reason why he would come down here.

Sailing through another yellow light, Ben turned onto Yale, and there it was before him.

Dead-Man's Curve. Tulsa-style.

He surged downhill, into the darkness. He checked the rearview. Yes, of course—the crazy was still behind him. Ben screeched around the first sloping curve in the road, taking it on two wheels, barely slowing at all.

And as soon as he was around the curve and out of sight, he pulled off onto the side of the road and slammed his brakes down for all they were worth.

The instant his car was stopped, Ben turned off the lights and killed the engine. A millisecond later, the maniac came whizzing around the curve. Ben could see him grappling to maintain control of his car. He saw the next curve coming, and the next one after that, but he was going much too fast. He couldn't possibly hang on. His car swerved wildly, first left, then right, then crossed the road and careened into a ditch, bounced out, plowed through a fence, and slammed into a tree trunk.

The sound of the crash was like the hammer of God.

Ben ran down the hill after him. The tree trunk had been driven halfway through the hood of the car. Smoke poured out; flames were beginning to lick at the engine. Debris was scattered all over the area. The car was totaled.

And the man crunched behind the steering wheel was not much better.

ABOUT HALF AN hour later, Dead-Man's Curve was a hubbub of activity. Four patrol cars and ten officers, including Mike, who had been searching for Ben since Christina called him, surrounded the accident site. An ambulance was pulling up, trying to get close. Spectators had gathered on the opposite side of the street. And predictably enough, a few reporters and minicams were pushing forward as well, trying to get a good shot for the late-night broadcast.

Ben watched as the rescue team used the jaws of life to pry the man out of the crumpled driver's seat. Eventually they removed him, lowered him onto a stretcher, and loaded him into the ambulance.

Ben stepped cautiously toward the ambulance. "Is he dead?" he asked Mike.

"Unfortunately, no." Mike pushed away from the wreckage, then wiped his hands on his trench coat. "He's going to be pretty miserable for a while, but he'll live."

"He needs help," Ben said.

"He needs to be put out of his misery," Mike replied, teeth clenched. "This world is bad enough without homicidal creeps like him running around."

"If things had only been different . . ." Ben said. He searched for the right words, words that didn't seem stupid and futile. "He might have been perfectly normal."

But then, he thought, so might we all.

"You're kidding yourself," Mike grunted back. "With someone this bad off, it's in the genes. Nothing you can do about it. He's just nuts. Psychopathic. Insane."

Ben shook his head. "He wasn't insane." He picked up a bit of glass and metal he found lying in the grass—a shattered stopwatch. "He was just sick at heart."

FOUR

Putting Away Childish Things

◆ ◆ ◆

CHAPTER

69

BEN SAT IN the back bedroom of their hotel suite, hidden away, while Jones dealt with the outside world. The phone had been ringing off the hook from the second the trial had ended. Clients of all classes, shapes, and sizes were banging down Ben's door, even though, technically speaking, he didn't actually have one. Scores of potential clients seemed desperate to have Ben represent them. Jones was setting up the client interviews. If he took only half the cases being offered, he'd have enough work to last for years. The cases ran the gamut—all the high-prestige and esoteric fields Ben had always wanted to try but had never had the clients for. He was getting other potentially lucrative opportunities as well; an outfit hawking some software called Legal Assist wanted him to be their product spokesman, and Channel Two had asked him to be their legal commentator.

In other words, for once, life was sweet. Ben had won an unequivocal and resounding victory, and everybody knew about it. It appeared that finally, after all this time and effort, the rest of the world was discovering the value of Benjamin J. Kincaid, Esq.

Ben was watching the news on the bedroom television. Even after the verdict had been delivered, the world still seemed obsessed with the Barrett trial. There were post-trial wrapups ("Sure, he's innocent, but what does this tell us about America?"); analyses ("Let's face it, the jury trial is an antique that doesn't work in the media age"); juror interviews ("I liked the cute little guy for the defense. He seemed so human, so fallible. Like he didn't know what he was going to do from one moment to the next"); and disgruntled prosecutors ("It is my position and the position of everyone in the justice department that we made no mistake. The jury's verdict is unfortunate but beyond our control").

Ben switched channels. On Channel Eight, he found Mr. Harvey Sanders, witness extraordinaire, being interviewed for at least the third time since the trial had concluded.

"Mr. Sanders," the female interviewer said, "some people are calling you the most critical witness in the entire trial. How does that make you feel?"

He blushed modestly, then flashed his million-dollar smile. "Oh, I think that's an overstatement. I just did my duty, that's all. The same as anyone else would do, I'm sure."

"All this publicity has had quite an impact on your acting career, hasn't it?"

"I have to admit it has. My agent says the phone is ringing constantly."

"People are saying you're the most famous witness in the history of the judiciary, or at least since Kato Kaelin. And your testimony was actually helpful."

"Yes, it's made a dramatic difference. We've got several commercials lined up now, a product endorsement, and an invitation to serve as the spokesman for the National Neighborhood Watch Program. And of course, the ubiquitous book offer. We may even get a TV movie."

"Well, that's wonderful. Thank you for being with us today."

"Thank you, Karen. Now I think I'd best go answer the phone."

Ben switched off the TV. He had a few calls to answer of his own. But first, there was one call he *wanted* to make.

"So, I guess you heard?"

"Benjamin, how could I not? It's everywhere."

"Even at Crescent Market?"

"Especially at Crescent Market."

Ben smiled. "The phone's been ringing constantly. It looks like I'm finally going to make a success of this law practice."

"I always knew you would." His mother's voice revealed her pride and happiness. "What a success you've turned out to be." She paused. "What has happened to . . . that man? The one whose father . . ." She didn't complete the sentence.

"He's mending. They expect him to make a full recovery. Physically, anyway."

There was a long silence on the line. "That's so tragic. Who could have known?"

Known what? That the problems his father had created could live on after him? That was no surprise. That evil could fester so long, so tenaciously? No surprise there, either. "I think he'll get some treatment. Psychiatric, I mean. Who knows? Perhaps he'll come around someday."

"Perhaps." Another pause. "And how are you, Benjamin?"

"I'm fine. Barrett owes me a huge fee, huge by my standards, anyway, and he has promised to pay up immediately. Coupled with all these new business prospects . . . well, I'd say I'm in good shape."

"That's excellent. That pleases me. I'm so proud of you, Benjamin." There was a small patch of static. "Your father would be proud of you, too."

They said their goodbyes, and Ben returned to the tasks at hand. There were stacks of files piled all around the room. If he was going to take on this huge new caseload, he needed to clear away the debris of the past. He had to decide what should go in the form files, what should be put in long-term storage, and what could be destroyed.

After a few minutes of digging, he came across a sealed manila envelope. Opening it, he found a thick stack of photocopied medical data. He stared at it, trying to figure out what it was. Oh, of course, he remembered. Barrett's medical records, the ones he had gone to court to prevent from being produced to the prosecution. Since Ben had won the motion, he had never taken the time to review the records.

He thumbed absently through the file, looking for the records pertaining to Barrett's psychiatric counseling. He didn't find any.

Now that was odd, Ben thought. If there was no record of psychiatric treatment, then why . . .

He continued sorting through the morass of documents. Until finally, somewhere near the bottom, he found something he had not anticipated, something he had not even dreamed possible.

His heart felt as if it had stopped beating in his chest. His jaw slackened; his eyes widened.

Oh my God, Ben thought, his brain racing through the recent past, retrying the case in his mind. How could I have been so stupid?

How could I have been so wrong?

BEN FOUND BARRETT at home, at the same house on Terwilliger that he had once shared with his three family members. The house had been cleaned, scoured. Like the charges against him, all traces of the crime had been eradicated. All the sins swept away.

Barrett was more than happy to see him. "Ben," he said jovially, arms extended. "My hero."

Ben bristled at his touch. He did not return the greeting.

"Something wrong, old man?" Barrett chuckled. "Hey, the check is in the mail. I promise. I wrote it out this morning."

Ben scanned the room. "Looks like you're getting things put back in order."

"Well, yes, of course. I mean, it's sad, but we have to get on with life, don't we? I suppose in time I'll have to sell this place; it's much too large for just me. Quite a change from the county jail. Still, in the meantime, I might as well restore some sense of order. Makes for a better home environment."

"Makes for a better backdrop for all those interviews you've been giving, too."

"That's true." He chuckled again. "I gotta tell you, it's nice having the press in your back pocket again. Hell, I expected that no matter how this turned out, my political career would be ruined. Now I'm beginning to wonder. This old dog might have some life in him yet."

Wordlessly Ben opened his briefcase, withdrew the envelope, and pressed it into Barrett's hands. "I was going through the files and I found this. It's your medical records. The ones you sent me to court to keep away from the prosecution's prying eyes."

"Ah, yes." Barrett took the file, thumbed through it absently. "And you're probably wondering where the records pertaining to my psychiatric counseling are. Well, look, Ben, I may have exaggerated that a bit, but whether I've been to a shrink or not, is it wrong for a man to want to keep his medical history off the evening news?"

"You've had a vasectomy," Ben said coldly, barely blinking. "It's right there, on page eighty-two. That's what you didn't want the prosecution to know." He took a deep breath and slowly released it. "It wasn't your baby."

"Ahh . . . no." Barrett dropped the envelope and took a seat on a nearby sofa. "No, I guess it wasn't." His face suddenly brightened. "Although sometimes miracles do happen. Those surgeons aren't perfect. But . . ." He smiled. "I suppose you're not buying that one."

"No, I'm not. You knew about the baby. And you knew it wasn't yours. And you didn't want the prosecution to know it couldn't possibly be yours because"—another deep breath—"because it gives you a motive for murder."

He stared down at his hands. "I guess it does, doesn't it?"

Ben felt a cold chill creeping up his spine. "You killed her, didn't you? You killed your wife."

"Well, I suppose there's no point in denying it. Not to Ben Kincaid, super-sleuth."

Ben collapsed into the nearest armchair. "I can't believe it. I can't believe I was so wrong, so blind. I saw you with your kids. I looked into your eyes. I was sure—"

Barrett's head snapped up suddenly. "Now, wait a minute, Ben. I think you've gotten the wrong idea."

"But you said—"

"I said I killed my wife. Yeah, true enough. But the kids? Never. No way in hell." He edged forward in his seat. "Don't you get it, Kincaid? *She* killed the kids. She did it."

Ben stared across the tiny expanse of carpet. "But I don't see—"

"It was her, Kincaid, believe me. If you search through those medical records long enough, you'll find that *she* was the one who had psychiatric treatment—though not nearly enough. There were times when she completely lost control, became absolutely insane. And violent. She hit me so many times I can't even count them all. I lost a tooth, thanks to her. She jabbed me so hard in the solar plexus once I almost lost consciousness." He took a deep breath. "We heard all that chatter throughout the trial about my so-called temper. But she was the one who had the temper. Sure, I got mad sometimes, but she went insane. I mean, totally out of control, violent, psycho-mommy. You're damn right the kids got bruised up a time or two. People always assume it's the man, that the male is the violent one. But it wasn't. It was her."

"But why kill them?"

"To get back at me, of course. In the only way she could. She hated me; she had for years. Why do you think she told those horrible stories to her sister, among others? She was jealous, cruel. Complained that I didn't spend any time with her, that all I cared about was my career, my image. She was tired of living in a goldfish bowl, of being known only as Mayor Barrett's wife. As an ornament. I'm sure you've heard this all before. The truth is, she was not well. Not well in the head."

"But there was never any indication—"

"Wasn't there? Do you remember what that clown at the ice-cream parlor said? He remembered the words, he just forgot who said them. It was her, not me. Hell, Fisher remembered her saying the same thing. 'The children are the only weapon I have against you.' I guess that was right. And finally she used that weapon. She played her last card."

Ben stared at the man, unable to come up with an intelligent comment.

"That was why she had the affair, too. To punish me. It was that creep Fisher, as you've probably guessed. Small wonder I don't much care for him. Remember that unmatched trace of blood the prosecution expert said he found in Caroline's bedroom? Fisher, I guarantee it. Apparently Caroline and her lover liked it rough—rough enough to draw blood. Anyway, after carrying this affair on right in front of my nose for weeks, she got pregnant, probably intentionally, to humiliate me. To give me an unwanted little public relations problem.

"But that wasn't enough. She didn't get what she wanted. Instead of flying off the handle, I calmly told her she could sleep with any piece of shit she wanted, what did I care? That infuriated her. That's what we fought about that fateful afternoon. She was desperate to get to me, and she couldn't do it. I just walked out on her and, well, I guess she decided to play her trump card, the only weapon she had left. She took away the only thing that would really hurt me. My children."

Ben gripped the sides of his chair. He wished he could doubt, could make himself disbelieve. But this was the truth. He knew it was.

"It was a shame she'd been reading *Medea*. I wonder if that was where she got the idea? People as unbalanced as her shouldn't be allowed Greek tragedy. Imagine if she'd read *Oedipus Rex*. What a mess that would've been."

He smiled, but soon saw that his attempt at gallows humor had fallen flat.

"I hit Caroline a few times, I have to admit. Locked her out of the house, all that. But what do you do with a wife who becomes a raving maniac at the slightest provocation, huh? I wish someone would tell me. The whole world is geared up to protect women from men. What happens when a man needs protection from a woman? Nothing, that's what. Don't bother going to friends, family, police. They'll laugh in your face."

"But—" Ben groped for words. "It was so . . . *bloody*."

"Yes, she did rather make a mess of it, didn't she? Caroline had been a nurse, you'll recall. She knew how to kill someone efficiently. She managed it with Annabelle—one direct thrust to the heart with a thin knife. Instantaneous death. But something went wrong with Alysha. I don't know what. Perhaps Alysha saw her kill Annabelle and tried to struggle. Perhaps she fought back. Anyway, things got out of control, and Caroline made a huge bloody mess. Poor Alysha—no wonder she cried out for her daddy. What she must have thought when her own mother came to kill her. At least it was quick. Still, Caroline's purpose was accomplished. She punished me. She took away my children."

Barrett's hand went toward his face, covering his eyes. "Imagine if you will—imagine what I faced when I came home, an hour or so after I'd left. I hadn't expected anything to happen. I just thought it was best to leave until Caroline's rage blew over, to keep her from hurting me or me from hurting her. If I had stayed, I knew one or the other would happen. So I left for a lousy hour, just to let her cool off, and I come home—" The color drained out of his face; his eyes became glassy and wet. *"And my children are dead!"* His voice was broken, hurt. "My two precious babies, the most beautiful things in my world—dead. Murdered. By their own mother."

He looked up suddenly. "And do you know what she said? *Do you know what she said?* She looked straight into my eyes and said, 'No more babies for you, you son of a bitch. Explain that at a press conference.'"

He shook his head. Tears streamed from his eyes. "I lost control. Truly and utterly lost control. I don't know what came over me. I was just enraged. I ran at her, grabbed the knife away, and just started pounding. Just started slicing away. Killing her. I couldn't stop myself. I was so angry. So . . . *angry*.

"We fought, but she was outmatched. I'm sure that's when she got my skin under her nail and made me bleed a little. She was no weakling. But I was stronger. And I wanted her to die. I really truly wanted her to die."

He looked up suddenly. "And then it was over. Just as quickly as it had started, it was over. The rage passed. I regained control. But Caroline—" He shook his head. "Next thing I remember, she was sprawled backwards over that dining room chair. Not moving. I checked for a pulse, tried to do CPR—but it was no use. She was dead." He ran his hand through his hair. "I just don't know what happened to me. The rage—the uncontrollable rage. I never felt anything like that before. I don't know how to explain it to you."

"Don't bother," Ben said quietly. It wasn't necessary. He knew all about it. It was a family trademark.

"I was so confused afterwards. I couldn't get my head together—didn't know what to do."

"So you ran."

"Well, I didn't see that hanging around would do my family any good, and I knew perfectly well what the chances were of a public figure getting a fair trial. Next to zilch. So, yeah, I ran."

"And when you didn't make it, when they caught you, you called me. And fed me that crock of bull about the city council."

Barrett stretched his neck, wiped away the tears. "Ben, you don't know how sorry I am about what happened. I know what I did was wrong. I've felt horrible about it ever since it happened. But I was not prepared to spend the rest of my life in jail because of it." He pressed his hand against his forehead. "I knew Whitman had some chump following me. Not to kill me. I think he was supposed to take pictures. That's why he was following me around, stalking outside the house. He was hoping to catch me in a compromising position, capture it on film, and feed it to the press. Whitman found out I was having an affair with my secretary—who could blame me? Anyway, that's what he meant when he told Buck to 'get the nigger.' He wanted color glossies he could spread across the front page. Some of my boys tipped me off to it, though, and when it became patently obvious that I needed a scapegoat, I let Whitman and his pet hood fill the role. Killed two birds with one stone, so to speak."

"He could go to prison."

"He won't. They don't have any evidence against him—because none exists. Besides, the DA obviously prefers to play the high and mighty part. Before they could institute further investigation, they would have to admit that they made a mistake the first time, which they appear to be unwilling to do. Whitman won't do time. And if his reputation is ruined—fine. He deserves it."

"But that meeting in the park. And your neighbor spotted Whitman in your neighborhood."

"Did he? I wonder. Whitman did meet Buck in the park. I think he saw that he was about to be dragged into this thing and wanted all the incriminating evidence—especially those photographs—destroyed as soon as possible. As for Harvey Sanders spotting Whitman in the sedan, that moron—" He grinned suddenly. "You may have noticed that the first time Sanders testified, he didn't know who it was he saw in the brown sedan. Despite his professed lack of knowledge about city government, he must've seen Whitman's picture at some time in his life, or seen him in the courtroom. But he didn't identify Whitman as the man in the car until his second time on the stand, and then only in the most protracted, melodramatic manner possible. You have to understand—Harvey is an actor. He saw his big break in this trial, and he wasn't going to blow it. His first trip to the witness stand had gotten him some publicity. He must've thought, Imagine what might happen if I became a critical witness, if I altered the course of the whole trial.

"So that's what he did. He embellished a bit, made himself important. Said exactly what you wanted him to say. And now the media drones are swarming around him, talking about how honest and charismatic he is."

Ben stared at the man wordlessly.

"So that's it then," Barrett said, clasping his hands together. "Now you know everything I do. I hope you're a lot happier for it."

Slowly, clumsily, Ben pushed himself out of the chair. "You must realize I'm not going to keep your dirty little secret to myself."

Barrett glanced up, a look of pure astonishment on his face. "Why, Ben, you have no choice."

"I certainly do—"

"Have you forgotten a little thing called attorney-client privilege? Anything I tell you must be held in the strictest confidence."

"The case is over."

"Yes, but your representation of me is not, as you very well know. This conversation directly pertained to a legal matter which you handled on my behalf. It's privileged."

"I don't care. I'm not going to be a part of this conspiracy of silence."

"Fine. Suit yourself. Go to the press. What will that accomplish? Well, first, you'll be disbarred, no question about that. You'll have your livelihood taken away as punishment for—what? For telling the truth. How ironic. Meanwhile, what will happen to me? Well—nothing! Nothing at all! I've already been tried and acquitted on this charge, the maximum possible charge. Double jeopardy has attached! They can't touch me. Hell, I could go tell my story to the press myself, and there would be absolutely nothing anyone could do to me."

Barrett smiled briefly, then sighed. "But I won't do that. I have my career to think of. And you won't do it either. Pious as you are, I don't think you're stupid."

Ben turned abruptly, feeling his way, tripping over an edge of carpet. "I can't believe I was so blind. It was all right in front of me. People kept telling me. Bullock, Mike. And I wouldn't listen. I looked into your eyes, decided that you couldn't kill your children, and stupidly thought that that meant you were not guilty. I'm so used to seeing things in terms of us against them, of right against wrong, defense against prosecution, that I missed the real truth. I was like a kid on the playground—I was the skins and the prosecution was the shirts. And we all wanted to win. And now, because I screwed up"—his head snapped around, and his eyes burned toward Barrett's—"a guilty man goes free."

Barrett nodded, eyes wide. "Life sucks, doesn't it?"

Silently Ben gathered up the medical file and the papers that were in it.

"I'll show you to the door," Barrett said.

"Please don't." Ben opened the front door, then stopped. "Don't come to my office again, Barrett. Don't come anywhere near me. You are no longer my client. And for God's sake, don't send any of your press groupies my way for quotes. Believe me, you wouldn't like what I'd give them."

Ben passed through the door and slammed it so loud that Harvey Sanders could hear the crash next door, even with his windows closed.

CHAPTER

70

WHEN BEN RETURNED to his apartment, he was surprised to find Joey crawling around on the floor, fiddling with a Fisher-Price music mobile.

He crawled on all fours to get to Joey-level. "Hiya, pardner. I stopped by the store and picked up some cool stuff for you. You're going to love it." A thought struck; he looked up. "Where's Joni?"

"I told her she could go home."

Ben whirled around. *Julia!*

She smiled. "Hi there, big brother. Surprised to see me?"

There she was, in all her glory. Ben's sister seemed firm and tanned, even more so than when he had last seen her more than six months before. Her long brown hair curled around her neck and down past her shoulders; her blue eyes sparkled.

"Julia," he said, his brain obviously not processing information as quickly as his eyes. "How—how did you get in?"

"Your friend Joni let me in." She pointed at the jumbo-size Toys Я Us bag in Ben's arms. "Picked up a few toys for yourself?"

"Huh? Oh . . . for Joey. I've had a pretty depressing day, and I was looking forward to spending some time . . ."

Julia sorted through the contents. "Tumbling mats, Nerf blocks, foam helmets—Ben, what's all this for? Gymnastic lessons?"

"Oh . . . well." Red blotches began creeping up his neck. "Joey has a . . . fondness for pratfalls."

"I see." She folded her hands and stood before him. There was a confidence about her, a sense of self-assuredness, that he had never seen before.

"Julia, we've been looking for you for months without any luck. What brings you back now?"

She smiled, a beatific, vibrant smile. "I got in!"

"You—"

"The graduate school program. I got in and got through my first term, shining colors. My professor says I'm one of the best students he's ever had."

"Really." He frowned. "You're not . . ."

"No, Ben, I'm not dating him. At least not yet. He is kind of cute, in a tweedy sort of way."

"We called every college in Connecticut—"

"Oh, did I say Connecticut? I meant Maine. I'm going to school in Maine." She tilted her head down at Joey. "So, how did you two get along?"

"Oh, well . . ." Where to begin? "We've done very well, actually. We've made a lot of progress, and the—"

"I can't tell you how much I've missed this little bundle of snot." She scooped him up into her arms. "I didn't think I would. I know that sounds horrible, but I'm just being honest. The first seven months, raising him on my own—well, I'd just had enough, you know? It was hell on wheels. I couldn't take it anymore and I didn't think I'd ever want to again. But I was wrong." She held the boy close against her cheek. "You can't separate a mother from her son."

Ben felt a sudden hollow sensation spreading throughout his body. "But—"

"I've got it all worked out now. There's this woman—the wife of one of the other students in the program—she needs some extra spending money to make ends meet, so she's going to watch Joey during the day, and during nights when I'm on call. We both live in adjoining condos, so it will be very convenient, very doable."

"Are you saying—"

"Get with the program, Ben. I'm saying I'm taking my baby back."

The room seemed to be moving, swimming, and all Ben could hear was the sound of the air conditioner blowing. It was so loud, so intrusive. "But—"

"Ben, what is your problem?" She bounced the baby to her other arm. "Jesus Christ, I thought you'd be relieved."

"But Joey and I, we've—"

"Oh, stop already. Help me gather up his things. I want to leave as soon as possible so I can get to Oklahoma City before dark."

"But, Julia—" He stared at her, his heart thumping in his chest. "You can't just stroll in and snatch him away!"

"Snatch him away? Ben, I'm his mother!"

"Maybe you were six months ago, but you abandoned him. You don't have any rights—"

"Rights? Is this a legal debate? Christ, should I hire a lawyer? Are we going to have a custody battle? You know you wouldn't win. Ben, I'm his mother!"

Julia started circling around the small apartment, obviously agitated, gathering together all Joey's things. It appeared to Ben that she had pretty well finished packing before he had even arrived. "I can't believe you're acting like this. I really can't. Why do we have to have a big scene? What did you think, that I was going to leave my precious baby with you forever?"

"How did I know *what* you were planning? You just plopped the baby in my arms and disappeared."

"And so what? So now you're Mr. Mom? Look at this place! Bad enough my brother lives in a dump like this, but my *baby*? No way. And some of the things that Joni person you dumped him with was saying make me wonder if he was even safe. Sounds like you have all sorts of loonies and crackpots looming around you. Making your money off murderers—"

"I took good care of Joey."

"Is that so?" She came right under Ben's nose and glared at him. "Look at him. Six months ago, he was already beginning to speak. Now I can't get him to say a word. He barely walks. He doesn't play like a normal child. My God, it's a good thing I got back here when I did."

Ben felt his jaw tightening. "That's not fair—"

"Well, this isn't a courtroom and you're not going to talk your way to victory." She threw two bags over her shoulders and headed for the door, baby in tow. "I'll send for the rest of this stuff."

"But, Julia—"

"Ben, it's what's best. A boy should be with his mother."

Ben stared at Joey. He was gazing up at his mother with obvious affection, brushing his cheek against her shoulder. Even after all this time, he knew who she was. And he wanted to be with her.

"Still, why not stay for a few days, and—"

"Don't make this more difficult than it already is, all right!" Her voice resounded off the walls and echoed through the small room. "We're leaving."

Ben raced to the door and took one of Joey's tiny little hands. "Joey?"

Joey peered back at Ben with wide and perplexed eyes. The excitement and activity obviously had left him confused and disoriented. "Baa, baa."

"Baa, baa?"

Joey giggled. "Baa, baa, Ungaben."

The door closed, and they were gone.

Ben stood there for the longest time, not moving, not really thinking, just staring with a hollow heart and eyes too dry to cry at the door that had closed so firmly and finally before him.

71

IT TOOK CHRISTINA two weeks, but she finally got Ben out to Heavener State Park for a backpacking expedition. They had spent the better part of the morning prowling through the sprawling elm trees and the thick twining brush, making a path toward the top of the mountain overlooking the Arkansas River. It was a lovely day, hot, but beautiful, and they had covered a fair amount of territory, despite the fact that Ben was lugging a huge backpack that seemed to be stuffed with several large, heavy objects.

"Ready to take a break?" Christina asked.

"You won't hear me complain." Ben fell down on a tree stump and worked the heavy backpack off his shoulders. Christina passed him the canteen and he took a long, refreshing drink.

"Another half an hour and we'll be at the Nordic runestone," Christina announced.

"Glory be."

"It's an impressive relic, for your information. The crème de la crème of Norwegian antiquities. And proof positive that my Viking ancestors were the ones who discovered America."

"That'll come as a big shock to the Native Americans."

She frowned. "You know what I mean. First Europeans. Columbus had a Norwegian map, you know."

"Spare me the Nordic propaganda." He stretched out under the nearest elm tree and tried to avoid the direct light of the sun.

Christina allowed a few minutes to pass quietly, listening to the humming-birds and kingfishers and swallows. Finally, she ventured into conversation. "You've been very quiet this morning."

Ben gazed across the mountaintops. "I've been drinking in the view."

"You've been thinking, and I know what you've been thinking about. Him."

"Him?"

"That kid. The bomber. The one whose father went for surgery with your father—"

"Actually, I haven't thought about that at all," Ben replied. "Not about him, or his father, or my father. I've had enough of that." He picked up a rock and tossed it across the clearing. "I've been obsessed with my father, with feeling guilty, blaming myself, wondering how he could do what he did. How he could—" Ben stopped, shook his head. "I've let him control my life after his death more than he did when he was alive. Well, enough already. Time to grow up. The truth is, my father was no better or worse than a lot of people, including me. We all have a temper. We all experience rage. We just have to learn to control it, that's all. Otherwise, we're not going to survive."

Christina plucked a nearby dandelion and blew, scattering its milky white fluff into the air. "You know," she said, "Jones and Loving are very worried about you."

"About me? Why?"

" 'Cause you haven't been by the hotel room for two weeks. And you don't appear to be looking for new office space. They're afraid you're never coming back."

"They're right." Ben picked up a small stone and flung it into the distance.

Christina scooted closer. "You miss Joey, don't you?"

Ben waited a long time before answering. "Of course I do. Except maybe in the middle of the night. Don't you?"

She grinned. "Yeah, I suppose I do. How do you think Julia will do as a full-time mommy? Think she can handle it?"

Ben's face darkened. "I don't know." His eyes seemed to turn inward, and he was silent again, with no apparent intention of speaking.

"Listen, Ben," Christina said, choosing her words carefully. "It wasn't your fault. What happened, I mean. With the Barrett trial. You did your job. It wasn't your fault the system didn't work."

"My job was to make the system work. I failed."

"You did everything you could."

He shook his head from side-to-side. "I was just like Whitman."

"What?"

He looked up at her. "I could only see one color."

A few more minutes passed. Then, abruptly, Ben jumped to his feet and began rummaging in his backpack. A moment later, he withdrew a shoebox-size wooden box. He opened it, then quietly touched the contents, the Magic 8-Ball, the marbles, the Krypto-Ray gun . . .

"Ben," Christina said, "that's your box! Your childhood treasures."

He nodded, closed the box, and gently set it down under a tree.

"But why?"

He wasn't listening. He was in his backpack again. This time, Christina was amazed to see him remove his briefcase, battered and scraped from so many court hearings and trials.

"Why on earth did you bring that?"

Ben didn't answer. He gripped the handle with both hands, spun around a few times like a discus thrower, and slung the briefcase off into the distance.

"Ben, what's come over you?"

Ben began gathering his gear. "Come on. Let's keep moving."

"But you're leaving—"

"I know. Come on."

"But, *Ben*!"

He threw his backpack, now much lighter than before, back over his shoulders. "Hey, less talking, more hiking, okay?"

Frowning, Christina gathered together her gear. After she had reassembled herself, she stood beside him, just at the edge of the clearing. Ben was gazing off into the distance, staring at the tall mountain before them.

"All right," she said, "I'm ready already. Where are we going?"

Ben pointed off toward the horizon. "To see what lies ahead. Over the next mountain."

They marched together down the trail, and within moments, both had disappeared from sight.

Three days later, a group of local children from Poteau found the wooden box and the briefcase, examined them and their contents, and took their new-found treasures home with them.

It made their day.

ACKNOWLEDGMENTS

◆ ◆ ◆

I WANT TO thank all those who have helped me put together this installment in the ongoing Ben Kincaid chronicles: Kirsten Bernhardt and Arlene Joplin, both of whom read an early draft of this manuscript and gave me their extremely useful comments; Gail Benedict, for converting my hand-scrawled corrections into a manuscript; and Vicky Hildebrandt, a good friend and great source for material.

I also want to thank again my editor, Joe Blades, who has been with me since Book One and is still with me here on Book Eight; Kim Hovey, who has been handling publicity on my behalf for just as long; Tamu Aljuwani, Brenda Brown, Clare Ferraro, Linda Grey, and all the rest of the gang at Ballantine.

I also want to thank Scott, Dee, Howard, Kerry, Rosalba, Sharon, Jackie, and everyone else at Novel Idea for allowing me to mention their splendid bookstore, and for having such a splendid bookstore, not to mention providing my favorite place to eat lunch.

Any cybernauts out there who would like to drop me a line are encouraged to do so. My e-mail address is: willbern@mindspring.com.

—William Bernhardt

ABOUT THE AUTHOR

◆ ◆ ◆

WILLIAM BERNHARDT made his debut as a novelist in 1992 with *Primary Justice*, a bestseller that launched what *The Armchair Detective* called "one of the best new series going." Bernhardt has since written seven more novels, five in the Ben Kincaid *Justice* series, leading *The Vancouver Sun* to dub him "the American equivalent of P.G. Wodehouse and John Mortimer." Bernhardt's novels include: *Blind Justice, Deadly Justice, Perfect Justice* (which won the Oklahoma Book Award), *Cruel Justice, Double Jeopardy* and *The Code of Buddyhood*. As an attorney, Bernhardt has received several awards for his public service and was named one of the top twenty-five young lawyers in the nation. He lives in Tulsa, Oklahoma, with his wife, Kirsten, and their children, Harry and Alice.